Meadowview
ACRES

DONNA M CAIN

ISBN: 0989012603
ISBN 13: 9780989012607

Library of Congress Control Number: 2013903556
Chiot Press, Crestwood, KY

CONTENTS

DEDICATION

For Chase, Eliot and my Du, for constant
fun, love and happiness...

PROLOGUE

He smelled the smoke before he saw it. There it was, coming from the science lab windows. The plumes were thick and white. Completely forgetting to call 911, Darren sprinted to the closest doors. Yanking them open, he was engulfed in smoke. He couldn't see his hand in front of his face. There was a chemical smell to the smoke that burned his nostrils. Darren took off his tee shirt and wrapped it around his nose and mouth.

He dropped to his hands and knees to try to get under the thickest plumes. The smoke was thinner down there; he could see a few feet ahead.

Darren knew the science lab was the third classroom on the right. If he crawled along the wall, he could count the doorways and know where he was. He started forward as quickly as possible, not knowing how long Hunter and Eli had already been inside.

His right hand came upon the first door quickly. Passing it, he tried to keep his eyes closed and feel his way. They were already tearing from the smoke and he would need as much sight as possible when he made it to the lab.

The second door was not much farther. He passed it and went quickly on. The hard floor was tough on his knees, but the smoke was worse. Even with the cotton shirt filtering the worst of it, Darren was already finding it hard to breathe.

Finally, his hand felt the entry to the third classroom. For a second, he questioned himself. Was he sure the lab was the third classroom, or was it the fourth one down? He was beginning to get a little lightheaded when he heard a voice from inside the room.

"Eli! Wake up!" It was Hunter. The voice was overcome by a series of coughs.

"Hunter!" Darren tried to shout through the entry. "It's Darren! Can you hear me?" He broke off then as his throat constricted causing him to cough roughly.

Darren listened through the sounds of wood and paper crackling in the fire. There were loud pops now and then as something combustible in the lab exploded.

Then Hunter's voice came out of the smoke, "Darren? Yeah! I hear you," followed by more coughing spasms. Hunter sounded weak.

Darren shouted, "Can you crawl toward my voice?" It was hard to communicate over the sounds of the fire. His throat felt raw.

"Yeah, I mean, no! I can't. Eli's passed out! I can't drag him! Get help!" He broke off coughing again.

"There's no time!" Darren responded, feeling desperate now. "Guide me to you!"

Darren started crawling once again as he recalled the layout of the room. The school desks were in the front of the room. Behind those, in the middle of the room was Mr. Just's main lab table with the rest of the lab tables in the back of the room. His hand touched the first desk. He tried to open his eyes, but the smoke in there was worse. It was so dense Darren couldn't make out shapes or light anywhere.

He heard Hunter's voice coming from the smoke. "Here, this way!" The voice broke off in a series of coughs. "We're beside Mr. Just's lab table!"

Darren counted the desks as he progressed towards Hunter's voice. *Two, three, four…* He prayed they could find their way out of the room.

"This way," Hunter yelled again and by the sound of his voice, Darren could tell he was very close.

"I'm close, almost there! Hold out your arm!" Darren coughed, still counting the desks as he passed. *Seven, eight, there!* Hunter's hand hit him in the head.

"I'm here, Hunter." He reached out and found Hunter's arm. Grabbing it, he yelled, "Where's Eli?"

More coughing, then, "I'm holding on to him. I think Mr. Just is here, but I haven't found him."

Darren wasted no time. "Pull Eli over to me; give me his hand." His breath was coming harder now. He reached into the emptiness of the smoke and felt nothing. After a moment, he felt Hunter's arm again. Hunter passed him a hand; this one was cold and dry. Grabbing it, Darren turned himself around and yelled to Hunter, "Follow me! Keep track of the desks! We'll pass eight of them!" He broke off coughing and felt a tightening in his chest. He took a quick moment to recover then yelled back to Hunter, "Eight desks then the doorway! Stay to the left, three doorways down! Let's go!"

Pulling Eli's limp body behind, Darren started to crawl.

BOOK ONE

CHAPTER 1

Claymont Jackson

Claymont Jackson climbed into the cab of his Caterpillar bulldozer. He had a lot on his mind. He had three acres left to clear before phase one of the new development could begin. As usual, his boss, Tony Clark, had started Claymont's day off with a threat. If he didn't clear the last three acres by today, his bonus was in jeopardy. Claymont couldn't blame Clark much, though. He knew Tony was hearing it from his boss, Gary Sam. And Mr. Sam was surely hearing it from the developer, Oakwood Homes. It was the trickle-down effect. Claymont was just the last one down the totem pole.

Oakwood Homes was responsible for the subdivision of around two-hundred fifty new houses. One thing Claymont knew from his years in construction was that time was money, and time was always short. Delays for weather or permits were always to be expected, and this job was no different. As of today they were only about a month behind schedule – mostly because of the cold snap about a month ago that brought a lot of rain. Today, Claymont was sure he could get them back on track. It was a beautiful day, and he was feeling good. He thought he could help Mr. Clark and Mr. Sam feel a little better, too. Claymont had plans for that bonus.

He stowed away his lunch box and his jacket, started the Cat and tuned into the Power Hits station. His son, Darren, had gotten him hooked on the music. He liked the upbeat tempos. The music seemed to give him more energy as he worked. He even found himself singing along sometimes.

Claymont never minded a deadline; it made him focus. Otherwise, he could be out all day mowing down trees and scooping up brush and sod. Claymont loved his work. It had a calming effect on him. Not that he was a boisterous man in the first place, but being inside his cab with some tunes playing made life nice. Scoop up that tree, level that mound – it was simple, mindless. Except today, of course; he had a lot on his mind.

The deadline was one thing, but the big thing was Darren. His son was starting in a playoff football game that night. A couple of scouts from the local colleges were coming to watch. If Darren had a good night on the field, his future could be set. *Wouldn't that be somethin'? My son a college athlete. Yessir, tonight's a big night!* Claymont started his work as a popular dance beat hit the airwaves.

Three hours later, he reached over and turned off the engine of the Cat. His back was aching, and his stomach was growling. What really made him stop, though, was his bladder. He was still holding his morning coffee, and he needed to pee.

He climbed from the cab and relieved himself by the big, back track of the Cat. "Good start," he said looking out at his progress. The morning work had gone smoothly. He decided to have an early lunch and retrieved his lunchbox from the cab. Unwrapping his sandwich, he noticed it contained pimento cheese again. He loved his wife Agnes dearly, but he didn't love her pimento cheese.

Agnes was his angel. They had met when he was on the cleaning crew of the Community College over in Shale. Agnes was finishing up her degree in business and would stay late at the library most nights. They first had exchanged pleasantries, then one conversation had led to another and before either of them knew it, they had been dating for a while. They married two years later, and their first baby came the Spring after that.

They built their dream home in Meadowview Acres eleven years ago. They were happy – still in love after all these years. Agnes had worked her way up to management at Shale Global Insurance, and he had moved into the construction business. He had worked construction for almost twenty years now and had been with Gary Sam Construction for the last twelve. They had a nice comfortable life, and Claymont counted his blessings every day.

One thing he didn't bless, however, was Agnes' pimento cheese. At least she had put three oatmeal cookies in his lunch, too. Claymont was nothing if not a huge, walking sweet tooth. He was halfway into his sandwich when he realized he was sweating. Not a little moist or damp – really dripping. *When did it get so hot?* Warm days were not uncommon in Hallston in late October, but it was not even noon yet. He finished his lunch and slugged back his bottle of water. His shirt was wet with sweat, so he stripped down to his undershirt. That was wet, too, but he would use the air in the Cat to cool off.

Starting his climb into the cab, Claymont slipped on the first step and sprawled onto the ground below. "Damn!" He spat. "What the hell's wrong with me?" He shook his head to clear it and saw bright-blue flashes in front of his eyes. His head was swimming, and he was sweating like crazy. He felt like his cookies were about to make a reappearance, too. He put his head in his hands, closed his eyes, and willed the episode to pass. He didn't have a heart problem that he knew about; no history of stroke in his family. He wondered if there was a virus going around. Claymont took some deep breaths and thought of Darren, his big strong boy.

Darren had worked hard in middle school to get noticed by the high school coaches and it had worked. His freshman year, he had caught a break when the full-back, who was a junior, unexpectedly injured his ACL. Darren walked right into the poor guy's spot and owned it for the last four years. Claymont was so proud. The boy worked hard on his grades, too. He was a good boy to his mother and polite to everyone. *So proud.* Claymont knew tonight was really going to be special.

Claymont opened his eyes and felt better. Thinking about Darren had calmed his nerves, and his stomach had settled. "Might be able to keep those cookies, after all," he said to the ground. He took it easy standing up and felt fine, so he started up into the cab again. "Maybe Agnes is trying to poison me with that pimento cheese," he chuckled as he started the Cat's engine. He positioned the air vents, so the coolness would hit his face then started back to the stand of small maple trees he had been clearing before lunch.

He felt okay, but he was still sweating hard. Little beads worked their way to the tip of his nose before falling into his lap, and his hands were slippery on the wheel. He felt like his movements were slow and strange.

He had just taken down a good sized maple when he saw something glitter on the ground in front of him. Usually, up that high, you couldn't see something small like a bottle cap or even a necklace. To make that glare it had to be something substantial. He backed up the bulldozer to see if he could get a better look at that angle and immediately felt hotness inside his chest. Sweat was dripping down Claymont's whole body, and he started to get a little panicky. He cranked the air in the cab and took some deep breaths. Out of the corner of his eye he could see the shimmer from the thing under the maple trees.

By the time the blue flashes started in front of his eyes again, Claymont knew he was in trouble. He quickly turned off the engine and fished his cell out of the pocket of his jeans. He tried to flip it open, but his fingers didn't seem to be working. He had to try three times when finally the phone slid open. Flashing lights were disrupting his vision, but his thoughts were clear. *Darren – Agnes*

–Pain. Where had the pain come from? His head was on fire inside.

He tried to push the buttons on the phone but couldn't see anything except blue flashes. "Darren. Agnes. Darren – big night. Agnes," he groaned. He had three numbers punched in when the flashes became one steady blue light.

There were two and a third acres left to clear when pain exploded inside Claymont Darren Jackson's skull. His body slumped down in the seat of the cab as a trickle of blood ran from his left nostril.

CHAPTER 2

Eli & Hunter

Eli and Hunter were cutting up in class as usual. Mr. Just had handed out the quiz on the Periodic Table not twenty minutes before, and they had finished in record time. Now they were bored and had to hang out for another forty minutes. To pass the time, they had resorted to flicking paper footballs through goals made with their fingers.

The two had been inseparable since Eli was born three and a half weeks after Hunter. That was sixteen years ago. Living next door to each other, it was only natural that they would become friends. The only thing that set them apart was their looks. Elivan was tall and lean with straight blonde hair and bright blue eyes. Hunter was broad and muscular – his wavy brown hair almost hiding his olive green eyes. Their play-dates started on the floor with stacking cups, followed by crawling races, hide and seek and super-hero fights in the back yard. As the years went by, they found cardboard boxes and lawn chairs could make awesome robots that reconfigured into tanks. Their focus changed, however, when a fourth grade field trip took them to the Science Center in Glover-croft. Their eyes filled with wonder as they went from exhibit to exhibit, each one seeming more impossi-ble than the first. From then on, every birthday and Christmas was greeted with a new chemistry set, erec-tor set or magic kit. They were hooked. They decided their professional name would be Shazaam Brothers and referred to themselves as such while performing more and more experiments and magic shows in the neighborhood.

Now they were bored. Twenty-seven more minutes until the bell rang and school would be out for the day.

Eli saw Mr. Just scan the room. A few more students were finishing up the quiz. "Come on, people," Mr. Just said. "This is not a hard quiz. Finish up." Eli couldn't understand how the kids could be so challenged. *It's memorization, not massive equation solving. Most of you are just lazy or idiots, like Hansen.*

They were still at the back of the room flicking paper footballs at each other when Eli's went high and hit

Hunter in the forehead. The mishap prompted them both to sputter out quiet laughter.

The bell finally rang, and school was out for the day. Hunter and Eli navigated the halls of Hallston High School as routinely as usual, first stopping at their lockers and then winding their way through the other students in the hallways toward the student parking lot. Passing Ms. Leezil's room, they heard the familiar voice of Hansen Reynolds.

Hansen was a typical high school jock. Part bully, part lady's man, the only thing he didn't have was intelligence. Hansen saw them coming and yelled, "Hey, Girls! Driving home together again, Fairies? You two ever spend any time apart?"

"No," Joe Eastman, one of Hansen's friends responded. "They haven't had their special alone time yet!"

The rest of the group broke up into giggles and went back to the stimulating conversation that had been interrupted. Hunter caught the eye of Hansen's girlfriend, Clara, and looked quickly away. Why she would ever want a guy like that was beyond him. Clara was always so nice, ever since grade school. Now she was just a side-kick to a jerk. *Man, girls make no sense.*

Finally, they made it out the door to the parking lot. They had both passed their driver's license tests, but only Eli had wheels – another guilt gift from his departing father – a nice 2010 Ford Fusion. It was bright red and Hunter had named it *The Flaming Tomato*. Eli loved the car, though he would never admit it to his dad. It had all the bells and whistles even that new hands-free system that played songs from an iPod.

Inside the Tomato, they discussed inventive ways to dispose of Hansen Reynolds and came up with a few really nice ideas. The day was warm but not hot, so they kept the sunroof open. The drive home was fast since their neighborhood of Meadowview Acres was only five miles from the school. As they pulled up to the house, Eli could tell that Heather was already home because the front door was open.

"Want to hang out later?" Hunter asked.

"Not today. Mom's gonna be late, so I have some stuff to do. We still going to the game?" Eli replied.

"Sure, I wanna see Hansen get pummeled by one of Glovercroft's linemen!" Hunter said with a nasty smirk.

"Alright then. See ya later"

"Yeah, I'll see ya."

As Hunter walked the short distance to his house, Eli got his backpack out of the back seat and locked the Fusion. He noticed the security gate in the front yard was open and cussed Heather. He ran inside, and, sure enough, the door to her room was shut and music was blaring.

He banged on her door. "Heather! Heather! Where's Brody? Did you let him out?"

Opening the door with her usual scowl for her big brother, Heather replied, "I didn't let him out. I just came home and came into my room. Now go away. Jake's picking me up to go to the mall, and I'm getting ready."

Before he could respond, she had shut the door in his face. He balled up his fists and banged them on the door. "Brat!" He yelled.

He took a quick look around the house and realized his suspicions were right. There was no sign of Brody. Eli was pissed. He always had to clean up after everyone else. He didn't understand why he was the only responsible one, the one always in charge of everything. It was the third time that week the dog had gotten out. All because Heather had left the gate open in the yard – again. He used to get along fine with his sister, but he had noticed that ever since she started dating Jake she could barely tie her shoes, much less latch a security gate.

He ran through the front door and bounded down the steps and through the front gate to the street. "Brody!" He yelled. "Here, Brody!" *Where is he?* He wondered why they even had a dog. His mom thought a puppy was just the thing to cheer up the kids after his dad left. All it was, though, was more for Eli to do. With his mom working all hours at the hospital and Heather in a fog of teenage love, the dog would starve if it weren't for Eli.

"Brody!" "Here, boy!" He yelled again. Eli saw a furry tail disappear behind the Miller's garage. He had to get the dog quickly. The Miller's was the last house before the woods and a Border Collie in the woods is not an easy catch – too many squirrels, birds, creatures and critters to smell out and chase.

He ran toward the Miller's garage and rounded it just in time to see Brody pounce into the rough foliage at the end of the woods. "Crap!" He spat. He ran calling for the dog until he got to the edge of the woods. There he stopped and peered in. There was no sign of the dog or anything else moving. He edged his way through the thick brush and started calling for Brody again. To his right, he saw movement and turned to see a squirrel racing up a broad oak. He started jogging at a steadier pace since the ground had evened out a bit. "Brody, where are you? Come!" He heard a bark in the distance, but it didn't sound too far away. He broke into a run.

There had been a lot of people in the woods lately – surveyors and builders. Eli had heard they were going to build a new subdivision there. All of his neighbors were upset about it because they liked the peaceful-ness of their secluded neighborhood. Eli really didn't care, though. It didn't matter to him if they built three hundred more cookie cutter houses for three hundred more cookie cutter families with three hundred more squalling kids running around the streets. *As long as they leave me alone.*

He heard another bark and determined that he was getting a little closer. He could see light up ahead from a clearing, and wondered if that was where the Border Collie had run. Eli was hot from running and sweat poured down his armpits and forehead. *It didn't feel this hot out earlier today.*

The barks came at a regular rate as Eli ran the last few yards to the clearing. He came up short when he burst into the bright sunlight. After being in the woods, it seemed like the sun was brighter than nor-mal. He could see Brody on the other side of the clear-ing. He was sniffing around a parked bulldozer; one of those huge yellow Caterpillars. He guessed the workers had left it there after a day of clearing. Eli heard them from time to time when he had the win-dows open at his house – the low steady hum and the "beep beep beep" when they backed up. He didn't mind the noise really, but his mother did. "Those things drive my head crazy!" She had said. Eli didn't think the machines drove her crazy. He thought the fact that her husband of nineteen years had run off with a much younger version of herself is what drove her head crazy.

Suddenly, Brody issued a low, menacing growl. The fur on his shoulders and haunches stood up, and he dropped his head forward. Eli didn't much care for being alone in the woods, and this new development didn't help matters much. Besides, he was wringing with sweat and had the beginnings of a headache. "Brody, come," he said with all of the authority his sixteen years could muster, "Come, now!"

The dog let out a searing howl, jumped back at least a yard, turned and started to run. Eli's eyes grew wide as he saw his dog racing toward him with its ears back and slobber foaming from its jaws. He was a little nervous by then and reached for the comfort of the dog as it neared. Almost upon him, Eli realized the animal's eyes looked frantic. Eli reached for Brody just as Brody flew past him back into the woods. Eli, thoroughly spooked now and imagining all types of fanged monsters on his heels, ran after the dog. Branches scratched his face, and he could feel his heart pounding.

When they both broke through the other side of the woods, the Miller's garage was like a beacon of safety.

Eli watched as Brody crossed the street to his own house, ran into their yard and through the opened front door. Feeling safer and a little silly for being scared in the first place, Eli cussed his sister in his mind and made a vow to do something hideous to her favorite CD.

CHAPTER 3

Mr. Just

The hallway after school was chaos, as usual. Mr. Just was monitoring the situation from outside his classroom door. Locker doors banged shut as kids laughed and screamed at each other from down the hall. Linda Baske was crying again about her boyfriend while the quiet ones just tried to get through the hallway unnoticed.

Mr. Just was always amazed at how loud it was. He never remembered his high school experience being this loud. It was like every sound had to be amplified for dramatic effect. "These kids just need to take it easy, Man. Chill out, calm down," he said quietly to himself. He caught Ms. Leezil's eye from her classroom across the hall, and they gave each other a look of exasperation. He knew she felt the same as he did. They had talked about this generation of kids over coffee in the teacher's lounge or drinks at his place. Her theory was that all of the preservatives in the food nowadays was to blame. She said it got the kid's hormones out of whack. He chalked it up to parents laying down on the job. He thought it was easy to give little Jimmy John or little Suzy Q everything they wanted without having to earn it. Every kid got a ribbon for just being in a race now, not for winning it. "Let's pat them all on the back every time they do anything," he thought. "How's that working out for you folks? You're raising a bunch of little darlings."

He watched those darlings now as they pushed, shoved, taunted and otherwise made life hell for each other. Some were worse than others, of course. Every school from every generation had its bullies and dumbasses. The one from his own experience was named Brad Knowles. Brad was a jock and not real forgiving of anyone who wasn't. That left Phillip Just directly in his sights. Phil was an easy going, laid back type of guy. He didn't sweat the small stuff. "Live and let live, Man." That was his motto. His long hair was clean and always tied in a long ponytail – not flying around free. He was chill. He was free. Mostly, he was high. Phil loved life and everyone in it, just as long as he had a smoke. Brad made sure that Phil was pushed around as often as possible to pay for the crime of not being like himself. That meant knocking books out of his hands, spraying his locker with shaving foam, throwing rocks to smack him in the head and all sorts of other punishments. Phil thought of it as an inconvenience, some moments worse than others. He heard at the last reunion that Brad had been killed in a drunk-driving accident. *Karma, Man.*

He was startled out of his trip down memory lane by the familiar teasing, "Ms. Weezil! Hey, Joe! Did ya see Ms. Weezil with her beady little weasel eyes?"

Of course it was Hansen Reynolds and his group of idiots. The rhyming jab at Ms. Leezil was nothing new and really didn't take much thought. Hansen just enjoyed it because he thought it was mean. Julie wasn't even bothered. Growing up Julie Leezil, she had always been teased about her last name. It didn't even faze her any more.

Something like a chewed up eraser went flying in Ms. Leezil's direction and missed her face by an inch. On his own, Hansen was more of a coward who didn't do much except verbally assault the world with his personality, but when his crew was around he had more courage. Phil didn't like the direction this was going.

"Hansen!" He yelled. "Over here now. You're in detention."

Hansen looked over at Mr. Just and grinned sarcastically. "It wasn't me, Mr. Just. It was Joe here. He's the one that did it."

Joe looked surprised and looked over at Mr. Just. "No it wasn't! I was headed out the door!"

Mr. Just really didn't want to play games with the idiot. "Hansen, you don't think I know you by now, Dude? You're in my detention more than any other kid in this school. Stop arguing and get in my classroom. The rest of you hit the road. Now."

He glanced at Julie who gave him a wink then slipped back into her classroom. He would be sure to collect on that debt later this weekend.

Hansen strutted over to Mr. Just's classroom and told the others that he'd meet up with them at the Hot Dog Hut later. "After I'm finished with my spankin'," he sneered.

Phil watched him strut by and felt disgusted. He was the type of teacher who found redeeming qualities in basically every student. Hansen, however, was a challenge. There just wasn't a likable aspect to the boob at all. He followed Hansen into the room just as the bell for detention sounded. Looking over the list, Mr. Just found no surprises. The usual suspects were all there, since Hansen had joined the group. "What is detention doing for them anyway?" He wondered.

They never changed. They didn't even seem to mind spending their free time in a classroom.

Mr. Just shook his head and settled down to grade the chemistry quizzes from his last class. No surprises there, either. The same kids got A's, the same kids got C's and Hansen got an F. He started to think what motivation the kid had for anything. Was there anything at all to drive Hansen Reynolds to excel? The kid had football; that was a no brainer. He was a big dude and could throw his weight around. He received accolades and praise from the coaching staff, but the student body as a whole rallied around him out of fear, not hero worship. What was the kid going to do when the cheers were gone and there were no more games to play? He knew the kid's home life stank. He had called two parent-teacher conferences already, and, at each one, the teacher was the only person to show up. He had called the home to discuss Hansen's failing grade only to be told by Mr. Reynolds not to worry about Hansen. "My boy is going to play ball and doesn't need a grade from a chemistry class to do that," he had said. The boy was screwed.

Finally, the bell rang ending detention and Phil breathed a sigh of relief. "Friday, thank God, Man." He thought. "I could use a beer."

He followed the detention kids out of the classroom and walked over to Ms. Leezil's door. "Hey, Jules. Did you recover from your trauma?"

"Ha!" She laughed. "It was hardly a trauma. Thanks for the intervention, though. That kid creeps me out!"

"No prob. Hey, I'm in the mood for Mexican. Want to keep me company?"

"I can't tonight. I'm on duty at the snack bar for the game. How about tomorrow night?" She asked with a little twinkle in her eye.

"Sure thing, Babe. Have fun feeding the masses!"

"Thanks. See you later, Phil." She winked at him as he left her room.

He went back to his classroom, grabbed his corduroy jacket and messenger bag and locked his door. Going through the visitor's parking on his way to the staff lot, he thought of Hansen Reynolds again. He couldn't seem to get his mind off the kid. He was still thinking that Hansen could be saved. He pushed the kid from his mind by planning his weekend. "It should be pleasant outside, maybe I could get in some yard work. Or I could take Jules to that Classic Rock Festival over in Glovercroft," He thought. He drove out of the parking lot thinking of what to order at Mexicali that night.

CHAPTER 4

Bug

"Sometimes you can hear a house breathe," thought Bug. "If you're super quiet, you can actually hear it inhale and exhale." Bug was lying on the couch with her eyes closed. She was trying to be still. She had muted the TV because she had already seen that episode of her cartoon. She knew, at twelve, she was really too old for cartoons, but she didn't care. It was her favorite show. Her Rubik's Cube was solved and on the table beside her. *When are they going to come out with another one? This one is super easy.*

Born Mary Ellen Hamilton, Bug had never actually answered to that name. Her parents nicknamed her Ladybug in the hospital because she was a tender five pounds, five ounces at birth with a head full of shocking black hair. Her Aunt Nicki had brought a blanket

23

with Ladybugs all over it to the hospital, and, curled up within, Mary Ellen had been referred to as the little Ladybug. The moniker was shortened to Bug over the years, and it was the only name she considered hers. Her looks hadn't changed much as she grew. She was petite for her age and her long straight hair was still as black as coal.

Bug was an extremely intelligent girl. With that came very few friends. The kids at school were just not excited about math or science the way Bug was. They had more important things to talk about, like sports, celebrities or the latest in the never ending dance of who's dating whom. Bug just shut them out and did her own thing. It didn't even bother her, really. She was quite content. She had her parents, Mark and Ann Hamilton, who were very involved in her life. Mark was the editor of the Hallston Daily Journal, the town newspaper. Bug loved when her dad came home armed with exciting stories of things happening in the world; places she had never even heard of before. She couldn't wait to read the paper with her dad every morning at the breakfast table. They would talk about the day's headlines and stories until it was time to leave for school.

Ann was a nurse who tried to fit her schedule around Bug's school day. She worked in the Neonatal Unit at Community Hospital. Bug loved hearing about the new babies when she and her mom worked in the garden, as they often did.

When her parents were both working, she had Shasta Port. Shasta was not quite a babysitter – more of a companion really. The big sister she didn't have. She was five years older and Bug always described her as "super nice and fun".

Bug was waiting for Shasta to come pick her up. Her mom had asked Shasta to take her for a haircut. Bug didn't really mind. She liked her hair, but it was too long and starting to get in her way. She closed her eyes and tried to hear the house breathe again, but the moment had passed and all she heard was the ice maker releasing its newly formed cubes from bondage. That made her want a Popsicle, so she hopped off the couch and skipped into the kitchen.

"Hmm, red or orange," she said to the empty room. "Red, super good." She un-wrapped her prize and looked out the kitchen window. It was very quiet out. She didn't hear the sounds of machinery from the other side of the woods. She was actually growing fond of the sounds. She thought the backup beeper was especially nice. She heard a bark and saw Brody, the Andrews' dog, pop out from behind the Miller's garage and run across the street and into the Andrews' house. Eli followed him. Bug liked Eli, but she liked Brody better.

The dog had found his way over to her house one time when he had gotten loose. Bug had loved how "super" soft his fur was and how he looked at her straight in the eyes. She and the dog had sat there for minutes just looking into each other's eyes. It had been relaxing for her. Most people didn't look at Bug much; she was curiously invisible. That was okay, though. She had Shasta. They talked about a lot of things, everything from Bug's favorite math class to Shasta's latest boy crush. Bug didn't quite get Shasta's interest in boys, but she liked to hear her talk about them. The one that came up most of the time was Darren. Shasta had liked him since she and Darren were in homeroom together in the eighth grade.

She had sucked the pop down to the stick and her mouth was frozen. As she threw the stick away, she heard Shasta's truck pull up in the driveway. Bug grabbed her bag and went out the side door, making sure it was locked behind her. *Never can be too careful – even in Meadowview Acres.*

She hopped down the steps and flung open the door to Shasta's Ranger. "Hey, Shasta! " Bug chirped, her mouth bright red from the frozen pop.

"Yum, Popsicle?" Shasta asked.

"Yup, how'd ya know?" Bug asked smiling.

Shasta just grinned and backed the Ranger out of the Hamilton's driveway.

"Okay, Miss Bug, off to get that hair trimmed. Where should we go when we're finished?" Shasta asked, already knowing what Bug would request.

"Oh! Can we get some tots at the Hot Dog Hut?" Bug asked. She loved the tater tots at the Hut. That was the place Shasta's parents owned. Shasta worked there part time when she wasn't hanging out with Bug. Bug loved going with Shasta because they always gave her extra tots when Shasta brought her by.

"Sure," replied Shasta. "I wanted to ask my dad about something anyway.

As they drove down the street, they passed the Andrew's house. Eli was washing Brody in the driveway beside the house. Shasta was about to honk a greeting but stopped when she saw the frown on Eli's face. "Somebody's in a grumpy mood," she thought. She took a right turn out of the neighborhood and headed toward town.

CHAPTER 5

Shasta

Bug fiddled with the radio as Shasta drove down Main Street toward Curls For Gurls. The song Bug settled on made Shasta kind of sad. It had been a special one for her and Darren. Shasta was still surprised at how quickly things could change in a person's life. Just a few short years ago, she and Darren were so close. They were best friends. Now, he would barely say hi when they passed in the hallway at school.

They had known each other since childhood. Living in the same neighborhood meant you went to the same schools. That combined with the never ending stream of neighborhood kickball games, cookouts, and Fourth of July parties made it impossible for them not to become friends. Shasta and Darren had an easy friendship. Shasta had a calm and mothering nature. If another kid got hurt playing or felt picked on, she was the first one to offer help or straighten out the bullies. Darren was much the same. He got along with everyone and never caused drama. The two of them always seemed to be picked first when calling teams for neighborhood games. The other kids in the neighborhood eventually thought of them as connected. They wouldn't say just Shasta or just Darren. It was always Shasta and Darren or Darren and Shasta.

By the time eighth grade came around, they were best friends. She could tell him anything and the same went for Darren. They spent most of their free time together, either outside or at each other's houses. Shasta never missed a football game; she was always sitting in the stands with Mr. & Mrs. Jackson. They were as close as two friends could be. That is, until the kiss ruined everything.

They were at a party in the basement of Joe Eastman's house after a big game Hallston had won. Lots of the football guys were there and they all kept taunting Darren. They were pushing him to kiss her, calling him chicken. Everyone thought they were a couple anyway, so they gave in to peer-pressure. Shasta had thought of it as a joke, but the joke was on her. She had come away from the kiss breathless and shocked at her body's response. She had never felt so alive!

She was also shocked at Darren's response. He had looked angry and immediately gone upstairs. She followed him and tried to talk, but he was distant. A little while later, he just left the party. From then on, their friendship felt awkward and forced. He wouldn't talk to her and didn't want to hang out. He was acting angry. She thought he wanted to go back to how things were before the kiss, but Shasta had developed genuine feelings for him. Either way, the friendship was doomed. Gradually, Darren began spending more time with his football friends, and Shasta just drifted away.

That was three years ago and Shasta still missed him. Not so much the love part, but the friends until the end part. She had other friends, but she never quite connected with them the way she had with Darren. She still went to all of his games, though. She knew she would never find another Darren.

Bug snapped Shasta out of her thoughts by singing very loudly to the song on the radio. They had reached Curls For Gurls and Shasta swung the Ranger into a parking space.

Forty-five minutes later with four less inches of hair, Bug was squirting ketchup onto a napkin to dip her tots into. Mrs. Port had given her an extra serving of them and Bug was in Tot Heaven.

Shasta left her in the booth and went in search of her dad. Mr. Port was a serious business owner and didn't like to be disturbed while working, but when he spotted his only child coming toward him with her deep auburn hair and dark brown eyes, he beamed. Shasta was the only thing he would stop everything for. She was his baby. After a squelching bear hug, he said, "What's my baby up to today?"

"Just bringing Bug by for a snack. Do you have a minute, though? I wanted to ask you about something."

"I've got all the time in the world for my best girl." He patted the seat beside him. "What's up?"

"Well," began Shasta, "You know it's my senior year and you know how I really want to get into a good journalism program in college?"

"Yep, I think you're on a really good track, Honey. How can I help?"

"Well, I just happened to mention it to Mr. Hamilton when I was picking up Bug last week. I really didn't expect anything; I was just making conversation." She stopped and took a big breath. "He offered me a summer internship. I mean, I didn't even ask him or anything; he just kind of offered. I didn't know what to say, so I told him I had to talk to you about it. I know you and Mom depend on me to work here part time, but this could really look great on my application, and the experience would be incredible. What do you think, Dad?"

Mr. Port knew the day was coming when his baby would leave him, but he thought that day would be at the end of summer, not the beginning of spring. He knew Shasta loved writing articles for the school newspaper, and she had dreams of becoming a really respected journalist. There wasn't anything she couldn't do, but he wished it didn't have to be so soon.

"Shasta, honey," he said, "There is no way a hot dog stand is going to come between my girl and her dreams of greatness. Of course you should take it. The Hallston Daily Journal is going to be lucky to have you."

Shasta was relieved. She loved her folks so much, she didn't want them to be short on help for the summer, but this internship was perfect and at just the right time. She hugged her dad tightly thinking how lucky she was to have caring parents.

"Thanks, Daddy, I really..."

"Stop it!" Bug screamed from the other side of the Hut. "Give those back you primate!"

Mr. Port and Shasta whirled toward the commotion to see Hansen Reynolds holding Bug's paper cup of tater tots up out of her reach. Standing on the seat of the booth, Bug was trying to stretch far enough to snatch them back.

"What's wrong, little Bookie Wookie Worm," Hansen taunted. "Did somebody steal your widdle snackie?"

He kept the cup of tots just out of her reach and would jerk them further away when she tried to snag them. His crew was laughing behind him and egging him on.

"Give them back! You're contaminating them with your idiot juice!" Bug wailed.

That insult was just biting enough for Hansen to mean business. Nobody embarrasses Hansen Reynolds in front of his subjects. He put the cup right in front of Bug's face, and, when she made to grab it, he stepped quickly to the side causing Bug to fall face first out of the booth and land on the cold cement floor of the Hut.

"Now listen here," Mr. Port bellowed. "I'll have none of that bullying in my place! You get out, Reynolds. And take your crew with you. If you can't behave in public, you're not welcome." He locked his steely gaze on Hansen.

Giggling and making quiet insults aimed at Mr. Port, Hansen and his followers moved toward the door. None of them were brave enough to actually be overheard because they knew Bill Port had been in the service. They also knew he kept a bat behind the cash register, and he wouldn't hesitate to use it.

As Clara Stagg passed the floor where Shasta was helping Bug to sit up, she quietly said, "Sorry, Buggie. You okay?"

"Yeth. Thankth, Clara," replied Bug holding a napkin to her bloody nose.

"Sometimes he can be a jerk, but he's not that way all the time," responded Clara, looking genuinely worried.

"I guess he keeps those other times secret," snapped Shasta. "Come on, Bug. Let's get you cleaned up."

As Shasta was helping Bug to her feet, Hansen, looking for Clara, turned from the door. "Come on, Babe. Don't keep me waitin'." His gentle tone was belied by the menacing look in his eyes as he kept them on Clara.

"I'm coming," said Clara and gave Bug and Shasta an apologetic glance.

"Out!" Mr. Port said sternly, glaring at Hansen. Hansen met his eyes in defiance for a moment before Clara caught up to him. They turned together and left.

Mrs. Port was rushing toward the booth with a tray. She placed it in front of Bug and smiled sweetly. "Here you go, Pumpkin, a brand new batch fresh from the fryer!"

"Thanth Mithus Pord," said Bug. The bleeding was easing up, and she felt better since the jerks were gone. Mrs. Port winked and hurried back to the front counter. The after school crowd was still trickling in, and she had a line waiting.

Mr. Port sat down opposite Bug and checked her nose. "Not too bad, Hon. I think you'll live." He smiled. "Try not to insult that guy so much, though. I know he's a jerk, but he knows you're smarter than he is, and that makes him a little afraid of you. Sometimes fear can make mean people even meaner, and I might not be around to stop him. Steer clear, okay? That goes for you, too, Shas." He looked meaningfully at his daughter.

"Got it, Dad-O," Shasta replied. "I think I'll get this one home now, though. Let's pack up and get going, Bug."

They got their things together and a to-go bag for Bug, said their goodbyes and hopped into the Ranger. They both sang along with the radio as they made their way back to Meadowview Acres. By the time they arrived, they had already forgotten the incident. As Shasta pulled the truck into the Hamilton's driveway, she noticed Eli and Hunter Massey walking into the woods behind the Miller's house.

"Wonder what they're up to." She nodded in the direction of the boys. Bug was interested at once.

"Ooh! I don't know! Let's follow and see. It might be an adventure! We can stalk them like the great cats of the Serengeti and scare the poo out of them!" She giggled at the thought.

"No, I don't like the woods. So many creepy crawlers and little rodents are in there. I'm always afraid something's going to drop on my head. Besides, they're probably just doing an experiment for the Shazaam Brothers or something."

"Haha! I forgot about that! They haven't had a magic show in so long. I miss those shows. Come on, Shas, let's go see what they're doing. Come on. You don't have to leave yet, do you?" She pleaded.

Shasta always had a hard time saying no to Bug, but this time she had to.

"Sorry, Bug. I've got to get home and change before I go to the game. Tonight's a big night for Darren, and I want to be there on time. We'll do something tomorrow. How about the library?"

"Sure, that sounds good," Bug replied, but she was still watching the boys make their way through the brush at the edge of the woods.

CHAPTER 6

Clara

Clara had been watching the scene play out in front of Ms. Leezil's room. She had a knot in her stomach. Ms. Leezil was her favorite teacher, and Clara was her student aide. She didn't know why Hansen was so mean sometimes. He was really nice to her when it was just the two of them, but when he got around all of his friends, he could be a major jerk. It was beginning to get old.

At first, when they were a new couple, Clara was thrilled. She was dating the school football star. She could hardly believe it; she was popular by default. No one could challenge her social standing now that she was attached to Hansen. Her mission had finally been completed with a simple make-out session behind the bleachers almost four months ago.

Clara had been very determined to make it happen. In ninth grade, she was a nobody. In tenth, she was noticeable enough for ridicule. Eleventh found her in the popular crowd "sub group". Then she was Senior Class Royalty. She had clawed her way up through the ranks. Sure, she had lost longtime friends and made enemies along the way, but she had no regrets. Well, maybe one, but he was a nobody and she couldn't take the risk.

Now, though, she was starting to get fed up. Hansen's antics were really stupid. All of their friends thought he was so cool and so quick witted with his jabs and insults. No one was brave enough to be on the hit list or the receiving end, so they went along to get along. Clara wondered if she could make it all the way until May. All of the good stuff was right around the corner.

Homecoming had been amazing for her. They were voted King and Queen at the dance and Clara was on cloud nine. She remembered dancing around with her crown atop her golden hair. She knew she had to hang in there. The holidays were coming soon with party after party. After that would be the Winter Formal, and then all of the senior activities, not to mention prom. That would be the culmination of four hard years spent clawing her way to the top –

Prom Queen. After that, she could ditch him, if only she could hold on that long.

Watching him made that incredibly hard. He had just spit a chewed up eraser at Ms. Leezil's face. Clara was embarrassed. She immediately pulled out her cell and acted like all of her texts were keeping her busy, and she had nothing to do with the situation. Thank goodness for Mr. Just sending him to detention. Clara would be free for an hour. She left with the others and caught a ride with Joe and Angie. Angie giggled the whole way to the Hot Dog Hut about how brave Hansen was to spit at Ms. Leezil. Joe was a little irritated that Hansen had tried to blame the whole thing on him, but he would get over it. He always did.

They all ordered and slid into a booth in the corner of the restaurant. The place was packed with after school kids. Mrs. Port was busy at the register, and Mr. Port was filling orders in the back with the two kids that worked there. Clara liked the Ports a lot. They lived just down the street from her. Clara had always loved trick or treats at their house because they both dressed up in costumes, and Mrs. Port gave out little bags filled with goodies instead of just one miniature sized treat. The Ports and Clara's own parents were good friends, as well, so Clara had seen them at her house on a number of occasions.

Clara was also good friends with their daughter, Shasta. Well, they used to be good friends. Shasta was one of those casualties of her social climb. She still saw her, but they didn't hang out at all. Clara glanced around the Hut and didn't see her. She thought Shasta was probably babysitting Bug. Clara had a soft spot for Bug. She liked rooting for the underdog.

The crew was reliving the event at school as if it were the most exciting thing that had happened in weeks. Clara kept her eyes on her french fries and silently wished she were home. "What is it with me today," she wondered. "I'm so sick of all of these people."

Somebody asked her a question, so she put on her popular girl smile and gave her best bubbly answer. Soon she was just as wrapped up in the school gossip as the others and she was able to get past her previous mood.

Hansen showed up a little while later after serving his detention. He slid into the seat beside her with his usual Loaded Cheese Coney and Tots. "Great," she thought, "Another oniony kiss later. Gross." Outwardly, though, she smiled and said, "How was the torture chamber with Mr. Just?"

"Easy! That old man don't bother me. I just played games on my phone for an hour. Who cares, anyway? I got a nice break before the game tonight!" Hansen shoved half of the wiener into his mouth and chomped down hard. Chili oozed down his chin and landed on the table below with a big, wet splat. He barely chewed before he swallowed the mouthful down and followed it with a chubby fistful of tots.

"Don't remind me. I feel so bad that I can't come," she lied. "I can't believe my parents are making me sit for my little brother!" Actually, she had volunteered for babysitting duty when she overheard her parents making plans for the evening. Clara was excited about playing video games with her little brother, pigging out on pizza and watching a movie in her PJ's after Charlie went to bed.

"You should be sorry, Babe," Hansen retorted around a mouthful of food. "You're gonna miss my moves on the field, and I might just show some other chick my moves off the field!" He laughed grotesquely at his own stupid joke.

Clara acted like she was hurt, but out loud she said, "You better be a good boyfriend and call me when the game's over. I want to hear all about it."

"You bet, Babe," he said, then turned to address his subjects. "Let's get outta here, guys. If we're late, Coach'll make us run sprints."

The guys shoved the rest of their food in and left the booth to throw away their trash. Clara was still gathering her things when she heard someone yell, "Stop it!"

She turned and knew before she saw that it was Hansen doing what Hansen did best – picking on someone. Poor little Bug was standing up on the seat of the booth trying to get to the food Hansen was holding out of her reach. Clara knew the situation was going to end badly before it ultimately did. It happened so quickly, and then Bug was sprawled on the floor. Shasta was beside her in an instant while Mr. Port was getting the boys in hand. Clara went over to Shasta and Bug and tried to offer help. Bug's little nose was bloody, and Shasta was pissed. She clearly wanted no help from Clara. When Hansen called for her to leave, Clara swallowed her anger and replaced it with her popular girl smile.

All the way to Meadowview Acres, Hansen talked about how great he was going to be in the football game. Clara was ignoring him and dreading the kiss that would inevitably come. Hansen pulled up in front of Clara's house and turned off the engine. Clara's hand was on the door handle when he shoved his face against hers. The smell of onions was strong and bitter on his breath, and he still had little particles of hot dog and tater tots in his mouth. It was all Clara could do not to throw up. Finally, the goodbye was over, and Clara couldn't escape the car fast enough. Hansen honked and pulled away.

Clara spit on the ground beside her and felt nauseous. "I'm never going to make it until prom," she said to herself. "Come on, girl, eyes on the prize, eyes on the prize." She took a moment to envision herself in a snow-white, flowing ball gown, her long golden hair shining with a huge crown on top of her head.

As she turned to go into the house, she noticed Hunter coming out of the side door to his house across the street. He happened to glance her way then turned back quickly. She felt the butterflies again and watched him as he walked the short distance to Eli's driveway. When he got there, he turned in her direction again. Clara raised her hand and waved. Hunter kind of nodded and then turned to talk to Eli who was washing his dog. Clara watched the back of his head for a moment before going into her house.

Hunter had been on Clara's radar for years. Unfortunately, he was not high enough on the social ladder to count for much. In Clara's mind, if she could just make it to graduation with Hansen the Neanderthal, the summer was reserved for Hunter. He was her dream – the one. Her first love, her first real kiss. "Hold on, girl," she told herself. "You can do this."

For tonight, though, her dream was a night without Hansen, and a lot of pizza...

CHAPTER 7

Darren

Darren was alone in the locker room. He liked to get there early on game days to clear his mind and go over the playbook. He went over everything in his head, so he would be able to react quickly and accurately when the coach called any play. Darren usually wasn't nervous before a game, but tonight was different. Tonight was big. Two different recruiters from two different colleges were coming to see him. If he did well tonight, he could write his own ticket. *If I mess up, though...* He shook his head to make the thought go away. That just wasn't an option. He had to play well. He had to. He wished for the millionth time that he could talk to Shasta. She would say all the right things to ease his mind. She could calm him down just by being there. He knew he would see her sitting with his parents in the stands, though. She had never missed a game. Not even after things went bad.

That night at the party was such a mistake. Darren still couldn't believe what he had let happen. Never to be one to let peer pressure get to him, Darren still didn't know why that night was different. They had all been in the basement. All of the football guys with their girlfriends and Darren and Shasta. He was sure everyone knew that their relationship was one of friendship, but something had happened. Some of the guys started egging him on, daring him to kiss her. They were being pretty harsh about it, calling him names. Usually, that kind of thing didn't faze Darren. At six foot two, he was a solid mass of muscles. No one bothered him, but that night was different. It was after a big game that they had won, so Darren was pretty pumped before they had even gotten to the party. Then with all the daring and pushing and everything, he gave in. He had moved in close to Shasta. "When did she start smelling so good?" He had thought. He remembered a clean, crisp, citrusy smell. He hadn't noticed how deeply brown her eyes were until he was looking straight into them. He felt a weird rolling in his belly, and he had started to sweat a little. As soon as his lips touched hers, his whole body seemed to feel it. He moved his hands into her silky soft hair and pulled her head closer to his own. He was melting. He wanted to stay like that, touching her forever, but she had pulled away, looking embarrassed. "Crap!" Darren had thought. She obviously hadn't felt the same way. The guys were being guys and saying stupid stuff like, "Get a room" or "Now he's whipped". Darren had gone upstairs to get a soda and hadn't gone back down. Shasta followed him up after a bit and tried to talk, but he had been cool to her. He felt rejected – not just rejected, but rejected by his best friend. His ego deflated, he made an excuse to leave the party. Things really just fizzled after that. He was too nervous to be alone with her anymore. He just wanted to grab her, hold her and kiss her again and again, but he knew she just wanted to forget it. She started hanging out with her girlfriends more, and he had no choice but to find a new group of friends. She never missed a game, though. Darren was happy about that.

Alone in the locker room, he pushed his mind back to the game. He concentrated on each play – on his part of each play. He couldn't mess up; not tonight. It could be amazing. What if both of the colleges wanted him? What if he could have his choice between the two? Darren knew his dad would be so proud. He had been supporting Darren for as long as he could remember. He remembered his dad outside playing ball with him even after a long day at work. He had made it to almost all of Darren's games, ever since middle school. He had only missed a few because of a deadline at work. Darren knew his dad was just as nervous as Darren about tonight. He would never let Darren see, though. "Just play like you always do, Son. Any school would be lucky to have you. And if they take a pass, well then, they're the losers, not you." He had said that to Darren just this morning at breakfast before he left for work.

"Thanks, Dad. See you at the game," Darren had replied.

He would see him at the game. They had a traditional salute to each other right after the National Anthem played. His mom thought it was silly, but she had filled in whenever his dad wasn't there, so he had never started a game without that salute. Tonight would be no different.

Darren started to undress and change into his pads and uniform just as the idiots arrived. Hansen, Joe, Clark, Jacob and Alan were the most irritating guys on the team. Grouped together, as they usually were, they were really hard to handle sometimes. They came in loud, smacking each other around and basically acting like lunatics. They never bothered Darren, though. They knew he could lay each one of them flat. Darren's crew trickled in a little after the idiots. Ethan, Chuck, Brian and Wes were the guys he had turned to when Shasta left. They were really good guys – real good friends. They all talked about the game, but it was almost like his friends were nervous, too – nervous for him. They knew how important the night was and what it could mean if it went well. Ethan, Brian and Wes were busy going over plays and getting dressed when Chuck came over and sat beside Darren.

"How ya feeling?" He asked.

"I'm good." Darren replied. "I've done all the prep work and I know I can perform. I've just never felt these nerves before."

"Man, that's understandable. But listen, you can't give in to them. You gotta go out there like you always do and play ball. Just play ball, D. You've got this." He smiled at Darren and let him have his space.

Coach Ripley came in a few minutes later to go over last minute plays and the starting line-up. Darren's nerves eased up as he listened to the coach go over the strategy for defeating the Glovercroft Mustangs. All of the guys gathered around in the locker room were amped up for the game; Darren was no exception. When he was finished outlining the strategy, the coach looked directly at Darren when he shouted his usual pre-game pump of, "Now let's get out there and show them what the Hallston Jaguars are made of!"

A testosterone fueled battle cry ensued as the team ran out to the field. Darren scanned the stands for his folks and Shasta. There in the usual spot was his mom with Shasta right beside her. "Where's Dad?" he thought. "He must've been held up at the construction site. Better hustle. I need my pre-game salute."

He warmed up with the team and kept checking the stands. Five minutes until the National Anthem followed by the coin toss and Darren started to feel anxious. He saw his coach motion to him and jogged over.

"Listen, Son," Coach Ripley said. "I know it's a big night for you. But you just have to do your job as usual. Now I've already had a talk with both those recruiters, so they know what you're capable of. I need you to go out there and show 'em. Got it?"

"Yessir, Coach. Have you seen my dad, though? Was he talking to the recruiters, too?"

"No, haven't seen Claymont at all tonight. But you know he's here somewhere, Son. You're damned sure he's not gonna miss this game." He clapped Darren hard on his shoulder pad and said, "Now get out there and get your mind on your work."

That was all it took to make Darren feel better. Of course his dad was there somewhere. Maybe he just got hung up talking to someone, or maybe the recruiters wanted to talk to him, and they were behind the bleachers. Darren's head was back on the game. When it came time for his salute after the National Anthem, Darren looked to the stands to find his mom standing up with two fingers touching her forehead. Darren grinned and returned the gesture. "Well, Mom doesn't seem worried," he thought. "So I guess everything's fine."

He jogged over to the middle of the field to join his co-captain for the coin toss. As the ref tossed the coin in the air, Peyton called "Tails" and the quarter landed to show its backside.

"Okay," thought Darren, "Time to go to work."

CHAPTER 8

Heather

"I look awesome!" Heather said to herself as she gazed at her reflection in the full-length mirror in her room. She had on low-waisted blue jeans that showed off her thin legs, brown suede boots with two inch heels and, the best thing of all, her brand new powder-blue sweater with a deep vee neck so a little of her cleavage peeked out.

She had gotten home from the mall just in time to change before Jake came back to pick her up. She knew buying the sweater had been an amazing decision, even if it cut into her birthday money. She thought her boobs looked incredible. "Jake won't be able to keep his hands off of me!" She giggled to herself.

As she examined the rest of her look in the mirror, she took note of just how great her teeth looked.

The braces had taken care of those unsightly buck teeth she had been forced to live with since they had replaced her baby teeth, and the acne wash she had been using for two years really made her skin almost perfect. Her crowning glory was her hair. Her shiny chestnut tresses cascaded down her back in perfect little ringlets. It usually took her about an hour to make those perfect little ringlets, but Jake loved her hair, so the time it took was no bother. She would do anything for him.

Heather wasn't surprised at all that she was the only sophomore in school to be dating a senior. *Just look at me! Any guy would be lucky to have this!* Jake was falling in love with her, she could tell. If things kept going like they were, Heather thought she and Jake could get married right out of high school, and then everyone would be so jealous of her. *More jealous than they are now!*

Heather turned and looked at her backside. "Perfect," she said. "Those butt lunges are really paying off!"

She danced around her purple bedroom as if she were a bride dancing at her wedding. *Heather Mitchell – Mrs. Jake Mitchell – Heather Andrews Mitchell*, which one would she use? "Hey! How old do you have to be to get married anyway?" She asked her room. Heather thought it was stupid to put an age on love – true love. She was sure the idiots that made up that law had never been in love before – at least not in love with Jake Mitchell.

Heather put the finishing touches on her lashes, answered two texts and went out to the living room. "Where is everyone?" She thought. "Oh yeah, Mom had to work tonight." She remembered Eli was there earlier, but she didn't hear anything coming from his room. Brody was asleep in his dog bed, but he smelled wet. "Maybe he got into something and had to get a bath," she thought.

She scribbled *At the game with Jake* on a napkin in the kitchen and left it on the counter. She had cleared it with her mom earlier in the week, but she didn't need Mr. "I'm in charge when Mom's gone" calling her cell all night.

She grabbed an energy drink from the fridge and ran out when she heard Jake's car in the drive. She jumped in the front seat and leaned over to give him a kiss.

"You look great," Jake said while looking directly at her chest.

"Thanks, Babe." Heather accepted the compliment without noticing his stare. She flipped down the car mirror to reapply the gloss she had lost kissing Jake hello.

"I was talking to Tessa, and she said just about everybody's going tonight," gushed Heather.

"Yeah," replied Jake. "It's going to be a good game. I know we'll win, though. Darren and Peyton are beasts. Not to mention our defensive line with Hansen and all those guys."

"Oh, I don't care either way. I just want to show you off to everyone!" Heather felt like all eyes were on her when she walked hanging onto his arm through the halls at school. A football game was even better, because there were people from other schools to witness their love.

Twenty minutes later, they were making out in the parking lot, and Heather was getting bored. "What's the point of dating a senior if you can't be seen at a major social event?" She thought while Jake's hands moved freely over her powder-blue sweater. She moved her head away from his and said, "Let's go on into the game now, Babe. Our friends are probably looking for us."

Jake shrugged and removed his sticky hands from their prizes. Heather reapplied her lip gloss again and fixed her disheveled chestnut ringlets. At the gate, they showed their school badges and went in search of their friends.

The scoreboard read Hallston Jaguars 14, Glovercroft Mustangs 7. The crowd was being stirred up by the cheer squad yelling, "Jaguars, Jaguars, GO, GO, GO!!" Pom-poms were shaking throughout the stands, and people had made signs out of poster board. It was all very exciting, and Heather was thrilled when she saw people looking at her with her future husband. *I really look fantastic tonight!*

The make out session had left her thirsty, so they wandered over to the concession stand. Ms. Leezil was working and gave them a big smile. Everyone loved Ms. Leezil. She was pretty and smart. Heather thought maybe she should be a teacher like Julie Leezil. That would be a good career to have when she and Jake got married. She could have summers off to spend with their babies. She thought they should probably start a family pretty soon after they get married. She wanted to be a young mom, so she could get her body back into shape.

"What'll it be, guys?" Ms. Leezil asked them.

"Cherry Coke for Heather and I'll have a Lemon-Lime," Jake answered.

"It's an exciting game tonight," Ms. Leezil said as she filled their cups with ice. "It sounds like our guys are tearing them apart out there. I just hope no one gets hurt like last year."

Last year, while playing Glovercroft, Mark Knichter was tackled so hard that he had flipped over and landed directly on his head resulting in a concussion and bruising on his brain. He was lucky his spine wasn't injured, but he had spent a week in the hospital. No one wanted a repeat of that scare.

Ms. Leezil handed the kids their drinks, collected the money and handed back the change to Jake. As Jake was looking down putting his change away, Ms. Leezil caught Heather's eye and made a hand motion like she was pulling up her sweater. "You're showing a lot of cleavage there, Hon." She whispered. "Pull your sweater up just a smidge." Ms. Leezil smiled and turned to help the next person in line.

Heather looked down and saw nothing out of place, so she just turned and walked back with Jake. They found Jake's friends standing by the forty yard line on the track circling the field. Jake's friends didn't play football; they were basketball and tennis guys. Heather thought a couple of them were really cute, but she and Jake were serious, so she tried hard not to flirt with anyone. She noticed them looking at her and smiled inwardly, confident about her "hotness" and loving it. "Maybe I should have a Plan B", she thought as she smiled at one of the tennis guys. As they were talking, Darren Jackson made a touchdown, bringing the score to 21-7. It was almost halftime, and Heather wanted to find her friends and watch the band and Dance Team perform, so she pulled Jake away, and they went to find seats in the bleachers.

On their way, Jake ran into another one of his friends and stopped to talk. Heather stood by his side and waited patiently for him to finish. "Like a good wife," she thought. She heard a crackling noise and turned to see Sheriff Buchanon talking on his walkie-talkie.

Heather couldn't hear much more than a few crackling words, but she did pick up "Meadowview on Route 68", "kids" and "in trouble". She strained forward to hear the rest, but Sheriff Buchanon had already turned on his heel and was making fast toward the parking lot.

A weird little feeling crept into Heather's belly. She knew it couldn't be Eli. *He was home, right?* Well, actually, he hadn't been there when she left with Jake. Heather felt a weird panicky feeling. Suddenly she wanted to go home right away. She didn't get nervous about many things, but the thought of something happening to her brother made her surprisingly anxious. He was a pain in her ass most of the time, but, after Dad left, it made her feel good that Eli was still there – more secure, safer. She tugged on Jake's arm and said, "We gotta go. Now."

CHAPTER 9

Eli & Hunter

By the time Eli had followed Brody back into the house, the dog was nowhere to be seen. He closed the front door and started for Heather's room to tell her off for being so forgetful and irresponsible. Halfway down the hall, he noticed the door to her bedroom was open. She had already left with Jake for the mall. *Doesn't matter.* He would definitely let her know the next time he saw her.

Next, he went in search of Brody. He just wanted to see if he was alright. The dog had been very agitated in the woods and that was unusual for Brody. He usually loved the woods and everything in them. Brody wasn't in his dog bed in the living room. He wasn't in the kitchen on the tile floor or lying in the patch of sunlight in the hallway. The only other place Eli could think to look was his own bedroom. Brody was there, under the bed. The poor dog looked completely freaked out. Eli got all the way down onto his stomach and reached for the trembling pup.

"Come here, Buddy. Come see me," Eli coaxed as he rubbed the Border Collie behind his left ear; the only part of the dog he could reach. He stretched a little farther and tried to grab his collar but Brody shrank back from Eli's hand.

Eli empathized with him. Whatever the dog had seen or heard had really shaken him up. Eli remembered his own fear while running in the woods. He still wasn't sure what it was that he had been afraid of, or what he had been running from. It was just that Brody had seemed frantic to get home, and that had made Eli very nervous. Dogs are known to have a sixth sense; it seemed like there was a reason for the fear. Eli reached the dog's ear once again and continued scratching it. He was trying hard to remember anything else about what had just happened when he discovered that his headache was gone. He noticed that he wasn't burning up and sweating any more either. He knew that those things could easily be attributed to chasing the dog through the woods and the stress of trying to find him.

As he scratched, Brody eased toward Eli, and, in a few minutes, the dog was out from under the bed with his black and white head in Eli's lap. Eli could tell that the dog was still afraid, though. He smelled too, and the froth from around his mouth was dry and crusty in his fur. Eli decided a bath would make Brody feel better, so he coaxed the dog out into the side yard. He gave him some dog treats to make him stay put while he got the shampoo, the garden hose and a towel.

At the last minute, while walking back to where Brody was waiting, he veered to the right and went to Hunter's side door. Hunter answered almost immediately since he was scarfing down cereal in the kitchen.

"Hey, Bro. What's happening?" He said as he opened the door to see Eli standing there.

"I'm giving Brody a bath. Come out here, I wanna tell you about something." Eli replied soberly.

"Sure. Give me a sec to finish and I'll be right out," Hunter replied.

By the time he was lathering Brody's fur, Hunter came bounding down the side steps and crossed the two driveways to where the Red Tomato was parked. Hunter glanced across the street to see Clara Stagg waving. Feeling awkward, he nodded his head then leaned against the car. Chomping on an apple, he said, "Okay, KemoSabe, the wise one is here. Lay it on me."

Eli didn't know exactly how to start telling Hunter about what had happened. He really didn't know himself. He was about to say forget about it and talk about something else when he noticed he was holding a huge ball of wet hair in his lathered hand. He looked down and saw more clumps of fur on the wet driveway beneath Brody. Hunter followed his gaze and his eyes narrowed. He looked at his friends face and, for the first time, noticed that Eli looked really worried. *And something else – afraid? Yeah, that's it.* Eli looked scared.

"I think you better let me in on what's happening with you," he said as he moved closer to where his friend was rinsing the dog. More and more fur was coming off of Brody as Eli washed the soap out of the dog's coat.

Eli started at the beginning. He told Hunter about coming home after school and the door being open. He told him about running through the woods to find the dog and about feeling hot, sweaty and headachy. He told him about the clearing and the bulldozer. Then he told him about the dog's reaction and its foaming jaws as Brody came charging back past Eli. He told Hunter about frantically running through the woods until he was home again. He even told him that he felt afraid in the woods – afraid of something behind him, but not knowing what it was. He ended his story recounting how he had found Brody under his bed and how long it had taken him to coax the dog out.

Hunter listened quietly. At first he thought his friend was overreacting, but then he looked down at the fur blowing away in the wind and realized that something had happened.

"Something happened," he thought. "But what? Eli didn't actually see anything. He didn't hear anything. He didn't even smell anything like a fire. What could have gotten him so bugged out?"

When Eli was finished, they both were quiet for a moment. Eli had finished rinsing Brody and had used the towel to dry him while he told Hunter his tale. The dog, clean but with somewhat less fur, sat quietly between the boys. He seemed a little better, so they led him into the house and settled him into his dog bed.

"Well, I think there's only one thing for us to do," Hunter said.

"What's that?" Eli asked.

"We've got to go back to where you and Brody were. Well, more like where Brody was, by that bulldozer. The fact that you didn't see, hear or smell anything is really weird to me. There must have been something that spooked Brody. We need to find out what that was. We have to go back and really look around."

"I don't know, Hunter. I mean, I doubt I could even get Brody to go into the woods anymore. And honestly, I don't know if I want to go back either." Eli felt a little ashamed, but the fear was still there, and if he couldn't tell Hunter, who else could he talk to?

"Listen," Hunter replied, "we don't even need Brody. He might even be a distraction. We'll just go in real quiet and listen for signs of anything weird. When we get to the dozer, if everything is still cool, I'll just go closer till I can see what's what. I promise if there's anything that looks off, we're out of there. Deal?"

Eli was reluctant, but still a little curious to know what had happened. "Okay. But really, Hunter, if any little thing is fishy, we're out, okay?"

"No worries, Bro. I got you covered," Hunter replied and clapped his best friend on the back. "Let's go out the back and leave Brody home."

They decided to be prepared for anything, so Hunter grabbed a Swiss Army knife and a flashlight. He threw them into a light backpack along with a couple bottles of water. At the last minute, Eli grabbed a garden spade to add to the pack. The boys headed out the side door.

Crossing the street to the Miller's house, Eli got a butterfly in his stomach. He had never in his life been afraid of the woods. He had played in them his whole life, ever since his mother had deemed him old enough to go in with Hunter. It felt strange for him to feel such trepidation about entering them.

They passed through the rough undergrowth at the edge and plunged into the shadowed world beyond. Nothing looked unusual or out of the ordinary. The leaves blanketed the ground, and a rough path was stretched out before them. All of the kids in the neighborhood played in the woods, especially the part closest to the houses. It was empty now, though. The trails were vacant, just as they had been earlier that afternoon.

Continuing down the rough path, they saw squirrels, chipmunks and birds galore. The smaller wildlife in the woods was abundant as evidenced by the fat cats in the neighborhood. They usually didn't see any of the bigger animals, maybe a deer once in a while, but nothing more than that.

The path ended causing the boys to make their way past tree stumps and clumps of rocks and branches while heading in the general direction of the clearing. Eli was feeling a little better since they were well into the woods, and they hadn't encountered anything out of the ordinary.

A few more yards in, Hunter stopped and turned slowly around to face Eli. "Do you hear that?" He whispered.

Eli stopped abruptly. "No. What?" The only thing he could hear was his heart beating.

"Nothing," replied Hunter, "nothing at all. Why aren't the birds chirping? When's the last time you heard something running around in the leaves or the trees? I haven't heard anything at all for the last few minutes."

Eli had noticed that it was quiet, but the strangeness of it hadn't occurred to him until Hunter pointed it out. A cold sweat broke out on Eli's brow. That in itself was weird because he felt extremely hot again, and another headache was coming on.

"Let's just keep going and get a little closer. My stomach's starting to act up a little. Probably nerves," Hunter whispered and started moving again.

A few minutes and yards later, they were close to the clearing. They could see where the shadowy woods ended in a bright sky. Both boys were sweating now, but neither wanted to turn back. They had come that far, and they wanted to keep going. Hunter got the bottles of water out of the pack and handed one to Eli.

"What do you think about skirting the edge of the woods over to where the dozer is?" Hunter asked. "I kinda think we should stay as hidden as possible until we see what's what. Plus, if it's this hot in here, it must be really hot out there." He poked his finger in the direction of the clearing.

"That's a good idea," said Eli. "I like the idea of having some cover."

Still sweating, the boys started to make their way along the edge of the woods. They had both sucked down their water bottles and put the empties back in the pack. They were halfway around the curve where the bulldozer sat when Eli saw a glimmer.

"What's that? Can you see it in front of the Cat?" Eli said, not realizing he was whispering.

"Yeah, that shiny thing? Can't tell what it is. The glare is too big. Let's get closer." Hunter had seen it earlier but didn't want Eli to become anxious, so he had kept it to himself.

"You know," said Hunter, "Mr. Jackson works out here on one of those big Cats. I've heard Mrs. Jackson tease him about driving to work when he could just clear a path to their back yard. You don't suppose that's his rig, do you?"

"I don't know," replied Eli. "I'm sure there are other people who work out here, too. He can't be the only one." An uncomfortable feeling had come over Eli when he realized that it could be Mr. Jackson's bulldozer. Eli had always liked Claymont Jackson. He was one of the grownups that actually played with the kids at the neighborhood parties. They would all be playing ball, and Mr. Jackson would leave a crowd of adults talking and run over to snatch the football then start running for the imaginary goal. He had always come to the Shazaam Brothers shows, too. He was one of the only parents beside his own and Hunter's to ever show up. Eli remembered him trying to buy a ticket and telling them to think of the money as an "investment". Eli really liked Mr. Jackson; he knew Hunter did too.

They were almost at the front of the cab. Still relatively far away inside the woods, they couldn't see inside, but it was turned off, and it looked to be empty. They were getting used to the quiet now and weren't as jumpy, so they continued to where the glare was coming from. As they got closer, Hunter could see that it was coming from a box – a steel box, half buried in the ground. It looked like the bulldozer had been digging it up along with the trees surrounding it. He got a few feet from it, with Eli close behind. Then, without warning, Hunter bent at the waist and vomited. Out came the bottle of water along with the apple chunks and half-digested cereal he had eaten earlier. Violent spasms racked his body until there was nothing left to empty.

Eli watched wide-eyed as his friend emptied his stomach. Hunter had not even said he was sick. It happened so fast! Eli's head was pounding, but he didn't feel nauseated. He stepped over to Hunter and relieved him of the pack on his friend's back. Hunter stumbled sideways and sat heavily down on the wooded floor.

"Whoa, Dude! Where'd that come from?" Eli asked his friend, still startled.

Hunter looked up and wiped his mouth with the back of his hand. His head was spinning, but he felt a little better. "Man, I don't know! It was like all of a sudden without warning, you know?"

"You okay now? We can sit down for a minute." Eli's head was beginning to pound; he thought they both could use a break.

"Naw, I'm good." Hunter rose shakily to his feet. "A little hot and kinda woozy but good. Let's see what that thing is." He stumbled over to the clump of trees and stooped down to look at the box. It looked like a work box or some kind of tool box, except that it had a bunch of chains with padlocks around it – at least five of them from what Hunter could see. "Whoa! This looks like some kinda secret treasure! This is a job for Shazaam Brothers!" Hunter said with a flourish that he didn't quite feel.

"I don't know. Maybe it belongs to the construction crew or something. We should leave it here." Eli's head was beginning to affect his mood.

"No way, Eli, this thing is half buried. It doesn't belong to the guys working on this site. If it did, they'd have it in the rig with them. Don't cha want to see what's in there?" Hunter asked. "Who knows how long it's been buried?" He leaned over and spit out more stomach acid. "Why do people bury things, Eli? To *hide* them because they're valuable and they don't want them to be found. But we found it. Shazaam!" He turned his head to spit again.

Despite Eli's anxious feeling, he was being sucked into everything that Hunter was saying. What if he was right? Eli's curiosity was getting the better of him. He looked at the box and said, "It is kinda cool. Makes you wonder why it would have to be locked up like that. Maybe it's money." Eli quickly forgot his headache and the fear that initially brought them both out there in the first place. This was a job for Shazaam Brothers, and they both knew it.

Hunter motioned for the pack, and Eli handed it over. He pulled the spade out and started to dig around the buried part of the box. They had to switch off digging a couple of times for Hunter to puke some more, or try to puke, but the digging went quickly. Soon the box was loose enough to be pulled from its grave. Eli reached in and tugged on the box until the remaining earth released it. As he pulled the box to his chest he felt a slight rumble in the ground below his feet.

"Do we have anything to cut these chains with?" Hunter asked as they sat looking it over.

"Sure, we got those wire cutters with that tool kit for Christmas two years ago. That'll work. If not, we can use a crowbar and our vice to pry apart one of the links. Nothing Shazaam can't handle!" Eli was pumped now. He was glad that they had returned to the woods. Nothing out there was scary. Although neither of them felt great, Eli's head really hurt, and Hunter couldn't stop dry heaving.

They decided to start back with the box. As they were leaving, Hunter turned back toward the bull-dozer.

"You know," he said, "maybe we should take a look inside the cab. Just to make sure it's empty. I mean, it looks like it from here, but we might as well check."

"Fine by me, Pukey," Eli said. "Think you can handle climbing up there?" He shifted the heavy box to his left hand and reached for the backpack with his right.

"Yeah, I'm feeling a little better anyway," Hunter replied.

Hunter handed off the pack and started toward the Cat. Eli followed and stopped a little distance away. He squinted into the setting sun to see if he could make out anything inside the cab. From his vantage point, there were only shadows within the cab of the Caterpillar. It looked empty.

Hunter climbed up two steps of the rig and had just come even with the window of the cab when movement caught his eye. He looked to the left along the edge of the woods and said to Eli, "We've got company."

CHAPTER 10

Hunter, Eli & Bug

Bug was standing at the edge of the clearing. She was thinking what a *super dumb* idea it had been to follow the boys into the woods. She knew she should have stayed at home after Shasta dropped her off, but she had been curious about the boys going into the woods with a backpack. She had wanted to follow them to see what they were up to, but she also wanted to pop out at just the right time and scare them. *That would have been super funny!*

Now she was hot, dirty and had a headache. Her dark hair was stuck to her head with sweat and her stomach was growling. She just wanted to go home, but she didn't want to go by herself, that was the problem.

Getting there was kind of an adventure. She had heard the boys up ahead most of the way. They couldn't hear her, though. Her featherweight frame barely disturbed the ground as she walked. Then, almost at once, everything had gone quiet. No animal's scurrying, no boy's voices, no leaves crunching underfoot up ahead, nothing. That was creepy. Then the headache had started. She had been on the lookout for those migraine headaches ever since she had read in a national health magazine that females are three times more likely to suffer from them than males. She was on the lookout for a few other maladies as well. *Never can be too careful. Knowledge is power.*

When she had made it to the clearing, she didn't see Hunter or Eli, and she became nervous. She expected them to be there doing whatever it was that brought them out in the first place. It never occurred to her that she wouldn't be able to find them. Alone and feeling sick, she had sat down on a fallen tree to rub her temples and cool down some. *Wow! It's super hot out here!* While she sat, she saw the boys emerge from the other side of the clearing by a big bulldozer. Relief flooded over her with the knowledge that she had an escort home. She watched as Hunter jumped up to the side of the dozer and started to climb up to the driver's door. Then he suddenly turned and looked right at her. He said something to Eli who turned and looked at her, too. They talked back and forth until Eli got up and started walking over to where she sat. He was carrying a big silver box. *Did they have that with them when they started out?* No, she remembered, just the backpack that Hunter was wearing. She was sure she would have noticed it because it was *super shiny*.

She looked back at Hunter who was climbing back up the side of the Caterpillar.

———

"We've got company," Hunter said to Eli from atop the Caterpillar.

"What? Who?" Eli looked around and saw Bug sitting on the other side of the clearing. "Damn! What's she doing here?"

"Don't know," replied Hunter climbing down from the rig. "But I do know she's going to ask a lot of questions about that thing." He nodded toward the box.

"That's no big deal," said Eli. "I'll go talk to her and if she asks, I'll tell her it's our tool box. That we came out here to do experiments or something."

"Right. A tool box covered with chains and locks. She'll catch on to that lie before it's all the way out of your mouth. Just tell her to mind her own business." He started to crawl up the side of the rig again. "I'll be over as soon as I check inside this thing." Hunter bent over once again to spit out more stomach acid.

Eli turned, taking the silver box with him, and walked toward Bug. He was feeling grumpy because his headache was worse than ever and he was getting tired of being in the woods. "Great," he grumbled to himself, "now I get to deal with a precocious twelve year old." He felt like this was all taking too much time. It was getting late and he still wanted to make it to the game.

———

Hunter went back to the task at hand and started to climb up to the cab of the Cat once again. He was sure it was empty, but he felt the need to look before they left. His stomach pain was subsiding a little now as he made it to the driver's side and peered into the dirty window.

His heart stopped and then started racing. His breath caught in his chest as he struggled to suck in air, finally succeeding with a great, gasping gulp.

The cab wasn't empty. It wasn't empty at all. Mr. Jackson was in there. At least Hunter thought it was Mr. Jackson. A man who once may have looked like Claymont Jackson was in the cab. He was covered in blood. It was coming from his ears, his nose, even his eyes had drops of blood under them. His head was drooped forward with his chin resting on his chest. The blood had run from his head and face to cover the shirt and pants worn on his slumped body. His hands were resting quite naturally in his lap – a cell phone in one. If it weren't for all of the blood and the way his face was swollen, he could have been taking a nap.

Hunter noticed a few flies stuck in the blood around Mr. Jackson's nose and felt sick to his stomach again. He imagined smelling the metallic odor of blood through the window. Suddenly, his body reacted. He turned and jumped the long distance from the cab to the ground and immediately started to dry heave. The contents of his stomach were long since history, but the convulsing waves were incredibly painful. He doubled over and his knees buckled, making him fall.

"AH! OH GOD!" He yelled and rolled onto his side. The image of Mr. Jackson's bloody body was seared onto the back of his eyelids. He couldn't make the picture leave his mind. That and the pain in his stomach was more than he could bear as he pulled his knees up to his chest and lay there fighting for breath in between the heaves.

———

Eli and Bug whirled in the direction of the Cat and saw Hunter jump down and then fall over. He was clutching his stomach and yelling. Eli had an awful feeling that Hunter's stomach wasn't the worst of it.

"Stay here," Eli told Bug sternly and took off running toward Hunter. He had dropped the box at Bug's feet, but she hadn't noticed. Her eyes were on Hunter who was lying on his side and moaning.

The convulsions were easing a bit by the time Eli got to his side. "Hunter! What is it? Are you hurt?"

Hunter pushed himself up to his knees and said breathlessly, "Eli, Man. It's bad. It's really bad. Mr. Jackson's in there, Man. Eli, he's dead."

It took a few seconds for Eli's brain to comprehend. He had been feeling anxious ever since they had started back into the woods, and he didn't really know why. He remembered hearing once that your subconscious picks up on all kinds of things, but your mind protects you from certain knowledge until you're able to deal with it. Eli had known that something was wrong ever since Brody flew past him on his frantic way home a couple of hours ago. Going there with Hunter, he had felt more secure, but, deep down, he knew something was wrong. Now he knew what that something was.

"Are you sure, Hunter?" Eli said in a trembling voice. "Maybe the paramedics could save him. Are you sure he's really d-dead?"

"Eli, he's dead. There's a ton of blood, Man. We have to call the sheriff." He turned his head and spat on the ground.

Eli took his phone from his pocket and dialed 9-1-1.

———————

Deputy Michael Clay was the first to arrive on the scene, followed quickly by an ambulance. None of the emergency lights were flashing on either vehicle. Eli had made it clear to Mrs. Putnam, the dispatcher, that there was no hope of resuscitation. Rachel had passed the information on to the ambulance driver and the deputy who had both gone quickly but quietly. A death in a small town has a tendency to elicit hysteria among its people. It was best to handle it as quietly as possible until the next of kin could hear it from an officer, not the town gossip.

Deputy Clay parked his cruiser near the kids, who had moved back over to where Bug was sitting on the fallen tree log. Hunter had wanted to put more distance between himself and the Cat. Funny thing was, his stomach felt worse than ever. He was sitting on the fallen tree beside Eli with his head hung over, the pain on his face visible. Eli had sat next to Bug and told her what was happening. All in all, he thought she took the news about Mr. Jackson well. She told him that judging from the description Hunter had given, it was probably a brain hemorrhage. Either that, or blunt force trauma to the head, but she couldn't be certain without viewing the body. Then she said, "Knowledge is Power."

They had relayed the information to Deputy Clay in somewhat disjointed sentences. Between the shock of the circumstances and each of their physical ailments, it was difficult to get a full sentence from any of them. Hunter kept retching, Eli was holding his head in his hands and Bug looked white as a sheet with sweat running down her face. Eventually, the deputy thought he had pieced together their entire story. He left them to talk to the paramedics who were hovering near the bulldozer waiting for instructions, not knowing if it was being treated as a crime scene. They had initially examined the body to confirm death, but needed permission to contaminate the scene by removing the body. Deputy Clay asked them to wait for the sheriff. He would give them the go ahead to take Mr. Jackson to the hospital for autopsy.

The sheriff radioed Deputy Clay that he was on his way. Michael Clay had started to feel sick to his stomach. He wondered if whatever had made those kids sick was catching.

CHAPTER 11

Sheriff Buchanon

Sheriff Donald Buchanon was a good man, a really good man. He was a good husband to Margy, a good father to Jeff and Jennifer and a good friend to a lot of people. He was also a very capable sheriff. A town the size of Hallston couldn't support a very big Police Department, so they had stuck with the Sheriff's Department that had been in place for years upon years. There were quite a few deputies and volunteers when extra hands were needed, but, all in all, Sheriff Buchanon was the law. He was the last word and the last person you saw leave the scene of any crime in Hallston.

He was a hands-on kind of man. Not so much a control freak, but someone who wanted the job done right and who was willing to put in the time and effort to see that it was. That part was probably a result from his time in the service. He had spent twelve years in the Army and had seen a lot in his two tours overseas. He had been well respected and highly decorated. His life in the Army made sense to him – well ordered, organized, a definite chain of command and a mission to keep people safe and secure. That's what drew him into the Sheriff's position after his time in the service was up. He liked the structure of the department, the mission to serve and protect, and the definite chain of command that ended with him.

He did miss the Army sometimes, though. He had made some really fine friendships over the years – not friends so much as brothers. He kept in touch with most of them, and they had reunions now and then, but he missed seeing them. Luckily, one of those brothers was right there in town. Bill Port had been a friend of his since middle school. He had also served with Don on his last tour. It was good to have Bill around.

As Sheriff Buchanon headed over to Bill's place to grab a drive-thru dinner, he looked forward to seeing his friend. Don's wife Margy and Bill's wife Val were good friends also, but they hadn't seen each other in a while. Kid's schedules seemed to leave them little free time this time of the year.

He pulled up to the drive-thru menu and waited for Val's tinny voice to come through the intercom.

"Hey, Don," she greeted. "What's it going to be tonight?"

"Hi, Val," he replied. "Lemme have a couple of corn dogs, a large waffle fry and a medium lemonade."

"Got it. See you at the window." The crackle of the speaker stopped.

The sheriff pulled around and waited his turn behind two other cars. By the time he rolled up to the service window, Bill Port was sticking his head out of it. He had a big grin on his face.

"Hey, Double D! It's been awhile! Have you been avoiding the Hut? Margy making you eat all that healthy crap?" Bill laughed at his friend's expense.

Bill was the only person left around town that called him that. It originated in middle school when the teachers would call out the entire name of each pupil on the first day of school. Donald Daniel Buchanon was a mouthful and William John Port had dubbed him "Double D" immediately.

"No, just haven't had time lately. I've been on the other side of town for the last few weeks working on those robberies," he said as he took his lemonade from Bill's outstretched hand.

That case had worried him. There were no clues at any of the scenes, no leads, no witnesses and the same MO for each case. The homeowners would be out of the house and come home to find the place ransacked – all computers, electronics, cameras and TV's gone. They never touched the jewelry or tried to get into a safe if there was one. They left a hell of a mess at each house, though. Then, finally a break came when a young couple that had been robbed remembered that their nanny cam was attached to their computer and they could access the footage online. There they were, two guys dressed in black going to work, when one of them looked directly at the camera before unplugging everything to take the computer. It didn't take long to find the perpetrator and his friend. The harder part was convincing them to rat out their accomplices. They eventually did, of course – no honor among thieves. It turned out they were a small part of a bigger gang from a neighboring town. They would rob houses in Hallston and sell the goods in Shale or Glovercroft. Sheriff Buchanon had handed over the evidence and perpetrators to the police department in Shale for prosecution in that town.

"Yeah, I heard about that. Nice job wrapping that up. Who was it, anyway?" Bill asked.

"A gang of guys from Shale. They had some connections in Glovercroft too, but most of the stolen merch was found in pawn shops in Shale. I've handed it all over to Captain Davis over there."

Val poked her head out beside her husbands and said, "Don, tell Margy to call me. We haven't been to dinner in weeks! I want to try that new Mexicali place that opened on Main a couple of weeks ago."

"Will do, Val. She's over at the middle school right now chaperoning the Fall Dance. She and Jennifer won't get home till late, I suppose. I'm headed over to the game to watch Jeff play." He accepted the steaming box of fried food from Val.

"We saw Jeff earlier with his buddies. Had to get Hansen Reynolds in line again. He was teasing Bug Hamilton and ended up with Bug falling and bloodying up her nose. That kid is a pain! I hope he gets some of that meanness out of his system by busting some linemen on the field tonight." Bill said.

"Hansen Reynolds. I've been hearing that name a lot lately," replied the sheriff. "I may have to sit that boy down for a discussion next time I see him."

A new car pulled up behind the sheriff's cruiser and the men said their quick goodbyes. Sheriff Buchanon pulled out of the Hot Dog Hut with his two corn dogs and fries in their little cardboard carton in the passenger seat. "Nothing better than food on a stick," he thought.

The parking lot at the high school was packed, so he made his own place close to the gate. One of the perks of the job was making your own parking place. He greeted the ladies at the ticket booth and paid for his entry. They tried not to accept his money, but he insisted and went on in. His stomach was happy with his meal-on-a-stick, but he was still thirsty, so he made his way over to the concession stand for a drink and a candy bar. "Margy will never know," he snickered to himself.

He looked onto the field as he made his way toward the concession, but the Jaguars had the ball so Jeff wasn't playing. Friends and neighbors greeted him as he walked. The air was warm for a late October night, and it felt good to have the night off. He hadn't realized how wrapped up in that case he had been until it was over. Stress can do that, just sneak up and live inside you until it feels like a normal part of who you are. It isn't until you feel the relief of it leaving that you realize how bad it had made you feel.

Sheriff Buchanon was quite content munching on a chocolate bar and watching the game. The score was 21-7 and the Mustangs had the ball. Jeff was lined up and ready for the snap. When it came a few seconds later, the crunch of pads was clearly audible. The father in him cringed, but the man in him yelled for his son. Jeff had made a good tackle, and he was proud of his boy.

As the teams lined up for the next play, Sheriff Buchanon's walkie-talkie crackled to life.

"This is the sheriff, what is it Rachel, you're making me miss a good game." He teased the dispatcher not anticipating anything serious, maybe a drunk kid in the parking lot or an unruly customer at the Gas N Go.

"Sorry, Sheriff," Rachel began, "but we had a call in from a couple of kids around where they're building the new subdivision on Route 68. They found something, Donald."

Sheriff Don Buchanon perked up immediately. The only time Rachel used his given name was when it was something bad – really bad.

"What'd they find, Rach?" He asked reluctantly.

"It's Mr. Jackson, Don. Claymont Jackson. Looks like he died on the site. The kids said he's still in his dozer." He could tell Rachel was upset.

"On my way. Over' n out."

He turned with a purposeful stride and made for the exit. His stomach was in knots. "Shit. Claymont Jackson. His kid is out there on that field playing right now. I know Agnes is here somewhere. Shit!" Sheriff Buchanon thought.

He made it to his car and called dispatch to talk while he drove. Rachel said that she had Deputy Clay and an ambulance on the way but with no lights. They didn't want to alert anyone yet, and the kids had made it clear that there was no hope of resuscitation. The kids, she said, were Elivan Andrews and Hunter Massey. Bug Hamilton was there as well.

The knot in his stomach pulled tighter as he passed by the construction foreman's trailer and headed toward the lights in the huge clearing. They were just car lights, not flashing. *Good call on Rachel's part.* News like that would travel quickly and he didn't want Agnes and Darren to hear any mixed up version of events.

He parked the cruiser and got out. He saw the kids sitting on a tree at the edge of the woods and walked over to them. They looked like they were in shock. "Are you kids all okay? Anyone hurt?" He looked each of them over.

He was thinking that somehow the big bulldozer had gotten out of control and wrecked. It was dark, so he really couldn't see if the Cat was damaged, but he could see that it was very close to a clump of maple trees.

The kids all mumbled pretty much the same thing. They were fine, just fine. Shaken up a little, that's all.

Deputy Clay walked over to him. He looked like he had aged a good ten years from the time the sheriff had seen him that morning. The worst part of their job is when you know one of the victims. Deputy Clay always seemed to take it a little harder, though. His family had deep roots in the community. His great-great grandfather had been one of the first Town Council members.

"Hey, Michael, what have you found so far?" The sheriff asked as he took out his notebook.

"Not much, really, Sheriff," Michael started in his thick southern drawl. "The kids said that Eli had been chasing Brody out here this afternoon, and the dog had acted kinda squirrely. He got Hunter, and the boys decided to investigate a little. They came up to the dozer but couldn't see inside. They thought it was Claymont's rig, so Hunter hopped up to look through the window. That's when he saw the blood. It's all over his face, poor guy. Paramedic says it's some kinda brain hemorrhage, most likely. He probably didn't even feel it come on. Says it probably took him pretty quick."

"What about Bug?" He asked. "Was she with Hunter and Eli?"

"Not at first. She had seen the guys goin' into the woods and followed 'em just as a prank. Try and scare 'em or somethin'. She came up just as Hunter found Mr. Jackson. They're all pretty shook up. Feelin' sick to their stomachs and what not. Tell you the truth, I ain't feelin' so hot myself. I'm sweatin' like crazy, and my head's killin' me," Deputy Clay responded.

"I know what you mean, Michael," said Sheriff Buchanon as his corn dogs rumbled around in his belly.

"Let me go take a look. Finish up with the kids and then give them a ride home. Have Rachel call their parents. Just tell them what their kid witnessed, and that they may be feeling a little upset. What's that box the Andrews kid has?"

Sheriff Buchanon had been looking at the kids as he spoke to Deputy Clay and had noticed Eli holding onto what looked like a shiny silver box.

"Oh, Hunter says they had that with 'em when they came out. Probably somethin' to do with all those experiments they do. I'll go get their statements and have Rach call their folks." Deputy Clay wiped the sweat from his forehead and headed toward the kids.

Sheriff Buchanon spoke quickly with the paramedics and got basically the same story as he had from Deputy Clay. Most likely a hemorrhage of the brain, couldn't tell more until the autopsy. No foul play from what they could see. Sheriff sent them to wait in the ambulance while he looked over the scene.

The corndogs were really churning as he made his way over to the bulldozer and climbed up the side to the driver's door. When he looked inside, the pain in his head was almost unbearable. He had started to see little flashes of blue light…

BOOK TWO

CHAPTER 12

Sheriff Buchanon

The florescent lights in the hospital corridor were hurting Sheriff Buchanon's eyes. The searing headache he had experienced at the construction site had vanished as quickly as it had come on, just after Deputy Clay left to take the kids home. It had left a remnant, however, and the lights were trying to coax it back.

He passed by the information desk and nodded to Adele, who worked the evening shift. Unfortunately, he was quite familiar with the way to the morgue. This time it was personal, though. Claymont Jackson was a good man. He was a kind person who always had a smile ready. He was well respected and liked within the whole community of Hallston. He was a hard worker and a good family man. His wife loved him, so did his son.

That had been tough. The sheriff had filled out all of his paperwork back at the scene and waited for the paramedics to remove Mr. Jackson from the bulldozer. After the ambulance left with Claymont, Sheriff Buchanon had gone straight to the high school. The game was almost over, so he waited by the ticket booth for Agnes to come through. He knew Darren would be awhile, meeting with the recruiters there and changing into his street clothes, but Agnes had come out quickly with Shasta Port by her side.

They both froze as they saw him. Although she was hoping to find her husband with the recruiters or in the parking lot, Agnes had known something was up when Claymont never showed up in the bleachers and didn't answer his phone.

"Evening, Ladies," he started. "I wonder if I could have a word with you Agnes." Leading up to it was the hardest part for the sheriff.

"Oh Dear God, it's Claymont! I know it is! I've been calling his cell phone, and I knew he would never miss this game! Something's happened!" She was immediately in tears as Shasta held her arm in case she collapsed. "What's happened, Sheriff? Where is he?"

They were still fairly close to the exit and people were starting to notice Agnes. He put his arm lightly on her back and led her a little way over to a more private area. It didn't matter, though. By then she was almost hysterical.

"You tell me right now, Don! You tell me where my husband is! I swear, Don, I swear! You tell me right now, where's my Claymont?" She was looking at him through dark brown eyes swimming in tears. Shasta was trying to blink back tears; her eyes were wide as well.

"Agnes, Honey, he's gone. There was an accident at the..."

"NO, NO, NO!" She collapsed pulling Shasta with her to the ground. The two women just sat on the black-top holding each other as he tried to finish telling them the rest of what had become of Claymont.

"Now, Agnes, listen Hon. He's at peace. It was a brain hemorrhage they think. It happened real quick. He didn't have any pain at all, Honey. It was over fast, Agnes." He looked at the teen holding onto Agnes and thought of his friend Bill. "Shasta, are you okay?" He made a mental note to call Shasta's dad soon.

"Y, yeah, I think," Shasta managed, but she was chalk white, and the sheriff knew she was thinking about how Darren was going to take the news. The two kids had been friends since they were little.

"If you're up for it, I think Darren could use a friend when he hears about this. Can you stick around?"

"Oh, Darren!" Agnes exclaimed. "He's going to be devastated. Shasta, you have to stay. Please stay and help him. He's going to really need you now, Sweetie."

The thought of her child seemed to give Agnes the strength to stand up and dust herself off. The shock was settling in, and her maternal instincts were now in control.

"Now listen, you two," she said. "That boy has had a big night. He's going to come out of that stadium on cloud nine and this news is going to crush him. We've got to stay strong," she said, her voice wavering, "for Darren."

"I'll tell him, Agnes," Sheriff Buchanon said while placing his hand on her shoulder. "It might come easier for him that way. You two can get in the back of the squad car, and I'll put Darren in front with me. That way, no one will overhear." He was looking around at the curious stares and could tell that there was already a murmur going around.

"Let's get you two in now to avoid any prying eyes." He led them over to his car and helped them gently in. Agnes was quietly crying, but he was watching Shasta. The shocked look she wore worried him more than Agnes' weeping. "Shasta, want me to call your dad and tell him what's going on? I think I'll have a few more minutes before Darren comes out."

"No thanks," she answered. "He'll hear soon enough. I'll call him after we see if Darren's okay." Clearly, her only thoughts right now were on her friend. Sheriff Buchanon was glad she was there, but hoped it wouldn't be too hard on the girl.

Agnes, dreading her only child's heart about to break, was moaning in the back seat. Her heart was broken as well, but Darren was her focus now.

A few of the football players were starting to come through the exit, so the sheriff told the women to stay in the car as he climbed out of the cruiser to wait. The boys were all on that endorphin high that comes after a big win. They were coming through the exit to cheers and applause by the waiting spectators and families. Sheriff saw the top of Darren's head, and his stomach rolled over.

The boy was scanning the crowd. He was looking for his parents – looking for Claymont. Sheriff Buchanon raised his arm and tried to grab Darren's attention. Finally, Darren looked his way, and the sheriff motioned him over. He could see the boys smile fade and an anxious look come over his face. Sheriff Buchanon walked forward to meet him and immediately took his arm.

"Hey, Bud. I've got your mom with me. She's okay, but we need to have a talk, okay? Let's get in my car."

He led Darren over to the passenger side and opened the door for him. Darren looked inside at his mother's face and then at Shasta. Looking back at the sheriff he asked, "Where's Dad? Is it my Dad, Sheriff?"

"I'm afraid so, Darren. Hop in the car, Son."

As Darren lowered himself into the cruiser, Sheriff Buchanon rushed to the other side and hopped into the driver's seat. When he was all the way in, with the door shut behind him, he looked at the boy. Darren's head was bowed and a look of grief was on his face before the sheriff could confirm his suspicions. He didn't cry; he just sat there as Sheriff Buchanon relayed the information. Agnes and Shasta listened quietly, since they hadn't had a chance to hear all of the details yet. When he was finished, Sheriff Buchanon put a strong hand on Darren's shoulder and said, "I want you to know something, Son. Your dad was a fine man. He was an upstanding, intelligent man of fine character. I respected him, Darren. The whole town did. You should be proud of him. I know for a fact he was damn proud of you."

Tears rolled down Darren's cheeks, and Don Buchanon pulled the boy into a tight embrace. "You get it out, Son. It's okay. It will all be okay. It's going to hurt a while. But you'll get through it, you and your mom. You'll get through."

The sheriff could hear soft crying from the back seat and decided to get them home. He released Darren and patted his shoulder. "I'm going to drive you all home now. Don't worry about your cars. I'll have Rachel dispatch some deputies over to get them to you. Just leave me your keys and we'll take care of the rest. Shasta, I'll let your dad know what's going on. If you need us to do anything, anything at all, you don't hesitate. Okay, Agnes, Darren, I mean it."

He saw the nods from the rear view mirror and the seat beside him and started the cruiser. They drove in silence the five miles back to Meadowview Acres. Sheriff Buchanon felt sick to his stomach. He didn't know why this had to happen to such a nice family. It just didn't seem fair.

When they got to the front of the Jackson's home, he helped Agnes out of the backseat and walked her up to the front door. He saw Shasta holding onto Darren and felt good enough about the situation to leave. He told Agnes he would be in touch the next day with the autopsy results and headed back to his car.

He called Bill Port on the way to the hospital and gave him a rundown of the events. Bill was as upset about the loss of Claymont as Don was but also concerned for Shasta. Don told him that she seemed fine, just sad. She was doing Darren some good by being there – Agnes too. Bill said that he would pick her truck up from the high school and give her a call after a little time had passed.

Walking to the morgue while being assaulted by the glare of the florescent bulbs, Don Buchanon was counting his blessings. He was thankful for his wife and his kids. He was thankful for his friends and neighbors. He made a mental note to make a doctor's appointment and get checked out. It'd been too long since his last checkup.

Deputy Clay was already sitting in the waiting room when he reached the morgue. "Hey, Mike. What's the word?"

The deputy looked exhausted. His eyes were glazed over and his whole body seemed to droop. He looked at Sheriff Buchanon with blood-shot eyes and said, "Hi, Sheriff. The ambulance just brought him in about an hour ago. Doc says he'll do the autopsy in the mornin'. Said there's a lot of blood loss, though. More than usual with a brain hemorrhage. Said he'll be done around noon tomorrow, and he'll give ya a call then."

"That's fine, Mike. I got the Jackson family home. It's going to be rough for them for a while. For the whole town, I'd imagine. Claymont was a popular guy."

"Yep, this one's tough alright," Deputy Clay responded. "Listen, I'm not feeling too good. I think we've got all the information the Doc's going to give us tonight. You mind if I go on home?"

"No, go on. You look like hell, Mike. You okay?" Alarm bells were sounding in Sheriff Buchanon's head. He'd had enough for one night.

"I'll be alright, just got a wicked headache. I thought I was going to faint while I's drivin' those kids home. Even had a nose bleed and started seein' spots and such. I was a lot better driving over here, though. Soon's they got outta my cruiser, I started feelin' better. I'm just goin' home and get some sleep. I'll see ya tomorrow at the station."

"That's fine, Michael. You feel better now," he said as he watched his deputy shuffle down the florescent hallway. He looked small in the light.

Sheriff Buchanon felt unsettled about something but couldn't quite place what. Something Deputy Clay had said sounded familiar. It had been a long night. He knew tomorrow would be longer still, so he decided to go home. All of the sudden he needed to see Margy, Jeff and Jennifer.

The nagging feeling stayed with him all the way home. Pulling into his driveway, a thought occurred to him. He had experienced terrible head pain at the construction site. He remembered seeing flashing lights and feeling like his head was going to split open.

Deputy Clay had said that he, too, had a headache at the site. He mentioned seeing spots. Claymont Jackson was at the site and died of what surely was a brain hemorrhage. Or was it? Was there more to this than a medical condition? Then he remembered how sick the kids had been. Hunter couldn't stop dry heaving, and Bug was all sweaty and weak. Eli had said he had a headache, too. Was there a connection?

Walking into his house that night, Sheriff Buchanon couldn't help but worry. What had happened to Claymont Jackson? Was the same thing going to happen to Deputy Clay – to Eli – to him?

CHAPTER 13

Eli & Hunter

The ride back to Meadowview Acres took less than a few minutes, but it was hell inside of Deputy Clay's squad car. Bug sat up front with the deputy while Eli and Hunter occupied the back seat with the shiny silver box wedged between them.

Deputy Clay was having a tough time driving while managing a nose bleed. He was worried about Bug beside him; she was white and clammy and Michael was pretty sure that she had fainted once during the drive. In the back seat, Hunter's stomach was heaving the entire drive. Eli seemed the least affected, but still had a very bad headache.

Deputy Clay parked on the street in front of Bug's house and helped Bug up to the door. Mr. and Mrs.

Hamilton met them there with looks of concern and puzzlement. Mrs. Andrews was there as well. The deputy spoke with them about the matter while still containing his nose bleed. Eventually, Mrs. Hamilton disappeared from the doorway with Bug, and Mr. Hamilton and Mrs. Andrews continued speaking with Deputy Clay.

Like two shell shocked victims, Hunter and Eli emerged from the car. Their bodies were exhausted and in pain. Their minds were blown with the events that had unfolded, and they were anxious about what was to come next. Eli was wearing the backpack while Hunter carried the box.

"Well, what do we do now?" Hunter managed to ask between acidic burps.

"Man, I just want to go home. This night has been hell, this whole day, really," Eli responded while rubbing his temples.

"No, Eli. What are we going to do now with this?" He gestured to the box dangling from its handle.

"Oh. Sorry. Let's just store it somewhere for a couple of days until things calm down. I think it's going to be a little hectic for a while with Mr. Jackson and all."

"That's fine with me," Hunter replied. "I just want to dump this thing somewhere and go to bed. I feel like crap."

"Where can we stash it so no one will find it and start asking questions? We don't need anyone nosing around – mainly Heather."

"Lemme think," said Hunter. "Got it, the storage shed behind my house. I'll take it there right now."

"Perfect. We'll get it in a couple of days and see what the heck's in that thing. 'Til then, I'm out of here. Take it easy, Buddy. And Hunter?"

Hunter stopped walking and turned back toward his friend.

"Thanks for going with me." He gave Hunter a sideways grin and walked into his house.

Heather was on him at once. "Eli! You're okay! What happened? I saw the police car bring you home! Are you in trouble?"

Before he could answer her, his mother rounded the corner of the kitchen and made a beeline for him. Squashing him with a huge hug she said, "Oh Eli! I'm so sorry for what you had to go through tonight. Are you okay, Honey?" She let go of him and stood back to take inventory of her son, looking him head to toe for injuries and, finally, taking in his face.

"Yeah, Mom. I'm alright, just tired is all." He realized as he said it that he wasn't just tired, he was bone tired. He was exhausted – mentally and physically. He slumped down into the chair beside him.

"Well I've just come from speaking to Deputy Clay over at the Hamilton's. He wanted us to know everything that you guys witnessed at the construction site. I really hate that this happened, Eli. Are you sure you're alright?"

"Yeah, Mom. Really, I'm fine. It's just sad, and I'm super tired." *I've been hanging around Bug too long. That kid says "super" in every sentence.* He gave his Mom a tired smile, and she couldn't help going over and hugging him once again.

"Wait," said Heather. "Who died then? I thought it was some kids. Were they with you and Hunter, Eli? Who was it? Oh no, was it one of Jake's friends? I better call him! He's going to need me to be there!" She was punching at her cell phone when Mrs. Andrews snatched it out of her hand and plopped it onto the kitchen counter.

"No, Heather!" She said exasperatedly. "This has absolutely nothing to do with Jake. Mr. Jackson is the person who died tonight, and your brother and Hunter found him. You should be thinking of the Jackson family right now, and your brother, not your ridiculous boyfriend."

Heather glared at her mother. She knew her mom didn't understand how much in love she and Jake were. She didn't have a clue about the depth of Jake's feelings for her. Heather didn't know what her mom meant when she said that she shouldn't be thinking of Jake right then. She thought of Jake constantly. Heather knew her mother just didn't get it. She swiped her phone off the kitchen counter and spat, "Just because Dad left you, you don't want me to have a boyfriend! You're jealous because Jake and I are in love and nobody loves you anymore!"

She turned sharply with her chestnut curls flying out behind her and stormed from the kitchen. A moment later they heard the door to her room slam shut.

"Don't let the hormones get to you," Lara winked at Eli. "Now, tell me what I can do for you. Do you want to talk about it? Are you hungry? Just tell me what you need." Lara Andrews sat next to her tired son and rubbed his shoulder. "He's so big," she thought. "When did that happen?"

"I don't need to talk about it, Mom. I'm sure Deputy Clay told you everything. I am kind of hungry, though. I could use a sandwich." His hunger had been masked by his headache, but now that his head was feeling better he could feel his empty stomach.

Lara, happy to have something useful to do that would help her son, jumped up from the table. She had gotten home from work just as Jake was dropping off Heather. Soon after, Rachel Putnam from the sheriff's dispatch had called to tell her that the deputy was bringing Eli, Bug and Hunter home, and he would speak to her when they arrived. She had been frantic with worry. Heather had evidently overheard something on the sheriff's walkie-talkie about some kids in trouble, but Lara had long since learned not to rely too much on things that Heather reported. Finally, as she made a ham and cheese sandwich for her first born, her heart was returning to its normal pace.

Mrs. Andrews placed the plate in front of Eli and poured him a big glass of milk. "How would you feel about me going to check on Hunter and Bug? Deputy Clay said they were both feeling pretty sick on the way back. I may be able to help."

"That's fine, Mom," he replied through a mouthful of sandwich. "I had a headache earlier, but it's gone now. Hunter was puking his guts out, though. And I don't know what was wrong with Bug, but she was really weak. I think you should go see if you can help. I'll be fine, I promise." He grinned up at her feeling mounds better now that his head had stopped pounding and his stomach was filling.

She smiled back and leaned down to kiss him on the forehead. "I'm so glad you're alright, Honey. I'll be back soon. Call my cell if you need me before, okay?"

He promised he would, and she left as he shoved the rest of his sandwich into his mouth.

When he finished eating, he went into the family room to watch TV and wait for her to return. He needed some down time, too, some time to decompress. He turned to the mindless chatter of a reality show and quickly forgot about watching. His mind was churning with the events of the evening. He felt uneasy. Everything had happened so fast. First he was chasing Brody, then he and Hunter were going into the woods, then the box and Bug. Finally, he thought of Mr. Jackson. He was still trying to process it all when he heard his mother come in the kitchen door. He was surprised to see that an hour had passed.

"In here, Mom," He yelled, anxious to hear what she had learned.

"Hey, Honey. How're you feeling?" Lara came into the family room, dropped her small medical bag onto the couch and sat beside it.

"I'm feeling a lot better," Eli said. "My head is fine and I'm not as tired as before. How's Hunter?"

"Well, surprisingly, he's doing pretty well. He says his stomach is feeling much better, and, judging from the way he was wolfing down a bowl of cereal, I believe him." She smiled as she remembered Hunter attacking his Sugar O's. She and Hunter's mom, Gina, often joked that they each had two sons. As close as Eli and Hunter had been since birth, both women had essentially raised both boys.

"Bug's doing well, too," she continued. Mrs. Hamilton is babying her like one of the newborns she cares for at the hospital, but her color was back, and she was talking non-stop about the medical facts that contribute to brain hemorrhages. She'll be fine. Why don't you go on to bed. You've had a heck of a day, Son. We'll go see Agnes and Darren tomorrow if you're up to it."

"Yeah, that's a good idea," he responded while pushing himself up from the recliner. "I'll see you in the morning, Mom. Well, maybe the afternoon." Eli felt like he could sleep for a week.

"Goodnight, Baby," Lara said. As she watched him leave the room, she said a silent prayer of thanks that her kids were safe.

Eli took a quick shower. He smelled like dirt and sweat, and he wanted to get the remnants of the day off of himself. After brushing his teeth, he went into his room to find Brody asleep on his bed. It occurred to him that he didn't get a chance to tell his mom about what had happened with the dog earlier in the day. He went to Brody and stroked his dog's soft coat. His hand came away clean. No fur. "Well I guess you're feeling better too, huh, Buddy?" he said softly to the pup. He crawled under his covers and was asleep within minutes.

Waking up the next day, Eli felt the effects from his adventure in the woods. His leg muscles were sore from running after Brody, and his arms were sore from digging the box out of the ground. His head still felt fine though, and he was not as freaked out about Mr. Jackson's death. He wondered if Hunter felt the same as he did.

Rolling over to look at the clock, he was surprised to see that it was only 11:41 am. He felt like he had slept for a whole day. He noticed that Brody wasn't on his bed anymore and listened to the sounds of the house. He could tell his mom was in the kitchen, on the phone. The one-sided conversation was plainly about the events of the previous night. Eli thought she was talking to a neighbor because it sounded like they were setting up plans to take meals over to Mrs. Jackson and Darren. He was glad. Not only had Eli liked Mr. Jackson, but he also really liked Darren, too. He thought Darren was a good guy. He was low-key and genuinely nice. He knew that he and Shasta used to be good friends, but Eli hadn't seen them together in a couple of years. He decided that he and Hunter should go see Darren today and tell him and Mrs. Jackson how sorry they were.

He padded off to the bathroom and then headed to the kitchen. His mom was just getting off the phone. She greeted him with another big hug. "How'd you sleep, Honey? You're up earlier than I expected."

"I slept fine. Who was on the phone?" He asked as he sank into a kitchen chair.

"Oh, that was Valerie Port. She and Mrs. Stagg are organizing some things for the Jacksons. I'm in charge of food tomorrow after the viewing and dinner for them in a few days. I think I want to go see Agnes today, though. The poor thing is probably a wreck. Luckily, I already had this weekend off. I wouldn't want to go in to work today. Do you have plans?" She asked as she gathered the ingredients to make Eli some pancakes.

"I think I'll see if Hunter wants to visit Darren. Maybe we'll go with you when you go over to see Mrs. Jackson. When are you leaving?"

"I don't know, but I'll wait for you two. Just let me know when you're ready, and we'll all go together. I'll grab Gina, too. Hunter won't mind if his mom goes."

"What about Heather?" Eli hadn't seen any signs of his sister since he'd been up. Usually there was a screech or a door slamming.

"She left early with Jake. They're going to the skate park over in Glovercroft today. Of course, none of this affects your sister. She's in her own little world. I do want her to come with us to the funeral, though. I think that'll be Monday." She whipped up the batter and poured out little circles onto the sizzling griddle.

Eli's mouth watered as he smelled the pancakes cooking. "You know, she's really been horrible lately," he said. "She never does anything around here. She even left the security gate unlatched so Brody could escape and when I told her about it, she screamed at me and slammed her door in my face. I think it's that boyfriend of hers. She's starting to act like she's better than everybody else."

"I know, Eli," Lara said as she flipped the cakes over to cook on the other side. "She's just having her first love right now. It kind of takes a girl over. Give her a little time to adjust to all of the emotions rolling around inside of her. She'll come back to us the same old Heather as before." She flipped three pancakes onto a plate and set it down in front of Eli. The steam coming off of them dissipated as he slathered them with syrup.

"Are you sure that's any better? The old Heather was a pain, too." He snickered to himself as he forked in a dripping mouthful.

Lara giggled and said, "Oh, come on! It's good to have a healthy self-esteem! She's our Heather, Eli. And she loves us both, even if she never shows it!"

They laughed together and Eli finished his breakfast. Lara cleared the dishes and started washing the emptied bowl of batter. As Eli left to shower and dress, Lara told him to let her know when he and Hunter were ready to leave for the Jackson's.

Before hopping in the shower, he shot off a quick text to Hunter. "Going to see Darren with Mom. Coming?"

CHAPTER 14

Darren & Shasta

Darren's world had come crashing down in a matter of minutes. The euphoric high that he had been on after performing so well in the game, followed by the exciting meetings with the recruiters, had turned into a devastating feeling of loss and bewilderment. Sitting in the police car and hearing the news from Sheriff Buchanon was dreamlike. He remembered looking for his dad's face in the crowd outside of the stadium. He was so pumped to tell him all the recruiters had said. He basically was offered a place on both teams, it was up to him to decide which scholarship he would take. He couldn't wait to give his folks the news.

Instead, he had caught the sheriff's eye and somehow he had known. He had pushed to the back of his brain the thought that something had gone terribly wrong for his father not to be sitting in the stands with his mom and Shasta. When he saw Sheriff Buchanon's face, he knew. He didn't remember walking with the sheriff to get into the cruiser. He didn't remember sitting in the car with his mom and Shasta in the back. His first memory of that time was of Sheriff Buchanon hugging him and telling him to be proud of his father because his father had been damn proud of Darren.

They had gotten home soon after, and Shasta stayed with them. Then people started to come, even though it was late. It was okay, though. It wasn't like he and his mom were going to sleep any time soon. They were reeling. First a few neighbors came, then family started to arrive. Most of his mom's side of the family lived in Shale, the next town over. There were very few left on his dad's side, though. They would be coming the next day.

The house was a flurry of activity – people bringing food, making calls and arrangements. Darren had staked out a corner of the living room, and Shasta hadn't left his side. She sat with him that night and throughout most of the last two days, only going home to change clothes or sleep a little bit. Otherwise, she was beside him just holding his hand. She spoke to people when he couldn't, and she brought him food and drinks. Mostly, she was there. No conversation had been needed. They were just Darren and Shasta again without skipping a beat.

More people had come throughout the past two days. Most of them wanted to give Darren a hug, but halfway through the first day he was done with hugging. He just stopped standing up when someone came over. That took care of that. A few people were crying but most were talking about what a surprise it was, and saying things like, "How could this have happened?" Some people were telling stories about a younger Claymont or something funny that he had done in the past at one the neighborhood parties. Darren knew that his dad was a great dad, but he was only now learning how much Claymont had been loved by everyone else.

Darren was thankful for all of the visitors. Not for himself, Shasta was all he needed. His mother had been so strong, and he was glad that she had so much love and support. He was worried what would happen when things started to die down, and not as many people were coming around anymore.

The first day Eli and Hunter and their moms had come over. That was kind of weird since they were the ones who had discovered Claymont in the Caterpillar. Darren was afraid that it would upset Agnes to see them, but quite the opposite happened. She saw them come in and immediately went to them and hugged each boy tightly.

"I want to tell you boys, Thank you. Thank you for finding my husband and calling for help. I know it was hard on you and I'm sorry for that. But I'm so grateful Hunter. Eli. So grateful."

Darren could tell that they were uneasy and didn't know how to respond, so he was glad when Lara Andrews moved forward to hug Agnes. Gina, Hunter's mom, followed suit and soon the three women were talking, so the guys slipped away over to where Darren and Shasta sat.

"Hey, Darren," Hunter began. "We just wanted to come over and say sorry about your dad. He was a really fun guy, and he was real nice, too."

"Yeah," Eli agreed. "He always came to our shows. Remember? He even paid for a ticket that one time. We didn't even sell tickets." Feeling sadder with the memory, Eli looked at the ground. "Anyway, we're sorry, Man."

Shasta was about to reply for Darren, when he stood up and awkwardly gave Eli a half hug. "Thanks, Man," he said.

He moved to Hunter and repeated the same half hug and thanks and sat back down. Shasta was a little taken aback but recovered enough to ask, "How're you guys doing? That couldn't have been an easy day for you. I heard that you three were pretty sick. Feeling better?"

Hunter replied, "Yeah. Actually, that was pretty strange. Eli here had a big headache, Buggie was almost fainting, and I couldn't stop puking. My mom says it was stress, but Eli and I felt that way before we even got to the clearing. Listen, I was thinking about that. I think there might be something in the woods. Some kind of chemical they used to kill off some of the vegetation or make the animals go away. It has to be something."

That's when the rest of the Jackson family had arrived, and Darren had to go speak with his relatives. Shasta went with him leaving Eli and Hunter alone. They left a few minutes later and Darren hadn't spoken to either of them again. He saw them at the funeral service that day, but he didn't feel much like conversation.

Now he and Shasta occupied the same corner of the living room as people trickled in to visit once again. The funeral had been short, the gravesite service even shorter and Darren was glad of that. Going on day three of the nightmare was just about all he could take. Shasta, sensing his mood, took his hand and led him out of the room into the back yard. Even though it was fall, the leaves were still green. She sat him down on the back steps and plopped down beside him. She had been at his side almost constantly for the last three days after not being alone with him for almost two whole years. Finally, it was time to talk.

It was simple and to the point. It was also everything Darren had been wishing for.

"I love you, Darren. I've loved you for as long as I can remember. I'm sorry to drop this on you now, but I think you need to know where I stand. I want to be here for you. I'm glad you've let me so far, but if you think things are just going to go back to the way they were before you kissed me, I can't. I really want to be your friend, and I'll really try if that's what you want, but I need you to know how I really feel."

Darren stared at her deep brown eyes and confusion turned into realization. "You love me? You've felt like this all along? Shas, why didn't you tell me? I thought you were mad about the kiss. I thought you wanted distance."

"What? No! What are you even talking about? You looked so angry and then you just left the party. I thought you were mad at me! Then you wouldn't talk to me and..."

"No," he interrupted. "not wouldn't, couldn't. I couldn't stand being around you because I wanted things to be different with us, and I thought you were the one that didn't feel the same. I'm so sorry, Shas. I handled this all wrong."

Shasta couldn't believe what was happening. "No, Darren, don't be sorry. It sounds like we were both wrong. We were both idiots. We've wasted so much time without each other. I'm sorry, too." She threw her arms around him and tears sprang into her eyes. "I'm so sorry for everything you're going through right now, and I promise I'll be here for you. I'm not going anywhere ever again. I love you, Darren."

Darren closed his eyes. He smelled her citrusy-clean smell and felt her soft auburn hair against his skin. "I love you too, Shasta. I always have."

They stayed that way for a little longer, savoring the comfort each of them felt in each other's arms. The sun was dipping in the sky, and the light was fading. They could hear people's voices from inside the house. The sound brought them back from the moment.

"My dad would be happy about this, you know?" Darren said. "He really loved you."

Shasta's eyes filled with tears again, and she said, "I loved him, too. I still can't believe he's gone. It happened so fast."

She put her head on his shoulder and squeezed his hand. After a few moments she said, "Do you think there's anything to what Hunter was saying? About a chemical in the woods or something put there purposefully that would make people sick?"

"Oh, yeah, I forgot he said that. I can't imagine any-one doing that knowing that people are in those woods a lot. I mean, not only the construction crew, but kids from this neighborhood are in there all the time," he replied.

"But not usually as deep as the site. When they play in the woods, they usually stay right around the paths. We hardly ever went past that when we played out there, remember?"

"That's true, but what about the people working in there – those surveyors and the people from Gary Sam Construction and Oakwood Homes? Did any of them get sick? I don't think there's anything to it, Shasta."

"You're probably right," she agreed. "Hunter, Eli and Buggie were just stressed. You know, I haven't seen Bug in a few days. I really should go check in and say hi. Do you feel like coming with me?

"I better stick around with Mom. I don't really want to leave her right now. Will you come back when you're done?" It was like she was his own, personal sun. When she was near, he felt better. When she was gone, the stinging loss and sadness surrounded him like a cloud.

"Of course I will," she said. "I won't be long." She leaned up to reach his face and kissed him softly. "I don't want to be anywhere else."

They got up together and went back into the house. People were starting to leave. Soon it would just be him and his mom. The future Darren had dreamed of had been ripped from his grasp. What were they going to do now? Would they leave Meadowview Acres? Darren put an arm protectively around Shasta and walked her to the door. "Come back soon," he said.

She smiled that sweet, gentle smile and left him.

CHAPTER 15

Heather

Two days after Mr. Jackson's funeral, Hunter and Eli decided to retrieve the box from the shed and open it. The suspense had been killing Hunter, but Eli had almost forgotten about it. That is, until Hunter said, "Dude! We have to open the treasure chest! We're probably sitting on a gold mine and we don't even know it!"

Eli was skeptical. "It's probably nothing, Hunter. I wouldn't get my hopes up if I were you."

"Well you're not me, and I know there's something cool in there. Who knows how long it's been buried? Plus, you can hear something sliding back and forth when you shake it."

"What if it's something that needed to stay buried? Did you think of that?" Eli was remembering the uneasy feeling he had when he thought of how sick

124

they all were at the construction site. He didn't believe, as Hunter did, that there was some kind of chemical placed around the site to kill off the vegetation. In Eli's mind, their illnesses were somehow connected to that box. They would never know, he guessed, unless they opened it.

It was after school on Wednesday. His mom wouldn't be home for another hour, and he could hear Heather in her room screeching at someone on her cell phone. *There's nothing better to do.*

"Okay. Why don't you go get it out of your shed and bring it into my room? I'll go get our wire cutters and the vice and tools. Let's get this thing over with," Eli resigned.

Hunter was off like a shot. He was so excited. Eli went to the garage and gathered the tools they would need and headed to his room. Halfway down the hallway, he heard Heather scream.

"No! I'm NOT going to forgive you, Jake! I don't care if you think Trish is making it up! She's NOT! You're guilty! You were kissing her! Trish said Joe walked in on you kissing HER! How could you DO this to me? We're in LOVE," her ranting continued.

Eli shook his head and made his way into his bedroom. He closed the door behind him. Brody was not on his bed as usual. His mom was picking him up from the veterinarian on her way home. She was nervous about the amount of fur he'd lost and wanted to get him checked out. Eli had told her a condensed version of the happenings in the woods, and she had wanted to make sure the dog hadn't gotten into anything poisonous.

Hunter, looking queasy, opened the bedroom door a few minutes later. "Man, I don't know what it is, but I'm feeling sick again. I puked up the pizza bites I had after school. Just threw 'em up out of nowhere." He put the box on the bed and sat beside it.

Eli noticed the faint but concrete evidence of a headache coming on. Warning bells sounded in his mind. "What is it about this damn thing?" He asked Hunter. "Every time we're around it, we start feeling this way. Maybe we should just take it back, Hunter. Let's just take it back to the woods."

Hunter was doubled over on the bed but managed to say, "Listen, Eli, if there is a connection to this thing and us feeling sick, and I mean "IF", we have to find out for sure. What if it's just a coincidence?" He burped a liquid sounding burp.

"Think about it, Hunter! You puking, my headache, Bug fainting and weak! Even Deputy Clay and his nose bleed! And what if something about this box hurt Mr. Jackson? Do you really still want to see inside?"

Hunter was curled up with his arms around his stomach on Eli's bed. He hadn't thought of it the way Eli had. He rose up on one elbow and thought a moment. Eli was rubbing his temples and sitting at his desk.

Finally, Hunter said, "Yes. I think we should open it. If what you're saying is true, we need to know. But I honestly think that whatever is making us sick is on the outside of this thing. The sooner we open it, the sooner we can ditch the box. I'm sure whatever is inside doesn't have anything to do with how we're feeling. How could it? What could penetrate a steel box? We've got to look inside, Eli, we have to." He got up slowly from the bed and retched into Eli's trash can.

Eli grabbed the wire cutters and said, "Fine, let's get this over with." He got the blades of the cutters around one of the links of one of the chains and pressed with all of his strength. Nothing, it didn't even make a dent.

Seeing the problem, Hunter got up from the bed to get the vice. He secured it onto the edge of Eli's desk. Next, he brought the box over and positioned a link into the vice's opening. Then he twirled the bar of the vice until it tightened upon the link. Once the link was secure, Eli reached for the small crow bar and threaded it through the link and pushed it forcibly sideways. The link bent at first then it popped open under the pressure.

The boys looked at each other as if to say, "No turning back now."

There were five other chains to get through before the padlock on the box itself would be freed. Eli did most of the work on the chains because Hunter was once again heaving into the trash can. When the fifth chain slipped off the box, Eli looked at Hunter. He was in a ball as he held the trash can in front of him in the corner of the room. Eli's head was hurting but not unmanageably.

"Look, this padlock is going to take a while to figure out. The cutters aren't going to get through, so we'll have to think of something else. Why don't you go home for a while, and I'll come get you if I can get the lock off," he suggested to Hunter.

"Yeah," Hunter replied weakly. "I don't think I'm going to be much help. Sorry, Man. Maybe you're right. Maybe that thing is what's messing us up. Fiddle with it if you want to, but if you still want to take it back to the hole in the woods, I'll go with you. Just not today. I feel like crap."

He pushed himself up from the floor. He was still holding tight to the can. "I'll bring this back later." He motioned to the trash can and left.

Eli sat looking at the silver box with the padlock on the front for a few minutes. "What in the world is this thing?" He asked himself. The fact that it made them sick was no longer disputed. Hunter even acknowledged that now. He wondered if there could be some chemical on the outside of the box like Hunter suggested and the inside was fine. He couldn't think of anything potent enough to penetrate steel and have an effect on people. Eli was stumped. He didn't know if he wanted to open it or not. He decided to grab a drink and take an aspirin for his head, so he left his room and made for the kitchen.

Passing Heather's doorway, he could still hear her crying on the phone to Jake. It sounded like the fight was dying down because he heard her say, "Do you know how many guys I don't flirt with every day? I do that because of you. I make that sacrifice for our future together! You need to remember that! You're not the only one who could cheat, you know! You're lucky I haven't so far!"

Eli rolled his eyes. That was far too much drama for him. He rounded the door to the kitchen just as his mother was coming in with Brody. The dog saw Eli and jumped up in the universal jump of joy greeting that all dogs bestow upon their families. Eli petted the dog and sat down in one of the kitchen chairs. "What'd the vet say?" He asked Lara.

"She said that he really did lose a lot of fur, but dogs can do that in instances of high stress. Something about the adrenaline. He'll be fine, though. How was school?" She asked.

"Fine, nothing special," Eli replied. "Heather and Jake are having another fight. Last I heard she was threatening to cheat on him."

"I'm afraid that relationship may be taking a turn into unhealthy territory. She asked me this morning what age is too young to get married." Lara's eyebrows furrowed as she remembered the conversation with her fifteen year old daughter that morning. At first the thing between Heather and Jake had seemed sweet, but now it was getting a little too serious for Lara's comfort level.

"Jeez," replied Eli. "That's a little much. What'd you tell her? Thirty?" He laughed at his own joke and then popped the aspirin into his mouth. He followed it with a big chug of water. "Well, Hunter and I are working on something, so I'll be in my room for a while."

"Oh, Shazaam Brothers at it again? I've missed those performances. What is it this time? Never mind, don't tell me. Just promise to go outside if it involves anything being blown up." She laughed and headed off to her room to change out of her work clothes.

Back in his room, Eli decided once and for all to open the box, find out its contents and go to Hunter to apprise him of the situation. He sat down at his desk and studied the padlock. It was completely sound. No getting around that sucker without the combination. Next, trying to find a vantage point, he looked at the box itself. *Bingo.* On the back were two hinges connected by screws. He started to work on them with his Phillips head.

It was going to be tough because they were in there tight. As he worked, he heard Brody sniff at the door, issue a low growl and pad off back toward the kitchen.

There! The first screw turned slightly under the pressure of the screwdriver, so Eli decided to get out his power driven one. It had been charging since he had brought all of the tools in from the garage. Once he started though, he found that it didn't have enough juice to be powerful enough. "I guess this is going to take elbow grease," he said aloud. Getting his Phillips head once again, he pushed down as he turned. A little at a time, the screw turned. It took a lot of energy, but a few minutes later he had one screw in his hand.

"One down, three to go," he said to the empty room. He started on the next screw and noticed his head thumping. *Damn it!* He tried to think of other things as he worked to keep his mind off the pain.

The door down the hall to Heather's room opened and slammed shut, followed by her voice yelling, "Mom! Mom! I need a ride!"

He heard the mumbled reply of his mother from the kitchen where she was cooking dinner and then Heather screeched, "Why? Why can't you now? I'm not hungry, I don't want to eat! I have to go see him!"

His mother's voice was raised a little in her response but still not loud enough for Eli to hear what she said.

Yes! The second screw released its hold and fell into Eli's hand. His head pounding now, he got out his flat-head screwdriver and jammed it under the hinge. At first it was stuck tight, but Eli worked at it until he was able to pry it off the box. He set to work on the third screw, but had to stop and close his eyes a moment. He had started to see little flashes of blue light. He took some deep breaths and opened his eyes. *Better, good.* He set to work on the third screw.

"Just take me now and you can come back and finish your stupid dinner!" Heather wailed at her mother. "You just want to keep me prisoner here! You don't want me to see him! You don't understand how in love we are!"

Lara finally had enough and yelled, "I said I will take you when I'm finished, Heather! That's maybe twenty minutes tops! Now sit down and stop this or you won't go at all! I'm tired of you speaking to me this way! You've been treating your brother and me horribly for the last few weeks, and this is going to stop!"

The rest of the argument came in waves of murmurs and overly dramatic teen cries as Eli rescued the third screw from its tight home and started work on the fourth. Excitement surged through him now that the end was near. His mind pushed his headache aside as he worked, allowing him to entertain ideas of what he would find in a mere few minutes. The fourth screw was turning along with his mind. *What could it be? A map to some adventure? Secret documents worth millions? A lost artifact?*

"Plop" the screw landed on the desk. Eli picked up the flat head and went to work on the hinge. Sounds from the argument in the kitchen picked up once again, but Eli was too psyched to listen to what they were saying.

The headache was almost blinding now as he worked, refusing to stop. He was so close, so close now. Spots were twinkling like stars in his eyes when finally the hinge popped off and the box was no longer sealed. Eli squeezed his eyes together in an effort to clear his vision. He took a deep breath and pried open the back end of the box. His ears popped loudly as if he were on a roller coaster then started to ring. Inside the box were two items – an old piece of some kind of rock and an envelope.

Eli was having trouble thinking because of the blinding pain. He needed Hunter. He needed to get away from that box! He grabbed his backpack off his bed and emptied the contents. Then he grabbed the rock and the envelope and put them into the pack. He zipped the backpack closed and slung it over his shoulder. His head felt like it would split open at any moment and he was having trouble seeing through the flashing lights. "Just like in the woods," he said. He had to run to Hunter's.

He bolted from his room down the hallway and into the kitchen.

The fight was still going full force, but his mother stopped mid-sentence when he burst into the room.

"Eli," she said, her face full of concern. "You look horrible, Honey. What's wrong?"

"Nothing, I. I'm going to Hunter's." He blinked and started again in the direction of the door.

"Oh, sure! Poor Eli! What's wrong with Eli!" Heather chided. "Nobody cares about Heather! Nobody cares what's wrong with me! I know! I'll go live with Dad! Dad will let me do whatever I want! He'll let me see Jake all the time if I want!

Heather's face was turning bright red as she continued her tirade. Eli and Mrs. Andrews watched as her eyes grew bigger and her face grew pinker, but she wasn't backing down. "Go on, Eli! Go to Hunter's house! I'm sure no one will care as long as YOU'RE happy! I'M going to pack and go live with…" suddenly she stopped. Looking shocked she said, "Wha…?"

A tiny trickle of blood rolled out of Heather's left nostril and she collapsed in a powder pink heap on the tiled kitchen floor. Her perfect chestnut ringlets made a weird, little pillow around her head. Heather was dead.

———————

Even through the blinding pain of his head, Eli knew it was bad. He had watched in horror as his sister's face had grown alarmingly red. Her eyes grew wider and wider. His mother seemed frozen in shock until Heather hit the floor. That broke the spell, and Lara was kneeling by her daughter the next instant.

Eli instinctively yelled, "I'll get help," and ran quickly from the kitchen out the door and over to Hunter's house. He didn't bother knocking; he just ran in the side door of the Massey's house.

Mrs. Massey was washing vegetables in the kitchen sink. She whirled around quickly when Eli burst into the room.

"Eli, what…," she began.

"Hurry! It's Heather! My mom needs help!" He kept running through the house to find Hunter. His eyes wide with fear, he flew into his friend's room.

Hunter had been lying on his bed and nursing his sick stomach, but was instantly alert when he laid eyes on Eli. Eli was frantic.

"It's this thing!" He yelled at Hunter holding up the backpack. "It's a curse or something! Hunter, it just killed Heather!"

Hunter's face was incredulous as he tried to comprehend what Eli had said. "What do you mean *it killed* Heather? What happened, Eli? What was in the box? What's wrong with Heather?" His heart was pounding in his chest.

Eli fell onto Hunter's bed and started sobbing.

"I don't know what it is! It's just a rock! I don't understand it! I threw it in the backpack and was on my way over here. Mom and Heather were in the kitchen fighting and, and," he had to stop a minute to catch his breath.

Hunter reached for the trash can and once again started to heave the contents of his stomach.

After a moment, Eli was more in control. "It's like it just stopped her, Hunter," Eli continued in a soft voice. Still sniffling, he said, "One second she was yelling at Mom and me and the next second she was on the floor. It was so fast. It just stopped her," he repeated.

He looked at the backpack in his hands. "I know it's this rock. It has to be, because the box is still on my bed. My head is killing me. You started to heave the second I came into the room with this thing." Eli looked at Hunter through his tears and said, "It kills people."

"That's it," Hunter said, angry now. "Give me that thing. What is it, anyway?"

"Like I said, just a rock. It just looks like a rock. I don't know what it is," Eli responded expressionless.

Hunter was putting on his shoes . "Go home, help your mom. I'm taking this thing back to the hell hole it came from. Give it to me."

Eli handed the backpack to Hunter who immediately choked back another dry heave. Throwing the backpack over his shoulder, Hunter flew out of his room and ran out of the house.

CHAPTER 16

Clara & Hansen

Clara had been having a pretty good week. The football team was having extra practices in preparation for playoffs, so Hansen was busy after school until late. That, coupled with Clara helping her mom and Mrs. Port pick up and deliver meals to Darren's house, had meant that she hadn't seen Hansen since Sunday. She thought it was a really nice break.

That day at school was no exception. She really didn't have to see him very much between classes because there was very little time and after school she would be helping Ms. Leezil grade papers. "Just lunch," she thought. "Make it through lunch and you're home free."

She grabbed her sack lunch from her locker and made her way to the cafeteria. Angie walked with her.

Angie was chatting about how Joe was going to get to play more now that Darren was sitting out the next football game. Clara had been sad to learn of Mr. Jackson's death. She liked Mr. and Mrs. Jackson – she thought they were nice. Darren scared her a little, though, because he was always so serious.

She and Angie found seats at the popular table next to Emily and Destiny. They were talking about Halloween costumes for Emily's party. Clara tried to be excited about the party, but the fact that she would be stuck with Hansen all night didn't excite her much.

Hansen and his cronies came in a few minutes later all amped up on some unseen testosterone high. Hansen went right to the cafeteria line and pushed a random kid out of his way. He grabbed a tray and, barking orders at the cafeteria ladies, went down the line. With looks of loathing on their faces, they served up what he wanted.

Clara inwardly groaned. "Why, why, why, does he have to act like that? What a jerk," she thought. She tried to eat quickly, so she could maybe make an excuse and leave. It was in vain, though. The next minute he was squeezing his bulky way onto the bench beside her.

"Hey, Babe. Did ya miss me?" He said and leaned over to try and kiss her.

She fake giggled and turned her head away from him acting like she had a mouthful of food. Hansen decided he didn't like to be denied in front of an audience. He grabbed the back of her blonde hair and forced her head toward him. He repeated maliciously and slowly, "I said, Hey, Babe. Did ya miss me?" and smashed his lips onto hers.

Clara was surprised. She knew he could be a jerk, but he never had been to her. He certainly had never laid a hand on her before this. She kissed him back dutifully and vowed that the kiss would be the last he would ever get from her. She could put up with his stupid and mean actions toward other people if it meant securing her popularity, but there was no way she would let him turn that meanness in her direction.

As soon as he released her hair, she started gathering up the rest of her uneaten lunch. She had caught Mr. Just's eye as he stood monitoring by the cafeteria door. That had given her an idea. She would tell everyone that she was supposed to take a make-up quiz for his class, but before she could make her excuses, Hansen had decided that the lunchroom was too quiet. He and his goons had chosen a victim and were busy emptying packets of ketchup into a milk carton.

Clara, about to serve her freshly prepared lie, rose from the table when Hansen grabbed her arm – hard.

"Sit down, Babe. You're not going anywhere until you see my latest show." He pulled her arm down forcing Clara to sit.

The poor kid across the room never knew what hit him. Clara didn't know his name, but she had smiled at him in the hall. She thought he looked nice. Hansen launched the ketchup filled carton in a perfect arc that caught the poor schmuck directly in the back of the head. The carton burst open and the ketchup splattered him from his head down the length of his back.

Hansen and his crew busted out laughing as the rest of the students in the cafeteria looked in horror at the boy soaked in the red sauce. No one else seemed to think it was funny.

Mr. Just was beside Hansen in an instant. "Get up and get to the office!" He yelled. His face was full of fury. "NOW!"

Hansen started to open his mouth and spew some kind of lie, but Mr. Just knew him too well. "Hansen Reynolds," he said with a steely tone. "If you don't get to the office now, I am going straight to Coach Ripley and telling him that you are off the team. Move."

Hansen seemed to take Mr. Just's threat seriously and got his wide load off the bench. Giving Mr. Just a "No harm done, Dude" look, he sidled past him and out of the cafeteria.

By then, the laughter from Hansen's table had subsided and the guy (Jeremy, Clara learned later) was being helped by friends to clean up. Mr. Martin, the Counselor was on his way over to Jeremy's table, too.

Mr. Just looked at the other guys at Hansen's table and said, "You're just as guilty; detention for each one of you for the rest of this week." The guys shifted their eyes around trying hard not to look at him. They weren't so brave without the main instigator around.

Clara felt really bad for Jeremy, but she was glad that Hansen was gone. Angie and Emily started talking about the party again, so Clara decided to stay and wait for the bell. She looked around the cafeteria as she talked and finally she found him. He was sitting at the table by the doors to the gym with Eli. Hunter looked great today. He had on a moss green shirt that matched his eyes. He was nodding at something Eli had just said. As she watched, he glanced in her direction, and she shot him a big smile. He looked a little confused at first but then smiled back. Clara's tummy did a little flip. "Hansen is history," she thought.

By late afternoon, Clara was using a key while grading papers in Ms. Leezil's classroom. She was having trouble concentrating, however. Her mind kept wandering, coming up with ways to break-up with Hansen. She thought the best idea was to do it when she was close to her house. Since he lived down the street, he would walk up to her house sometimes to see her. She could just tell him and go inside the safety of her home. Clara kind of hoped he would come over today. She was finally ready to pull the trigger. She hadn't seen him after school and nobody knew what had happened after he had gone to Principal Harrison's office.

Ten minutes later she found out. Her phone chimed an alert that she had a new text. It was from Hansen. "Had to stay after for detention. Can't go to football till next week. Give me a ride home."

"That's nice," thought Clara. "No hi, how are you. No please, no thank you. Well fine, I'll give you a ride home. To *my* house. Then I'll tell you it's over and go inside. You can walk home from there."

When it was time to quit for the day, Ms. Leezil and Clara walked out of the classroom. As Ms. Leezil locked her door, she said, "Thanks, Clara. Have a good night, Hon." Then she walked over to where Mr. Just was waiting for her.

Hansen was there in no time. As they walked to the student parking lot, he gave Clara a play by play of his conversation with the principal. Clara didn't care and only half listened. They made it out to her car and climbed in.

"Yep! They'll be sorry when my dad calls the school tomorrow! He won't stand for this! The coach'll be mad, too. The team has NO defense without me." Hansen's tirade was unending.

Clara was more interested in why her car wasn't starting. When she turned the key, a series of little clicks sounded instead of the purr of her little VW Bug's engine. She tried it again only to hear the same little, "click, click, click, click, click".

"Oh, great! Your piece of crap car is shot! That's just great, Clara! What'd you do, flood it? Don't you know how to drive? Geez! Women drivers!" Hansen railed at her.

"I did not flood it; it sounds like the battery to me." Clara's dad was serious about his little girl driving. Before handing her the keys, he had taught her how to change her own oil, fill the wash fluid and made her watch a DVD titled *Automobile Care and Maintenance.* She remembered the same sound coming from a car on the DVD that was having battery trouble. "And if you want to get out and walk home, be my guest!"

Hansen was about to respond when there was a tap on Clara's window. It was Mr. Just. Clara opened her door since she couldn't roll down the window. "Hey, Mr. Just. I think my battery's dead."

"Yeah, that's what it sounded like to me, too." He had just said goodbye to Julie and was walking to his car when he had heard Clara's VW refusing to start.

"Can you call someone? I don't keep jumper cables in my Jeep." He looked over at Hansen's angry face and was immediately reluctant to leave Clara alone with him. There were very few cars left in the lot at that time of day, and he didn't see anyone else around. Julie had just pulled out, too.

"I don't think so. My dad's flying until Friday and Mom works at the courthouse in Glovercroft. I'm not supposed to call because she might be in the middle of a trial. She does the court reporting."

Mr. Just looked over at Hansen and asked, "What about you?"

Hansen sneered and replied, "It's not my car. My dad's not gonna come over and fix it."

"Yeah, I figured," Mr. Just said. "Hansen, you're really a piece of work, Man." He was not about to leave Clara alone with that beast, so he did the only thing he could. "Come on, then. I'll ride you both home real quick. Where do you live, Clara?"

"Oh! Thanks, Mr. Just! We live really close, just in Meadowview Acres. We both live there." Clara was relieved not to be stuck alone with Hansen.

They walked together to the staff parking and got into Phillip's Jeep. Clara got in front with Mr. Just, and, Hansen shoved his bulky self into the back. The top was off, and the fresh air felt nice. Clara closed her eyes on the way home and felt the wind in her hair. She knew Hansen was pissed in the back seat, but she didn't care. She felt free. She hadn't realized how trapped she had been feeling.

They arrived at the subdivision too soon. Clara could have ridden around in Mr. Just's Jeep for hours, but reality came crashing back when she heard Hansen say, "I'll just get out at her house. We have things to discuss."

Mr. Just's eyebrows furrowed as he looked squarely at Clara. "That okay with you? I can take him on to his house if you want."

Clara said, "No, it's alright. Really. Thanks a lot for the ride, Mr. Just. I'll tell my mom about the car and we'll handle it."

"Ain't nothin' but a thing," he replied. The kids were both getting out of his Jeep when his phone rang. Looking at the screen, he saw that it was Julie. He put the Jeep in park and took the call while still in front of Clara's house. They had talked about getting together for dinner that night, and he wanted to know the plan.

Hansen was walking with Clara to the sidewalk in front of her house when she stopped. Turning to look him square in the face she said, "So here's the thing. I'm done with you. I'm done with your stupid pranks, I'm done with your mean comments and teasing and most of all I'm done with kissing you. It's gross. And if you ever try to grab my hair again, I'll kick you in the crotch. Don't think I won't. So that's it, we're over." She stopped talking and stared right at him. She could tell that he was furious, but he was shocked as well. She was a little afraid, but she knew that Mr. Just was still parked in his Jeep a few feet away, and she knew lots of her neighbors were home. When Hansen didn't say anything, she turned to go into her house. That's when he blew.

"You bitch! Nobody breaks up with me! Who do you think you are? You're a nobody! I MADE you! You're nothing without me! And you think you can just dump me? Think again!" He looked like he was about to lunge at Clara.

Just then, the door across the street to Hunter's house flew open, and he came running out. He ran across the street and was about to run past Hansen and Clara toward the woods when Hansen reached out and grabbed his backpack. He gave it a hard yank causing Hunter to fall backwards onto the lawn. "What's this, Sissy Boy? Did you come over to save your little friend?"

"Give it back!" Hunter yelled at him. "I have to go! Give me that back!"

Realizing that he had found a perfect victim, Hansen pushed Hunter back down again and decided to toy with him. "Why? What's so important, Pansy Boy?" He started to unzip the pack and Hunter yelled, "Stop, don't unzip that! Give it back to me!"

Hansen was having fun now. All the rage he had toward Clara was now being directed at Hunter. He unzipped the pack while still holding off Hunter. "Stop! No!" Hunter was almost begging him now.

"Oh," Hansen said. "It's a pretty widdle rock! Does the widdle Pansy Boy like collecting rocks?"

Mr. Just had looked up from his cell right as Hansen had called Clara a bitch. "That kid just doesn't know when to stop," he thought. He was telling Julie that he'd call her right back when Hunter Massey had run across the street and been snagged by Hansen. Mr. Just jumped out of his Jeep and walked quickly over to the scene.

He could tell immediately that something was terribly wrong. Hansen's face was turning bright red and his eyes bulged. The other two kids were just staring, not knowing what to do. Phillip didn't know what to do either. He thought that maybe Hansen was choking and was trying to remember how to perform the Heimlich Maneuver. Hansen started to claw at his throat frantically as Phillip ran to position himself behind the boy. He was reaching around Hansen's generous middle trying to get a hold, when Hansen bucked Mr. Just off of him and fell to the ground. He lay there on the grass convulsing – his face turning purple. Mr. Just ran back to his Jeep to retrieve his phone and dialed 9-1-1. She answered after the first ring.

"9-1-1, what's your emergency?" Rachel's voice was steady and calm on the other end.

"This is Phillip Just, I'm in the neighborhood of Meadowview Acres and there's a teenage boy here having some kind of attack," he relayed while his heart sped up.

"Meadowview Acres?" Rachel asked, stunned. "I just had another call not two minutes ago from there. "Is this about the Andrews girl?"

"The Andrews girl? No! This is Hansen Reynolds! He's having some kind of problem breathing! Hurry, I don't think he has much time," Mr. Just said shakily. *I'm getting a little freaked out here, Man.*

"We already have a crew on the way. I'll radio and tell them your situation. Sit tight. It won't be long." Then she was gone.

Phillip Just looked over to where Hansen had been scratching his throat and rolling on the ground. He saw that the boy was perfectly still; his throat was raw and bloody where he had tried to scratch open an airway.

Shocked, Mr. Just shook his head and thought, "Karma, Man."

CHAPTER 17

Peaceful Hearts

Bug sat in an overstuffed chair in the foyer of the Peaceful Hearts Funeral Home. She was waiting for her parents. Unfortunately, they had two sets of families to console today. Since Peaceful Hearts was the only funeral home in Hallston, Hansen Reynolds had been laid out in one room, while Heather Andrews occupied the other. Practically everyone Bug knew had passed by her going to one viewing or the other as she sat. Most people went to both.

Bug had been curious about everything that had transpired the past week. It had all started with her decision to follow Eli and Hunter into the woods last Friday. She remembered the cold, clammy feeling that had come over her. She was sweating but still felt cold, and she remembered feeling weak. She also remembered Eli telling her about Mr. Jackson and the deputy driving them home. She didn't remember fainting in his squad car, but they said she did. *Super weird*. She had never fainted in her life before that night.

Her parents had been so happy to see her that she didn't even get in trouble for going into the woods in the first place. That was lucky. She knew Mr. Jackson hadn't been lucky, though – Bug had read about brain hemorrhages in the same magazine that she had read about the migraine headaches. Her headache had gone away as soon as she had gotten home, though.

She also remembered something else. She remembered Eli and Hunter passing a shiny silver box back and forth to each other. She knew that they hadn't had the box with them going into the woods because she had watched them. All they had with them was the backpack Hunter was wearing. Where had they gotten that box? What did they have in it? *Also super weird.*

Then, just a few days later, Heather Andrews had an aneurysm. That's what most people were saying had killed her. At about the same time, Hansen died from his throat swelling. They were saying he had an allergic reaction to something. Bug felt bad for the Andrews family, and she was still trying really hard to feel bad for Hansen.

All in all, the last week had been very curious, and if there was one thing Bug Hamilton needed the most – it was answers. It was almost like some puzzle that she needed to solve, and Bug knew that she was up to the challenge. *Knowledge is power.*

She already had her first clue. Shasta had come to see her Monday, and they had talked about Mr. Jackson. Bug had asked Shasta for as much information as she knew about Mr. Jackson's previous health problems. Was there any family history of stroke? Had he been feeling anything out of the ordinary? Shasta had tried to answer, but just didn't have that kind of information. She did have some other information, though. She told Bug that Hunter had a theory that there was some type of chemical in the woods that the construction people had used to help kill vegetation and ward off animals. Bug slipped that bit of information into her iron-clad memory.

Next up was research. Bug searched online for any widely used chemicals that could be used in clearing vegetation that could trigger health problems. That was futile. Almost every chemical on the planet can trigger health problems. Next, she researched Gary Sam Construction and Oakwood Homes. There wasn't anything in either company's history that pointed to a similar occurrence. Then Bug hit a wall. She didn't know where to go next.

That was, until Wednesday. Bug had been watching a documentary on the ecological ramifications of forest clearing when she first heard the commotion. Someone was yelling outside. She went to the front room and looked out the window to see who it was. The yelling was coming from further down the street, so she opened the front door and stepped out.

The scene was in front of Clara Stagg's house. There was a Jeep parked on the street, and she could see a man getting out. Clara was there and her boyfriend, Hansen, was yelling at her. Bug was about to go back inside when she saw Hunter running across the street. She gasped as she witnessed Hansen first grab then yank Hunter's backpack off of him. Bug, feeling a little ashamed for watching but unable to stop, sat down on the front step. Hunter was yelling at Hansen, and Hansen was unzipping the backpack. He reached inside and pulled out something. *What is that?* To Bug it looked like a piece of concrete. That's when things went from bad to worse. Even from her house two houses up the street, Bug could see Hansen's face getting red. Bug was suddenly afraid. Her instincts told her to go inside, and she listened.

Once inside the safety of her house, she decided to keep an eye on things. She peeked out of the side window that faced the opposite end of the street and had a clear view of Clara's sidewalk. Clara and Hunter stood side by side. They were looking at the large, still form of Hansen sprawled out on the lawn. The man in the Jeep was on the phone. Bug saw Hunter turn away from Clara and throw up on the sidewalk. Then, he grabbed his backpack up off the ground, went over to where Hansen had dropped the rock, scooped it up and put it back in the pack. Once Hunter had zipped it up, he said something to Clara and then ran back across the street and down his driveway. Bug lost sight of him after that. *Super curious. What's that piece of rock thing? Why's it so important? Was that in his backpack on Friday going into the woods – or was it in that box?*

That was about the time the first ambulance showed up, and Bug got worried. She was worried because it didn't stop at Clara's house. It went to the Andrews' house. Bug called her dad. He had been home within minutes, followed by her mom an hour later. By then, the neighborhood was crowded with people talking in little groups. Family members of the Andrews' started arriving at their house. Hansen had been taken away in the second ambulance, and Clara's house was relatively quiet. The man in the Jeep was gone. Bug didn't know what was going on with the Reynolds family since Hansen's house was further down Meadowview Drive.

Bug's parents had quizzed her endlessly about what she had witnessed. Then she had been allowed to go with them when Mark and Ann ventured out to join one of the groups of neighbors discussing the events. That had been disappointing to Bug. No one knew any more than she did.

Bug was lost in thought as she sat in her puffy chair at the funeral home. She had initially gone in to show her respects to both families. She saw Heather laid out in her casket. She was plastic looking, and Bug didn't think that they did her hair the right way. When she had seen Heather before, her hair was always curled into a bunch of loose ringlets that fell down her back. Whoever styled her hair for the last time had made a bunch of jumbo curls that lay awkwardly around her shoulders. Bug thought Heather would be upset about that.

She hadn't bothered to look at dead Hansen. She had had enough of him while he was alive. "Oops," she thought, "don't think ill of the dead." She tried hard to think of something nice about Hansen. Finally she had it and went up to Mr. and Mrs. Reynolds and said, "Hansen was the biggest one on the football team. I'm sorry you lost your son." *There! Super job!*

She was still in her puffy chair and lost in thought when Clara came up to her and said, "Hey, Buggie. How are you?"

"Oh! Hi Clara," Bug replied. "I'm fine. Sorry about your boyfriend."

Bug noticed one of Clara's eyebrows twitch up when she said, "Yep, poor Hansen. Hey, have you seen Hunter? I thought he'd be in Heather's room with Eli, but I didn't see him."

"No," Bug said. "He hasn't come in yet. I've been sitting here for at least an hour and a half and he hasn't passed by me yet. Why do you want to talk to him? Is it because he was there when Hansen died?"

Clara looked shocked at Bug's question but recovered quickly. "Uh, no. I wanted to talk to him about something else. Well, I'll see you later, Buggie." She turned and started back down the hall to Hansen's room.

As soon as Clara went into the room with the Reynolds family, Eli came out of the room where Heather was. He looked tired to Bug. He saw her looking at him and made his way to the foyer.

"How're you doing with all this, Bug?" He asked.

"Oh, I'm doing fine. I'm sorry for you, though, Eli. I think Heather was the prettiest girl I've ever seen. She never talked to me at all, but she was nice to look at."

Eli grinned at that and replied, "You know, Bug, I think hearing that would have made her happy."

"Do you have to stay here all day?" Bug asked.

"Yeah, I don't want to leave my mom. Dad's here, too, and that's kinda awkward. He's acting like he's all broken up over it, but he hadn't even talked to Heather in weeks. I wish he'd leave." Eli sat down in the puffy chair next to Bug's.

"Clara was just out here looking for Hunter. Is he coming?"

"Yeah, that's why I came out. He just texted that he and his folks are on their way. I'm going to wait for them out here and give them the head's up about Dad. Mr. Massey has been pretty mad at my dad since he left us, and I want to warn him." He paused, then said, "Why does Clara want to see Hunter?"

"She didn't say, but I think it's because he was there with her when Hansen died. I don't know for sure, though."

"Huh," said Eli.

"Can I ask you about something, Eli? Not about Heather or anything. About last Friday."

"Sure, what is it?" Eli was happy to talk about anything other than Heather. He was fighting the guilty feeling that he had caused her death by having the box in their home. He had been struggling with that every moment since she died.

"What was in that silver box that you and Hunter had at the construction site?" Bug watched Eli's reaction.

Eli's head popped up with a look of shock and guilt on his face, and he stared right at Bug. "What do you mean? Why? Why do you want to know?" All of a sudden, Eli was on his feet and pacing the small foyer. "It was nothing. A toolbox. That's what we keep our tools in." He stopped pacing and looked at her.

Bug felt bad having caused him to get upset, especially today. She thought this could all wait a few days.

"Oh, okay," she said. "I just thought it was something else. Oh, look! There's Hunter."

She had managed to divert his attention and calm him down at once. He still looked agitated, but she didn't think he was angry anymore.

The Massey's came in, and Eli hugged them all. He told them about his dad and let them know how his mom was doing. Mr. and Mrs. Massey went on into the room with Heather while Hunter stayed behind with Eli. They were a little farther down the hallway and Eli was talking in whispers. Bug saw Hunter's eyes get big and he looked over at her. "Bingo", she thought. "We have a super clue."

Not long after, Hunter and Eli disappeared into Heather's room. Bug was turning ideas over in her mind about what could be in the box when Shasta and Darren arrived at Peaceful Hearts. It was probably pretty tough on Darren since he was just there for his dad's funeral Monday.

"There she is." Shasta went directly to her little friend and gave her a big hug. "Waiting for your folks?"

"Yup," replied Bug to Shasta. "Hey, Darren." She looked at the big young man and smiled.

He returned the smile but didn't say anything. Bug knew from Shasta that he was the strong, silent type. Bug was happy that they were together again. She had never seen Shasta so happy.

Shasta turned to Darren and said, "If you don't mind going into the Reynolds' room on your own, I'll stay here with Bug. Then we can both go to see Eli."

"That's fine. I know there's no love lost between you and Hansen. I need to say something to his parents, though. They've been helpful to Mom this week." He gave her a quick kiss and left them.

Bug was happy to have Shasta to herself. Shasta was smart, too, and Bug thought that she might have some insight into the mystery.

Shasta sat in the puffy chair that Eli had vacated and looked at Bug. "I see those wheels turning," she said. "What are you thinking about so hard?"

"I have a theory," Bug started. "A theory about these deaths. I think they're all connected."

Shasta's eyes narrowed as she said, "Bug, you have to be careful here. A lot of people are really upset right now. This might not be the best time to start on a conspiracy theory. We know for a fact what killed all three of them."

"Do we?" Bug said. "I don't. Take Mr. Jackson. He was a perfectly healthy man of fifty-one. I overheard my mom talking to Agnes Jackson when we took a cake over last Sunday. According to her, this was a surprise because he had no family history of stroke or any medical condition that could cause this. He wasn't on medication for anything, either. There was no trauma, he was sitting in his bulldozer fine as could be, then WHAM! Out of nowhere! He's dead. Also, the amount of blood at the scene was remarkable – it said that in the autopsy report."

Bug looked over and could tell that she had gotten Shasta thinking. "Now look at Heather, a perfectly healthy girl of fifteen. According to my dad, she had an aneurysm. Once again, no family history or medical condition. She took no medications. There's only a two to three percent chance of an adult female having an aneurysm, and she was too young to be in that category. There's an even less chance than that in kids. She had none of the risk factors like hypertension or diabetes, and she didn't have any symptoms. It happened fast, just like Mr. Jackson."

Bug stopped again to let Shasta absorb the information, then continued, "Then there's Hansen. He had an allergic reaction to something? What? He wasn't eating or drinking anything. I saw him. I saw him reach into Hunter's backpack and pull out a rock type thing. Can people be allergic to rocks? According to my research, it's extremely rare. I know there's more to this, Shasta. I'm going to find out what it is. And there's one more thing. A big thing."

Shasta listened to Bug and was curious in spite of herself. Bug had a way of making things sound so plausible. She made a lot of sense. "What big thing?" she asked.

"Eli and Hunter went into the woods that night with only a backpack on Hunter's back. When I caught up to them in the clearing, they had a silver metal box with them. It had a bunch of chains around it with locks. I just asked Eli about it right before you got here, and he was super jumpy. Whatever is in that box has something to do with all of this." Bug, feeling somewhat lighter now that someone else was burdened with this load, sat back in the puffy chair.

"Okay, Bug, you've sold me. But what do we do from here?" Shasta was reluctant to get involved with this, but the journalist inside of her was intrigued.

"Well, I think the first thing we need to do is more research. I think we should go to the newspaper offices and look through the archives."

"And what exactly are we looking for?" Shasta asked.

"Any unexplained deaths that have occurred within the same type of time frame. You know? Super close together for no apparent reason. Sometimes, things like that get overlooked. We'll start with the most newsworthy ones and go from there. Are you in?" Bug smiled at Shasta. She was eager to get started.

Shasta thought for a moment and decided it was worth looking into. Then she smiled back at Bug and said, "I'm in".

CHAPTER 18

Clara

Clara hadn't had to use her popular girl smile in days. It was so nice to just be Clara again – Clara without Hansen. She really felt badly about how that day had gone down with Hansen, though. She'd had no idea what would ultimately transpire once she had broken up with him. She remembered saying the words, "We're over," and watching his expression change from one of surprise to hatred. That's when she had gotten scared.

Right after Hansen had called her a bitch, she saw Mr. Just get out of his Jeep. Thank goodness he was there. She knew Hansen wouldn't be able to actually hurt her. Not with an adult present, but looking at his face, she hadn't been so sure. Then, when Hunter came flying across the street, Clara had initially thought he was coming to save her, the Damsel in Distress thing. Turns out, he was bolting for the woods for some reason. That's when Hansen had nabbed him. Clara had been surprised at how quick Hansen was when his arm shot out, and he snagged the backpack off of Hunter.

The rest she didn't understand at all. Hunter was yelling about whatever it was in the backpack. He kept yelling to Hansen, "Give it back." She wondered why. It turned out to be just some kind of rock. She didn't get it. Then Hansen's face started to get all red and puffy, and he started to scratch out his own throat. Clara shuddered at the memory.

The whole thing, it seemed to her, took less than a couple of minutes. Suddenly, Mr. Just was there trying to reach around Hansen to do the Heimlich but his arms hadn't been long enough. Then he had gone racing back to his Jeep for his cell to call for an ambulance. That's when she and Hunter had just stood there, frozen to the sidewalk and watched Hansen convulse and die.

Clara had never seen anyone die before, not even a pet. Mostly, she was grossed out at the color his face had turned. It was a very unnatural blue-ish. *Yuck.*

After that, she remembered that Hunter had puked. Surprisingly, Hunter was a little more freaked out than she was, and she was Hansen's girlfriend after all – well, ex-girlfriend. Then Hunter had turned to her and said,

"You never should have been with that guy, Clara." He had grabbed his backpack and run back behind his house, and Clara hadn't seen him again until in the hallway at Peaceful Hearts.

While all of that was going on with Hansen, Heather had already died. That one shocked Clara. She wondered how in the world that could have happened? Heather was so young and healthy, but then, so was Hansen.

She and Mr. Just had been waiting for the ambulance to come and were surprised when it turned into the Andrews' driveway. One of the paramedics had gone into the Andrews' house and the other had come over to where she stood with Mr. Just. The paramedic checked Hansen's vital signs and then called the information in to the dispatcher. A deputy's car had arrived soon after that, and Clara and Mr. Just had had to give statements. It was funny, but both of them had left out Hunter's part altogether. They had just said that Clara and Hansen had been talking after Mr. Just had dropped them off. Then Hansen had started having some sort of reaction to something and couldn't breathe. They both told of how Mr. Just had tried to administer help but couldn't, and then Hansen had finally died.

Clara was so thankful to Mr. Just for helping her by driving them home and for staying until they took

Hansen away. Her mom had been contacted at work in Glovercroft and was on her way home, but her dad was a pilot and not expected to fly back in until Friday. Mr. Just had been a comfort to her that day. She made a mental note to bake him some cookies and take them to him at school.

The neighborhood had been crazed that night. Everyone was out talking about not only Heather and Hansen, but Mr. Jackson, too. It was rare to have any unexpected deaths around their quiet town. To have three in the same town, let alone the same neighborhood, was unheard of. They had stayed outside in little clusters talking late into the night.

The next couple of days were like the ones after Mr. Jackson had died. Clara's mom and Shasta's mom had organized the same kind of food chain for the Andrews' and the Reynolds' families. Clara was happy to help. She hadn't told her mother that she had just broken up with Hansen before he died. She hadn't told anyone. She thought Mr. Just might have a clue, but he couldn't have heard what she had said to Hansen. Clara just decided to keep that part to herself.

She had known that Hunter would be at the funeral home to support Eli and his mom. She had been looking for him all morning. Clara had been expected to get there early and portray the grieving girlfriend, and she didn't mind doing that last thing for Hansen. Then, when she saw Bug and Bug asked her about Hunter being with her when Hansen died, Clara was thrown. It wasn't like they had anything to hide, but something instinctual made Clara want to protect him. The only person who knew about Hunter was Mr. Just, and he didn't mention it to anyone. How did Bug know? She guessed it didn't really matter.

Finally, she had found Hunter in the hallway and been able to have a conversation. He looked really stressed out, and Clara felt sorry for him. She knew how close he was with Eli and the whole Andrews family.

"Hey, Hunter," she said looking at him sadly.

"Hi," Hunter responded tersely. Clara thought he seemed a little angry with her, and that confused her.

"Um, how's Eli doing? I was in there earlier and didn't really get a chance to talk to him." She asked, trying to be sensitive.

"He's pretty upset. We all are." His answer was short and to the point. Now Clara was really confused.

"Well, I'm going over to their house later on with some casseroles and desserts and stuff. You know, so they don't have to think about feeding themselves and all of their guests. My mom is organizing the food donations."

"Seems to me you should be doing that for the Reyn-olds' family," he said sullenly.

Clara thought she might understand what was bothering him. "You know, Hunter. You didn't have anything to do with what happened to Hansen. Mr. Just and I didn't even mention your name to the deputy asking us questions. Hansen had been really upset with me right before you came running over. If anyone is responsible, it's me."

"You don't get it, Clara. I was responsible. I can't explain it, but he would still be alive if I hadn't run over there." He bowed his head and said softly, "Heather would still be alive too."

Now Clara was really confused. Heather would be alive too? What did that mean? "Hunter, this is ridicu-lous. Hansen blew a gasket because I had just broken up with him. And not in a very nice way, I might add. I had just told him what a jerk he was and how I couldn't stand him. He had gotten totally pissed at me and was about to hit me when you came over. You basically saved me. Thank you for that. There's no reason for you to think you're the cause of anything. You're just upset." Clara suddenly wanted to get out of there. "Do you want me to drive you home?" She asked.

He looked up at her through his wavy hair and said, "You don't have to stay with Hansen's family?"

She rolled her eyes. "No! I've done enough for him. I mean, I'm sorry he died and all, but he had been very mean to a lot of people for a very long time. Mr. Just called it Karma." She looked behind her and the hallway was clear. It looked like a good time for a getaway. She took Hunter's arm and said, "Let's get out of here."

Hunter texted his parents and Eli. He wrote that he needed to leave for a while and would be back soon. They were probably going to stay there with Lara and Eli for the rest of the afternoon since his dad wanted to keep an eye on Mr. Andrews.

They got to Clara's VW, which had a brand new battery thanks to the automobile club, and climbed in. "Where to?" Clara asked Hunter.

"I don't care. Let's just drive." Hunter was glad to be away from all of the crying and sad faces. He was also glad to be alone with Clara. When she had told him that she had broken up with Hansen and how she really felt about him, Hunter was elated. He had been waiting for Clara to see the light. He had really liked her since freshman year, but she never had given him the time of day. It was weird because they had been close while they were growing up in the neighborhood, and they had hung around together in middle school. She had always been one of Hunter's favorite people. Once they hit high school, though, she just dumped all of her old friends and started hanging out with the popular crowd.

They drove toward the edge of town. The radio was on, and Clara had put the windows down. It was another beautiful day, and they were both feeling relieved to be away from everyone for a while.

They were heading east on Route 68. They passed by the entrance to Meadowview Acres and then drove past the construction site where the new housing development was supposed to be built. Clara noticed as Hunter looked out at the site and frowned deeply as they passed. She wondered what he could be thinking about and figured that he was probably remembering the terrible night when they found Mr. Jackson. What she didn't know was that Hunter was remembering finding the box and unearthing it that night. He was thinking if they had only left the box there, Heather would be alive now – Hansen, too.

Clara drove past the "Thanks for Visiting Hallston" sign and kept going on Route 68. Except for woods, it was fairly empty from here until the town limits of Chester some twenty miles on down the road. She drove a little further then pulled over onto a gravel road that led into the woods. At the outskirts, she parked the VW and said, "Let's just sit for a little bit. Then we'll go back to Eli."

"Sounds good," said Hunter. They got out of the car and wandered out into the grass at the edge of the woods. It was so peaceful. Neither one wanted to ruin the quiet, so they sat down in the grass and turned their faces upward. They felt the warmth of the late October sun.

Clara was still processing everything that had happened the past week. Sometimes, she forgot that Hansen was dead. She felt like she had broken up with him, and he had just gone away. The feeling of freedom made her feel guilty. She was glad that she was free of him, but she had never wished him dead. If she was honest with herself, she would admit that she was thankful for Hansen. By dating him for only four months, she had secured her place in the popular crowd. Now she was High School Royalty. Even more so now that she was seen by everyone (except Hunter and Mr. Just) as the grieving girlfriend left behind by his tragic death. She could call her own shots now, but was that what she wanted?

Clara felt a little ashamed when she thought about her old friends. The ones she had dumped in order to climb the ladder. What if she were to go back to them now? Would they accept her? She had felt so good these last couple of days without having to put on her popular girl smile and put up with the dingbats. It felt good to be Clara again. It especially felt nice with Hunter sitting next to her. She looked over at him and noticed that he was looking at her.

"Why did you date Hansen in the first place?" He asked. "He's always been a world-class jerk."

Clara thought for a moment, and answered, "I was trying really hard to be someone that I'm not. I thought it would make me happy to be popular, you know? Not to be picked on any more. But it didn't make me happy, it made me tired. It was a lot of work." She sighed and closed her eyes as she felt the warmth of the sun.

"Are you saying that you don't want to hang out with your friends anymore now that Hansen's gone?" He asked.

"I'm not even sure they are my friends. They're fun and nice to me for the most part. But I don't think they'd miss me if I were gone." She turned then to face him.

"Hunter, do you think any of my old friends would want me around again? You know, like Shasta? Do you think she'd forgive me for the last few years?" The thought made Clara hopeful. She would love to have her old life back. Suddenly, the idea of Prom Queen had lost its appeal.

Hunter shrugged his shoulders. "I don't know, probably. I mean, you two grew up together. We all did.

We're all kinda connected in a way. You should talk to her. She could probably use a friend right now."

Clara nodded. "I've been pretty stupid, huh? I think I just lost track of important things like true friends and having self-esteem. The truth is, even though they let me into their group because of Hansen, I never really felt like I fit in. Something was missing."

Hunter grinned at her and said, "Well, welcome back to mediocrity. We've missed you. I've missed you."

Clara felt the butterflies again as she looked at Hunter's smile. Then, she remembered something he had said at the funeral home.

"Hunter, what did you mean when you said that Heather and Hansen would be alive if it wasn't for you?" She watched the smile fade.

"It's complicated," he answered. "It started the night we found Mr. Jackson in his bulldozer."

Clara could tell that he didn't want to talk about it, so she said, "Well, I'm here if you ever want to talk. But don't be so hard on yourself, Hunter. I can't imagine how any of this could be your fault.

A silent tear rolled down his perfect face. Alarmed, Clara scooted closer and put her arm around him. He leaned his head on her shoulder and stayed there; his tears wetting her green plaid blouse. "Something else is going on here," Clara thought. "What else happened in those woods and why does he feel like Heather and Hansen are his fault?"

Whatever it was, Clara was determined to help him through. She leaned her head against his and let him cry.

CHAPTER 19

Shasta & Bug

It was Saturday before Shasta and Bug could get away to start their research. Both of the funerals had been held – Heather's only that morning. Shasta picked Bug up around lunch time, and they headed for the Hut. Shasta didn't have to work that day, but she had promised Bug that they could take their lunches with them and eat while they worked.

After ordering their standard number two meals with lemonades from the drive thru, they headed off to the offices of the Hallston Daily Journal. The paper itself had been in existence since the mid 1940's, making it around sixty-seven years old. The neighboring towns of Shale and Glovercroft also had newspapers, and, since they were bigger towns, the Hallston Daily Journal would often pick up the top stories from those papers to run.

Shasta parked the Ranger in the deserted lot. There was a skeleton crew on the weekends covering anything newsworthy, but otherwise it was empty. Walking through the front door to the reception area, Bug mentally went over the plan that she and Shasta had put in place to get them through to the archive room. It wouldn't be hard.

Mrs. Beatrice Walton was the weekend receptionist and had known Bug since she was Ladybug. "Bug, Sweetie! How good to see you! Come give old Mrs. Bea a hug," the old lady cooed at her.

Bug went obligingly around the desk to be squished by Mrs. Bea's ample bosom. "Hi, Mrs. Bea, it's good to see you, too."

"Hi, Shasta. How're you dear?" She said, acknowledging Shasta at last. "What brings you two out here today?"

Shasta smiled and said, "I'm starting a summer internship here, and Bug said that she'd show me around."

"Yeah," said Bug. "Dad can't wait for Shasta to start. She's going to be a big help!" Bug was overly enthusiastic, showing Mrs. Bea a mouthful of teeth.

"Okay girls," Mrs. Bea replied. "Just stay out of the second floor offices. Those are for the big dogs!" Mrs. Bea giggled and went back to her gossip magazine.

Once the girls were out of sight, she would forget about them altogether.

The girls shot each other a quick look and headed for the elevators. The offices of the Hallston Daily Journal were set up in a straight forward manner. The offices used most often were on the first floor. Those were the reporters, classified ads, business advertising and reception. The second floor housed Mr. Hamilton, who was the Editor-in-Chief, his assistant editor, the assistant's assistant and miscellaneous secretaries and other assistants. The actual printing was done in the lower level. That left the third floor for the Resource Room and the Archives. That's where Shasta and Bug headed. They hopped into the waiting elevator, and Bug jabbed a finger at the button marked "3".

Shasta was feeling a little anxious, like she was doing something sneaky. Bug had told her dad that she was taking Shasta around the offices today, so they really weren't doing anything wrong.

They made it to the third floor with a "ding" from the elevator. The doors slid open, and the girls walked out. Shasta followed Bug to the left and down the narrow hallway. It was an old building, and it smelled like must and dust and newspapers. Shasta loved it. She couldn't wait to start working there for the summer.

They made it to a large door with a big glass pane in the middle. Shasta reached for the doorknob, but Bug said, "Hang on. We need this." She pulled a key out of her pants pocket and held it out to Shasta.

Surprised, Shasta said, "Did you take that from your dad? Bug, I don't think we should do this."

"No," Bug replied. "I've had this key for ages. Whenever I come here with Dad, I always go in here and read. It's super interesting. I bet I've read most of the newspapers in this place."

Shasta should have known. Bug wasn't the devious type. She took the key from Bug's outstretched hand and unlocked the door.

Walking into the room, Shasta was elated. The whole room was filled with newspaper memorabilia. There were stories that had been framed on the walls and a great big table covered with plexi-glass in the middle of the room. Shasta walked over to find the very first issue of the Hallston Daily Journal under the glass. It was dated July 4, 1945. The headline read, "Independence for Hallston". The story was about how the town of Hallston had split itself off from the larger neighboring city of Glovercroft.

Bug walked over to a rectangular table by the windows and started to take her things out of her bag. She arranged her spiral notebook and pens neatly and then took her Hot Dog Hut Go-Box out and placed it on the table beside them. Shasta took her cue and joined Bug at the table. As they ate their lunch, they discussed their plan of action. They were going to double team – Bug looking through headlines, while Shasta took the Obituaries.

Bug had been coming to work with her dad off and on since she was about seven years old. She had always loved that room. There were so many things to learn about. The lady who worked in there was Ms. Shelbourne. She had always been so nice to Bug. She taught her how to use the different machines, and she showed her where they kept all the back issues. She also showed her the boxes of discs that represented each year of the newspaper. There wasn't a disc for each paper but one for every month. Since Bug had read so many of the newspapers already, she knew that she hadn't yet seen anything out of the ordinary. The last time she was there, she had left off at May of nineteen eighty-seven. She left Shasta to retrieve that box of discs.

Their saving grace was that Hallston was a very small town. Even the larger neighboring towns were small. Any death or accident was front page news, much like Heather, Hansen and Mr. Jackson had been. Bug had watched her father struggle with those stories. They had been so personal.

Shasta had settled down in front of one of the computers when Bug came out of the back room with two boxes. One was for nineteen eighty-seven and the other was nineteen eighty-six. The girls settled in and started to scan through the information. Shasta found that there were very few deaths in the town, sometimes none at all. She concentrated mostly on the Sunday papers. She made sure to read the dates and the circumstances of death if it was available.

Bug absolutely flew through the headlines. She was so familiar with how the paper was formatted that she knew where to find the most interesting stories and which ones were fluff. She also felt like she should know what she was looking for. She and her father had talked at length about all kinds of stories that had made headlines over the years – even the ones that had happened before her birth.

An hour later, Bug was on November of nineteen seventy-nine and Shasta was studying July of nineteen eighty-two. Shasta's eyes were getting tired, so she got up and stretched. She wandered over to the window and looked outside. It was a beautiful late-fall day and the sky was soft-blue with puffy-white clouds.

"You know, Bug. We might just be on a wild goose chase here," she started. "I was thinking about a different strategy. Why don't I go over to Eli's house and talk to him? You know, at the funeral home he probably was not in the best frame of mind. I could go over tomorrow and ask him about the box. Maybe Darren would go with me. Eli might feel more comfortable with a guy there."

"You could do that anyway," Bug replied. "But I just feel like there's something here. It's driving me super batty."

Shasta could tell that her little friend had tunnel vision, so she went back to her computer and started on nineteen eighty-one. She read more obits, some from accidents, some from old age, a couple from a fire or drowning. It was starting to get a little depressing, but Shasta kept on. If she was going to be a good journalist, she needed to get used to tedious research.

———

Bug's stomach was growling, but she didn't want to stop. She felt like she would stumble upon something any minute. The sun was starting to go down, and they would need to leave soon, but that itchy feeling in her brain was telling her that she was close to finding something. She just couldn't stop yet. She was on August of nineteen sixty-eight when something caught her eye.

The headline read, "Two Mystery Deaths in Hallston". Bug sucked in her breath and motioned Shasta over. They read the article together.

A man had been found just outside of the town limits of Hallston. There was no clear sign of death, no identification of the man and no clue as to where he had come from. About a mile down the road, inside the Hallston city limits, was an abandoned car. The gas tank was empty but the license was registered to a Gerald Bell. Gerald Bell was not with his car, however. Mr.Bell was evidently waiting for the bus to Glovercroft. He had a ticket and was waiting for the arriving passengers to get off before he could board. He died on the spot. A massive head trauma is what they called it. Witnesses said he was talking to a white-haired man who had just gotten off the bus, and the next thing anyone knew, that man was gone, and Gerald was on the ground dead.

The girls finished reading at about the same time and looked at each other.

"Well," Shasta said. "Maybe the dead guy on the outskirts killed this guy at the bus stop and stole his car. It ran out of gas and he had to walk. Then he had a heart attack or something."

"Maybe," Bug wondered, "But let's just see."

She scrolled down to find the paper for the previous day, and there was another headline.

"Woman Dies Waiting For Bus to Hallston"

This article had been borrowed from the Glovercroft Gazette. It told of Jenny Littrell who was waiting at a bus stop close to the docks in Glovercroft. The witnesses to this death had said that she must have had some sort of fit. She had been fine as she waited with the others. Suddenly, she started choking and grabbing her throat. She had convulsions and died right there at the bus stop.

Shasta looked at Bug. Both girl's eyes were wide as they remembered how Hansen had bought his ticket to Heaven (or wherever). "Keep going," said Shasta.

Bug scrolled down some and, on the same day, found yet another headline.

"Dock Worker Dies, Family in Shock"

The sad story was about Donny Lane who had been a well-liked young man of twenty three. His family was shocked when the physicians had reported that he had died of a brain hemorrhage. There was also an "excessive amount of blood".

"These can't be a coincidence," Bug said. It's just too perfect if you know what to look for. Even the way they all died. It fits."

"You're right. It does fit. But what started it in motion? See if there's anything else."

Bug scrolled down and found no other deaths. There was, however, a different kind of headline.

The headline read "Professor Preston Monroe only passenger to disembark from Death Ship".

"I think we found our guy," Bug said.

The girls started reading the article.

CHAPTER 20

Bug & Shasta

As soon as they had read the article about Professor Monroe, Shasta and Bug knew that they were on to something. Evidently, Professor Preston Monroe, age thirty-two, had been the only person to disembark from the cargo ship *Tritoria* on that August day in nineteen sixty-eight. The ship had then immediately left port. One of the dock workers reportedly had spoken with a deck hand and found that more than fifteen crew members had died on the journey from a small island in the South Pacific. "The guy had been acting very nervous," reported the dock worker. "He said that they must've had some kind of virus on the ship, and they wanted to get out of here real quick, so they wouldn't spread it." The article said that the professor was in poor health as well.

"So what does this mean?" Shasta asked.

"Okay," started Bug. "We've got this professor getting off of a ship in Glovercroft. A ship that had a lot of crew members die during the journey. After the professor got off the ship, a dock worker died. That Donny Lane from the article. He died from a brain hemorrhage and his family was shocked, remember? Then, at the bus stop near the docks, Jenny Littrell has a fit and choked to death. That bus leaves for Hallston. Gerald Bell dies at the bus stop in Hallston after greeting some man who just got off the bus that came from Glovercroft. You with me so far?"

Shasta narrowed her eyes and tried to follow the trail. She nodded, "Go on".

"So Gerald Bell dies at the bus stop, but his car runs out of gas down on Route 68. How did his car get there? Whoever was in the car walked down Route 68 and ran into the vagrant man. That guy dies, and the trail ends."

Shasta was still trying to piece it all together. "So if I'm following you correctly, you're saying that Professor Monroe got off the ship in Glovercroft – Donny Lane dies. Waited for the bus to Hallston – Jenny Litrell dies. Got off the bus in Hallston – Gerald Bell dies. Stole Mr. Bell's car and drove it till it ran out of gas. Then he walked the rest of the way out of town where he encountered the last guy who also dies. Right?"

Bug nodded her head enthusiastically.

"Okay, I've got that part, but how does that get us here today? How does that connect with what's happening now?"

Bug explained, "Well, if my theory is correct, I think that Professor Monroe had something with him. I think he knew it was bad, and he wanted to get as far out of town as he could and bury it. And I think Hunter and Eli unburied it. It's a super theory, and I know I'm right. Want to know why?" Her eyes were twinkling.

Shasta smiled despite the seriousness of the matter. "Yes, please."

"Mr. Mystery Man that died outside the city limits in nineteen sixty-eight was found at marker post 143. That's where Meadowview Acres is. The town has grown since nineteen sixty-eight. It used to stop way up around where Main Street hits Olive. But Hallston's been built up a lot, the new high school, more houses and stores. Hallston has expanded. Back then, this guy was way out of town. The guy probably thought that it'd be buried forever, but he didn't foresee the town growing so much. Then Oakwood Homes decides to build more houses and, POOF, thar she blows!"

Bug sat back in her chair and folded her arms across her chest. She felt confident that her theory was right.

"That makes a lot of sense. So to find out what he buried, we need to do a little investigating on this Professor Preston Monroe and find out what he was working on and where that ship had come in from. But that was so long ago." She furrowed her brow thinking. "Hey, you don't think we could find him, do you? He would be in his seventies now, but he might be living around here somewhere."

"The article said he was in poor health, though," replied Bug. "That doesn't sound good, but we might as well try."

Bug made a copy of each of the articles that led them to their theory, then she put all of the discs back in the back room. Shasta, looking for information on the professor, was already cruising the internet.

First, she searched for images and found two that were shocking. The first was taken in late nineteen sixty-seven and showed a handsome man with dark brown hair and bright blue eyes. The second shot was taken at the dock in Glovercroft in August of nineteen sixty-eight. There was a ship in the background and he was holding a metal box. In this picture the man was rail thin and stooped over. His hair was completely white and his eyes looked lifeless as he gazed at the camera.

"Wow," said Shasta. "That's totally weird. Look at the difference! It's like he aged fifty years in the span of a few months."

Bug said, "Let's try to find what he was working on and where that picture was taken." She pointed to the picture with the ship. They could just make out the ship's name in the photo – *Tritoria*, the one that had brought him to Glovercroft.

Finding information on Professor Monroe turned out to be quite easy. He had been the top in his field and had written numerous papers and a couple of books. His concentrated area of interest was myths and legends. He had taught a class at the State College in Chester titled, "Histories, Legends & Myths" before leaving the college in May of nineteen sixty-eight.

As Shasta delved deeper into his background, she found that he had never married and had no children or family to speak of. After a brief interview in August of nineteen sixty-eight, the paper trail ended. The last interview was conducted by the school newspaper at State College. Shasta tried in vain to find that online, but it wasn't available.

While Shasta was busy, Bug decided to research the shipping vessel that had brought him back to Glovercroft. She started with the ship's name *Tritoria* and went from there. A cargo ship based out of Tahiti, it was no longer in commission. It had mainly transported fruit and occasionally cloth and other locally made materials. It wasn't a passenger ship, but it looked like the ship had made an exception in Professor Monroe's case. After much digging, Bug found that the ship, indeed, had reported an alarming case of seventeen crew members who had contracted a serious virus and perished on a trip to the states in nineteen sixty-eight. There wasn't much other information aside from the list of the dead crewmen. There was no elaboration on the symptoms or cause of each man's death.

"Here we go," Bug heard Shasta say quietly. She rolled her chair over to where Shasta sat and started to read over the girl's shoulder.

Shasta had found an excerpt from one of the Professor's books entitled, *The Legend of The Varuupian Tribe and It's Ties to Our Culture*. There were only a few sentences from the excerpt, but they brought chills to Bug as she read them.

"While curses this strong have existed in other cultures, the Curse of the Varuupian Tribe is remarkable in its ability to harm not just by touch, but by proximity. I have heard directly from a tribe member that he had witnessed the curse claim a victim simply by walking past the artifact. Also, once the curse has touched a victim, very rarely can the effects be negated."

The girls looked at each other with wide, fearful eyes. "What is this? An artifact? What does that even mean? And how do we know what to look for?" Shasta's mind was reeling. She understood and accepted the fact that something strange had been happening. But until then she hadn't really let herself believe how bad it could be.

Bug was remembering the look on Hansen's face after he had reached into Hunter's backpack. She knew exactly what the artifact was and exactly where to find it. Something else seemed more important to her at that moment, however.

"I know what it is, Shasta. Hunter has it. Remember I told you about the backpack and Hansen grabbing it off of Hunter's back? Remember what I told you was inside?"

"That's right," Shasta said wonderingly. "The rock, or piece of rock that Hansen took out of the pack before he started choking."

"Yeah, but here's the thing. We know what it is, and we know Hunter and Eli have it. That's good, but what do we do with it? How do we get rid of it so that it doesn't hurt anyone else?"

Shasta, quietly pondering the question, sat for a moment. They couldn't just take it back to the woods and bury it again. It would eventually be dug up by someone else. How could they dispose of it once and for all? "We need Professor Monroe," Shasta said.

Bug nodded her head and scooted her chair back to her computer. In less than a couple of minutes, she had found his last known address by going through the university's old files. The address was in Shale.

Shasta looked at the address and then back at Bug. "I'm almost afraid to check this out," she said. "You know if he's still alive we have to go talk to him, right?"

Bug nodded her head and felt the anticipation grow. They went to the white pages online and typed in the address. There he was, 141 Wickwood Drive, Shale.

The sun had gone below the tree line and Shasta knew that both of their parents would be wondering where they were. She told Bug to call her dad and tell him that they were on the way home, so he wouldn't worry. They would go tomorrow, Shasta said, and then they would go straight to Hunter and Eli and tell them what they had learned.

Turning out the lights in the Research Room and locking the door behind them, both of the girls were quiet, lost in thought. What had started out as mild curiosity had grown into a life-threatening event in a matter of days. They wondered if they could stop the town from enduring any more heartache. For the first time in her little life, Bug was sorry that she was so smart. She thought how nice it would be to be unaware of their situation.

The drive home was subdued – no radio, no singing. Finally, Bug broke the silence and asked, "Shasta? What should I tell my folks that we're doing tomorrow?"

Shasta thought of the drive to Shale and wondered what they would find on the other end. All they could hope for was some answers.

"Tell them the truth, Buggie. We're doing some research on a project."

CHAPTER 21

Professor Preston Monroe

After days of beautiful, warm sunshine, Shasta awoke to the sound of rain pattering at her window. As the sleepy fog slowly evaporated from her mind, her thoughts turned to the events of the day. She would shower and dress, then pick up Bug. After that, who knew? It would all depend on what Professor Monroe had to say.

She did know that at some point today, she and Bug would have to talk to Hunter and Eli. Shasta decided to text Hunter later and tell him that they needed a pow-wow this afternoon. He would be curious, but he would agree. She didn't know what frame of mind Eli would be in after burying his sister just yesterday morning. Shasta had trouble believing that had only been yesterday. So much had happened since.

Shasta, fueled by the importance of her mission, jumped from her bed and gathered up a pair of jeans and a hoodie. It looked cold outside. She could hear her parents talking in another part of the house. She was glad that she had the weekend off from the Hot Dog Hut. They wouldn't question her plans with Bug. That part, at least, was normal. Shasta planned to tell her parents everything as soon as she and Bug finished with the boys. She wanted to be armed with all of the facts first.

Showered and dressed, she pulled her thick, auburn hair into a ponytail and unhooked her phone from its charger. She had been with Darren just yesterday before she and Bug had gone to the newspaper, but she missed him already. She texted him, "Morning! Got to hang with Buggie for a while today, but can I see you tonight?" While she waited for a reply from Darren, she looked up Hunter's number and shot off another quick text. This one read, "Hey, It's Shas. Can Bug and I talk to u and Eli 2day? 4ish?"

A ping alerted her that she had an incoming text and she smiled as she read Darren's reply. "Can't wait. See you then."

Not yet hearing from Hunter, she dropped her phone into her bag and left her room.

Her folks were just leaving for work at the Hut, so she kissed them both goodbye and told them vaguely about doing some research with Bug. Grabbing a breakfast bar from the pantry, she locked up and headed for the Ranger. She noticed that her tank was close to empty. They would need to stop at the Gas N Go on the way out of town.

Pulling into Bug's driveway, she noticed the girl's round face peering out of the front window. She had probably been there over an hour waiting for Shasta. Shasta knew that Bug was a little anxious about this whole thing, but so was she.

Bug hopped into the passenger side and greeted Shasta with a toothy smile. "I'm ready," she said. "I thought about this a lot last night, and I think this is a good thing. Knowledge is power. We know what we're working with here, now we just need help with the problem solving." She paused and said, "And I'm telling my dad the whole thing when we get back. He's a smart man who'll be able to help."

"I love the positivity, Bug," Shasta replied with a smile. "Let's keep that up. And I agree that you should tell your dad, but let's talk to Hunter first and get more info."

They backed out of the driveway and headed west on Route 68 for the Gas N Go. Shasta filled the tank while Bug got some snacks inside the quick mart. Shale was about an hour's drive, on the other side of Glovercroft.

Shasta just hoped they would be able to see the professor when they got there. She had toyed with the idea of calling first, but she thought the professor might tell them not to come. The element of surprise was on their side.

The radio was on and the windshield wipers made a little squeak with every swipe. The girls chatted about other things to lighten their anxiety. Shasta talked about Darren, of course, and Bug told Shasta all about a documentary she had just watched on the changing weather patterns and what could be the cause.

Before they knew it, they had hit the city limits of Shale. Shasta pulled to the side of the road and entered the address into her GPS. The automated voice told her to proceed ahead for eight point six miles and turn left on Marion Street.

The guided system easily found the way, and they were at their destination within fifteen minutes. Shasta parked in front of 141 Wickwood and turned off the engine. The house was modest and well kept. The lawn was trimmed as were the bushes anchoring the walkway to the front door.

Shasta looked at Bug and said, "If you want me to go by myself, I will."

"No way," said Bug as she opened her door and hopped out onto the curb. "Let's go see what he says."

Shasta popped her hoodie up to guard against the rain and followed Bug up the walkway to the front door. Bug had already rung the bell by the time Shasta joined her on the stoop.

The door opened to reveal a muscular looking woman in a nurse's uniform. She had a very kind face, but her voice was lower than a typical woman's register.

"Hello, how can I help you?" The woman smiled at the girls.

"Um, hi," Shasta began. "Um, we would like to see Professor Preston Monroe, please."

The nurse looked puzzled and asked, "Is the professor expecting you?"

"Well, no," Shasta replied. "But we're students over in Hallston and we've come to ask him some questions about his book."

"I see." The nurse seemed to think for a moment and said, "Why don't you come in out of the rain and wait here. I'll go see if he's up to having any visitors today."

She motioned the girls in and closed the door after them. Shasta and Bug stayed right by the door, not wanting to intrude any further. They were both feeling anxious.

The nurse gave them a little smile before walking down the hall and disappearing through another doorway.

The girls could hear muffled speech coming from that direction and continued to wait quietly. Shasta could hear little drops of rain falling off of Bug's slick yellow raincoat and hitting the wood floor. The nurse returned momentarily and held her arms out. "Let me have that wet coat, Dear. The professor said he has a few minutes to talk to you."

Bug took off her slicker and handed it to the nurse who then hung it on a peg near the door. Shasta slipped out of her rain clogs, and both girls followed the nurse back down the same hallway. Stopping in front of the doorway, she held her arm out directing the girls to go through. Shasta went in first, followed by Bug.

The room was decorated in dark wood finishes. Bookshelves lined one whole wall. There were soft, comfy chairs and a sofa under a painting of a dense tropical forest. The professor sat in a green leather chair facing the only window in the room. He didn't get up to greet them when they walked into the room.

Shasta spoke first, "Um, hi Professor Monroe. My name is Shasta Port and this is my friend Bug Hamilton. We were wondering if you could answer some questions about your book."

He turned his head slowly toward her as she spoke, never looking at her directly. "Bug. Let's hope that's a nickname. To which book are you referring, Ms. Port?"

Shasta cleared her throat. She hadn't known what to expect, but for some reason she hadn't expected him to be anything other than friendly. She pushed forward and said, *"The Legend of The Varuupian Tribe and It's Ties to Our Culture."*

The Professor's jaw tightened for a second before he said, "I'm afraid that book is out of print. I can't help you. You can show yourselves out." He looked back out the window.

Shasta looked down at Bug with a defeated expression. Bug decided to give it a try.

"Yes, it is a nickname. My birth name is Mary Ellen Hamilton and I go by Bug because Mary Ellen is super boring. I'm twelve years old, almost thirteen. Shasta and I came to talk to you about your book because our friends have died in Hallston. They died because someone dug up the box that you put the cursed thing in. We need to find out what we're supposed to do to get rid of it before anyone else dies. We came to you because we know you're the only one who can tell us what to do to get out of this super bad situation. I'm sorry if that bothers you, but we need information. Knowledge is power."

The moment Bug had mentioned the box Professor Monroe's mouth had opened in shock. Then he bowed his head and slowly shook it from side to side.

Bug thought he was crying. She was about to apologize again when he said, "No. I had prayed that this would never happen. How? How did it get discovered?"

Shasta moved slowly forward into the room as she spoke. "Our friends were in the woods around a construction site. A developer is building a new subdivision and some bulldozers had been clearing the site. One of the bulldozers unearthed the box. The man driving that rig died from a brain hemorrhage. Or else, that's what they're calling it. Anyway, our friends had found the box and brought it home. We don't know the details, but one of the guy's sister died, and then Bug here watched another boy on the street choke to death while he was holding the rock."

"Holding the rock!" The professor was stunned. "What do you mean "holding the rock"? No one should ever be in contact with the artifact! Where is it now?" As upset as he was, not once did he rise out of his chair or look at them directly. His hands gripped the armrests of his chair.

"We know our friends still have it, but we're not sure what their plan is. They know that there's something about it, but we don't think they know the full story. That's why we're here. As soon as you tell us what we can do, we're going straight over to see them."

The professor seemed to weaken. He motioned them over to the sofa under the lush painting. "Have a seat, please. I'm going to tell you everything I know from the beginning. It may take a while. Then maybe you can help solve this catastrophe that I created."

Bug and Shasta settled in on the comfy couch and listened to the professor recall how it had begun.

He had been teaching his Histories, Legends and Myths class at the college when he had come across a book about a tiny island called Shaali and a tribe of people who inhabited that island. They were known as the Varuupi. The Varuupi had one of the most intricate practices of dark magic and curses that he had ever encountered. One legend in particular had impressed him so much that he had decided to take a few years off from teaching and go to the island in search of material for a book.

Getting to Tahiti was easy. Going from Tahiti to a smaller island called Banno was a little more difficult, but manageable. Getting from Banno to Shaali proved to be almost impossible. The natives who chartered planes or boats between the islands wouldn't touch the island of Shaali. They believed the island itself to be cursed. Finally, Monroe had found one captain who would take him. It helped that the captain was not a native, and Monroe had plenty of cash to persuade him. They set off the next day.

Monroe had asked the captain to wait for six hours, so he could explore the tiny island and take pictures. The captain had agreed, and Monroe had set off. There was nothing remarkable at first, just overgrown vegetation and a few odd animals in the trees, but then he had come across what looked to be the site of an ancient people. He could still make out the dwellings arranged in a circle around a large pit that could only have been for fire. On the outskirts of the settlement was a graveyard. Rocks had been placed in rectangles, row upon row. In the middle of each rectangle was a different totem. Some carved from wood; some etched in stone. Monroe had felt a little uneasy being alone there bearing witness to an extinct people. He was getting ready to leave, when he saw what he had been looking for all along. A tomb made of a large slab of rock was at the very end of the gravesite.

Professor Monroe took hundreds of pictures chronicling every detail of the site and the dwellings. When he was leaving, he returned to the tomb. A small chunk of the slab had broken off and lay on the ground beside the tomb. Professor Monroe picked it up and stowed it away in his backpack. He remembered feeling as if the earth had shifted a little under his feet.

"I chalked it up to not eating and the intense heat of the island. That wasn't what it turned out to be."

The girls had been breathlessly listening to his story. They knew what was to come. They had seen a picture of this man in nineteen sixty-eight, before he left for the island. The man sitting before them was a shell. His white cotton shirt was barely concealing the bony frame underneath. His hair was snow white and sparse. He was in his mid-seventies but looked much older. They listened as he continued.

He took a big breath and said, "I made it back to the boat after only four hours. The captain was glad to see me but acting very strangely. Just minutes after we set off for Banno, it happened. The captain started screaming. He was clawing at his eyes and screaming in some language I didn't understand. I didn't know what to do to help. I tried to talk to him, to comfort him in some way. I kept asking what I could do, but he just kept speaking in that same strange language. I was looking for a rope. I thought, if I could restrain him, I could get us back to Banno and get help there. I had just found the rope and turned back to him when I heard the splash. I was frantic. I looked over the side of the boat and couldn't see him. He wasn't anywhere. Looking for him, I went from side to side, but he just wasn't there. Not knowing what to do, I cut the boat's engine. I just sat there waiting for him, looking for him. But there was nothing. He never resurfaced. Finally, about three hours later it was getting dark. I knew I'd never find my way back to Banno in the dark, so I started the boat and followed the coordinates back. It was dark when I made it to port. I shored up the vessel and left the keys in the engine. I was exhausted, but I was able to find a native to try to explain what had happened. I thought someone should know. I recognized the guy from that morning; he had helped us to shove off. I remember walking toward him, and his expression changed as I got closer. I was about to speak to him when he started to yell. I recognized the word he was yelling at me. It was the native word for "Demon". He ran away from me. I barely made it back to my room and collapsed on the bed. The next morning, when I woke and went into the bathroom, I saw myself in the reflection. My hair had turned completely white. I didn't recognize myself."

He stopped and took some deep breaths. Shasta could tell that this was tiring him out, mentally as well as physically. She felt sorry for him, but they needed to know the rest. "Is that when you found the *Tritoria* to bring you here?" she asked.

His head came up suddenly as if he had forgotten the girls were there. "Yes, I went back to Tahiti the next day and was able to book passage on the *Tritoria*. I wish to God I hadn't, though. At that point I still hadn't thought that the captain from Banno's death was anything but coincidence. And my appearance? Well, stress maybe. I didn't really start to believe in the curse until we had almost made it back to the states. The ship was hell. Men were dying every day. And I, not knowing it was my fault. I thought it was some type of jungle fever like everyone else. But then something just clicked and I knew. It was the curse of Varuupi. I thought I had found the answer when I found the metal box on board and put the rock in there. I wrote a letter, even put in instructions and money in case something happened to me. Then I chained it with as many chains as I could find and kept it under the bed in my cabin. There were no deaths for three days. I thought that had solved it, until the day we docked in Glovercroft."

Bug chimed in. "That's how we found you. We followed the string of deaths from the docks to outside Hallston. We followed your path."

"I remember how glad the crew was to be rid of me. They were almost pushing me off of the ship. They knew. They knew I had been cursed somehow. Then, that nice boy at the docks. I had put my luggage down along with the metal box and was turning to give the deck hand some money. It was all I could do for them. When I turned back, that young man had picked up my luggage, the box too, and was headed down the plank. I ran after him and grabbed my things. I thought he was alright. He was alive when I left him. I was still under the impression that the box was containing the curse. My plan was to go all the way through Hallston and bury it deep in the woods. There were so many miles of woods between Hallston and Chester back then. I never would have imagined that it could have been uncovered. Then, at the bus stop, I put my suitcase down beside me but held onto the box. I remember it was down at my side and a lady was standing very close to me. I switched hands to get it further away from her. When the bus came I got on and went to the very back. I put my luggage in the seat in front of me, so, I could put more distance in between myself and the other passengers. We were about to pull away from the bus stop when the commotion started with Ms. Littrell. She was the lady standing so close to me. I knew. I knew at that point that I had to get as far away from people as I could. I was beside myself that whole bus ride. Everyone on the bus was fine, though, which gave me another false sense of confidence."

Bug shifted in her seat and Professor Monroe cocked his head in their direction. Shasta thought that Monroe was very peculiar, but she couldn't pinpoint the cause.

"Getting off the bus in Hallston gave me hope. From there I just needed to find a car and drive as far away from town as possible. I was starting to feel pretty weak at that point. Having been cursed for that long was taking its toll. It was a wonder I was still alive at all. The curse seemed to affect people differently, and I had some kind of tolerance."

"How did you get Mr. Bell's car?" asked Shasta.

"He was too close to all of us getting off the bus. You know the kind? Always wanting to be first to get on? Crowding up too close to the people who haven't even gotten off yet? He was one of those. I suppose his tolerance to the curse was very little. All the box did was graze his arm as I went past. I could hear the reaction to him falling to the ground. I didn't even need to turn around. My focus was clear – get away from people. It was just coincidence that his was the only car in the lot with the keys under the mat. People did that all the time in those days, especially in small towns. I didn't even think to look at how much gas the car had. I just drove as fast as I could toward the town limit. I didn't make it, though.

"When the car ran out of gas, my head was pounding. I was exhausted. My legs would barely carry me. I grabbed the box and got a spade that I had taken from the ship out of my suitcase. I left the luggage in the trunk and started walking. I had made it pretty far when I saw someone ahead. At that point, I could barely see, my head hurt so badly. It didn't take much for him to overtake me. He was looking for my wallet, but took the box instead. I guess he thought that it was valuable since it was chained up. I must've passed out for a few minutes because the next thing I remember, I was on the ground. The box was a few feet away from me and he was on the ground a few feet away from it. I picked it up and ran. I ran until I thought I'd die. When I was as deep in the woods as my body would let me go, I started to dig. That was a chore, let me tell you. I'm still not sure where the energy came from."

"Adrenaline," Bug said. "Adrenaline is caused by fear."

He replied with a small, weak grin. "I was afraid alright. But I got that thing buried. Not deep enough, it turns out. After that, I sat back and cried a good long cry. When I felt that I could stand, I got up and slowly made my way back out of the woods. I made it all the way back to the car and got my luggage, left the key under the mat. I had a bit of luck then when a stranger offered me a ride back to the bus stop. You can't take rides from strangers nowadays, however. I jumped on the first bus to Shale and came back here, to my home. I fell into bed and cried some more. I still felt very ill. I was probably traumatized as well. And that's it, the whole story. Well, except for one thing."

"What's that?" Shasta asked.

"The next morning I woke up blind." He looked in the girl's direction. They could see the vacant stare coming from his pale blue eyes. "I've been blind ever since."

BOOK THREE

CHAPTER 22

The Rock of Varuupi

The last piece of the puzzle fell into place for Shasta as Professor Monroe faced them with his vacant stare. She had known something was off when they had first walked into the room – the way he had turned his head in their direction without looking at them, not getting up to introduce himself, staring out the window as he told his tale. Now she could see how obvious it had been.

She felt the need to say something to him. She had still been processing his story when the last revelation had been disclosed. Her head was spinning with all of the new information. Still, she felt pity for the man. Even if it was his fault that this nightmare had been set in motion, she felt as if his whole life had been a punishment.

Shasta was about to speak when the nurse came back into the room. "I'm sorry to interrupt, but the professor has to take his lunch now. I hope you've had a nice visit." Her tone was pleasant, but final. It was time to go.

She walked over to the professor's chair and helped him to stand. As the kind nurse guided the frail man to the door, he stopped at a bookcase and held out his arm. The nurse released him so he could move closer to the bookcase. Feeling along the shelves, he touched the spines of each book until he came to a battered leather bound book. He obviously knew it by touch as he took it from its place in line. He held the book closely to his chest for a moment.

Turning back to the girls, he said, "This is all I can give you to help. Everything I learned came from this book. This is where it all started for me. I was so enthralled with this legend above any others. I thought I could write a book that would explain the curse and the people it came from. Instead, it ended my career, and almost ended my life as well." He held the book out.

Shasta moved forward and took it from his outstretched hand. Still feeling sorry for the professor, she said, "Thank you. And thank you for talking to us today."

"No, young lady. Please don't thank me. If it weren't for me, this wouldn't be happening to your friends. Good luck finding the answer."

The nurse smiled at the girls and resumed guiding her patient from the room. As she led him out the door, she said, "You can just gather your things and let yourselves out." She smiled again and was gone.

Bug looked at Shasta. "I feel bad for him." She hadn't had a clue that the professor was blind. His confession had caught her off guard.

Shasta looked at her little friend and said, "I know, but he's right. If he hadn't brought this rock back from Shaali, all of those people would still be alive. And Mr. Jackson, Heather, even Hansen. And the professor would still have his sight." She handed the book to Bug and said, "Let's get going. We need to see Hunter and Eli."

Bug looked at the book in her hands, *Legends And Myths From Around the Globe*. She hoped the answer would be easily found inside, but something told her that none of this would be easy.

The girls gathered their rain gear from the front hall and let themselves out the door. The rain was still coming down, but not as heavily as before. Hopping over puddles, they dashed to the Ranger and got quickly inside. Shasta started the engine and turned on the heat. The dampness of the day had made her chilly.

"Before we start back, I need to check my phone to see if Hunter texted back, yet." She pulled the phone from her bag and saw that she had one missed call and two texts. The missed call was an automated reminder of her dental cleaning scheduled for Tuesday. The first text was from Darren, "Mom seems down today. What should I do?" It read.

Worried about Mrs. Jackson and Darren, Shasta furrowed her brow. A part of her felt guilty for not spending more time with them. She texted back, "Tell her I'm coming over tonight with a pizza and a DVD." It was the only thing Shasta could think of to do. Maybe it would take Agnes' mind away from Mr. Jackson for a couple of hours.

The second text was from Hunter. "Sure, 4's good. My house."

"Okay, good," she said. "We're going to Hunter's at four o'clock. We'll be back in plenty of time. It's only one thirty now." She pulled away from the curb and headed back to Hallston.

Bug was studying the table of contents in the Legends & Myths book. "Here it is, Chapter 14, The Rock of Varuupi. Want me to read it to you?"

"I'm a little afraid of what it'll say," Shasta said. "But we need to know. Go ahead."

The Rock Of Varuupi

The tiny island of Shaali in the South Pacific was home to a tribe of people called the Varuupi. The Varuupi were a people with deeply rooted beliefs in dark magic, rituals and curses. Of the known curses the Varuupian people are recognized for, the most remarkable is the curse of the Rock of Varuupi. Its far reaching and menacing disposition has been chronicled as extremely fatal.

As with most other tribes, the Varuupi were led by a chief. The position was always inherited, never elected nor challenged. With that being the case, the chief was encouraged to have many sons, thus ensuring an heir. To that course, the chief of the Varuupian people could have as many wives as he chose, even another man's wife.

There was, however, one woman that was strictly forbidden to the chief. That woman was the daughter of a high priest. Any daughter of a high priest in the tribe was considered sacred. Her blood was thought to be magical and was often used in many rituals and spells. The daughters were also sacrificed if the need arose. The most chilling fact is that other tribe members would sometimes murder the daughter of a high priest, believing that the blood they spilled would gain them favor in the afterlife. For these reasons, daughters of high priests rarely lived long.

If, however, the daughter of a high priest was fortunate enough to survive her fifth birth year, she would then be allowed to become a part of the tribe and taught to be a high priestess. High priestesses were highly sought after as their magic was considerably stronger than their male counterparts. The reason behind this is unknown, but some attribute it to the power of intuition. They were also quite feared as many in the tribe would attribute her living past age five to a guiding hand from the spirit world.

In the Varuupian tribe credited with the curse, the chief had already acquired nine wives and had twelve sons. Upon his death, the eldest would succeed him. The chief, however, known as Chief Maalini, became aware of the daughter of the high priest as she grew and became a member of the tribe. He thought her to be quite beautiful and was intrigued by her skill at dark magic. He knew of her training to become a high priestess and would regularly have her come to him to treat any number of maladies. Eventually, Chief Maalini became convinced that he must be able to marry her, as well.

Chief Maalini took his request to the high priest who immediately protested. He called it taboo and against the wishes of the spirits. The chief heard his protests, but was unable to be deterred. He planned to marry the daughter, Thuuni, at the next tribal ceremony.

The high priest was outraged. He knew he could not stop the chief from marrying Thuuni, but he decided to make him pay. For the safety of the tribe, he would kill the chief. He then placed a curse upon his daughter causing any man who touched her upon a marital bed to be stricken down dead. The curse ensured Thuuni would remain pure, as tribal law dictated. By the time of her marriage, Thuuni was quite emotionally involved with the chief and very happy about the upcoming wedding. She was unaware of the curse her father had placed upon her.

The marriage ceremony was held and Chief Maalini was wed to Thuuni. The celebration carried on for many hours until finally, the chief took his bride to their hut. Moments later, the screams of Thuuni were heard throughout the tribe when she discovered that the chief was dead.

Thuuni was an incredibly powerful high priestess by this time and recognized the hand of a curse at work. Knowing it could only be the work of her father, she vowed revenge. She also vowed to reverse the high priest's curse on Chief Maalini, thus bringing him back to life.

After the burial ceremony was held for Chief Maalini, Thuuni placed a very strong curse upon his tomb. The curse was to protect it until she could find a way to make him live again. She used her own blood in the curse, making it extremely potent. Anyone touching the tomb would die. There are accounts of innocent Varuupian people being stricken down after passing beside the tomb. Clearly the curse of the High Priestess Thuuni is one of the most powerful curses known today.

The last account that was made by an observer, simply states that the high priest died by his own hand the day following the burial of Chief Maalini. No other descriptions were provided. One can only deduce that Thuuni made good on her threat to kill her father in retribution.

Soon after, the tribe of the Varuupi suffered mass casualties. Some believe it to be the curse of the rock; others theorize that an illness swept through the tribe. Nevertheless, in less than six short months after the chief was buried, the Varrupian people ceased to exist.

A team of archaeologists went to the small island of Shaali some years after and found the gravesite of the tribe. The tomb of Chief Maalini was also found. No tomb nor marked grave was found for High Priestess Thuuni. It is the belief of the team that the high priestess was the sole living Varuupian. There is no evidence, however, that Thuuni lived on. The team lost fifteen people on the trip. Whether their deaths were from an illness in the region or the Curse of The Rock of Varuupi one can only speculate.

Bug put the book down on the seat beside her and started to cry. Alarmed, Shasta quickly pulled over to the side of the road, put the Ranger in Park and scooted over on the seat to hug her.

"It's okay, Sweetie. It'll be alright. We'll find a way to get rid of it. Maybe the boys will have some ideas. Remember? They're the Shazaam Brothers!" She was rocking Bug back and forth trying to say anything to make her stop crying. Shasta had never seen Bug cry, not once. Not even when she had hurt herself, Bug had always just laughed instead. This was very unnerving to her.

"It's o, o, okay, Shas. I'm j, j, just sad for Th, Th, Thuuni. She loved the chief so much and her dad just k, k, killed him. That's so mean!" Bug started wailing again, and Shasta was more surprised than ever. She wasn't afraid of the curse, Shasta realized, she was sad about the love story. Shasta smiled and thought to herself, "Maybe my little Buggie is growing up."

After a couple of minutes, Bug sniffled and sat up. "Sorry, I think I must be super stressed out. I usually don't cry about things like that. I usually don't cry at anything." She wiped her nose with the sleeve of her raincoat. "You know, crying is the natural way for your body to release tension. I actually feel better than I have in days!" Through bright blue eyes made puffy by all the tears, she looked at Shasta.

Shasta couldn't help but giggle a little and said, "I'm glad you feel better, Bug. But that kind of scared me." Feeling a little relieved, Shasta pulled out onto the road again. They were only about half an hour away. Shasta decided to change the subject for a while. She and Bug had been immersed in the research for what felt like days.

"So we have about an hour and a half before we need to be at Hunter's. Why don't we get some ice cream and then go to the Movie Vault? I need to pick out a DVD for tonight," Shasta suggested.

"That's a great idea! I could use a little Rocky Road!"

They drove in silence for a few miles until Bug finally brought it up again. "I've been trying to come up with an idea to get rid of that piece of Chief Maalini's tomb. The only thing I can come up with is to disintegrate it. Do you think that would work?"

Shasta thought a moment. Then she said, "I really don't know. It seems like it would. Maybe there's some kind of chemical to eat away at it until nothing's left. I'm sure the boys will know if there's something like that. We need to remember to ask them. Keep thinking, though. If that doesn't work, we'll need a backup plan."

There was one thing that worried Shasta that she didn't confess. Who could get close to the rock and not be affected? Shasta herself had never been around it, but, judging from the way it had affected other people, the idea really scared her. Bug couldn't do it. It had made her so sick that night when she had followed the boys into the woods. Mrs. Hamilton said that she hadn't seen Bug that sick in years. She decided that was a good question for Hunter. Who can actually stand to be around the thing without getting sick, or worse?

Finally they reached the Dipping Station and went in. The place was empty. Evidently, not a lot of people think of ice cream on a cold, rainy day. Shasta's nerves were fully awake as she looked at her watch. It was almost three o'clock. One hour until they would talk to Hunter and Eli. She wondered, "Where is the rock, now? Where do they keep it?"

The thought was still with her as she ordered two cups of Rocky Road.

CHAPTER 23

Eli & Hunter

Hunter and Eli were sitting in lawn chairs in back of Hunter's house. It was around three in the afternoon and they were going to meet Shasta and Bug at four. Neither of them was looking forward to meeting with the girls. Eli had told Hunter what Bug had asked him at the funeral home. At the time, it seemed like she had believed his "tool box" answer. They figured that Bug had told Shasta about the box, and that was what the girls wanted to discuss.

Eli had been feeling guilty ever since last Wednesday when Heather had died. He knew it was because of the rock. The Rock of Varuupi, the letter called it. Professor Preston Monroe had brought it back from some island and the thing was cursed. Eli wasn't one to believe in such things; he was more into the concrete findings of science, but from what he had seen since the box had come into his possession, it was believable.

Heather's funeral had been brutal for Eli with his dad showing up all heartbroken and his mom in total shock and disbelief. It was all Eli could do to get through that day. Thank goodness for Hunter's parents. Mr. and Mrs. Massey were like a second family for Eli, and he had felt much steadier with them around. Eli had been happy when his dad left Saturday afternoon. He had given Eli a hug and said, "I'm always here for you, Son. Please remember that."

Eli hadn't said anything back to his father, but in his head he was thinking, "Yeah, Dad. You're always around, aren't you?"

That had been just yesterday, but Eli felt like it had been weeks ago. He was exhausted – mentally and physically. Hunter was pretty freaked out, too, but Eli could tell that Hunter was trying to act like everything would work out. He was trying to make Eli feel better. Eli knew that he would do the same for Hunter if the situation was reversed.

Hunter tipped back and rocked on the back legs of the lawn chair. "So we have a good idea of what they want to talk about," he said to Eli. "How much should we tell them?"

"Well," Eli started. "I don't think it would be a bad idea to just tell them everything." He saw Hunter's eyebrows go up in surprise and continued. "At this point, we know what it is and what it's capable of. We also know the name of the guy that brought it here and buried it. If we had some allies, especially smart ones like Shasta and Bug, maybe they could help us track this guy down, so we can give him his damn box back." Eli squinted his eyes together. He had been nursing a nearly continuous headache since Wednesday.

"Jeez, I hadn't thought of that! That's a great idea! We could get it off our hands and make it someone else's problem." Hunter paused, thinking. "You saw the date on that letter, though. And we don't know how old the guy was when he wrote it. I wonder if he's still alive."

"I wouldn't worry so much about his age. It's the curse that makes me wonder if he's still alive. We don't even know if the guy made it out of the woods after he buried it." Eli started to rub his temples.

Both boys were lost in thought when Shasta's Ranger pulled into the Massey's driveway.

"Someone's early," Hunter said after looking at his watch. It was three forty-two.

They watched as the girls got out of the truck and headed for the side door. They rerouted themselves when they saw the guys in the back yard.

"Hey, guys," Shasta said. Bug smiled at them both.

"Hey, Shas. Hi Bug," Hunter said.

Hunter got up from his chair and walked over to the back patio to grab two more chairs. He brought them over and set them up for the girls.

"Is this going to be a private enough spot?" Bug asked. "Our subject matter is pretty sensitive."

"Hunter's mom and dad are at my house and his little brother is inside playing video games. We should maybe talk softly, but we're okay." Eli wasn't going to act like he didn't know why they were there. He was too tired, and his head hurt. He continued by saying, "We know you saw the box with us after we found Mr. Jackson that night. And we know you didn't buy my story about it being our tool box. So we guess you two are here out of curiosity?"

Shasta was the one who answered. "Actually, we know quite a bit. And we're here to help, or try to help, if you'll let us."

The boys both looked skeptical, so she continued.

"When Bug told me about the box you had found in the woods, I didn't think that there was a connection to Mr. Jackson, but she did. She didn't know exactly what was going on, but she was curious. She did a little research on her own about chemicals and things, but nothing really panned out. Then, unfortunately, she saw Hansen die."

Hunter and Eli wore the same look of surprise on their faces.

"She heard the commotion and yelling, so she looked out the window. She saw Hansen grab your pack, take out the rock and... well, you know. Anyway, when she heard about Heather that same night," she looked at Eli and said, "Sorry, Eli, but when she heard about Heather that same night, she knew that there was a connection for sure."

Hunter interjected with, "So you saw Hansen holding the rock, and you knew what it was?" He asked Bug.

"Oh, no!" Bug replied. "I was just super sure at that point that there was something fishy going on. So, I told Shasta and we did some digging at the newspaper. We were looking for old articles about people who had died under strange circumstances in quick succession, and we found a trail." Bug tried not to sound excited.

"What kind of trail?" Eli, realizing that these two might have even more information than he and Hunter, was more interested. Forgetting his headache for the moment, he said, "Go on."

Bug looked at Shasta who nodded at her. "Well, we found a string of mysterious deaths that had happened way back in nineteen sixty-eight. The descriptions sounded a lot like what was happening here now. We kept digging and found an article on a man who had gotten off of a boat in Glovercroft. The paper said that there were a lot of deaths on that same boat. We researched the man, and then everything just fell into place."

Hunter looked at Bug. "Professor…"

She finished for him, "Preston Monroe."

Eli and Hunter were stunned. It seemed that neither of them could speak, so Shasta did. "Bug and I researched what the professor was working on. When we found out that he was researching the Curse of the Varuupian Rock, we knew we had to talk to him."

Hunter found his voice. "Talk to him? Talk to him? Are you saying that you actually know where he is? That we can all go talk to him?"

Bug shushed him with a look and a finger to her lips. All four of them looked at the windows of both houses before Shasta continued.

"We talked to him this morning. He lives in Shale. He's in his mid-seventies now, but he looks much older. He told us all about going to Shaali and finding the rock. He told us about the trip back on the ship and about making his way to Hallston, or back then it was outside of the town limits, and burying the box." She looked down at her shoes. She was thinking how hard this must be on Eli. "And he told us about all the people that had died along the way." She stopped talking then and looked at them both.

Hunter and Eli were quietly absorbing everything the girls had said. Shasta and Bug stayed silent, waiting for the questions that they both knew were coming.

Finally, Hunter said, "Eli was thinking that we could take the box with everything in it back to this professor guy if we could find him. Couldn't we still do that? It was his problem to start with – he should have to fix it."

"Well, that's not really possible." Shasta paused, thinking how to tell them the rest. "Professor Monroe didn't actually come away from this unscathed. He was cursed, too. He's blind."

Eli's eyes opened wide. "He's blind? He should be dead! How can he have been around that thing and ended up living so long?" He was feeling very angry with Professor Monroe. It was his fault that this was happening – his fault for bringing the damned thing here in the first place. Eli wished that Professor Monroe had died instead of Heather. He looked away from the group as tears sprang into his eyes.

Shasta could read his thoughts. "I know what you mean, Eli. And he knows that. He knows that he should have died, and I think he sort of wishes he had. Either way, he can't help us. Even with his sight, he's just too weak. He said that there was a letter with the rock?"

Hunter leaned forward, reached around and pulled an envelope out of his back pocket. He handed it over to Shasta.

Shasta opened the envelope and took out the money – two hundred cash. Not so much to travel with these days, but back then, it would have been a lot. She handed the money to Bug and pulled out the map. She glanced at it then handed that over to Bug as well. She pulled out the last item and unfolded it.

She read it through twice; her forehead wrinkled in confusion, then handed the letter to Bug. Looking at Hunter first, then Eli, she said, "But, that doesn't say how to get rid of it. It just says it's a cursed artifact and shows where it came from on a stupid map. How are we supposed to know what to do to get rid of it?" It was Shasta's turn to be angry. The whole morning, Professor Monroe never said anything about what to do with the rock, how to dispose of it. What were they supposed to do now?

That's when Bug spoke up, "Well, we know that Professor Monroe isn't the sharpest crayon in the box, or he wouldn't have brought that piece of the tomb back from Shaali in the first place. Also, it took him a super long time to figure out that the rock was what killed the captain of his little boat and the crewmen on the ship. I, for one, am glad that he doesn't suggest how to get rid of it. For all we know we would all end up cursed."

She looked around at the group, then back at Shasta. "What about what we were talking about on the way back from Shale? Remember? We were going to ask the Shazaam Brothers about a chemical that could disintegrate rock."

"That's right," said Shasta. "We were thinking that if you guys knew of some kind of chemical that would just dissolve the rock; the curse would cease to exist. What do you think?"

Hunter looked at Eli and thought for a moment. Then he said, "That may be a pretty good option. We would need to test some things out, though. And we don't really have anything stronger than bleach in our kits, but, with some research, we might be able to come up with something."

"Just," Eli said.

"Just what?" Hunter asked.

"No, Mr. Just. Mr. Just at school. He has all kinds of stuff in the lab. And he has a ton of knowledge about chemical components. What about taking it to him? He's really cool, I know he'd help us."

The time had come for Shasta to finally voice her main fear. "We can't do that. What if it hurts him? Or worse. We know what that rock can do, we've seen it. And it seems to affect different people in different ways. We don't know what affect it would have on him. Should we really take a chance on someone else's life?"

Eli and Hunter exchanged a look. Then, Hunter said, "We know how it affects each of us, and you too, Bug. But you're right, Shasta. No one else should be around it that hasn't already been exposed. We'll take it with us to the school and keep it outside when we talk to him. We'll find out what he suggests and then Eli and I will ultimately be the ones to deal with it."

"Well, that sounds like a super good plan," said Bug. "But I'm going to tell my dad about this whole thing. He'll know what to do if your plan doesn't work. That way, we'll have a Plan B."

Bug then reached down and pulled something out of her bag. It was the book that Professor Monroe had given them. "Read the chapter on the Varuupi. It'll fill in the gaps from his letter." She handed the book over to Eli who accepted it and started to flip through the pages.

"Eli?" Shasta said. "Does your mom know about any of this?"

"No," he replied looking guiltier than before. "I'll need to tell her soon, but I just can't yet."

"You know," she continued. "You can't blame your-self for what happened to Heather. There's no way you could have known what was in that box. It was normal curiosity. If you had even the slightest belief that something in there could hurt your family, you never would have opened it at all. Much less in your own house."

Shasta was trying to be kind, but her words had a stinging effect on both Eli and Hunter. They both had an idea that the box was responsible for Mr. Jackson's death and for making them sick, as well. The boys had wanted to open it anyway. Thinking back, they should have taken it deep into the woods and buried it, but they had wanted to see what was inside. Two more people had died because of them. Eli knew that guilt would be with him forever.

They had a plan and all of the information had been shared, so it seemed like a good time to call it quits. Shasta stood up and motioned for Bug.

"Let us know what happens. We'll help any way that we can, except, I don't think either of us should get too close to the rock. We know how sick it makes Bug, and who knows what it'll do to me?"

Bug added, "I'll tell my dad what's going on and let you know if he comes up with anything. When will you go to the school to see Mr. Just?"

"I think we should talk to him after school tomorrow. We'll keep it in Eli's trunk until then. That way, if he has an idea, we can work in the lab, and he can be on a cell phone nearby or something. That may work." Hunter looked at Eli to see if he agreed with that plan. Eli nodded and said it sounded good.

"Okay, bye then." Shasta got her bag from the ground, and Bug followed her to the truck. Shasta was thinking how in the world she was going to explain all of this to Darren and Agnes.

Eli looked at Hunter and said, "I feel a little better. Just the fact that we've got a plan and some friends who are going to help makes me feel better."

"Yeah," agreed Hunter. "Do you really think Mr. Just will know what to do?"

"I think if anyone would, it would be him. He's got a great scientific mind. He's really our only hope at this point. It's got to work."

Eli reached up and started to massage his temples once again. His headache was back.

CHAPTER 24

Shasta & Darren

Shasta had picked up the pizza from Hot Slice! and was on her way back to Meadowview Acres. She wasn't very hungry because her stomach was in knots. She had been going over scenarios of different conversations in her head. How was she going to tell Darren and his mom all that she and Bug and the boys had learned? She knew it sounded crazy and didn't even know how to begin.

As she pulled into the Jackson's driveway, she felt even more nervous. Should she be the one to tell them, or should it come from Sheriff Buchanon or Bug's dad? No, she decided, coming from her, someone so close to the family, was better. She stuck the DVD in her bag and got the pizza from the passenger side of the Ranger.

Darren opened the door and gave her a hug. Looking at him, she saw that he had bags under his eyes, and he looked very sad. It must've been a hard day with Mrs. Jackson. Shasta had to remind herself that it had only been a week since Claymont died. So much had happened within that week but not to Darren and his mom. To them, the only thing that had happened was that they had lost a husband and a father.

Balancing the pizza box in her other hand, she returned Darren's hug. "Tough day?" She asked.

He looked behind him to ensure that they couldn't be overheard and said, "It was bad today, Shas. I don't know why this day has been harder on her than any other, but today was really bad. I didn't know what to do. All I could do was sit with her and make sure she ate something." He glanced at the box and said, "Thanks for bringing that and the movie. Maybe it'll help her think of something else for a while."

"That's what I'm hoping, but..." she stopped short, nervous about the information she was about to relay.

Darren looked confused and said, "What? Is something else wrong?"

Shasta knew that it would be worse if she dragged it out. She needed to do it quickly, like ripping off a bandage.

"Nothing's happened exactly, it's just that I have some information. Information about what may have caused your dad's brain hemorrhage."

Darren's eyes narrowed as he said, "What do you mean? What kind of information? Shas, what are you saying?"

Shasta walked into the adjoining dining room and set the pizza box and her bag on the table. When she turned around, he was right behind her. She took his hands and said, "When your dad died, everyone just thought it was a medical condition and left it at that, right?"

He nodded, still too confused to ask any questions.

"Well," she went on, "that kind of made sense. But when Heather died a few days later from the same thing, and then Hansen on the same day, it started to seem a little too coincidental."

Darren's eyes widened in partial understanding. "You mean it wasn't just a brain hemorrhage. That something caused him to have it? And caused Heather's death and whatever it was that got Hansen?"

She nodded, still holding his hands. "That's right. We've tracked down a reason that this has happened. It's not something that I would ever have believed possible. But it is, Darren. And it's happening here now."

He dropped her hands and started pacing the small dining room. "Who's we? Who told you about this?"

"At first it was Bug. You know how smart she is, how she notices things that most of us don't. She thought there was probably a connection between the three deaths. It was just too coincidental for three people who lived so close to one another to die so suddenly. She witnessed Hansen die. She knew something was off by what she saw that day. She also was curious because she was there with Hunter and Eli when they found, well, the bulldozer. She noticed something that day as well."

"What? What is it?" Darren looked tired and worried. Shasta hated doing this to him, but his family had the right to know everything she knew.

"Darren, it's kind of an involved story. And I think you both deserve to know all of the facts. Do you think we could get your mom, and we could just go sit down and talk?"

For a moment he looked unsure, not wanting to cause his mother any more grief, but then, his mind made up, he gave her a little grin and said, "You're right. She deserves to know everything there is to know. It might even help if she has some answers. Go on into the living room and I'll get her."

Shasta's stomach was still in knots. Facing Darren was hard enough, but how could she tell Agnes? She had always been so nice to Shasta. The last thing she wanted to do was to give her more pain.

She sat down on one end of the sofa in the living room. She could hear Darren's voice in the back of the house talking to Agnes. After a couple more minutes, they both showed up. When Agnes saw Shasta, she crossed the room and gave the girl a weak, little hug.

"Shasta, it's always so good to see you. Darren says you've brought us a movie." She was trying to sound perky, but it wasn't working at all.

"Hi, Mrs. Jackson." Shasta returned the hug. "I did bring us something to watch. But there's something I need to talk to you about first."

She was on alert immediately. Agnes' emotions had been on a hair-pin trigger ever since last Friday. Her eyes were wide as she asked, "What's happened? What's happened now? Is it someone else?"

Trying to calm her as quickly as possible, Shasta said, "No, nothing has happened to anyone else that I know of. It's just that there's some new information that I wanted to share with you both."

It was Agnes's turn to look confused. Darren went to his mother and guided her to the comfy blue chair across from the couch. "It's okay, Mom, Shasta has some news about what may have caused Dad's brain hemorrhage, and Heather and Hansen too. They all might be related."

Agnes was calming down but more confused than ever. She had never once contemplated that the three deaths were connected. To her, those other two were just really sad things that had happened after her world had collapsed. She could vaguely remember talking to Lara on the phone and trying to console her. She hadn't talked to anyone from the Reynolds family. They didn't know each other well, and Agnes just hadn't had it in her to make any more calls. As a matter of fact, she hadn't thought of those other two deaths at all. Her thoughts were only on Claymont. And now Shasta was saying that they might all be related somehow?

She settled herself in the blue chair and looked across the room at Shasta. Agnes knew the girl was no drama queen. She was smart and mature. She had been almost a member of their family for years. If she was bringing them information about her husband's death, Agnes was sure that it was reliable.

"Tell us what you know, Shasta. Don't leave anything out." Darren could tell that his mother could handle hearing the news.

Shasta took a deep breath and began with what she had already told Darren. "So, Mrs. Jackson, after Mr. Jackson died, everyone just accepted that he'd had a brain hemorrhage. That seemed to be the case until Heather and Hansen died. You know Bug across the street? The girl I sit for? Well she's extremely smart. She's curious, too, and she was with the boys when they found Mr. Jackson. She also witnessed Hansen die when she was looking out her window. There were a couple of things she noticed that made her question whether the deaths were related. When someone told her about Heather, she was sure that they were." She shifted herself on the couch a little bit and continued.

"Bug had noticed that Hunter and Eli had a box with them at the construction site, a box they hadn't had going into the woods. That made her curious. The other curious thing was when Hansen died. He had yanked Hunter's backpack off of him and had taken out a chunk of rock from the pack when he started to have his attack. We found out later that the same rock had been near Heather when she died."

Darren interjected here. "What could a rock have to do with brain hemorrhaging?"

"That's what Bug wanted to know, so she told me that she wanted to research other deaths from around here and see if anything added up. We went to the newspaper's archives and searched for hours for any mysterious deaths that had happened in close succession. Finally, we found four from back in nineteen sixty-eight. We also found that a man had gotten off of a ship that had lost a lot of crew members to a mysterious virus. We kept checking and were able to place the man at each of the four deaths."

"Who was this man? Did he kill these people?" Agnes was very interested, and much calmer. Her mind was focused on something more than her grief.

"No," Shasta said. "He didn't kill them, but what he had with him did. His name is Professor Preston Monroe. He studied legends and myths and taught a class on them at the State College in Chester. One of the legends that he studied made him curious enough to quit his job and go on a fact finding mission so he could write a book." Shasta stopped there and reached for her bag. Before she had driven to Hot Slice! she had stopped at Hunter's house to retrieve the book that the professor had given to her. She handed the book to Darren. "This isn't the book that he wrote. This is the book that started his curiosity and set him off on his quest. Read Chapter fourteen, Darren."

Darren looked the book over before opening it to the table of contents. "The Rock Of Varuupi?" He looked up at Shasta, and she nodded.

Agnes was motionless as Darren read the chapter about Chief Maalini, Thuuni, and the curse. As Darren read the last piece of information about the fifteen archaeologists who died while on the island of Shaali, his eyes grew wider. He stopped reading and looked up at his mother.

Agnes was still. She looked resigned. Finally, she spoke. "This curse – the rock that has the curse. Are you saying that somehow this rock found its way here to Hallston? How is that possible?"

Shasta told them of her meeting with Professor Monroe. She told them the story that he had told her and Bug that morning. How, by the time he had gotten off the ship, he knew what he had in his possession – how he made his way to Hallston with people dying along the way. They watched her as she spoke, but Shasta wasn't certain if they really believed all she was saying.

"So that's how he made it to the woods and buried the box. Mr. Jackson inadvertently dug it up while he worked, and Hunter and Eli brought it home. They were thinking that there was something exciting inside. There is one more thing about the professor, though. He's blind. He was struck blind within hours of burying the rock. The curse touched him as well." She stopped talking and waited.

Darren spoke first. "Where is it now? The rock?"

"After meeting with the professor, Bug and I went to Hunter's and talked to him and Eli. They have it stored in the shed behind Hunter's house. The plan is, tomorrow after school, they're going to talk to Mr. Just to see if it can be dissolved using some chemical composition. If that doesn't work, we'll go straight to Sheriff Buchanon."

"Why not go to the sheriff now, Shasta?" Agnes asked. "Now I'm not sure about many things, but one thing I know is that you don't mess with any type of voodoo or black magic. If that's what's really going on here, why leave it for a few kids to take care of? Let the authorities take it over. That's what they're there for."

"Well, you're right. But the thing is, that curse is so strong that it killed Hansen within minutes of him touching it. It affects different people in different ways. What if we handed it over to someone like the sheriff only to see it kill him, too? Right now, we think it's just safer if no one else gets near it." Shasta was still questioning that decision.

Looking more peaceful than she had in days, Agnes eased back in her chair. Her voice was soft when she spoke. "You know, I had an old great-aunt who lived way south of here. She used to scare the devil out of my sisters and me with her stories of voodoo and dark magic. My sister Shelley said the stories weren't true, but I believed them. I believed every one of them. If my Claymont unearthed some cursed box, I believe that too. It makes more sense in my mind than my healthy fifty-one year old husband suddenly contracting some kind of brain problem." She looked up at Darren and Shasta and said, "You know that autopsy wasn't conclusive. That's what's been bothering me this whole time. The autopsy report said that there was more blood loss than normal with a brain hemorrhage. That means it could have been something else. Things just didn't add up for me, and, as crazy as a cursed rock sounds, it makes more sense."

Almost dreamlike, Agnes rose from her chair and started slowly walking toward the door to the living room. "I'm going to sleep now, I'm awfully tired."

Darren and Shasta watched her leave. Then Shasta said, "Do you think she's okay? She's acting a little strange."

He replied, "I think she's exhausted. And this explanation gives her more answers than anything else. I'll check on her in a little while." He looked at her then. "Do you really believe this? A curse? It's kind of out there."

Shasta thought a moment and said, "Yeah, I do. It sounds a little far-fetched coming out of the blue like this I bet. But when you read the documentation and see the newspaper articles, it's more believable. The big thing, Darren, was meeting with the professor this morning. He even looks like someone who's been cursed. I totally believed everything he said. He's lived the majority of his life knowing that he is responsible for all of those deaths, all because he brought a relic home from an island in the South Pacific. It's haunted him his whole life. Now, knowing that he's responsible for your dad, Heather and Hansen, he must be in a living hell."

Darren wanted to say, "Good, he deserves to be in hell," but he was just too tired. He laid his head on her shoulder and said, "I'm so glad you're here. Can you stay a while?"

Shasta laid her head on top of Darren's and answered, "I'll stay as long as you need me."

"Well, I'll need you forever. Can you handle that?"

She smiled, and thought how strange it was that she could feel such happiness in the midst of all the challenges they were facing.

"Just try and stop me," she said.

CHAPTER 25

Bug

It had seemed silly for Shasta to drive Bug home after talking to Eli and Hunter. After all, she just lived next door. Nevertheless, the girls had gotten into Shasta's truck and backed out of the Massey's driveway. Shasta pulled up in front of Bug's house next door and parked.

"Are you okay, Bug?" She asked. The day had been long and filled with all kinds of information that people usually didn't hear. She was worried about how all of it was affecting Bug.

Bug was looking past Shasta to her house. "I'm fine. I need to tell my dad, though. He'll know what to do, and I'll feel better once he knows."

"Okay, then. I'll talk to you soon. If you need me tonight, I'll be at the Jackson's." She leaned over and gave her little friend a hug. "Try not to worry. We'll sort all of this out."

Bug hugged her back. She loved Shasta. To Bug, Shasta represented security, strength and acceptance. She could tell her anything and know that Shasta would not only listen, but not judge, ridicule or tease her. That in itself was remarkable, but it was also out of love. They had become as close as sisters.

Bug jumped from Shasta's truck and walked up her driveway. She could smell dinner cooking as she stepped into the kitchen. *Spaghetti? No, baked ravioli, super yummy!* Bug's tummy rumbled as she closed the side door.

Her mother was taking the bread out of the oven. She smiled at her and said, "Hi, Sweetie! Did you have a good day with Shasta?"

Bug put her bag down on the kitchen counter and sat down on one of the stools. "Yeah, we had a productive day."

"Well what did you girls get into today? The library, a little shopping?" Ann Hamilton cut the hot bread into slices and started to spread butter on them.

"We actually did some research on some curses and how they may still be affecting people today. Where's Dad?"

Mrs. Hamilton got the parmesan cheese from the fridge and started to sprinkle the hot, buttered slices of bread. "I think he's in the living room watching the news. I was about to call him for dinner. Why don't you go wash up and get him for me. I'll set the table."

"Okay." Bug slid from the high stool and walked to the bathroom to wash her hands. She was trying to figure out just how to start the conversation with her dad. She decided not to do it before dinner. There was no use wasting a good meal, like baked ravioli, with bad news. She would wait until afterward.

She wiped her hands dry and went in search of her father. Mark was indeed in the living room watching the news. His serious face was glued to the reporter who was speaking about the latest catastrophic weather event – another earthquake. The poor people were still rebuilding from the last one.

He noticed her standing beside his chair and said, "Hey, Sweetie! How's my girl?"

Bug bent down and hugged her father around his neck. She felt better already. Everything would be alright. She felt like he would make everything better because that's what dad's do.

"I'm fine. Mom says to come eat now."

Jumping up from his chair and turning off the TV, he said, "Good, I'm about to waste away. I'm starving! Did you have a good day?"

"Yes, I did. But I need to ask you about something. Can we have a talk after dinner?"

Mark was used to his daughter's curiosity. She regularly asked him about current events or documentaries that she had watched. The request was nothing new. After the events of last week, he had been expecting it. He had a feeling that she was a little shaken about the recent events. To have known one person who passed away was hard enough, but she had known all three of those people. He put an arm around her tiny shoulder as they walked down the hall to the kitchen. "Sure, right after we eat."

Dinner was as great as Bug had predicted. Soon all three of their plates were clean and none of them had left room for dessert.

"Wonderfully tasty as usual, Ann," Mark complimented. Rubbing his belly, he turned to Bug and said, "Let's go work off this meal with a good discussion." He winked at his wife, and let her know that Bug had requested this conversation. She picked up on it and said, "Don't worry about clearing the table, Bug. I'll do it tonight. You go on and talk to Dad."

Bug left the table and followed her father down the hall back to the living room. She chose the overstuffed loveseat with the ottoman and Mark plopped down beside her. That was their talking spot. They always ended up there when Bug had questions that needed answering. Mark would stretch his long legs out on the ottoman and Bug would stretch her short legs atop her father's lap. Once they were cozy, Mark waited for Bug to start.

He was expecting her to ask questions about Heather and Hansen, so he was surprised when she said, "You know how knowledge is power? Well, sometimes it can be scary, too." She unexpectedly started to cry.

Alarmed, Mr. Hamilton scooted closer to Bug and folded her up into his arms. Ann had obviously heard because Mark saw her head pop around the doorframe. She had a look of concern on her face. He mouthed, "She's okay," to his wife and let Bug cry it out. There were many times that Mark Hamilton had worried about his daughter – the first day of every school year, or meeting new people. She had always been a little quirky, but he and Ann thought it to be endearing. From what he witnessed of other people reacting to her, they seemed to feel the same way. For the most part, she was accepted as she was, but not at school, however. She was just so much smarter than kids her own age. The middle school principal and the school counselor had recommended that she skip a grade, but he and Ann had felt that she was not mature enough. She was a young girl with a brilliant mind.

As she nestled closer and the tears quieted, he wondered what could have her so upset. What did she mean that knowledge can be scary? He was used to her signature line of, "Knowledge is Power." A day didn't go by that he didn't hear her say the phrase at least a couple of times. That and the word "super". Just tonight at dinner she had said how "super yummy" the ravioli had been. He smiled to himself and squeezed her a little tighter, as he waited for her to be able to talk.

Finally, her dark, little head rose up, and she looked at him. "You know," she sniffled, "Crying is the body's natural way of releasing tension."

He smiled at her. "I know. Now start at the beginning."

So she did. She started way back at the Hot Dog Hut when Hansen had caused her to fall out of the booth and bloody her nose. She could tell that made her dad mad, but what could he do now? Hansen was dead.

Next she recounted the night she followed Eli and Hunter into the woods, and they had found Mr. Jackson. Her dad wasn't happy about that, either, but he didn't interrupt. He had been so worried about her that night after Deputy Clay had brought her home. She also told him about the box the boys had brought home with them.

Then, she told him about watching Hansen die. He knew about this, of course, because she had called him when it was happening, and he had come straight home. They had learned of Heather together later on that day.

She came to the day of the funerals. To Bug, that's when it all started. Sitting in the puffy chair in the foyer of Peaceful Hearts, she had started to put things together. She told her dad of the feeling she'd had that the deaths were somehow connected. She started to tell him the commonalities of the deaths and their circumstances. As she spoke, the newspaperman in Mark Hamilton perked up. He could see her line of thinking and was intrigued.

"So then I told Shasta. At first she didn't believe me, but she was curious enough to help me research."

"Don't tell me," Mark interjected. "That's why you two spent so much time at the newspaper on Saturday. Mrs. Walton called to tell me that you and Shasta had been there for quite a while. I told her no worries. Is that what the two of you were doing?"

"Yes, but we didn't make a mess; we put everything back where we found it. We made four copies and I left forty cents on the copier with a note for Mrs. Shelbourne. But, Dad! We found something. We found a connection." She was excited about the mystery; her fear and stress forgotten. "Way back in nineteen sixty-eight, a series of deaths occurred that are very similar to the ones that just happened. They were from Glovercroft to Hallston. They happened all in one twenty-four hour period and we were able to trace them all back to one man." Here she jumped off the loveseat and ran from the room.

Mark waited and tried to absorb the information that his twelve year old had just presented him with.

Bug jogged back into the room with her bag and sat back down. She opened her bag and pulled out what Mark recognized as some photocopies of articles from his newspaper. Handing them to him one at a time, she started with the vagrant on the outskirts of Hallston.

"This one was a thief who tried to rob the man." She handed him another. "This was Gerald Bell. He came into contact with the man at the bus station." She handed him the next. "This lady was at a bus stop in Glovercroft with him." Finally, she showed him the last clipping. "And this Donny guy helped him with his luggage at the docks." She waited a couple of minutes for her dad to skim through the articles.

"Okay, I see that there could be a connection with how these people died and the ways that our three people died. But who is this man and how did he cause their deaths?" Mark was still intrigued, but he couldn't see how those deaths from so long ago could have anything to do with what had happened in Meadowview Acres.

"The man had just disembarked from a ship. The ship had lost seventeen people to a strange virus on their journey. This man is the key. Shasta and I found this article next." She handed him the article on Professor Preston Monroe.

Mark's eyes narrowed as he read the article. Still trying to find the connection, he said, "What had this professor been working on?"

Bug smiled. He was following the same logic that they had. She handed him the last photocopy. It had the excerpt from his book, *The Curse of the Varuupian Tribe and its Ties to Our Culture*.

Bug watched as understanding registered on her dad's face. "So what you believe is that this curse is somehow at play here?"

"Dad, I watched Hansen take the rock out of Hunter's backpack. The backpack with the rock in it had been in Heather's kitchen just minutes before. And the rock had been dug up by Mr. Jackson at the construction site. When I was around the metal box that Hunter had, I was really sick, so were he and Eli. Even the deputy was. But I haven't told you the rest."

Mark looked at his daughter and steeled himself for what was to come.

"Shasta and I went to Shale this morning and talked to Professor Monroe in person."

Mark Hamilton's eyes flew wide open. "You? And Shasta? You went to Shale? Bug, you should have told me. If you wanted to talk to this man, I should have taken you. That wasn't safe. You should know better!" Even while admonishing her, he was too curious to be angry. "Well, what did he say?"

Bug recited almost word for word the story that Professor Monroe had told her and Shasta that morning. Mark listened in silence as all the pieces fell into place. When she finished, he said, "That is some story! And you say he's blind now? And has been since the night he buried the box with the artifact?"

Bug nodded. "So there's more. When we came home this afternoon, we met with the boys. They do have the box with the rock and they showed us the envelope that the Professor had put inside. It had two hundred dollars in cash, a map showing the island of Shaali and an explanation of what the rock is, and what it's capable of doing. The only thing not in there is what to *do* about it. We don't know how to get rid of it."

She stopped there and watched as her father got up from the loveseat and started to pace the room. She could hear him mumbling to himself.

"Okay, so we've got the artifact that's cursed. No one needs to be around it. Need to tell Sheriff Buchanon ASAP. Boys are okay, Bug's alright, anyone else touch it? No, okay." She heard him mumble some more but couldn't really make out what he was saying. Finally he stopped and said, "I need to talk to this professor. I'll go first thing in the morning. He'll be the one to tell us how to rid ourselves of the thing."

He crossed the room, took her by her shoulders and looked her straight in the eye. "Buggie, I'm really proud of you for piecing all of this together, but you took some risks here, you know? You and Shasta should not have gone to Shale without me or another adult. That professor could have been a crazy person. You could have been in danger. Now, from now on, you don't go anywhere near the boys or that box. If you see it, you go the opposite direction. Do you hear me?"

She nodded her head and promised that she would stay away. "What are you going to do?"

"First thing in the morning, I'm calling Sheriff Buchanon. I'll take him to Shale with me and tell him the story on the way. Together, maybe we can get some information out of this guy. Where did you say the rock is now?"

"Well, Hunter and Eli are going to ask their chemistry teacher, Mr. Just, if there is any way to disintegrate rock. They're going to see if they can dissolve it and the curse along with it. Right now, it's either in Hunter's shed out back or Eli's trunk."

Mark thought that over for a moment. "Mr. Just. Phillip Just. Yeah, I know him. I had to talk to him a few months ago for some facts about an article we were running. Real smart guy. Okay, we'll let that stand for now. But as soon as the sheriff and I get back from Shale tomorrow, we'll have an answer."

"Thanks, Dad. I feel better now that you know. I was super stressed out." She went to him and put her spindly little arms around his middle. He hugged her back, still amazed at the brain inside of her small head.

"You go to bed now, Bug. You've had a rough week. I have to go to the office and sign off on tomorrow's paper before they send it to print. I'll see you first thing." He squeezed her one last time and kissed the top of her black hair. "I love you, Baby."

"Love you, too, Dad." She smiled and left the room.

———————

It seemed to Bug that she had only just put her head down on the pillow when she was startled awake. She opened her groggy eyes and, through the dim light, she made out the shape of her father sitting on her bed.

"Bug!" He half-whispered. "Bug! Wake up!"

She rose up on one arm and rubbed her eyes. "What? What is it, Dad?"

"I've just come from the newspaper. I was looking it over before sending it to print and I saw something on the Obit page. Honey, Professor Monroe died today. It says that he passed away earlier this afternoon from natural causes."

CHAPTER 26

Hunter & Eli

Even with all of the precautions that he and Eli had taken, Hunter was still nervous. Eli had retrieved the rock from the storage shed and put it back into its box. Then he had put the box in the backpack, and put the backpack inside a suitcase. After a little more thought, he had put that smaller suitcase into a larger one. That suitcase was now secured in the trunk of the Flaming Tomato. All together, the rock was five levels of material away from them as they drove to school that Monday morning. Even so, Hunter was nervous, and queasy. He didn't know if the nerves were messing with his stomach, or if it was the rock. It was probably a combination of both. He had skipped breakfast that morning in anticipation of puking on the way to school. *So far, so good.*

Hunter looked over at Eli behind the wheel. He was very quiet this morning. Hunter knew that his friend had been under tremendous pressure, but there was something else. Hunter had noticed that Eli looked older somehow. There was something in his face that hadn't been there before. He knew that Eli was still grieving and feeling guilty about Heather. Hunter felt guilty as well. But Eli had a strange look to him. He looked haunted.

Hunter looked out the window and decided to try to lighten the mood. "I'm feeling good today, Eli. I've got a good feeling about this plan. Mr. Just has an awesome, scientific brain. I'm sure he'll be able to do something. Then all of this crap will be over. Hey, my stomach's not even upset!" He lied.

Eli just nodded and kept his eyes on the road. After a few minutes of driving in silence, he said, "I hope so, Hunter. I really do. I just don't want anyone else to get hurt."

Hunter felt the sting of guilt as he remembered bringing the box over to Eli's house that day. If only they had decided to take it back to the woods and bury it.

They pulled into the student lot and decided not to park in their usual place on the third row. The seniors were allotted the first two rows of prime parking spaces, followed by the juniors with the last two rows. Today, though, they needed to park as far away as possible. They couldn't risk the rock affecting anyone walking too close to the car. Eli found a good spot on the far end of the visitor's lot. After turning off the engine, Eli sat still, not making a move to get out of the car. Hunter just waited to give his friend some time.

"This is going to be the longest day of school ever," Hunter said after a few minutes. "But let's get going. The sooner it starts, the sooner it's over, and we can talk to Just."

Eli nodded again and got out of the car. Hunter followed and soon they were in their first period classes. Hunter worried about how Eli would manage his day. He guessed that his odd behavior would be attributed to Heather's death, but Hunter wished that he could keep a better eye on him. When the bell rang for lunch after third period, Hunter waited beside his locker as he usually did. He was starving, having skipped breakfast, but he was anxious to see how Eli was holding up. After some time had passed, he finally saw Eli walking slowly toward him.

"Dude, you look terrible," he said as Eli caught up to him. "Do you need to go home or something? I can take care of business this afternoon on my own."

"No, I'm fine, really. I just have a huge headache. I need to be here, Hunter. Let's go eat something, maybe that'll help."

Hunter made Eli stop at the nurse's desk on the way to the cafeteria. Without any questions, she gave him two tablets for his headache. All she needed to do was look at him. She tried to get him to lie down for a while, but he said he wanted to eat something. Satisfied that the food and medication would help him to feel better, she had let him go.

The cafeteria wasn't as noisy as it usually was. Hunter knew immediately that it was the absence of Hansen that made the difference. The table where he usually held court was filled with the same kids, Clark, Jacob, Jeff and Alan, but they didn't seem to be making any trouble for anyone. Hunter thought without Hansen, those guys might actually be cool.

He scanned the other end of the table and saw Emily, Destiny, Trish and Clara. Clara was looking at him when he found her. She smiled her bright, beautiful smile and Hunter felt warm. The day that she had driven him out to the field by the woods had been so nice. She was Clara again – sweet, down to earth, no one to impress Clara. He smiled back and grabbed a tray to follow Eli down the lunch line.

The food and medicine did help Eli. His color came back a little, and he was a little more talkative, too. They discussed ways to break the news to Mr. Just. They were divided in their ideas with Hunter wanting to tell him just the bare bones and Eli wanting to spill the whole story. They decided to go with telling him as much as possible without all the details.

The bell rang, and lunch was over. Eli told Hunter that he would see him in chemistry class sixth period and left. Hunter took the chance to walk over to where Clara was still sitting. He was half expecting her to act like she didn't know him, like she had for the past three years, but she didn't.

"I was hoping you'd come say hi," she smiled her dazzling smile at him, and her friends all looked at him and smiled, too. "You guys, this is Hunter Massey. We're old friends."

The girls all said hello and, leaving Clara behind with Hunter, gathered their things to walk to fourth period.

"It's funny that I've gone to school with them for years, and this is the first time they've ever acknowledged me," Hunter said to her.

"I know," replied Clara. "Popular girls, what're you gonna do with 'em?" She rolled her eyes dramatically, and Hunter laughed.

"Yeah, right!" He said and Clara laughed back.

As he walked her to class, she asked him how Eli was doing.

"He's pretty stressed out and upset right now. I think it'll just take time. His mom offered for him to stay out of school this whole week, even Principal Harrison said it was fine, but he wanted to come."

"I hope they'll be okay. I really like Mrs. Andrews and Eli, too," Clara said sadly.

They made it to Clara's class with time to spare so Hunter hung out and talked for a few more minutes before going on to his own class. The next two classes were the longest Hunter had ever experienced. When the bell rang for sixth, he all but ran from the room.

Eli was already talking to Mr. Just when Hunter made it to the classroom. He walked to where the two were talking and heard the tail end of Eli's sentence. "... that we could really use your help with."

"Sure thing, Man, what's up?" Mr. Just said. He was easy going and unperturbed as usual.

Eli looked at Hunter and continued, "It's really important and can't wait. Can we talk after school today?"

"Well, yeah, Man. Hey, you dudes aren't in any trouble, are you?" He gave Hunter and Eli the once over and looked back to Eli.

"No, we aren't in trouble. It's just very important that we talk as soon as possible." Hunter spoke for Eli, knowing what Eli was thinking. Of course he was in trouble. They were all in trouble.

"No sweat, guys. Right after school I have about ten minutes until detention starts."

"This will take longer than ten minutes," Eli said.

Mr. Just had a quizzical look on his face. He was also full of compassion when he said, "I've got all the time you need. Let's talk before detention and then you can come back when it's over for as long as you need."

Hunter and Eli went to their seats in the back of the room as Mr. Just started talking about how an oxide is formed. As he spoke of oxides having an oxygen atom as well as another element, neither of the boys listened. Eli put his head down on the desk and was asleep within minutes. Hunter saw Mr. Just notice Eli sleeping. He paused his lecture for just a moment before continuing. He knew something was up with them and was giving Eli a pass. "I sure hope he can help," Hunter thought to himself.

After what seemed to Hunter like a million years, the bell rang and most of the class headed for the door. Eli had woken up, looking surprised at where he was, halfway through the class.

Monitoring the halls, Mr. Just was standing right outside his doorway when the boys came out behind the rest of the class. Mr. Just saw them and smiled.

"I've got to stay here while the halls are full to keep an eye out for any hooligans, but we're free to talk." He waited as they looked at each other, trying to decide how to start.

Hunter plunged in. "We know you're a scientist and all, but do you believe in things like curses?"

Mr. Just raised his eyebrows as he considered. He was very open-minded. There wasn't a lot that he didn't believe or accept, but he had never thought much about curses.

"You know, Man, I've never thought about it much. I don't suppose I should say that I don't believe in them, since I haven't fully researched them. So yeah, sure I believe there are things out there that are unexplainable. I like for things to be proven and concrete. But I accept the fact that some things just aren't."

Eli took it from there. The fact that there was very little time made him more blunt than he would have liked. Students, showing up for detention, filed into the room past him, making him speak very quietly.

"We have a strong reason to believe that we are in possession of a relic that has been cursed. We can show you documentation if you need it, but time is really short right now. This thing – it's a rock. It's the reason behind the deaths. Mr. Jackson, Hansen Reynolds and my sister. It affects people in different ways, so we don't know if we can protect you. We have to destroy it. Hunter and I can be around it for short periods of time, but we have to do this as soon as possible. Do you have anything that can dissolve a rock?"

Mr. Just involuntarily took a step backward. He wasn't afraid, just a little freaked out. *Either this kid is on the list for Sister Mary's House of Crazy, or he's still in shock from his sister's death.*

"Whoa, Man, take it easy there, Eli. Now I know a lot has happened in the last few days, hell, you shouldn't even be at school. But everything you just spewed on me is really out there." He looked at Hunter. "You on board with all this, Cowboy?"

Hunter said, "I know it sounds crazy. But it's true. If we had time to tell you the whole story, we would. Listen, can you surf the web while you're doing detention?"

Mr. Just said, "Sure, no problem."

Hunter went from the door to Mr. Just's desk at the front of his classroom and scribbled something down on a scrap piece of paper. He came back to where Eli and Phillip Just were standing and held the paper out for Mr. Just. "Here. Do this, please. Look this up. This is what we have. It was dug up behind our neighborhood, and Eli and I brought it back to our houses. We shouldn't have, but we did. And now we need help, we're desperate. We'll go grab something to eat and come back when detention is over. Hopefully, by then you'll believe us and you'll know what we can do."

Mr. Just looked at the kids. He knew these guys weren't the ones always making trouble. They didn't goof off; they made good grades, and one look at Eli told him that something other than grief was at play here. He had made up his mind.

"Absolutely. You got it, Man. Come back in an hour and I'll do what I can to help."

Eli looked at him and said, "This shouldn't be happening, and it's my fault that my sister's dead. We have to end this."

Mr. Just put a hand on his shoulder and said, "I'll do whatever I can, Eli. Hold it together, Dude, hold on. I'll see you in a little while."

He watched Eli and Hunter walk down the hallway to the doors to the student parking lot. He could definitely tell the two were seriously freaked. Seeing them like that, when Mr. Just knew that they were usually laid back and light hearted, really made him curious. Maybe there was something at work here other than coincidence. When they had gone, Mr. Just opened the scrap of paper and read what Hunter had scribbled – "The Rock Of Varuupi" and "Professor Preston Monroe". He frowned and went in to take roll for detention.

It was still a few minutes early but he wanted to get started. He had heard that professor's name before and had an uneasy feeling. He had read the man's obituary just this morning along with a short article on his life.

By then, Hunter and Eli were back inside the Tomato. They had decided to go to the Hot Dog Hut and grab a snack. Hunter was a little reluctant, though.

"Hey, Eli," he said. "What if we're too close to people at the Hut? It's always so crowded after school."

Eli was surprised that they had overlooked that. "You're right. It's too risky."

Eli noticed they were low on gas. There was no getting around that. "We need gas, though. How're we going to do that without getting too close to anyone?"

The boys drove past the Gas N Go a few times before it looked empty enough to pull in. Eli parked on the far side of the mini mart while they waited for the last car to fill up and leave. A few minutes later, the opportunity presented itself. All of the bays were free of cars. Eli hurriedly pulled the car into the bay furthest from the mini mart and closest to the exit back to Main Street. He hopped out and stuck his debit card into the self-pay pump. He was jittery as he waited for the machine to tell him to select fuel type and begin pumping. He groaned loudly as he saw the familiar words pop up on the pump's screen, "Please see attendant".

Eli opened the door and told Hunter, "It says I have to go inside. I'm gonna throw him a twenty. Start pumping when you see me through the glass." He turned and ran to the mini mart.

Hunter hopped out of the car and put the hose into the fuel tank of the Fusion. Watching through the window, he saw the attendant take Eli's money and then an audible click came from the pump. Hunter squeezed the handle and the fuel started dispensing. By then, Eli was running back toward the car.

Both boys were feeling a little more relieved as the price clicker ascended. $10.49…$11.01…$12.34…$13.45. They were silent, willing it to go faster, with their eyes glued to the pump. They didn't see Ms. Leezil's car pull into the bay beside them until she had almost parked.

The boys looked at each other in fear as she got out of her car and said, "Hey, guys! How's your Monday?"

Hunter kept his eyes on the pump as Eli replied, "Um, good. We're just in a hurry." He looked at Hunter who instinctively knew what Eli was trying to say. Hunter stopped the pump at $16.87 and replaced the nozzle. He ran around to the passenger side and got in.

Ms. Leezil looked confused as she watched the boys hurry to get in the car. Then, almost out of nowhere, she stumbled sideways. Her hand reached out to steady herself and found the side of her car. She had broken out in a cold sweat and was feeling faint.

Eli had just gotten into the driver's side when he saw her stumble. Hunter saw it too and yelled, "Go, Go, Go! Hurry!"

Eli's sweaty fingers were fumbling with the key, and he couldn't make it fit into the ignition. Out of the corner of his eye, he could make out Julie Leezil falling to the ground. Panicked, now, he shoved the key in and turned it making the engine come to life. He stepped on the gas, and the car bolted forward out of the bay and down to the street. He narrowly missed another car as he swerved to get back onto Main Street.

Hunter was looking behind them. "Oh,God! She's on the ground, ELI, SHE'S ON THE GROUND!"

Eli knew. He had seen her fall. The despair that filled him was almost too much. He gritted his teeth and tried not to cry. He drove straight to the high school and parked on the far side of the baseball field. There was no one to be seen. They were completely alone.

Breathing heavily, Hunter slumped against the seat. He was exhausted. The stress of the last few days was just too much. His body was rebelling against him. He had put on a brave front for Eli's sake the last few days, but he was just too tired to continue.

They sat, not speaking, in the car, each trying to gain composure. The sight of Ms. Leezil falling to the ground was still fresh in their minds. Was she alive? Did they leave fast enough?

Eli looked at the clock on the dashboard of the car. They had left school only twenty minutes ago. Another forty until they could talk to Mr. Just. He closed his eyes and prayed for the time to pass quickly.

CHAPTER 27

Sheriff Buchanon

Sheriff Buchanon was worried about his town. In just over a week, three people had died. Claymont was first, followed by Hansen and then Heather Andrews. He remembered seeing Heather at the game the Friday that Claymont had died. She had looked so healthy and happy. Then Hansen died. No one had seen that coming either, or had they?

Donald had been bothered by the coincidence even before the last two deaths. He didn't like the way that he and Deputy Clay had gotten so sick at the construction site, the kids, too. No one at the site had escaped without feeling some sort of illness. The more he thought about it; the more he was convinced there was a connection.

After Claymont's funeral on Monday, Sheriff Buchanon had sought out the paramedics that had been on the scene. They worked out of Community Hospital and were easy to find. The sheriff had asked them a number of questions about that Friday night, but what he really wanted to know was how each of them had felt physically. Danny Kurr was one of the paramedics that night. He said that he remembered feeling extremely hot and dizzy. Jeremy Listle, his partner, had been nauseated and had vomited most of the way to the morgue. That was one reason it had taken so long to get Claymont's body there that night. They'd had to keep stopping for Jeremy to throw up. Both men had thought they were reacting to the amount of blood at the scene. That can happen sometimes. Even professionals who deal with death on a regular basis can have sensitivity to it occasionally.

Sheriff Buchanon didn't think they were being sensitive. He thought they were affected the same way that he, Deputy Clay and the kids were.

Tuesday had been a busy one at the department and he hadn't had much free time, so it wasn't until Wednesday afternoon that he'd had a chance to return to the site. The bulldozer had been removed. Gary Sam Construction had hauled it off to be cleaned. That was going to be a tough job. The inside of that cab was a mess. He didn't envy the guy in charge of that. He didn't have any trouble finding the clump of maples that Claymont had been clearing when he'd had his attack.

Sheriff Buchanon walked slowly around, waiting for a headache to begin or to feel sick to his stomach. Nothing happened. He felt right as rain. He wandered over to the spot where the bulldozer had sat. He stood right on the spot and felt nothing. Walking back over to the clump of maples, he noticed a hole in the ground – not a scrape made by the Cat, a hole. Looking closer, he could tell that something had been dug up. The hole was at least two feet deep and a foot and a half to two feet wide as well. It looked oddly out of place. The ground around it had been scraped with the bucket of the bulldozer and where the bucket had pulled vegetation out of the ground, roots and brush were left. He could tell the hole was different. The sides were clean, and there were marks left behind by a small shovel or spade.

The Sheriff thought back to that night. Had the hole been there? It had been too dark to see, but he had used his flashlight to poke around while the paramedics had worked to release Claymont. He remembered nothing out of the ordinary. He supposed that the bucket could have made the hole, but no. The bucket of the Cat was much larger than that.

Then he remembered the kids. Hunter had sat next to Eli on the fallen tree. Hunter was dry-heaving and Eli had his head in his hands. Bug was white and clammy and looked like she was in a daze. They had a backpack with them and something else. He had asked the deputy. He remembered it was one of those metal boxes with a hinge for a padlock. If he remembered correctly, it had been secured with chains as well. He had asked Michael about it and had been told that the kids had it with them all along. He wondered if they had lied to the deputy. But then, what could it be? Nothing he could think of would have affected people that way just by being in its proximity. Could it be some kind of chemical? He knew the boy's reputation of playing with science experiments sometimes. Could they have concocted something so strong that it would be able to make them all sick? He decided it was worth a trip to talk to them.

That's when Rachel had radioed and told him about Heather Andrews. She said that she had just gotten another emergency call about Hansen Reynolds and thought there might be a connection. It had taken him a couple of minutes to get back to his car, so, by the time he made it to Meadowview Acres, the ambulance was already pulling into the drive. He noticed a deputy talking to a man in a Jeep and a young girl. The paramedic was headed in the direction of the boy on the ground. The sheriff started toward the Andrews house.

Inside was a flurry of activity. Heather's mom and her friend were holding onto each other as the paramedic worked to start Heather's heart. He looked around for Eli, but didn't see him. He turned to look outside the door and almost ran right into the other paramedic rushing in. The two guys were different than the ones who had worked Claymont's scene.

The paramedic that had just come on the scene said, "Nothing to do for the boy. Allergic reaction, he's gone."

The paramedic working on Heather sat back on his heels and looked up at Mrs. Andrews. "I'm sorry, Ma'am, there's nothing more we can do for her."

There was a moment of complete silence and then the screams came. Lara Andrews was inconsolable as her friend, who was also crying loudly, tried to comfort her. The two women clung to each other as the paramedics went to the ambulance to get the gurney.

Sheriff Buchanon walked slowly down the drive toward the deputy's car. Another one was just pulling up behind. "Good," he thought. "It's Michael." He changed direction and met Deputy Clay as he was exiting his squad car.

"Sheriff," Deputy Clay tipped his hat. "What's the status here?"

"I'll be damned if I know, Michael. We've got little Heather Andrews dead in her kitchen and this boy, Hansen, over here I haven't looked at yet. He's one of Jeff's friends. Paramedic says it was an allergic reaction.

Looks like Stephens is getting statements from a couple of witnesses."

"Wish I knew what was happening around here," Michael responded. "Seems to me the whole town's goin' ta hell." He looked from the Andrews' house back over to where Hansen lay on the ground.

Sheriff Buchanon felt the same way. As Deputy Clay went to the Andrews' house to get the information, Sheriff Buchanon looked around. He was searching for Eli, Hunter or Bug. He saw no signs of any of them, so he went back to his car and called dispatch.

Rachel's voice crackled to life. "What can I do for you, Sheriff?"

"Rachel, have there been any more calls today? Has anyone else been sick, needing an ambulance?"

"No, Sheriff. Missy Davis over on Plum Street caught a dishtowel on fire and panicked, but the Volunteer FD got her under control without much trouble. That was my only call today besides Meadowview."

"What about yesterday, anything out of the ordinary?" He was still looking for some kind of connection.

"No, Sir, nothing remarkable. Same stuff as usual." Rachel was beginning to get curious. "Is there something I should be on the lookout for, Don?"

He didn't want to start a panic. "No, Rach, not at all. I'm just trying to fit something together in my head is all. Let me know if you have anything else come in that involves more than one person, alright?"

"Yessir, over 'n out."

Deputy Clay was approaching his squad car, so he let the window down. "What'd you find out, Mike?"

"This sounds just like Mr. Jackson. The girl's fine until she goes down. Happened real fast, though not nearly as much blood as Claymont. No history of any problems, just came outta the blue." He looked over at the paramedics removing Hansen. The second ambulance had arrived by then and they had already assessed the situation. The two paramedics were struggling under Hansen's bulk to get him onto the gurney. "This one over here is clearly an allergic reaction. Maybe somethin' he ate, could even be somethin' growin' around here. No big mystery, though."

That made Don feel a little better, at least the two weren't related. Maybe there was some kind of virus going around. He would have to check with the doctors at Community. His theory of the kids having some weird chemical in that box didn't seem very realistic anymore. He would still talk to them but not today. Not with Eli losing his sister like that.

He gave Deputy Clay orders to wrap up the two investigations as quickly as possible. He would see him back at the station. He also wanted autopsy reports on his desk in the morning. Deputy Clay assured him that it was handled, and Sheriff Buchanon left Meadowview Acres.

The autopsy reports last Thursday hadn't shown any unusual signs. The cause of death for Heather had been listed as an aneurysm. Hansen's death had been classified as an acute allergic reaction to an unknown substance. The contents of his stomach were so vast and varied, it was all but impossible to differentiate the culprit. His parents had not wanted to prolong the investigation and were satisfied with the findings. It was obvious that his throat had closed, and that was the cause of his death.

Sheriff Buchanon had gone to both funerals and paid his respects to both families. He had seen Eli and Hunter briefly while at Heather's but was no longer interested in interviewing them. The box theory just didn't hold up under scrutiny. He believed it was just a very harrowing coincidence for the community of Hallston. It was jolting for such a quiet town to experience the deaths of three citizens.

He had heard from Bill Port that Shasta had been keeping the Jackson's company. They were still deeply grieving but dealing with their loss. He knew the community would rally around the other two families as well.

Monday had been quiet. Everyone seemed to be getting back to business as usual. A couple of petty thefts and a drunk behind the wheel on Saturday night had been the work of the weekend. With that having been cleaned up, Sheriff Buchanon had decided to leave work a little early and catch up on raking the leaves that had started to litter his front lawn. He didn't see the note asking him to call Mark Hamilton at the Hallston Daily Journal.

He said his goodbyes and headed for the cruiser. It was another bright, crisp fall day, but still not too cold. He loved the fall weather. He didn't even mind the winter. Hallston didn't get really cold through the winter, and, it never snowed, but some of the nights could get pretty chilly.

He stopped at Hardware on Main for some biodegradable lawn bags and a new pair of gloves. He had gotten a nasty cut last year when he had scooped up a mound of leaves only to be sliced by a rusty piece of discarded metal. He had ended up getting a tetanus shot and a couple of stitches.

He left the hardware store and started down Main toward home. Passing by the Gas N Go, he noticed Randy Garner from the mini mart squatting down beside someone who was leaning against a car. He pulled in at the last minute and swung around to park. He noticed, as he got out, that it was one of the teachers from the high school.

"Hey Randy, need some help?" He asked as he approached.

"Hi Sheriff. I think we're doing a little better now. Ms. Leezil had a little fainting spell."

The Sheriff looked at the woman on the ground and recognized her as Jeff's English teacher. *That's it, Ms. Leezil.*

"How're you feeling, Ms. Leezil?" He asked, noticing her pale complexion and the sweat on her brow. He had seen the same symptoms on someone else recently.

She sat up a little straighter and accepted the water bottle from Randy with a sweet smile. "I'm feeling better, Sheriff. I just don't know what happened. One second I was about to pump my gas, and the next I just couldn't keep my footing. I felt so hot, too. It was really unusual." She took another sip from the bottle.

The sheriff was remembering Bug Hamilton sitting on the fallen tree in the clearing. She looked exactly like that, damp hair clinging to her forehead, ghostly white and weak. "Have you been feeling this way all day?" He asked.

"Oh no, not at all. As a matter of fact, I felt great. I pulled into the station and got out. I said hello to a couple of students and then, boom, down I went! I must've looked like a rag doll. I'm sorry if I scared you, Randy. You were so nice to come out and help me." She started to get her feet under her, and Randy steadied her as she stood.

"No, Ms. Leezil. It was no bother at all. I'm just glad you're alright." Randy glanced back to the mini mart. Another car had just pulled up. "I'm sorry, but I've got to get back in there. No one's manning the cash register."

"I'll take it from here", Sheriff Buchanon said, taking her arm.

"Thanks again, Randy!" Julie Leezil called after him. "You're my hero!"

Randy turned back and smiled. Sheriff Buchanon could see the man blushing.

He took hold of Julie's elbow and guided her around to the driver's side door so she could sit down for a minute. She was feeling better, but he thought she would need to rest a bit before driving.

"You said that you said hello to some students?" He had a weird feeling that he knew what she was going to say.

"Yes, Eli and Hunter were gassing up when I pulled in. They were in such a hurry, though. You should have seen them take off. Anyway, that's when my little episode happened. I think I was falling right as they were driving away." She dabbed at her forehead with a paper napkin she had retrieved from her glove box.

That was exactly who Don thought she would name. "Do you remember smelling anything unusual, or maybe seeing anything?" He wanted her to say that she had seen a metal box and that there was a sickening smell coming from it but no such luck.

"No, not a thing. They weren't even here long enough for me to notice anything. They left right when I got out of my car." She dabbed her forehead again and looked up at him with that sweet smile of hers. "I hate to be a damsel in distress, Sheriff, but would you mind? I didn't pump my gas, yet."

He looked at her and realized that she was asking him to do it for her. "Oh, sure, no problem. You just sit there." He took the card from her and stuck it into the machine at the pump. It accepted the card and told him to select the type and begin pumping.

His mind wandered as he filled Ms. Leezil's car with gas. What in the world could those boys have to do with all of this? He had been ready to chalk it up to coincidence, but this was getting to be a little too much. The pump kicked off, and he replaced the cap.

She looked much better now, so he felt comfortable letting her drive. "Are you going straight home?" He asked.

"Yes. No more stops for me. And thank you, Sheriff Buchanon. You've been such a sweetheart today." She smiled and closed her door. As he watched her drive away, Sheriff Buchanon tried to remember the last time he had been called a sweetheart.

He looked at his dashboard clock when he got back into his cruiser. School was out for the day. "I think it's time I sat down and had a little talk with Mr. Andrews and Mr. Massey," he thought to himself.

He pulled out onto Main Street and made his way toward Meadowview Acres.

CHAPTER 28

Eli, Hunter & Mr. Just

"That's the last one," Eli said as they watched the white pickup exit the student parking area. He started the engine and slowly drove down to the now vacant lot. He parked in the fourth row just in case another student were to return to school for some reason.

"Okay, here we go. Are you good with the plan?" Eli was more focused now. They had talked the last half an hour about how to go about getting the relic into the lab without coming into contact with anyone, even Mr. Just.

Hunter was still exhausted. His body was betraying him at a crucial moment. He looked at Eli and said, "I'm ready. I know my part. I stay here with the suitcase while you go in and talk to Mr. Just. When you text me to bring it in, I wait until I see Mr. Just come out of the building and then bring it in."

"Right," said Eli. "Hopefully, he'll have told me what to try, and we can get started right when you come in."

Eli noticed that Hunter was looking pretty bad. He had known that his friend had been acting like he wasn't worried for Eli's sake, and now he was just too tired to continue the farce. Eli felt guilt rise up in him again. He was responsible for getting Hunter involved, too.

"I'm going in. Take it easy and I'll text you soon."

Eli got out of the car and went into the school straight to Mr. Just's classroom. It was empty except for the teacher behind his computer screen. He obviously heard Eli come in because he said, "Just hang tight a sec. I need to finish reading this."

Eli propped himself against the main lab table and waited. He noticed that there were still beakers of chemicals that had been left on the table from experiments earlier that day. He read the labels – alcohol, boron, potassium chlorate, picric acid and a few other beakers with substances that had no labels. There were safety glasses lying around haphazardly along with rolls of paper towels and notebooks. Eli had never seen Mr. Just's table so messy before. All of the lab tables were positioned at the back of the room, behind the classroom desks. Mr. Just had the biggest lab table at the front of the others. Eli guessed that he hadn't had time to clean it up before getting started at the computer.

Mr. Just finished reading and looked up. Sitting back in his chair, he gave Eli a level look and said, "I believe you." He got up and crossed the room to where Eli stood. "When you two left here earlier, I was a little concerned about your frame of mind. I thought that maybe losing your sister and coming back to school so soon after was making you a little freaked. But when I read the name on the paper that Hunter gave me, I started to wonder. You see, I had read the name of that professor before, as early as this morning."

Eli was confused. "You know about Monroe?"

"No, not exactly, but, I know more now. This morning I read his name in the Hallston Daily Journal, in the obituaries. Eli, he died yesterday afternoon." He reached out and steadied the boy. Eli had wobbled a little after hearing the news.

"He's dead, but, how? Just yesterday morning he talked with the girls. How could he be dead?" Eli was feeling light-headed.

"What girls? Who talked to Professor Monroe?" Mr. Just asked.

Eli sat down in one of the lab chairs and said, "Shasta Port and Bug. Bug Hamilton, she's the daughter of the editor of the paper. They're in on it, too. They were trying to help, so they found the Professor and went to talk to him yesterday. Shasta said that they left around lunch time."

"Well, they must've been the last people this dude talked to. The paper says he died yesterday afternoon of natural causes. It also mentioned that he was a blind man. I'm assuming that wasn't the case before he started researching this rock?" Mr. Just walked back to his printer and picked up a few papers. "According to this, he quit his job to go to a remote island to research the Varuupian Curse." He handed the papers to Eli.

"Now, listen. I'm a scientist. I usually don't go in for all that mumbo-jumbo crap, but this curse is well documented. There was another crew that went in before Monroe and lost like half of their people. And read that last page. That was an interview with some native of Shaali who, lucky for him, left the island before the chief's burial. According to him, curses were commonplace."

Eli glanced at the papers then put them down on the table beside the beakers. "Look, Mr. Just," he said. "I don't need to read these. I've seen firsthand what the Rock of Varuupi is capable of. It's nothing to take lightly. That's why you can't be here when we try to dissolve it. We just don't know how it'll affect you. Just tell me what to do and then go out to your car. We'll have you on speaker phone the whole time. That way, we know you're safe."

Mr. Just looked at Eli like he was crazy. "No way, Man! There is no way I'm leaving. Now look, I'm not a fool, I know it could get dicey, but I'm not leaving you kids to do it yourselves. We're going to be working with hydrofluoric acid; I'm not letting you do that unsupervised." He saw Eli's expression and understood what he was feeling.

"Eli, I saw Hansen die, remember? I didn't know it at the time, but he was holding the rock. I was standing right next to it when I tried to give him the Heimlich. It didn't make me sick. It didn't seem to affect Clara, either. You may not have realized that I was there that day with everything else going on, but Eli, I've already been exposed."

He was right. Eli hadn't remembered or connected the fact, but he thought Hunter should have. Hunter was as exhausted as Eli, though, and, things had been getting overlooked lately. Anyway, the revelation solved the problem. Eli was more relieved than he wanted to admit.

"That does make sense," he told Mr. Just. "If you have already been in contact with it and you don't remember having any symptoms, I guess it should be alright. Are you sure that you didn't feel anything that day?"

"Not a twinge, and I'm sure that'll be the case today, too. Now let's get going and get this over with. Where is it?" He glanced around the room.

"In my trunk, Hunter's going to bring it in. Just let me text him."

While Eli composed and sent the text to Hunter, Mr. Just slid most of the clutter to one side of the lab table. Next, he got out a heavy plastic tray, a hammer and a chisel. Finally, he went to the locked cabinet where all of the chemicals were stored and brought back a small plastic jug filled with clear liquid. He placed it on the table beside the other things.

"Hunter's coming in with it now," Eli said as he walked over to Mr. Just and looked over the materials. "Do you really think this will work?"

"It's a great place to start," Mr. Just replied. "Hydrofluoric acid is highly corrosive, it can dissolve glass with no problem. That's why it's stored in heavy plastic. It's actually quite coincidental that we need to use this. If you had been awake in class today, you would have heard me explaining oxides. An oxide is a compound that contains at least one oxygen atom along with another element in its chemical formula. Most of the earth's crust consists of solid oxides, the result of elements being oxidized by the oxygen in air or water. This rock is an oxide; hydrofluoric acid dissolves oxides."

Eli was about to ask Mr. Just another question, when Hunter appeared at the classroom door, the suitcase on wheels trailed behind him. "Are you sure it's okay for him to be here?" Hunter asked nodding his head at the teacher.

"He's already been exposed and didn't seem to be affected. When Hansen died, remember? I do think that we should watch him really closely while we're taking it out, just to make sure," Eli answered.

"Hey, Dudes," Mr. Just interjected. "I'm here. You don't have to talk about me like I'm not. And I'm fine. Look." He walked over to Hunter and took the handle of the suitcase from him. He rolled it over to his desk, then picked it up and laid it on the top. To demonstrate even further, he unzipped the large suitcase and took out the smaller one nestled inside.

The familiar feeling in Hunter's stomach started again. The bile rose in his throat, and he was clammy. He looked at Eli and could tell that his friend was getting another headache, although he wasn't sure if Eli's headaches ever truly went away. Looking at his teacher, Hunter could see no affects whatsoever. Mr. Just got down to the backpack and stopped.

"Are you guys alright? Do you want me to stop?" He asked looking at the pain registered on their faces.

"No," Eli said forcefully. "This has to happen. I'm fine." He looked over at Hunter.

"I'm sorry," Hunter said. With that, he grabbed the nearest trash can and went to the front of the classroom, as far away from them as he could get. There he commenced to reacquaint himself with the lunch he had eaten a few hours previously.

"Tell me if you want me to stop," Mr. Just told Eli. "Otherwise, I'm just going to keep truckin'."

He saw Eli nod his head and returned to the backpack. He unzipped it and pulled the metal box from within. He still felt nothing. He hadn't told the boys, but, when he had touched the handle of the suitcase, he had felt a jolt, like the earth shifting just a little. It didn't hurt, it was just an odd feeling. It reminded him of that last little bump that an elevator makes right before the doors open. Right now, though, he felt nothing. He could hear Hunter at the front of the room still retching.

He took the metal box from his desk over to the lab table. Phillip placed the metal box carefully beside the large plastic bin. Then, he opened the box. As he inspected the artifact with his eyes, he surveyed his body for any discomfort. *Nothing, continue.*

He put on his gloves and reached into the box. It looked like a piece of ordinary rock that had been broken off of a bigger one. Its shape was not quite a triangle but looked like it had been part of a corner. It was much larger than he had expected, about six inches at its widest point and around two at its tip. Phillip picked it up and brought it to his face for a closer examination. There were no markings on the rock at all. Nothing remarkable could be seen by the naked eye. He placed it in the bin.

"Mr. Just?"

The sound of Eli's voice startled Phillip. He was so intrigued with his experiment that he had almost entirely forgotten about the boy. "What is it?"

"Are you feeling alright?" Eli asked.

"So far, I'm cool." Something in the way Eli was looking at him made him ask, "Why?"

Eli pointed to the sink in the corner of the classroom. There was a mirror attached to the wall above. "I think you should go look." The boy's eyes were a little wider than normal causing Phillip's stomach to do a little flip. As he walked over to the mirror, he could still hear dry heaving at the other end of the room. Then he heard Hunter say, "Whoa!"

More curious than afraid, he got to the mirror and peered at his reflection. His mouth became an "O" as he stared. He still wore his hair in a long pony tail down his back. That was about the only thing he had saved from the seventies. But while just a few moments ago it was mostly dark brown with a few gray strands running through, now, it was completely white. *What the hell?*

He reached up and shook it loose from the elastic band. He ran his fingers through it from scalp to ends. Every strand of his hair was white, through and through. It was amazing. He couldn't seem to look away until he heard Eli again. He sounded defeated.

"You're not untouchable. We don't know what else it's doing to you. We can't see what's going on inside of you. I think we should stop now. Or you should. Hunter and I'll finish."

Phillip Just turned from the mirror and walked quickly back to the lab desk. "No way, Kiddo, I'm in this now. We're moving full steam ahead. Go get those safety goggles and put them on." He motioned to Eli and then got his own goggles fixed in place.

Reaching for the hydrofluoric acid he said, "I don't have enough for the whole artifact. I wasn't sure of its size, but looking at it now I know I don't have enough. The good news is, once we test this out to see if it works, I'll be able to get more and we can finish the job. For now, I need to break off a little chunk to see how gnarly this will get."

Eli watched as his teacher got the chisel and placed it on the very edge of the pointiest end of the rock. Then, he took his hammer and hit the end of the chisel. What happened next surprised them all.

The second the chisel's sharp end went into the rock, a huge spark flew from the crevasse that was created. The spark jolted them both. Mr. Just jumped back and lost his footing, causing him to fall. On the way down, the back of his head connected with the desk directly behind him with a loud "CRACK!" He slumped to the floor unconscious.

Eli involuntarily jumped at the sight of the huge spark. His elbow hit the stand of beakers to his left causing their contents to spill. Reaching out like long fingers over the top of the lab desk, the chemicals soaked through the paper towels and notebook papers that had been strewn about. Eli looked quickly back at the rock and saw that a flame was now issuing from the crack. The last thing Eli remembered seeing was a spark from the rock igniting the wet desk.

Hunter was on his feet in an instant. He had been watching their progress as he held the trash can to his chest. He saw Mr. Just raise the hammer and bring it swiftly down. Then, unexpectedly, Mr. Just startled and fell. He heard a loud crack! Hunter could see the rock. A flash of fire was emitting from the rock itself. He saw

Eli's shocked face looking down at the table, then Eli slowly closed his eyes and collapsed. Hunter watched in horror as the entire lab table burst into flames.

Panic spurred him into action. His adrenaline masked the nausea enough that he dropped the trash can and started toward the back of the room. The smoke was getting thicker by the instant. It was happening too fast, he had to get to Eli and Mr. Just. "Eli!" He yelled. "Mr. Just? Eli?" There was no answer.

He dropped to all fours to get out of the thickest part of the smoke. He could smell the acrid odor of chemicals burning which made it hard to breathe. He made his way on his hands and knees slowly. The smoke was thicker still. He could see a flame up ahead. He knew he had to get Eli and Mr. Just out of there somehow, but he couldn't see anything. He was coughing, and tears clouded his vision. He bumped into something on the floor in front of him. Grabbing it, he recognized the backpack. *The rock!* He had to get the rock out too.

He knew he was close when he found the pack. He remembered Mr. Just had put it on the desk behind him when he had taken the box out. Hunter reached into the smoke before him, stretching out his arms as far as they would go. He felt something. It was one of the lab table's legs. He pulled himself up and coughed uncontrollably. The odor was so intense up there. He could barely make out the rock from around the smoke. Being careful not to touch anything else, he opened the back-pack and scooped the rock inside. He immediately felt the heat coming from inside the pack.

Hunter dropped back down to his knees and felt around. There was nothing. He crawled slowly for-ward, still feeling the ground in front of him. It was so hard to breathe, he was getting lightheaded, but still he pushed onward. His left arm grazed something, and Hunter reached out with his hand – a shoe. "Eli!" He sputtered. His voice sounded odd and somehow far away. Eli didn't answer.

Hunter crawled forward, feeling first the shoe, then a leg. He made it to Eli's shoulder and tried to shake him. "Eli, wake up! We have to get out of here!"

There was no response from his friend. Hunter could barely breathe. He was beginning to feel dizzy and dis-oriented, when out of the smoke came a voice.

CHAPTER 29

Darren

Darren couldn't stop thinking about the Rock of Varuupi and the legend of the curse. He just couldn't get his mind around it. He was trying to make himself believe that the curse had killed his father. Even after Shasta had left the night before, the possibility wouldn't leave his mind. He had stayed up late into the night reading anything he could find online about the curse and the people of the Varuupian tribe. He had gotten very little sleep.

All day at school he had been in a fog. He had seen Eli and Hunter in the cafeteria at lunch and had wanted to talk to them, but he didn't know what he wanted to say or ask.

Shasta had told him about the plan to take the rock to Mr. Just after school to see if it could be destroyed.

For some reason that didn't sit well with Darren. It seemed very risky. If something were that powerful, powerful enough to harm people without even touching it, what could it do to someone trying to destroy it? The idea bothered him. From what he had learned online last night, in ancient times with some tribes, if a curse did take hold, it was too powerful to be destroyed without some sort of ceremony or counter curse. Darren didn't think Mr. Just had any knowledge of counter curses.

Shasta had to work at the Hot Dog Hut after school, so Darren went home to check on his mother. It seemed that she was coming to grips with the idea that her husband's death was more supernatural than medical. For some reason she had an easier time accepting that.

Darren got a snack and watched television. Even while watching the sports network, he couldn't help thinking of Eli and Hunter at the school with Mr. Just. He tried to push it out of his mind, but it kept creeping in. He wondered what was happening, and if Sheriff Buchanon knew about the rock yet.

Finally, he couldn't stand it any longer. He texted Shasta, "Going to check on things at school, call you later." He told his mother that he was going to the school, and he'd be back soon. She just smiled and nodded her head.

On the drive over, his mind came up with different scenarios – some good, some not so good. When he pulled into the parking lot and saw Eli's car, he felt a little twinge in his stomach. Darren had a bad feeling about this. He parked next to the Flaming Tomato and got out.

He smelled the smoke before he saw it. There it was, coming out of the windows of the science lab. The plumes were thick and white. Completely forgetting to call 911, he sprinted to the closest doors. Yanking them open, he was engulfed in smoke. He couldn't see his hand in front of his face. There was a chemical smell to the smoke that burned his nostrils. Darren took off his tee shirt and wrapped it around his nose and mouth.

He dropped to his hands and knees along the right side of the corridor. The smoke was thinner down there; he could see a few feet ahead.

Darren knew the science lab was the third classroom on the right. If he crawled along the wall, he could count the doorways and know where he was. He started forward as quickly as possible, not knowing how long Hunter and Eli had already been inside.

His right hand came upon the first doorway quickly. Passing it, he tried to keep his eyes closed and feel his way. He would need as much eyesight as he could get when he found the lab. The second door was not much farther up. He passed it and went quickly on. The hard floor was tough on his knees, but the smoke was worse. Even with the cotton shirt filtering the worst of it, Darren was finding it hard to breathe.

Finally, his hand found the entry to the third classroom. For a second he questioned himself. Was the lab the third room or the fourth one down? He was beginning to get a little lightheaded when he heard a voice from inside the room. "Eli! Wake up!" It was Hunter. Darren heard coughing.

"Hunter!" Darren yelled through the entrance. "It's Darren, can you hear me?" He broke off then as his throat constricted causing him to cough roughly.

Darren listened through the sounds of wood and paper crackling in the fire. There were loud pops now and then as something combustible in the lab exploded.

Then Hunter's voice came out of the smoke, "Darren? Yeah, I hear you," followed by more coughing spasms. Hunter sounded weak.

Darren shouted, "Can you crawl toward my voice?" It was so hard to communicate over the sounds of the fire. His throat felt raw.

"Yeah, I mean no! Eli's passed out! I can't drag him! Get help!" He stopped talking and coughed strongly.

"There's no time," Darren yelled. "Guide me to you!"

Darren started crawling once again as he recalled the layout of the room. The school desks were in the front of the room. Behind those, in the middle of the room, was Mr. Just's main lab table with the rest of the lab tables in the back. His hand touched the first desk. He tried to open his eyes, but the smoke in there was worse. It was so dense Darren couldn't make out shapes or light anywhere.

He heard Hunter's voice coming from the smoke. "Here, this way!" Hunter guided him toward the back of the classroom.

Darren counted the desks as he progressed toward Hunter's voice. *Two, three, four.* He prayed they could find their way out of the room.

"This way!" Hunter yelled again, and by the sound of his voice, Darren could tell that he was very close.

"I'm close, almost there! Hold out your arm!" Darren coughed. *Seven, eight, there!* He felt Hunter's hand hit him in the head.

"I'm here, Hunter!" He reached out and found Hunter's arm. Grabbing it, he yelled, "Where's Eli?"

"I'm holding on to him," Hunter sputtered. "Mr. Just is here, too, but I can't find him."

Darren wasted no time. "Pull Eli over to me, give me his hand!" Darren's breath was coming harder now. He reached into the emptiness of the smoke and felt nothing. After a moment, he felt Hunter's arm again. Hunter passed him another hand; this one was cold and dry. Grabbing it, Darren turned himself around and yelled to Hunter, "Follow me! Keep track of the desks. We'll pass eight of them." He broke off coughing and felt a tightening in his chest. He took a quick moment to recover then yelled back to Hunter, "Eight desks then the doorway! Stay to the left, three doorways down! Let's go!"

Pulling Eli's limp body behind, Darren started to crawl.

———————

Shasta didn't like the text from Darren. She didn't want Darren anywhere near that lab. Who knows what the rock would do to him? It had killed his father with the curse.

Shasta took her apron off and handed it to her mother. "I'm sorry, Mom, I have to go. Darren needs me."

Her mother looked surprised that she was leaving so quickly. "Is everything okay, Honey?"

"I'm sure it will be. I just need to go. I'll call you in a little while." She ran out the door of the Hut and hopped into her Ranger.

It took her no time at all to get to the school. She saw Darren's car parked next to Eli's and pulled up beside them. Her stomach rolled over as she noticed smoke billowing out of the door that had been propped open. She grabbed her bag and pulled out her phone.

Rachel answered on the first ring. "911, what's your emergency?"

Shasta's trembling voice answered, "There's a fire at the high school! It's coming from the science lab! The entrance by the student parking lot is the closest! Hurry!" She punched "end" on her phone, not waiting for any questions.

She jumped out of her car and ran to the entrance. The smoke had an awful smell to it. It was so thick. Shasta yelled, "Darren! Darren!" She listened for a response and heard none. She made up her mind then. She knew that help was on the way, but it could be too late already. She took the Hot Dog Hut bandana from around her neck and secured it over her mouth. Taking a deep breath, she plunged into the entrance.

She knew the science lab was one of the first few classrooms on the right. She would just crawl in that direction and call for Darren on the way. Dropping to all fours, she started out.

The first doorway was there in no time. She was sure this one wasn't it, so she kept going. At the second doorway, she tried to peer in through the smoke. "Darren!" She coughed out. "Darren, are you in there?"

She heard his voice, but couldn't make out what he was saying. "I'm coming in!" She called and started to make her way forward. She could feel more heat now. It was getting a lot harder to breathe.

Once inside the room, she couldn't figure out which way to go. She called out for Darren again and listened. She felt like she could hear him, but he sounded so far away. Shasta tried to yell again, but the smoke was restricting her throat. She moved in the direction she thought the voice was coming from. She had gone only a few feet when she felt very disoriented.

"Darren!" She tried to yell, but her voice was only a whisper. She heard Darren say, "Follow me," but she couldn't get a sense of where he was. She was getting really tired now. She crawled slowly on.

"Follow me!" Darren called back to Hunter. He was worried that he would be able to drag Eli out but lose Hunter on the way. "Two more doorways on the left and then we're out!" He heard a faint cough and thought it was Hunter, but it seemed like it was coming from beside him, not behind. Maybe Hunter was closer than he thought. Darren couldn't see anything of his surroundings. He was still dragging Eli with his right hand and hopping forward while feeling his way with his left. Passing the second doorway, he thought he heard something.

It was sirens. Someone must have called to report the fire. Hope spurred him on. "Come on, Hunter. We're almost there now, push on buddy, push!"

The sirens were getting louder. Darren could tell that they were in the student parking lot just a few yards away. He felt the first classroom doorway on his left and pushed himself to the exit. Just as he made it to the door, it swung open revealing a yellow and red clad member of the Hallston Fire Department. The man looked down at him and yelled, "Got survivors," to his counterparts who came running.

Strong hands grabbed him and carried him out of the school to a safe spot away from the smoke. He was coughing heartily now. He noticed Hunter being carried out and Eli as well. "Thank God." He thought. Then he remembered Mr. Just. Grabbing the sleeve of the firefighter closest to him he said urgently, "There's a teacher in the third classroom to the right along the hallway! He's in the middle of the classroom!" He broke off coughing.

The firefighter ran to relay the information to the others. Darren looked over to where Hunter lay. He was lying on the ground fighting for breath. A firefighter was giving him oxygen. Darren looked at Eli. Paramedics were giving him CPR. Suddenly, Darren felt a plastic cup attach to his mouth and a rush of sweet, pure oxygen. He laid back and closed his eyes.

A few minutes later, one of the firefighters came to him and asked, "Do you know the girl who called 911? Is she here somewhere?"

Darren didn't know who he was talking about. He had assumed it had been a passerby or a staff member who was still in the building. "No," he replied. "I don't know who it was."

The firefighter then said, "Well, we have you three out and we've located the teacher now. They're getting him out. So the three cars in the lot belong to you three?" He nodded towards Eli and Hunter.

Darren thought, "Three cars – no, just mine and Eli's." He craned his neck around the fire truck and saw the third. *No!* A girl called 911! *Shasta!* At once, Darren remembered the faint cough coming from the second classroom doorway. He had thought it was Hunter.

Darren was on his feet in a flash. Running toward the entrance of the school he yelled, "She's in there! In the second classroom! Hurry! Hurry!"

A fireman grabbed him around the waist as he tried to reenter to school. "Hang on there, Son. Who's left in there?"

Darren was breathless. "Shasta! Shasta Port! The second door on the right!" He slumped back to the ground in a coughing fit.

He watched the man relay the information to the team still inside the school. There were tears in his eyes. His heart was pounding out of his chest.

Hunter was at his side then, asking what was happening. "Shasta's in there," Darren said.

"Shasta? Where did she come from?" He asked through his coughs.

"I don't know. I didn't know she was here." He put his head in his hands and tried to breathe.

Hunter was still using the oxygen mask, but he pulled it away to say, "Don't worry, Darren. They'll get her out. They'll get her out the way you got Eli. He woke up, and he's going to be fine. You'll see. They'll bring her out any minute."

The next time the firefighters came out, it was with Mr. Just. The boys watched as they took the teacher over, put him on a gurney and loaded him into the ambulance. The emergency siren and lights roared to life as the vehicle sped away to Community Hospital.

Another ambulance sped into the parking lot and parked close to the entrance. They had obviously been called and given some information. One of the paramedics got out and opened the back to retrieve the gurney. Just as he finished, two men carried Shasta from the school and placed her immediately on the gurney. The paramedic jumped in the back with her and closed the door. The lights came on and it was speeding away before Darren even knew it was happening.

"Shasta!" He jumped to his feet and tried to run after the ambulance. The same, kind firefighter that had stopped him before stopped him this time. "Come on, Son. You need to get checked out at the hospital anyway. You can see her there." He led Darren over to a deputy's cruiser and asked that he be taken to Community. Darren got into the car and prayed.

As he was riding out of the parking lot, he noticed Hunter putting the backpack into the trunk of Eli's car. It occurred to him only then that he hadn't been affected by the rock at all. He was well within its range the whole time he had been guiding Hunter out of the school.

Fury built up inside of Darren as he thought of the curse, the rock. It had killed his father, now had it killed Shasta?

BOOK FOUR

CHAPTER 30

Bug & Mr. Hamilton

Everything was out of whack for Bug. Hearing about Professor Monroe had made her feel strange. She remembered the frail, white-haired man that she and Shasta had spent time with only yesterday morning. She could still see his peculiar stare. He was weak, yes, but Bug didn't get the sense yesterday that he had been close to dying. Yet, he had; a mere hour or two after they had left – he had passed away.

Bug felt weird about his death. She was not a big fan of the man who had set this curse upon them over forty years ago, but she felt empathy. He had lived all of those years knowing that the Rock Of Varuupi could be discovered. Bug thought he must have been constantly afraid of that possibility, and now the possibility had been realized. She wondered if the knowledge that more people had died because of him was what ultimately had killed him. Bug was having trouble reconciling her anger with her pity for the man.

"Finish eating, Hon. We'll leave right when you're through," Mr. Hamilton said to his daughter sitting across from him at the kitchen table.

It was Monday morning and Bug's father had told her that he needed her to come to the office with him that day. She would miss a day of school, but this was more important. They had talked it over last night after he had broken the news to her about Professor Monroe. The plan was to do more research on the curse. More specifically, counter curses, breaking curses or anything else that they could find out about the rock.

Bug shoveled in the rest of her Wheat Squares and drank the cereal flavored milk from the bowl. Wiping her mouth with her sleeve, she said, "I'm ready. Just let me grab my bag." She jumped from the table and ran to her room.

Mrs. Hamilton had already left for the hospital. She was on the early shift that morning. Mark had woken her up the night before and told her everything. There were no secrets in the Hamilton household, and this was a biggie. Ann had taken the news well enough. Even as crazy a story as it was, she hadn't questioned her husband. After almost twenty years of marriage, she knew that Mark was serious and reliable. Ann had been extremely worried about Bug, but Mark had reassured her that Bug would stay by his side until the mess was over. He had also asked her to keep her ears open at the hospital. If there were any other emergencies or unexplained deaths in town, he needed to know ASAP.

Bug was back in no time. The two hopped into Mark's car and headed toward the offices of the Hallston Daily Journal.

"Are we still going to try to get Professor Monroe's books?" Bug asked as they drove.

"I think that would be a good start. I plan to call his home when we get to the office. I'm thinking I can say that we want to do an article about him for the paper. Hopefully, whoever's in charge of the estate will be flattered and cooperate. You said the only person you saw in the home was a nurse?" He took a right onto Main and headed east.

"Yep," Bug replied. "She was very friendly, but her voice was super low, like a man almost. She was super nice to the professor, too."

"Well, maybe she would be someone to interview about this. After caring for him for so long, she may know more than she thinks."

They pulled into the parking lot and Mr. Hamilton parked in the space designated "Editor-In-Chief".

There were lots of people around, Bug noticed. When she and Shasta had been there it had been the weekend and only a few people were working. Today, however, the place was busy. People were running from one office to another, some were going up the stairs while others were in line for the elevator. Bug's dad said hello to the lady at the desk as they made their way over to the stairs.

On the second floor, Mr. Hamilton told Bug to wait in his office while he spoke to his assistant. Bug selected the huge, brown leather chair opposite her dad's desk and sat down. She was running things over in her mind trying to solve the puzzle that had so quickly become the center of her world. *Knowledge is Power.* She needed more power.

Bug felt so small. Her petite frame had never really bothered her before, but the events of late had left her feeling vulnerable. *Knowledge is Power.* Willing an idea to spring forth, she said it over and over again in her mind. She took herself back to Professor Monroe's house. She remembered reading some of the titles on the bookshelves, *Ancient Tribes, Tribes FromThe South Pacific, Legends of Dark Magic* and, the one that had bothered her, *Quiet Death.* She wondered if any of those books would hold an answer. She didn't remember seeing any titles of counter curses or destroying cursed relics. That would have been too easy, she guessed.

She then remembered a book that had been on the table in front of the sofa where she and Shasta had been sitting. It had looked just as tattered as the book the professor had given to Shasta. "What was the name of that one?" She thought. "Oh! That's it! *Curses of Ancient Tribes.* Super!" She thought that was a great place to start her research today.

Mr. Hamilton came back in just as Bug had remembered the title of Professor Monroe's book. "Dad, I remembered something that may help! There was a book in the professor's house, *Curses of Ancient Tribes.* We should look it up!"

Mr. Hamilton scribbled the title of the book on a scrap piece of paper and said, "Good, Bug. Let me know anything else you remember. Right now, let's try to call his home and see where that takes us."

He had a number on a post-it note that he had carried into the room. He had his assistant look it up for him while Bug was waiting. He sat behind his desk and pulled the telephone closer to him.

Mr. Hamilton punched the "speaker" button and Bug immediately heard the dial tone. They both remained quiet as he punched in the phone number to the house in Shale. One ring sounded then two rings. On the third a voice answered, "Hello?" The voice on the other end of the line was very deep, yet pleasant.

Bug looked at her dad and mouthed the word "nurse" to him.

Mr. Hamilton was very professional in his manner, "Hello. My name is Mark Hamilton. I'm the Editor-in-Chief at the Hallston Daily Journal. I'm calling today first, to convey my sympathies to the loved ones of Professor Monroe, and, secondly, I'd like to speak with someone about the possibility of running an article about the professor in my paper. His achievements were so impressive and his tenure at the State College in Chester was also quite notable. Who could I speak with about this possibility?"

They waited. There was silence from the other end of the phone. Mr. Hamilton was about to speak again when an audible sniffle came through.

"I'm sorry," the voice replied. "I'm still coming to terms with his passing. This is his wife, Truly Monroe."

Bug looked at her father. Her eyes were wide. The nurse was his wife? She hadn't guessed that one. There had been nothing between the two of them yesterday that would have given it away.

Mr. Hamilton said quickly, "Oh, I'm terribly sorry, Mrs. Monroe. I realize that it only just happened yesterday. We were just hoping to do a bit more than an obituary considering his contribution to the community."

"Yes," the voice responded. "That would be nice. Preston was always working on something. The college was always asking him for his input on one project or another. He would never ask for it, but I would appreciate the recognition."

"That's wonderful," Mr. Hamilton said. "You know, Mrs. Monroe, I'm sure that the college is planning a remembrance as well, so I'd like to focus more on his books. Do you have any copies that I could borrow? Of the three, two are out of print."

Again the line was silent. The friendly voice that had started the conversation had turned into one of cautiousness. "Why do you need the books? Can't you just say that he wrote them?"

"Yes," Mark said, afraid that he was about to lose her. "We could just mention the titles, but I was hoping to go into more depth. I wanted to convey the passion and dedication that Professor Monroe had in his research. I've never been able to read his books and was hoping that by reading them, I would have a better understanding of his area of expertise."

They waited for a response. Bug looked at her dad and mouthed "she knows". Mark nodded his head in agreement.

"I'm sorry, Mr. Hamilton. I'm afraid that's impossible. We don't have any copies of Preston's books. They were out of print at least thirty years ago. If you'd like to write an article about my husband, please do so, but you'll have to get your information elsewhere. Thank you for calling." With that, the line was dead.

Mark punched the speaker button again to disconnect the line. "Well that didn't go well. I guess it's you and me, Kiddo." He winked at Bug and then said, "But I'm calling the sheriff on this, too. He needs to have all of this information."

He picked up the phone again and dialed the Sheriff's Department. Asking for the sheriff, he was told that Sheriff Buchanon was busy with a case and asked if the sheriff could return his call. Mark left his name and a request for the sheriff to call back as soon as he was able.

"Time to get this party started," he said to Bug. He grabbed the scrap paper with the book title and held his other hand out to Bug. "Let's go!"

She smiled up at her father and took his hand. There was little that Bug loved more than focusing on a problem to solve. She only wished that this problem didn't have such dire circumstances. She wondered how Shasta and the boys were doing today at school. They must be nervous. It was still well before lunch time, and they would have a long day before talking to Mr. Just.

Stepping into the research room, Bug smelled the familiar newspapery smell again. *Yum.* She loved that smell. She said hello to Mrs. Shelbourne and went to her favorite computer desk by the window. That was the same computer she had used to find out about the professor. Now she was going to use it to solve the mess that he had created.

While her father spoke to Mrs. Shelbourne, Bug went to the search engine and typed in the title of the book from the professor's house. It popped up right away. She clicked on the site and found that it had no excerpts. It did, however, list places that the book could be purchased. She wrote down the address of a bookstore in Glovercroft. She hoped her dad could pick that up today.

Next, she searched breaking curses. Those results were less stellar. They ranged from information on a video game to a list of curses from a popular wizarding novel. It would take a while to go through them. She settled in and started to read.

———

By lunchtime, there were no real leads. Bug had finally narrowed down the search to exclude games, movies and fantasy. She was reading a page on voodoo when her father came over.

"Hey, Hon. I've got a couple of leads, but I have some work to do downstairs. I'm going to leave this in your very capable hands for a bit." He put a piece of paper on the desk that had two titles written. "Oh! Also, Jerry should be back soon with that book from Glovercroft. I'll have him bring it to you as soon as he's back."

Bug had told her father where to find a copy of *Curses of Ancient Tribes* in Glovercroft. He had sent a runner out for it that morning. Hopefully, something in there would be useful because Bug was not finding much online.

"That's fine, Dad. I brought my lunch and I'm fine right here. I do want to see that book, though. I'm not finding much here." She picked up the paper with the titles. "What are these?"

"Those are two books that were listed as references in Professor Monroe's syllabus for the class he taught at State. We might get lucky." He kissed her forehead and rushed away.

She looked at the titles he had written, *Curses: Fact or Fiction* and *A History of Affliction by Curse*. She typed the first title into the search engine and was pleasantly surprised. It came right up and had numerous excerpts. Reading through the excerpts was quite interesting but not helpful for her cause. She tried the next title. Not as many excerpts were available, but they were more informative than the first book. Bug was happy to see that a curse described in this book had been resolved by burning the object carrying it. Maybe Eli and Hunter would be successful after all, she hoped.

She kept reading and jotting down notes until she was interrupted by Jerry, her dad's runner. She thanked him as he handed the book off to her. It didn't look like the same book at all. This one was brand, spanking new. The spine wasn't even creased. This book looked nothing like the copy in Professor Monroe's home.

She decided to have some lunch while she read, so she moved from the computer table to the couches in the corner of the Research Room.

"Bug, Honey, you doin' okay?" It was Mrs. Shelbourne who worked in the room full time. She was responsible for re-shelving and re-filing all of the books, newspapers and CD's that the staff worked with every day. Bug had known her since she was about seven years old.

"Thanks, Mrs. Shelbourne. I'm fine, just going to break for lunch and read a little," Bug said as she settled into the comfy couch.

"You just let me know if you need something. I'll be around here someplace." She smiled at Bug and made her way to the back room with her arms full of CD's.

The spine of *Curses of Ancient Tribes* cracked when Bug opened it. It smelled like a new book, all crisp and clean. New books were Bug's favorites. A new book meant that she was going to learn something that she hadn't known before. She took a big bite out of her American cheese on wheat, no mayo, and started to read.

The book was very interesting. In the first chapter alone she learned that there were still many different tribes thought to use curses as part of daily life. Some were in the Amazon, others in little islands up and down South America. There were different beliefs and customs for almost every tribe. The range was amazing. Some tribes used animal blood; some used plants. There was no rhyme or reason to any of it. Everything was much too varied.

She scanned the Table of Contents looking for something to catch her eye. She needed to find the reason that Professor Monroe kept this book and used it so much.

A half an hour later, Mr. Hamilton came back. He found her curled up on the couch reading. Her half eaten sandwich was discarded beside her.

"Hey, Buggie. How're we doing?" He asked, sitting down beside her. "Have you made any headway?"

Bug looked up at him soberly and said, "Yep. It seems to me that the professor knew what he was doing after all. We have two choices. One is super risky and the other might not work."

CHAPTER 31

friends & Neighbors

Bug had just finished explaining the two choices for ridding themselves of the cursed rock when Mark's cell phone rang. It was his wife. He answered with a certain amount of anxiety, knowing that she only called from work when it was important.

"Hey, Honey. What's up?" He said, dreading her reply.

"Mark," she started, "two ambulances just got to the ER." Mark noticed the tremor in her voice and felt his stomach roll over. "One has Phillip Just, you know, the science teacher at Hallston High? And Mark, the other is Shasta. There was a fire at the high school. It looks bad, Honey."

Shasta, no! Mark then thought of Hunter and Eli seeking help from the teacher with the rock. "Are there any others?" He asked.

"No, not so far. You should probably send someone to the high school, though. I'm not hearing much information other than their medical conditions." She paused then, adding, "I don't think the teacher's going to make it." He could hear her holding back tears. "Shasta is critical. I'm so worried about her, Mark. I'm waiting here for Val and Bill. How's Bug? You have to break the news to her about Shas."

"She's fine." He looked at his daughter who was listening intently. "I'll tell her and we'll be right over. We'll see you soon, Honey. Call me back if you hear anything else." He ended the call and looked at Bug. She knew something was wrong. Her eyes were big and worried.

"What happened?" She asked in a small voice.

"Bug, Honey." Mark said as he took her tiny hands into his big ones. "There's been a fire at the high school. A teacher has been hurt."

She interrupted him then. "The science teacher, Mr. Just." She said it matter-of-factly, like she had been expecting to hear that news.

"Yes, but someone else was hurt." He paused, not knowing how to break it to her.

"Eli? Hunter? Who is it, Daddy?"

Bug hadn't called him Daddy in years. "Honey, it's Shasta. She was hurt in the fire, and she's in critical condition at the hospital."

Bug's mouth opened as she took in a little gasp of air. "Shas? What was she doing there? It was just supposed to be Hunter and Eli!"

"I don't know, Honey, but let's get to the hospital and see what we can find out." He nodded toward the book on the couch beside her. "Throw that in your bag. We're still going to need it." He put his arm around her as they left the Research Room. On the way down, they stopped on the second floor so he could tell his assistant to get a crew over to the high school as soon as possible. They needed to get all the information from the firefighters at the scene.

The hospital was crowded. Bill and Valerie Port had arrived and were standing with Ann. Eli and Hunter were there speaking with Deputy Clay. The boys were covered with soot and looked shaken. Sheriff Buchanon was talking to one of the paramedics. Darren was there, too. He was standing off to the side and looking down one of the hospital corridors. Mark guessed that that must be the direction they had taken Shasta.

Ann saw them arrive and came running over to Bug. She gathered the girl in her arms and held her tightly. "Bug, Shasta will be okay. The doctor said that she's regained consciousness and they're looking her over now. She'll be alright, Honey."

Bug didn't feel like crying. She just felt tired. There had been so many emotions rolling around in her lately.

She wasn't used to dealing with so many at once. She hugged her mother back and sighed.

Mark made his way over to the sheriff. He was just finishing his discussion with the paramedic who was walking away.

"Sheriff, I tried calling you earlier today. I have something incredibly important to talk to you about," Mark began.

"Hey, Mark. I'm sure you can understand I'm in the middle of this investigation right now. Can we talk later? Tomorrow, maybe? I may be tied up here a while." The sheriff was looking past Mr. Hamilton at the boys with the deputy.

"No, it can't wait. As a matter of fact, the information I have is directly related to what's going on here." He followed his gaze. "And if you're thinking that those boys have something to do with it, you're right. But it isn't their fault. It's simply a series of events that started innocently enough. It's going to take some doing for us to stop it, though."

By the time he finished speaking Mark had Sheriff Buchanon's attention. He was looking at Mark with a quizzical expression. "I'm listening." He motioned to a stand of chairs along the hallway. The men walked over and sat down.

———— ————

Eli's head was pounding as he answered the deputy's questions. Yes, they were with Mr. Just when the fire broke out. No, it was not intentional. Yes, they were working in the lab. No, the fire was not due to any negligence on the teacher's part.

The guilt weighing down both boys now was enormous. Mr. Just had been pronounced dead when they had arrived at the hospital ER. When they heard the news, Hunter had looked at Eli with a mixture of shock and grief. Eli's head had exploded with pain. He wasn't sure how he was going to survive this nightmare. It just kept getting worse, and now Shasta was hurt.

Eli looked over at Darren who was guarding the hallway down which they had taken Shasta. He had saved their lives. If it hadn't been for Darren, he and Hunter would be dead now as well. Eli didn't remember anything from the time that the lab table had ignited until he woke up on the grass outside of the school with an oxygen mask over his face. Hunter had filled him in. He had been so overcome with the smoke that he had lost his way in the room. He had found Eli but didn't know how to exit the classroom. Thankfully, Darren had shown up then.

The deputy finished with his questions and walked over to speak with Darren. Hunter turned to Eli and said, "Man, Shasta has to make it. I don't think I can handle one more person dying because of us. I feel so bad about Mr. Just. I can't imagine losing Shasta, too."

"I know. I'm freaking out, too. This is way too overwhelming. It's time to go to the sheriff, Hunter. We can't handle the situation ourselves anymore." Eli had tears in his eyes.

"You're right. We've tried everything we can. We need help."

Hunter looked over at the sheriff. He was talking to Bug's dad, but staring at him and Eli. Hunter felt uneasy and looked away. "I think he might know already," he said to Eli.

Eli followed his glance and saw the two men talking, the sheriff looking right at them. His guilt overwhelmed him. Eli walked over to another section of chairs and slumped into one. Just then, Lara Andrews and Gina and Hank Massey came rushing into the emergency room. They scanned it quickly then made a beeline for their sons.

———————

Darren was having a tough time with the deputy's questions. He was about to come unglued. His worry over Shasta's condition was making him crazy. She had regained consciousness, but she was still in pretty bad shape.

He finished quickly with Deputy Clay. Mainly, he needed to confirm everything that the deputy had already learned from Eli and Hunter. Darren was angry, but he wasn't sure why or at whom. He wasn't angry at Eli and Hunter. He understood that the guys were just trying to take care of the problem and it had gotten out of hand. From listening to Hunter, it sounded like the initial flame had come from the rock itself. So who was he mad at?

It wasn't Shasta. He was sure that she had gone into the school looking for him. He would have done the same. He wondered if he was mad at himself, but didn't think that was it either.

Darren saw the doctor walking back up the hallway and stood up straight. The Port's made their way over to hear the news of Shasta's condition.

"Well," the doctor began, "she's awake and responding. We still have her on oxygen, of course, she continues to be short of breath. Her airways and lungs are irritated because of the chemicals in the smoke. I've found no burns on her body, which is lucky, considering where she was found. Her skin is tender, however, which is common in people who have suffered smoke inhalation. She'll be a little red for a while, but that will subside. I saw no damage of either cornea from the heat."

"Is she going to be alright?" Val Port asked the doctor. Her voice was shaking. Her husband put a protective arm around her while Ann held her hand.

"Our main concerns at the moment," he continued, "are her mental state. She's very confused which is also a normal side effect. Her breathing is also a problem. She's still having some bronchospasms and her nasal passages are swollen. The soot that has infiltrated will work its way out, but it will be a few days. She's nauseous at the moment, but that will subside, as well. I'd like to keep her here a couple of days and run some tests, but I'm expecting her to make a full recovery."

"Oh, thank God!" Ann Hamilton said as she hugged her friend.

"When can we see her?" The question came from Darren who had been listening quietly.

"Yes! Can we see her soon?" Val repeated the question.

"Let's give her some time to steady her breathing. She needs to concentrate on that right now instead of talking. I'll come get you when I think she's up for visitors." With that, the doctor nodded at the four concerned faces and strode back down the hallway.

Bill Port laid a big hand on Darren's shoulder. He knew how much the two kids cared about one another. The boy had just lost his father, and, now Shasta had been seriously injured. Bill couldn't imagine the pain that Darren was in.

"Why don't you go in to see her when the doc comes back? I think you'd do her a world of good. Val and I can wait a while," he said to Darren.

Darren nodded and thanked him.

———

Sheriff Buchanon, Bill Port and Mark Hamilton stood on the front lawn of the Hamilton's home Tuesday afternoon. They were watching friends and neighbors arrive for the scheduled meeting. Sheriff Buchanon had contacted all of the families that had been involved with the situation. As a result, most of the neighborhood of Meadowview Acres was filing into the Hamilton's house.

The story Mark had told him was admittedly far-fetched, but after their discussion at the hospital, Mark had taken the sheriff back to the offices of the Hallston Daily Journal and shown him the trail of information. He had started with the articles from August of nineteen sixty-eight and ended with the professor's death. The thing that got Don Buchanon was the book – the one that Professor Monroe had given to Shasta. After reading the chapter on the Varuupian curse and listening to Mark compare the deaths from nineteen sixty-eight to the deaths happening in Hallston, it was hard to argue.

Mark Hamilton, being a newspaper man, was all about informing the public. This time the sheriff concurred. That was the purpose for the meeting. All of the people were going there for answers, but hopefully to find a solution as well. The men were skeptical about how the story was going to be received. Mark had to make them believe that the curse was real. Bug had come up with two alternatives to get rid of the rock and she was right. One was very risky and the other may not work. Sheriff Buchanon had listened as Bug laid out both plans. When she was finished, Don thought what a brilliant girl she was. He also thought, "We're screwed".

Everyone was accounted for and taking their seats as Sheriff Buchanon and Mark walked to the front of the makeshift assembly. Ann had moved all of the living room furniture to the walls of the room and set up as many chairs as she could find. Mark watched as the sheriff called everyone to attention.

"Everyone," he began. The room quieted as they heard the sheriff beginning to speak. "I'd like to thank you all for coming today. I know you're all wondering what we'd like to talk to you about, and I'll get to that in a moment. First, let me thank the Hamilton family for allowing us to gather in their home. This is an important conversation and it will be much more comfortable here than in a room down at the station. So thank you Mark, Ann." He paused then, letting them be recognized.

"Now, our community has been having a tough time lately, and it hasn't been easy on any of us. We've lost some good people very suddenly. A lot of us are grieving." He glanced at Agnes and Lara, and then over at the Reynolds family. "Most of us were thinking what a bad coincidence that all of this was. That's what it seemed to be, just a really bad chain of events. But recently, Mr. Hamilton here brought me some information. This information changes everything. I'm going to let him tell you all about it." Sheriff Buchanon motioned for Mark to address the group.

The murmurs of the crowd were getting a little loud with speculation. Mr. Reynolds looked angry and stood up to say, "What exactly are you trying to say here, Don? That my boy didn't die of what they said he did?"

More murmuring was heard as people looked to one another for answers.

"Now calm down, Mr. Reynolds," Mark said gently. "It's quite an involved story. I know you're still grieving Hansen, but this may give you some answers."

Mr. Reynolds sat back down red-faced, and the crowd seemed to quiet. Eli looked at Hunter. They were thinking the same thing. "Like father, like son."

Mark began again. "I'm going to tell you a story. I'd like to ask for your patience, though. The story may not make sense to you in the beginning or even the middle. But I hope when I get to the end, you'll all understand what we believe to be happening to us here in Meadowview Acres."

He looked out at the crowd. They all had expectant faces. The Massey's were there with Lara Andrews, sitting by their boys. The Reynolds' were sitting close to the Staggs, but Clara was over by Hunter. Agnes and Darren sat together with Bill Port beside them. Val was at the hospital with Shasta. Margy Buchanon was there with Jeff and Jennifer sitting next to Ann. There was another woman that the sheriff had told him was a friend of Phillip Just – Julie Leezil. Deputy Clay was also there standing in the back of the room. The last face he looked at before he began was that of his baby. Bug was sitting on the floor in the hallway just outside the living room. She had been very quiet since finding out about Shasta yesterday. Mark looked at her now and smiled a gentle "everything will be alright" smile. Bug winked at her dad, and he began the story.

"Back in August of nineteen sixty-eight, a ship came into port at Glovercroft..."

CHAPTER 32

A Plan Is Born

"And that's where we are now," Mr. Hamilton concluded and looked at the faces in the room. No one spoke. Finally, Bill Port stood up. "So what you're telling us is that this rock carries a curse from some ancient civilization? That's how these people have died? That's quite a story, Mark."

"Listen, everyone," Mark tried to explain, "I know it sounds a little unbelievable, but look at the facts. Claymont died almost immediately after digging up the box with the rock inside. The next people around it were terribly sick. Then, Heather, who was a young, healthy girl, died suddenly when the rock was near. That same day Hansen died while actually holding the rock. It's just too coincidental, especially when you compare the circumstances with the information from Professor Monroe."

Sheriff Buchanon stepped forward and said, "We almost had another fatality."

All eyes were on him, looking questioningly. "Julie Leezil," he said nodding in the teacher's direction.

She had put the pieces together as Mark Hamilton spoke. She remembered her run-in with the boys at the Gas N Go. She had tears in her eyes as she said, "It's true. I didn't know at the time, but I was close to it. I was fine and then, the next moment I felt as if my whole body had shifted. It was like nothing I'd ever felt before. Then I just saw black." A sob caught in her throat.

Sheriff Buchanon finished for her. "She was at the Gas N Go the same time as the boys. It was in Eli's trunk. Luckily, the boys high-tailed it out of there."

"I believe it." Julie said strongly. "After feeling it firsthand, I believe it. All of you would too."

The room was quiet once again. Mark felt uneasy. He was having trouble reading the room. He wondered what they would do if no one believed the theory. He decided they would have to carry out the plan themselves. He was about to speak when another voice was heard.

"This is a super weird thing that's happening," said Bug. "But it's nobody's fault, not yet. It will be though if we all don't get together and fix it. If someone else dies or gets sick now, it's because you're all too scared to make it right." She sat back down on the floor in the hallway.

"You're right, Bug. You're absolutely right." Hank Massey's voice was deep and loud. He had been listening to Mark lay out the story and had been shocked at Hunter and Eli's involvement. They could just have easily been killed. "No matter how bizarre it sounds, it's damn well happening. You all know it is."

"What do we do, Sheriff?" Deputy Clay asked. "How can we get rid of it?"

"I'm glad you asked, Michael," responded the sheriff. "Bug, would you mind telling everyone what you've learned?"

Bug looked up at him from her place in the hallway and saw the sheriff wink at her. He had been nice when Bug had talked to him before, so she felt comfortable going to the front of the room to stand beside him. She knew it was her job to tell everyone the facts. *Knowledge is Power*.

Bug held up her copy of *Curses of Ancient Tribes*. "I've been researching this problem for quite a while, and I believe that there are really only two choices here."

Just then, Mr. Reynolds interrupted. Standing up from his chair, he said, "Oh, so now we're supposed to listen to a little twelve year old? Wow! I feel better already! It's great to know that the law in this town has a tweenager on speed dial! Ha! This is bullshit! You can't tell me that my boy died because of some mumbo-jumbo from some island! He had an allergic reaction, people! He didn't die from some damn curse!" He looked down at his wife and said curtly, "Get up! We're leaving!"

Mrs. Reynolds looked embarrassed, but rose from her seat and followed her husband from the room. The front door slammed loudly as they exited the Hamilton home.

Sheriff Buchanon looked around at the people still seated. "Maybe now's a good time for anyone else to leave. You won't be judged. We know you all have been through a lot lately."

Friends and neighbors looked around at each other waiting for another exit.

"I'm sorry." It was Ms. Leezil's soft voice. "I simply can't take any more of this." Her eyes were still damp, and she kept her head bowed as she stood. "I just lost Phillip yesterday. And after my close call with the curse, I'm just too afraid to be involved. I apologize. I'm sure you'll all do the right thing. Good luck."

Ann Hamilton went to the teacher and put a tender arm around her. "Don't think a thing about it, Honey. We all understand completely. Let me help you out to your car."

As the two women walked slowly to the door, Ann shot her husband a worried look. Mark knew what she was thinking. This thing was more real now. Julie Leezil was badly shaken with the mere thought of coming into contact with the rock again. He looked around the room to see if anyone else had decided to leave.

"Okay, Bug," he said when no one else made a move to go. "You can continue."

"So as I said before, there are only two options. This book was one that the professor had in his home. It's the only resource I've found that has any suggestions at all. I'll read you what it says about our choices. She opened the book to her first bookmark and began to read.

"All research and findings to date seem to be decidedly pessimistic pertaining to the countering or reversing of curses. There are, however, some who believe that in the case of a cursed article or object, returning it to the site of the original event can diminish the effects. This is most effective, obviously, the more distance there is between the object and the person/persons that it was created to harm."

She stopped and turned to the next marked page. "And here's choice number two:

"Additionally, there has been some documented success with the physical burial of the object/article. There are specifics with this method, however. The cursed object must be wrapped in heavy cloth then placed in an un-penetrable container, sealed shut. The container holding the wrapped object must then be buried no fewer than twelve feet below the ground and covered with a mixture of sand, gravel and dirt, thus entombing the curse. This method has been shown to be successful in two separately documented cases."

So those are our options." Bug closed her book and walked back over to her spot in the hall.

Sheriff Buchanon stepped forward once again to address the crowd. "Thank you, Bug. So what we believe is that the professor was trying to use the burial method, but he either didn't know about the particulars or his health stopped him from burying the box properly. It was only a few feet down when the boys dug it up." He paced the room as he spoke, something he usually did when he was trying to put together the facts in a case.

"Now, the first choice we have is to take the box back to that island where Monroe found it. This idea has a lot of risks. Number one: who's going to take it and will they be able to survive the trip? Number two: There's a strong possibility that innocent people will be encountered along the way and have a reaction, possibly die. Number three: Will the designated person even be able to reach the island of Shaali? It's pretty remote and the natives don't go to it at all." He stopped pacing and looked around the room. "Does anyone have any input?"

Bill Port stood up then. "Don, I agree with your assessment. This route seems very risky not only to one of our people but also to strangers. How could we do this knowing that someone out there might die as a result? I think we should move on to the other option." He sat back down.

"Okay," Sheriff Buchanon said. "Does anyone have any objections to moving on to the second choice?" He saw people shaking their heads and started pacing again.

"So option number two isn't easy either. We need to find a place for the actual burial, gather all of the materials and figure out who's going to take care of what. I know that I'll be involved the whole way, my exposure to the rock was painful, but not fatal. The main thing is to make sure that no one comes into contact with the rock who hasn't already been exposed. We can't gauge a new individual's reaction, and I won't take that chance."

It was Eli's turn to speak up. "Sheriff, Hunter and I can handle being around it. I mean, we're both kinda used to it now, and it doesn't seem to do anything more than make us both sick. We'll help with the burial."

"NO!" Lara Andrews jumped to her feet. "I've lost one child to this thing, I will NOT lose another!" She flew from the room in tears. Gina Massey followed to comfort her.

After a moment passed, Hunter said, "Eli's right. We're okay around it now. I mean, it makes us feel like hell, but we can handle it. Plus, we're the ones who dug it up, it only feels right that we take care of it." He slumped back into his seat then.

"No one is blaming you boys," Mr. Hamilton said. "There is no way you could have predicted what was in that box. Everyone here knows that."

"He's right, though," the sheriff said. "These two have the most experience being around the thing. They know its effects. Is there anyone else here that has experienced any exposure?" He looked around the room.

"I have, Sir. When I got to the construction site the night Mr. Jackson died." Michael Clay remembered feeling clammy and having a never-ending nose bleed. "I can deal with the effects, count me in."

"Good man, Deputy," the Sheriff said. "Anyone else?"

Clara raised her hand as if she were in class. "I was standing right by Hansen and the rock was on the ground. I didn't feel a thing." Mr. and Mrs. Stagg looked at their daughter, shocked. They obviously didn't want her involved.

"Okay, Clara, thank you. We'll keep that in mind." The sheriff really didn't think her parents would allow her involvement, but he might be able to use her for something.

The room was quiet again when an unexpected voice said, "My Claymont set this in motion without even knowing it. And he died as a result. You know, it seems to me that you'll need something to dig a hole that big. Mr. Clark might see his way clear to letting you use Claymont's rig."

Mark was surprised. Agnes was still in deep mourning yet she had been handling all of this very calmly. "Thank you, Agnes. That's really a great help. I don't know if any of us have experience operating a bull-dozer though."

When Darren heard his mother say that Claymont had started the whole thing, he finally understood what he had been feeling. The anger that he was experiencing was toward his father. He was angry that he had dug up the box, angry that he had died as a result of it and angry that more people had been hurt because of it. He knew what he had to do next. "I do." The voice came from the seat beside Agnes. "My dad taught me how to use that rig when I was eight. I've been on it more times than I can count."

"Well, that's true, Son, but I don't think any of us want to take any chances with your health. Your family has been through enough." Sheriff Buchanon couldn't imagine Agnes losing her son, too.

Hunter spoke up then, "Darren isn't affected at all by the curse. I had it in my backpack the whole time he was leading me out of the fire with Eli. Then outside, while the paramedics were giving us oxygen, it was on the grass right beside him."

"It's true." Darren said. "Nothing, I didn't feel anything."

Sheriff Buchanon looked to Agnes who just nodded her head. She understood what he was asking and gave her permission. "Well, alright, then. I guess we have some able bodies, and a way to drive the machine and dig the hole. What's left?"

Bug spoke up and said, "Where will you dig the hole?"

Bill Port spoke first, "You know there's a good twenty miles of woods between here and Chester. Why couldn't we scope out a good spot in the middle? I'd be happy to scout out a place where the dozer could get through."

"Great idea, Bill," said Mark. I'll go with you. I've got some maps of the area at the office and we'll go from there."

"So the last thing that we'll need is the dump truck with the gravel and sand. I'll talk to Tony Clark about getting those things when I ask him about Claymont's rig." Sheriff Buchanon was feeling hopeful. Things seemed to be coming together. "What are we missing, Bug?"

"A heavy cloth to wrap it in, I would suggest leather. And a non-penetrable container that can be sealed shut," she answered.

"Well," Sheriff Buchanon said. "It's in a steel safe right now, that pretty un-penetrable. We'll take it out and wrap it then we'll need to solder it closed. How can we do that?"

Eli said, "Hunter and I have soldering equipment. We'll do that."

Mark looked at the sheriff with raised eyebrows and said, "Are we missing anything? That seemed to come together relatively easy."

Before he could answer, Agnes said, "Coming up with the plan may be easy, but the execution is a different story. The devil's in the details." With that she stood and left the room.

As they watched her leave, many of the residents felt uneasy about the task before them. The meeting was over for all intents and purposes, so Sheriff Buchanon made his way to the back of the room to speak with Bill.

The crowd had started to converse in small groups. The information was still overwhelming, and they needed to discuss it to understand it more. Some people were looking over the articles that Mark had put on a table nearby. Others were looking through the book titled, *Legends and Myths from Around the Globe*. Mark walked over to Don and Bill.

"So what are we missing? I still feel like we're overlooking something." He looked from one man to the other. They had been saying the same thing before he had joined them.

Don said, "I'm going to call Tony Clark tonight, so I can meet with him in the morning. Can you two scout out a site tomorrow morning?"

"Sure," said Bill. "I can do that." He looked at Mark.

"I'll make time; this is too important. I'll go to the office tonight and pick up the maps and meet you here at, what, seven?"

Bill nodded his head. "What else?" he asked Don.

"The boys," he answered. "I'm going to give them the safe with the rock in it so they can take it out and wrap it up then solder it shut." He motioned to Hunter and Eli who were standing with Hank. They had been waiting for Lara to come back into the room with Gina.

The three walked over and Sheriff Buchanon relayed the boy's part of the plan to them. "After you get it sealed shut, do you think you can keep it in your car and follow us out to the site to help dig?"

The boys looked at each other and Eli said, "Sure, we'll do anything we can."

Hank looked worriedly at the sheriff and said, "Take care of the boys, Don. I know they're used to being around that thing, but if you see anything squirrelly, take care of them."

"You bet I will, Hank. Try not to worry."

Clara came over then and took Hunter's hand. "Do you need me to help? I don't seem to have any reaction at all, Sheriff." She looked up at Hunter and smiled, happy to be at his side.

"Right now we seem to have everything under control. But I'll let you know if anything comes up."

Mark Hamilton spoke. "Clara, I have something that I could use your help with."

She tore her gaze from Hunter to look at him. "Sure, Mr. Hamilton. What is it?"

"I wonder if you might have some time to spend with Bug. She seems to be a little lost with Shasta in the hospital." He looked over at his black haired daughter. She was curled up on one corner of the couch next to Ann. She looked so small. "All of this has really been a lot for her to handle, and, you see, she thinks of Shasta as an older sister. Do you think you could fill in for a while?"

Clara looked over at Bug. She was so sweet. Suddenly, Clara had an image of Bug on the floor of the Hot Dog Hut with a bloody nose. A bloody nose caused by Hansen. That made her angry. "Absolutely, Mr. Hamilton. It would be my pleasure. As a matter of fact, I think I'll start right now." She leaned up on her toes to kiss Hunter's cheek and then made her way over to where Bug sat on the couch.

Resuming their discussion, Sheriff Buchanon said, "We'll reconvene tomorrow after I've talked to Clark, and you two have scouted the woods." He turned to Eli and Hunter and said, "You boys are out of school because of the fire, but hang tight at home and we'll let you know what's going on."

"When should we wrap the rock and solder the safe shut?" asked Hunter.

The sheriff looked from Mark to Hank to Bill, then back to the boys. "Well, no time like the present. Mark, you go on to the office and get the maps. Bill and Hank, you guys can't be around. I'll grab Deputy Clay and we'll go with the boys. That okay?"

They all muttered their agreement and took off in different directions. Sheriff Buchanon, with the boys, grabbed Deputy Clay on his way out the door. "I've got an old leather coat in my cruiser that we can use to wrap the rock. The thing is so thick, it must weigh fifty pounds. I'll get that and the safe out of my car and bring it, where?" He looked at the boys for information.

Hunter said, "There's a shed behind my house. It seems to be far enough away that we haven't had a problem. Bring it there and we'll meet you with the soldering tools."

The boys and Deputy Clay left him there on the sidewalk. Sheriff Buchanon started walking to his cruiser. He was going over the plan in his head trying to see if they were forgetting anything. He knew one thing for certain. He was ready for this whole thing to be over with. He unlocked the trunk of his cruiser and looked at the safe inside. He had bought it at Hardware on Main after Hunter had handed the backpack over to him at the hospital. The twinge of a headache started immediately and began to grow. He reached in and grabbed the safe, pulling it from the car. As he reached back in for his heavy leather coat, he thought, "Let's get this son of a bitch sealed."

Bright blue stars sparkled in his vision.

CHAPTER 33

Darren & Shasta

Darren was still really concerned about his mother. She had been acting so strangely since finding out about the curse. She was so calm, so quiet. Her weeping and fits of anger at her husband's death had gone away as well. She seemed oddly at peace.

He had been surprised when she offered his dad's bulldozer to help dig the hole for the burial of the artifact. No one had expected that, but he had been shocked when she had given her permission for Darren himself to be the operator. Darren didn't know what to make of that.

After Agnes left the meeting, it had come to a close. Their path had been decided. People now were talking in small groups or looking over the books that Bug had left out on a table. Darren had already seen the books, and the only person he wanted to talk to wasn't there. He needed to get back to the hospital. He had promised Shasta that he would tell her everything that had been discussed.

Shasta was doing better today, but her voice was very rough and her skin was still tender. She coughed a lot, too. He was surprised at how he, Hunter and Eli had managed to get out of the fire with very few problems. He and Hunter seemed to be fine after breathing the oxygen given to them by the paramedics. Eli had come around pretty soon after being pulled from the building and seemed no worse for wear. Shasta had been in there much longer than they had, though, and she was paying a price. Still, Darren knew that they were all very lucky. He was especially; he still had Shasta.

He stood up and dug for his keys in the front pocket of his jeans. On his way to the door, he was stopped by Shasta's father.

"Going back to the hospital, Darren?" Bill Port asked.

"I promised Shasta I would tell her what happened at the meeting," he replied.

Bill looked at the young man in front of him, but couldn't read his expression. "How're you feeling about your part in all of this?"

Darren answered truthfully. "I'm honestly fine with it. I've been exposed to the artifact and didn't feel any weird effects. I really don't see much risk in my involvement." He looked down at the floor and said, "I'll just be glad when it's over and all of this is behind us."

"I can't imagine what you and your mom have been going through." Bill said. "You're one tough guy, I'll give you that. If you or Agnes need anything, and I mean anything, you call us, okay?"

Darren said that he would and started to leave when Mr. Port said, "So are you going to break this to Shasta or should I? You know she's not going to like the idea of you being such a big part of this plan."

Darren thought for a moment then said, "I'll do it. I think she'll understand why I feel like I need to be involved."

"Well, good luck." He winked at Darren knowing the boy was in for a tough argument with his daughter. "I'm headed to the hospital, too. Want a ride?" Mr. Port admired the soft spoken young man. He was full of a quiet strength that Bill respected. The way he had handled himself since his father died had been remarkable.

"Thank you, Sir. But I'd better have my car there in case I stay later than you."

"Alright, then, I'll see you over there." Bill clapped him on the back and made his way out the door.

On his way to the car, Darren went over the plan that had been discussed at the meeting. The whole way over to Community Hospital, he was trying to dissect it to find a weakness. Everything seemed to be in place, but he remembered what his mom had said. The devil's in the details. Darren, looking for holes, tried to walk through the plan step by step.

By the time he pulled into the parking lot, he had gone over the plan three or four times. He was missing information on exactly where they would be digging and if they could get the materials to pour on top of the box, but everything else seemed sound.

He could hear Mr. Port's voice coming from Shasta's room before he got there. It sounded like he was giving Shasta and Mrs. Port a play by play of the meeting.

Darren walked into the room as Mr. Port was saying, "Lara had to leave the room. The idea of Eli being in harm's way was just too much after losing Heather. Oh, here he is!" He broke off when Darren stepped into the room.

Darren greeted the Port's then went to Shasta's bedside and gently kissed the top of her hair. It seemed to be the least tender place on her body.

She smiled weakly back, the skin on her face and hands bright pink. "Dad was just catching us up on the meeting. How do you think it went?" She asked him in her gravelly voice.

"Well," Darren started. "I thought about the plan the whole way over here and I'm not coming up with any holes or anything. I know there are unforeseen aspects, but I can't figure out what those might be." He looked at Mr. Port, then. "I feel pretty confident that we'll do the job right and put this thing to rest."

Shasta caught the look between Darren and her father. "What? What aren't you saying? What do you mean by "we'll do the job"? She looked at Darren as understanding came into her eyes.

"Honey, I think Mom and I will go on home and leave the two of you to talk." Bill went to the bed and kissed his baby's auburn hair. Val did the same then gave Darren a hug on her way out. "We'll see you in the morning, Sweetie," she said to Shasta.

Once they were alone, Darren scooted his plastic hospital chair over so that he was next to Shasta. She was looking at him with a measure of fear in her eyes. She waited for him to speak, already knowing what he was going to say.

"Now, listen. I've already been around that thing. In the fire, remember, and then again when we were out of the school with the paramedics."

Shasta, still waiting for an acceptable explanation, glared at him.

"I didn't realize it at the time, but the backpack was right beside me. I noticed a couple of the firefighters vomiting and one of the paramedics had to go lay down, but I just thought it was because of the smoke." He took her tender hand gently and continued.

"I didn't feel anything, Shas, not a thing. No headache, nausea, weakness, nothing at all. And I was around it for a pretty long time." He could see tears forming in her deep brown eyes.

"Let me try to explain. This whole time, I've felt not only grief for my dad, but I've also been really mad, too. I didn't know why until today at the meeting. Mom said something about how Dad was the reason for all of this. She wasn't blaming him at all, she was just saying that he unknowingly started this in motion by digging up the box. That's when it hit me. I've been mad at Dad." He stopped a minute trying to find the words to explain what he was feeling.

Shasta had started to understand a little of what he was saying. She knew that he was grieving, but she had also seen something else in him. Now she understood what that had been.

"So you think being a part of the solution will make up for the deaths the rock caused? Darren, none of that was your dad's fault. He's completely innocent in this. So are you." She could see the hurt in his eyes.

"I know that. I get it, but I don't feel it. That's the difference. The reasoning makes sense to me, but I can't help how I feel. And I feel like I need to make this right. Then, maybe I can just grieve my dad and get rid of the anger." He looked at her then, hoping she would understand.

Of course she did, they were Darren and Shasta. They were completely connected. He could see acceptance in her eyes and relief flooded over him. The last thing he wanted to do was hurt Shasta any more than she already had been.

"I promise you two things," he said. "The first one is that I will be incredibly careful and observant. If I feel the slightest twinge of anything, I'll get out of there. We'll get this done as quickly as possible and get out."

"And the second thing," Shasta prompted, curious.

He brought her little pink hand up to his lips and kissed it tenderly. "The second thing is, that when this is over, you and I are going to make up for lost time. We're going to sit on the couch and watch movies, eat pizza and gummy worms and do absolutely nothing for at least a month."

She laughed then, thinking how heavenly that sounded. A simple evening at home with nothing to worry about seemed like a distant dream. "Oh Darren, I can't wait for that. It's pretty bad when your dream is eating gummy worms on a couch watching a lame movie."

Darren grew serious again. "Really, Shas, I don't want you to get worked up about this. I feel like it's the right thing to do. And when it's done, it's done. The nightmare will be over."

Shasta thought for a minute about what Darren had before him. She knew that he was big and strong and smart, but those things didn't seem to matter if the curse got to you. She understood why he needed to do this, why it was so important to him.

"Tell me the whole plan," she said. "Let's go over it and see if anything's missing."

On the drive home, Darren felt better. He and Shasta had picked the plan apart. What if this happened? What if that happened? Every instance had a contingency. Darren had a Plan B and a Plan C. He was going in with his eyes wide open.

As he pulled into the drive, he could make out his mother's small shape sitting on the front stoop. He parked and walked over to sit beside her.

"How's Shasta doing?" Agnes asked.

"Much better. She's still coughing and her skin still hurts, but she's feeling a lot better. How're you, Mom?" Darren was still concerned and didn't know how to help.

"Oh, Honey, I'm fine. I really am. I think in the last week I've gone through every emotion known to man. But I'm coming out the other side." She reached over and squeezed his hand.

"I'm sorry I haven't been able to help you much with all of this," she continued. "I couldn't seem to climb out of that hole I was in."

"It's okay, Mom. I've been alright. Shasta's been with me, and you've been here too, no matter what you think. Are you sure you're feeling better?" Darren could see her face; she looked calm and relaxed.

"Yes. I'm still missing your father something awful, but I imagine that will just be a way of life now. He was such a good man. I'll miss him every day."

"I know," Darren said sadly. "I will too."

"They say it gets better with time. I suppose we'll have to hope for that. I'm getting used to it a little, though." Agnes was talking to Darren, but also talking to herself. "I'll be alright again. We'll be alright." She squeezed his hand again then changed the subject.

"Now, how're you feeling about burying that thing?"

Darren was surprised that she wanted to talk about it, but he was glad, too. "I'm feeling pretty good. Shasta and I went over the plan and I'm feeling confident. Thanks for understanding that I need to do this."

"You've been angry since he died, Darren. We both know this isn't your dad's fault, but we both sort of feel like it is. Isn't that right?" Agnes had known exactly what Darren had been feeling. She knew her son well.

"Yeah, that's right. But we'll take care of it and that will be the end," Darren said determinedly.

"God, I hope so. I hope so," Agnes said. "Now, this old lady is going to bed. It's been another long day." She got up from the stoop and bent to hug her son. "I love you, Darren. You be careful."

That night Darren woke from a dream. He had been inside the cab of his father's bulldozer, digging the hole for the artifact. The hole was huge and very deep. The sheriff had just put the safe at the bottom and was climbing back out. Darren was waiting to start covering the safe with dirt, when all of the sudden, the bulldozer started to tip forward. He frantically tried to back up the rig, but the controls weren't responding. The Cat was tipping, tipping... Darren tried to open the door of the cab, but it wouldn't budge. He could feel the momentum of the Cat falling forward into the hole. Darren tried to brace himself as the dozer fell down, down, into the depths. In his dream, the hole was never-ending, he just kept falling and falling and falling...

CHAPTER 34

Sheriff Buchanon

The day turned out to be gray and dismal. It wasn't raining, but the air was thick and humid. The dark gray clouds seemed to bring an ominous feeling to Sheriff Buchanon as he drove west on Route 68 toward Tony Clark's construction site.

He had just come from visiting Agnes. They had finalized the paperwork which opened an investigation into Claymont's death. As his widow, it was within her rights to request an inquiry. Sheriff Buchanon had explained to her that the only way to get their hands on Claymont's Caterpillar was to have it impounded as part of an investigation. As of eight forty-seven that morning, the Hallston Sheriff's Department had been allowed to take Claymont's rig. Agnes had been happy with her decision. She told the sheriff that she hadn't known what she could do to help, but she wanted to do something. The sheriff assured her that this was a big way to help. Having that rig to dig the hole for the burial was a lifesaver, possibly literally.

The sheriff hadn't really passed this information on to the rest of the department, yet. He was sure that no one would understand why he was agreeing to open an investigation into such a cut and dried medical incident. They certainly wouldn't get why he had impounded a Caterpillar bulldozer. He thought if they could get this done in the span of one or two days, no one would have to find out anyway. He would work out the details later. First, he had to inform Tony Clark.

He had called Tony just that morning to ask for a meeting. Mr. Clark had been accommodating but guarded. Sheriff Buchanon had an idea that the man thought the meeting had something to do with Claymont's death. He was right, of course, but it certainly wasn't going to be the conversation Tony expected.

His cell phone rang, and Don answered quickly. He was expecting an update from Bill on the scouting excursion into the woods. He knew that he and Mark had started out early. He wasn't disappointed when he heard Bill on the line.

"Hey, Don," Bill said. "We've made some headway here."

Sheriff Buchanon knew that Bill and Mark were going to head down the existing gravel road as far as it would go. From there they would discern the next course of action. They needed to find the best way into the woods for the bulldozer and other vehicles to travel.

Bill continued, "The old gravel road washes out a couple of miles in. After that, there's an old dirt path, narrow, but enough room for us to pass. That goes another six miles, so far. We're still on it."

Don interjected then, "Have you come across anything looking inhabited? An old shack, a deer stand, abandoned cars? Anything at all that would signify people around?"

"No nothing," Bill answered. "The woods are empty. We haven't come across anything like that. There have been no tracks on this path either, not foot nor vehicle. Mark's maps show an outbuilding further ahead. We're expecting it to be overgrown. We'll see when we get there. We're about eight miles in total and we'd like to at least double that."

"Do you have a specific site in mind, Bill?"

"We have a fair idea after studying the maps. Mark thinks if we can make it in roughly seventeen miles, we'll be as far away from Hallston as we will be from Chester, around twenty seven or eight miles. That puts us seventeen miles away from Route 68 and the other side drops off steeply another nineteen miles past. That'll mean we're smack dab in the middle of the woods."

Don thought for a moment. He knew the cliffs that Mark's maps indicated. "What about moving more toward the cliffs? With that massive drop off, no one would think about building in that area in the future."

"You're right, Don. We thought about that, too. It's all going to hinge on how hard it'll be to get the equipment through. These woods are getting denser as we go. We'll exhaust this path then see what we're faced with. I'll call with another update in a couple of hours. We should have some more information then."

"Sounds good, thanks, Bill." Sheriff Buchanon pushed the END button on his phone. He had reached the trailer at the head of the construction site and swung the cruiser into a roughly outlined parking space.

Getting out of the car, he felt the first small raindrops on his face. He hoped it wouldn't be a downpour. They needed the weather on their side if they were going to bury that thing tomorrow.

He was a few minutes early but didn't really care. Sometimes being sheriff had its perks. If he wanted to talk, people talked. He still hadn't decided exactly how this conversation was going to go. He battled with how much information Clark really needed. The sheriff decided to play it by ear.

Entering the trailer, Don heard Tony's voice booming. He closed the door behind him and glanced around. It seemed larger inside than he had expected. To the left was a big drafting table with plans and graphs strewn about. File cabinets flanked the table, and a small desk was in the corner. To the right was Mr. Clark's desk, heavily covered with papers, file folders and maps.

Tony was behind the desk and on the phone when he saw the sheriff and motioned him to the two plastic chairs in front of his desk. Sheriff Buchanon took off his hat and sat down.

"That's not good enough," Tony yelled into the phone. "George, this has put me more than a month behind. Don't you get it?"

His face was red with anger as he paced back and forth behind his desk.

"You gotta get me another operator now. Do you think Howard Brig cares about the reason? He's all over Gary Sam. And you're up there sending guys out to job sites in Shale? What the hell?" He stopped to listen to the man's response then yelled, "Well, fine. The next time I hear from Howard Brig at Oakwood Homes, I'm giving him your phone number, your home phone number." He continued to pace as he listened. After a moment he said, "I don't care what you have to do. I'm sick of hearing it from Howard and Gary, too. Send me a bulldozer operator tomorrow. No excuses." He slammed the phone down.

Sheriff Buchanon cleared his throat. Tony looked up as if he had forgotten the big man sitting in the plastic chair.

"Oh, Sheriff." He laughed nervously. "I can't seem to get my point across today. Ever have one of those days?" He said while motioning to the phone.

"Quite a few actually," responded Sheriff Buchanon. "Sounds like you're in a little bit of a bind."

Tony shook his head and said, "It's too bad about Claymont and all, but damned if he didn't put me in a pinch. I'm getting further behind every day without a replacement for him."

The sheriff decided to get to the point. "Well, I'm afraid I might be about to rain on your parade a little more."

Tony sat down in the frayed leather chair behind his desk and looked squarely at the sheriff. The man was in no mood for more bad news. "What are you talking about?"

"Well, I'm here to inform you that I need to impound Claymont's Caterpillar. Agnes has requested an investigation into his death. I talked to her just this morning. We'll be taking it today." He waited for the fallout. It came.

"What the hell are you talking about, Sheriff? Claymont died of a brain thing, a hemorrhage, right? What's there to investigate? What's that bulldozer going to tell you?" The man's face was getting red again, and he was throwing his arms around as he continued his tirade.

"This is ridiculous! Here I am trying to find a replacement for Claymont's rig and now you're telling me that I don't even have the bulldozer?"

Tony was pacing faster now while shaking his head. Don was getting a little concerned about the man's blood pressure. He decided to take a different approach.

"Now settle down a minute, Tony. Come here and sit down. I may have an idea that could help us both out."

Tony Clark looked at him like he was crazy. Don could tell that the man lived his life full of stress. Some people thrived on stress, even made some up if things were going smoothly. He thought Tony Clark was such a person. Nevertheless, he sat back down in his chair.

"We're going to be building an outpost for training, most likely over in Chester, closer to State College. We'll need to rent a dump truck from you along with a load of gravel and sand. No drivers, just the equipment and the load. We'll, of course, pay the going rate."

He stopped to let this sink in. With a man like Clark, the minimum information was the best way to go. Tony didn't care what they were doing as long as he got paid. Sheriff Buchanon could tell the man was turning the information over in his mind and trying to come up with a way to take advantage of the situation.

"It won't take me too long to go over the rig for the investigation. One, maybe two days, and then I'll have it right back to you." Then the sheriff dangled his morsel, "I may have a bulldozer operator for you, too."

"I'm still behind two more days without that rig," he said still glowering. Don thought he seemed to be pouting and had finally had enough of this guy. He wasn't only disrespectful about his twelve year employee's death; he was now trying to work Don for more money.

"That's tough now, isn't it," Sheriff Buchanon said icily. "You realize that I didn't even have to have this chat with you? I could have just picked up the Caterpillar without notifying you at all. Aren't you lucky that we're having this discussion?"

Tony changed his tone immediately, realizing that the deal could go south. "Yeah, yeah, Sheriff, I get it. I'm just a little worked up because of that phone call. Now, you need gravel and sand was it?"

"That's it," Don replied, glad that Tony was back to playing ball. "One of the smaller dump trucks. You can just fill it with a gravel and sand mixture. Bill the department for that load and for the dump truck rental for two days."

"Can do, no problem. Who'll be picking that up? And when?" Tony was all business now.

"Have it loaded and ready with the keys in it tomorrow morning. I'll pick it up myself with Deputy Clay." Don was getting sick of this guy.

"Consider it done, Sheriff, now, about that bulldozer operator. When will he start?" Tony asked.

"He'll start when he returns the dozer in a couple of days. It'll just be part-time work for him, but that's enough time for you to get another full-timer and get you over this hump. That's worth a little inconvenience, isn't it?"

Don was being accommodating and extremely political. The bulldozer was the property of the department on paper already. He didn't need anyone's permission to take it, especially Tony's, but he wanted to make Tony happy in case they needed something else for the job.

Sheriff Buchanon knew he was going to pay a pretty penny for the dump truck and the load of gravel and sand, but that didn't matter. The burial was the most important thing.

Finally, Tony smiled and stuck his hand out for the sheriff to shake. "That's a deal, Sheriff. A dump truck, a

load of gravel and sand, and you get me a dozer operator."

Sheriff Buchanon shook the man's hand and thought,
"What deal? I'm paying for some equipment and doing
you a favor, Jackass." He smiled at Tony as they shook
hands. The smile on his lips didn't quite make it to his
eyes.

Of course the next thing out of Tony's mouth was,
"So who is this guy, the rig operator?"

Sheriff Buchanon didn't see much use in hiding
the information. Tony would find out soon enough.
Besides, he hadn't even talked to Darren yet. He stood
and put his hat back on making his way to the door of
the trailer.

"I'll send him over to pick up the Cat today and you
can talk to him. His name's Darren Jackson." He saw
Tony Clark's face register a look of shocked confusion
as he walked out the door.

The sheriff was happy to be leaving the trailer. Tony
Clark had left a bad taste in his mouth. He had met men
like Tony before, men who only cared about themselves,
and had no respect for them.

Back in the cruiser, he checked his voicemail – nothing from Mark or Bill. He checked in with Rachel at Dispatch. She said things were pretty quiet, so he told her
that he was going to check on something and wouldn't

be back to the office until that afternoon. He then dialed Darren's cell phone and waited for him to answer.

"Hello," came the young man's voice.

"Hey, Darren, Sheriff Buchanon here. I'm about to head over to the woods to check on Mr. Port and Mr. Hamilton's progress. Interested in going with me?"

Sheriff Buchanon could hear a rhythmic beeping in the background. Darren answered, "Sure. I'm at the hospital with Shasta. When will you be here?"

"I'm heading your way now, give me ten minutes then meet me by the Emergency Room."

They said goodbye as the sheriff pulled out of the gravel parking lot and headed east toward Community Hospital. The rain was steady now, much to the disappointment of Sheriff Buchanon. He was hoping for dry conditions for the burial. He thought wet weather would make things more difficult.

He made it to the hospital and swerved into the half circle entrance of the ER. Darren came trotting over to the cruiser as he stopped. The young man hopped into the passenger seat and fastened his seatbelt.

"How's Shasta today?" Sheriff Buchanon asked. He hadn't thought to ask Bill earlier; they had had other things on their minds.

"She's better," Darren responded. "Her skin isn't so touchy and she's breathing better."

Darren looked out the window at the rain and asked, "Have you heard from them, Mr. Port and Mr. Hamilton?"

"A little earlier, yeah. They had gotten about eight miles in, so they had quite a bit to go. I didn't tell them I was coming out. I just decided after I met with Tony Clark." The sheriff grimaced as he remembered the conversation.

"Oh, yeah, how'd that go?" Darren asked. The wipers were squeaking as they swiped the rain off of the windshield.

"It went fine, I guess. I don't see how your dad was able to tolerate that man for twelve years, Darren. He must've had the patience of a saint." Sheriff Buchanon shook his head.

He turned left and headed down Main Street. "I told him the department is building a training center in Chester. He doesn't need to know the real reason. Anyway, he bought the story and he'll have the dump truck with the gravel and sand mixture ready first thing tomorrow."

Darren asked, "What about Dad's Caterpillar?"

"Well, I wanted to talk to you about that," Sheriff Buchanon started. "Of course he blew a gasket when I told him that we were going to impound the Cat. He had been looking for another operator when I got there this morning. I told him that I'd only have it a couple of days, and that I may have someone to drive it for him after that." The sheriff stopped there, waiting to see if Darren figured out yet that he was the replacement. Of course, he did.

Darren furrowed his brow. The sheriff knew that the young man was mulling the idea over and waited quietly. They were going through the middle of town. People were running to and from their cars, trying to dodge the raindrops.

Finally, Darren said, "I guess that might be okay. I'll have to talk to Mom first, though."

Sheriff Buchanon said, "I told him that it's only after school and weekend work for you, not permanent. You have school to think about. And honestly, Darren, if you just don't want to do it, then I'll tell him I was wrong. We'll be finished with the rig by then, and I won't give a crap if he's angry."

"No," Darren replied. "It's really okay. I just don't know what Mom and I are going to do long term, you know? I don't know if she'll want to move closer to her family in Shale or if we'll stay in Meadowview. I don't even know about school."

The Sheriff noticed the worry on Darren's face. "It'll all work out, you'll see. Your mom's a strong woman. I'm sure she has a plan, and I'm more than sure that her plan includes you going to college. Weren't you offered a football scholarship from State?"

Darren's answer was a little quiet. "Yeah, but we haven't really talked about that yet. Things kinda happened, and we haven't had the chance."

"Well, you make the time to talk to her, Son. Your mom's going to know how important it is to you and what an achievement it is. After tomorrow, things will settle down, and you can decide. As for the work with Gary Sam Construction, you do it if you want."

He got to the end of Main and took a right, then headed west on Route 68 out of Hallston.

"If you do decide to work for Tony Clark, remember something. You don't need that job, but he needs an operator. Don't let him make you think that he's doing you some kind of favor by hiring you. And don't let him take advantage of you." He looked over at Darren, and the boy was smiling back at him.

"Don't worry, Sheriff," he said with a little sideways grin. "Nobody takes advantage of me."

Sheriff Buchanon chuckled and knew the boy was right. He might be soft spoken, but he was a mountain of muscle and very smart. That boy was going to go a long way in life.

A few minutes later they made it to the rough gravel road and started down. The sheriff could tell they wouldn't get far in the cruiser and wished he had a truck. He had decided that he and Deputy Clay would ride in the small dump truck leading Darren in the bulldozer. The boy's car would be a problem. Fusions are nice, but not for this terrain. He hoped they could find a truck to borrow for Hunter and Eli. *Shasta – Shasta has a Ranger.* He made a mental note to mention it to Bill.

The cruiser was struggling on the rough road. Sheriff Buchanon could feel his tires searching for purchase in the wet rubble. He decided not to risk getting stuck and stopped the car about a hundred yards into the woods.

"That road's pretty rough," said Darren. "Do you think Eli's car can make it?"

"Probably better than mine, but it gets even rougher further down. I was thinking that maybe they could borrow Shasta's truck. I was going to mention it to Bill."

"That's actually a great idea," Darren replied. "The Ranger's a good little truck; it would take this road with no trouble. I'm sure Shasta won't mind."

"I think I'll try Bill's phone and see where they are," said Sheriff Buchanon as he reached for his cell on the dashboard. He punched in Bill's number and waited.

The rain was easing up; the only drops now coming from the trees above. It looked like that would be the end of the wet weather.

"Huh. It went straight to voicemail," said the sheriff. "I guess I'll back us out of here, and we can try him again in a bit."

The road was too narrow to turn the cruiser around, so they navigated in reverse until they were out of the woods. Sheriff Buchanon swung the cruiser into the field next to the road and cut the engine off.

They sat there for the next hour discussing the plan. The sun had started to peek out from the clouds, and a gentle breeze was blowing. Darren was thinking about telling the sheriff about his dream. He was in the bulldozer, and it had started to fall into the hole that he had dug to bury the Rock of Varuupi. Darren had thought of the dream a lot. It made him a little uneasy. He was about to tell the sheriff about it when they heard the sound of a vehicle coming down the rocky road.

"It's them," Sheriff Buchanon said excitedly as he opened the door to the cruiser.

Darren followed suit and was standing beside the sheriff as they watched Bill Port's black Blazer emerge from the tangled brushy entrance to the woods. Bill pulled the SUV over and parked by the cruiser. Both men got out. Sheriff Buchanon could tell that they were excited. That was a good sign.

"Hey!" Bill Port greeted them both with a big smile of excitement. "Sorry we've been out of touch, but cell reception gets a little hairy in there."

"Yeah, it's pretty much a dead zone past a certain point," Mark Hamilton agreed. "But we've found a perfect spot for the burial."

Sheriff Buchanon looked from one man back to the other and finally had to say, "Well, one of you start talking. What did you find?"

Bill and Mark looked at each other, and Mark said, "Go ahead, Bill. You can tell them."

Bill said, "Okay, so we followed the dirt path past the gravel one and got in around eighteen miles or so. Then, it starts to get really narrow. It was a little tough on the Blazer, but the bulldozer and the dump truck should have no trouble. The sides are mostly saplings and feeders which can be mowed over as you go."

The man was so excited he kept shifting his weight from one leg to another. Darren thought he looked like a little kid who needed to pee.

"After about two miles of the really narrow part of the path, it opens up quite a bit. It's not a path anymore, though. It's just woods, but they aren't dense, so you can just wind your way through them. The ground evens out a lot there, too. It's not as rough."

Mark interjected, "We found the outbuilding. It wasn't where it shows on the map. It's way closer to the cliffs." They were like two kids talking about their first day at camp.

Bill picked the story up again. "Right, and here's the best part. Out of the four walls, only two are still standing! They'll be easy to knock down."

Sheriff Buchanon was confused. "And why do we want to knock them down?"

"Oh," It was Mark again, "because the floor of the outbuilding is a slab of concrete! It's at least four inches thick, guys!"

"Yep," Bill said, "all we have to do is knock down the walls, lift up the concrete slab, dig the hole underneath and place the slab back on top. It's perfect!"

Sheriff Buchanon thought about what he was hearing. "So how far into the woods are we with this outbuilding?"

Mark spoke up immediately, "Almost thirty five. That's the best part. We'll only be around three miles from the cliffs! No one would ever think about building anything substantial that close to the drop off. That thing'll be buried forever."

Sheriff Buchanon had to admit that it did sound ideal. "Nice work, guys. It doesn't sound like we'll find anything better."

Darren had a thought. "So how are we going to find it tomorrow? Neither of you can be around the artifact."

Bill motioned to his Blazer. "I plugged it into the GPS. You can take my truck."

"Well that solves the problem of Hunter and Eli borrowing a truck. I was going to ask for Shasta's Ranger, though," Sheriff Buchanon said.

"That would have been fine," replied Bill. "But this way, you have the coordinates and we already know that the Blazer can make it through."

"Thanks, Bill," the sheriff said. "You too, Mark. You've set my mind at ease. I think we might just pull this off after all."

Don Buchanon always had a little trepidation before confronting a perpetrator or busting up a crime in progress. A little fear was healthy, it kept you on your toes. Something about this job felt different, though. The unpredictable nature of the curse had him spooked. He reminded himself that they were armed with all the facts. They had done everything possible to ensure that the plan was carried out successfully.

He looked at Darren. "First light?"

Darren nodded his head and said, "Let's get to work."

CHAPTER 35

Down the Gravel Path

B ug was waiting for Clara to pick her up. She was already fifteen minutes late. Bug was a little anxious because this was new to her. Shasta was never late. Shasta was always right on time or a little early.

Bug hadn't minded having Clara fill in for Shasta at first. She had been friendly and fun. It was almost like she was trying to make up for something. Bug didn't know what that could be, but it didn't matter. She was glad to have someone to hang out with while Shasta was in the hospital.

Bug had gone to see Shasta the day before, too. Monday night when the fire happened, Bug was seriously freaked out, but after the meeting on Tuesday when Clara came to sit with her, she had felt much better. That was only last night, but to Bug it felt like a long time.

Her dad had made her go to school. He said it would do her good. The middle school was still in session, but the high school kids were out for the rest of the week because of the fire. The school officials had to figure out what to do without one science teacher and three large classrooms. It was a mess.

Bug had talked to herself a lot the last couple of days. She did a lot of research online, too. She looked up Smoke Inhalation Treatments, Smoke Inhalation Side Affects and Basic Driving Skills. She had decided that she needed to know how to drive, just in case of emergency. *Knowledge is Power.*

She looked at her watch again. Clara was now twenty-two minutes late. She decided to wait on the front stoop so she let herself out the door and locked it behind her. *Never can be too careful.*

Bug remembered the last time she had sat on the front stoop. A shiver went through her little body as she thought of Hansen convulsing on the ground. She wished for the hundredth time that Clara would get there. *Where is she?*

A car turned into the entrance of Meadowview Acres. Bug recognized it at once. Her dad had gone just that morning to scout out a site in the woods to bury the rock. Bug hopped up from the stoop and ran to the driveway.

Mark honked a greeting when he saw his daughter. She waved fiercely. She was excited to hear what had happened that morning. All of the sudden, she was glad that Clara was late.

"Hi Dad," she greeted as she ran to hug his middle.

Hugging her back warmly he said, "How's my Ladybug?"

"I'm fine, just waiting for Clara to take me to see Shasta. What happened this morning?" She could barely contain herself.

Mark knew the feeling. He and Bill had been so thrilled to have found the perfect spot that they had tripped over themselves trying to tell the sheriff and Darren. He decided not to make his daughter wait.

"Well, we found the perfect spot," He said as she followed him through the side door to the kitchen. Loosening his tie, he put his briefcase down on the kitchen table and sat down in one of the chairs. Bug's eyes were wide as she sat across from him. She was eager for news.

"It's almost to the cliffs, so there's no chance anyone will want to build there in the future. It's halfway in between here and Chester and the best part is there's already a big slab of concrete that we can use to top it off with." He was still so proud of their discovery.

"That sounds great. So we can dig the hole and put the safe at the bottom, cover it with the gravel and sand

and then put the concrete on top?" Bug was hopeful about the process.

"Yep, that's what we're thinking. I'm feeling pretty confident about the success of this plan." He sat back and sighed. It had been a long day. He and Bill had started out bright and early to do the scouting, then he had come home to shower and change before going in to work for the rest of the day.

"You know, it sounds like another part of *Curses of Ancient Tribes*," said Bug. "That book had the two suggestions we discussed at the meeting, but I remember reading part of another chapter that talked about entombing an object. This way, we're kind of doing both. First we bury it then we entomb it, Super!"

A car horn honked outside. "Oops, I bet that's Clara. I better go, Dad." She hopped up and kissed her dad on the cheek.

"Tell Shasta hi for me. I'll see you tonight," Mark said. "And Bug?"

She turned at the door to see her father's face full of concern. "What is it, Dad?" She asked.

"Nothing, just be careful, Honey." He winked at her and then she was gone.

Clara's Volkswagon Bug was parked behind Mr. Hamilton's car. Bug hopped in the passenger side, as Clara turned the blaring music down.

"Okay, how late am I this time?" Clara asked good-naturedly. She didn't mind being reprimanded by her little friend; she actually found it amusing. One thing Clara loved about Bug was that she always spoke her mind and was never concerned about what anyone thought of her. How freeing that would be. Clara was learning to let go of her "popular girl" alter ego, but it still crept up on her.

"Twenty-seven minutes," Bug said. "That's a new record for you and you've only been taking me places since yesterday."

Clara laughed and turned the tunes up again. That was another difference between Shasta and Clara. Shasta didn't like the radio up too loud. Bug was on Clara's side, though. She liked car music playing loud. The girls sang to the radio all the way to the hospital.

Darren was in the room with Shasta when the girls arrived. It looked like they were having a serious discussion. Clara felt like she and Bug were interrupting, so she tried to back out of the room. The movement caught Shasta's eye, though.

"Hey, Buggie," She said happily. "I was hoping you could come see me today."

"Oh, I had to go to school first, and then I had to wait for Clara to pick me up. She was twenty-seven minutes late. Hi Darren," Bug said.

She went to the side of Shasta's bed and stopped. Bug didn't know if she was supposed to hug Shasta or shake her hand, so she just stood still.

Clara came further into the room and said, "Hi Shasta, Hi Darren. Is it okay if I come in?" Clara hadn't talked to either of them since Hansen died. To them, she was still the old, popular girl Clara.

"Um, sure," Shasta said. "Thanks for driving Bug over." Shasta was a little confused at how her adopted sister could have ended up with Clara as a chaperone.

"Oh, it was no problem at all. I love hanging out with Buggie. But don't worry, Shasta, I'm a poor substitute for you. You have to hurry up and get out of here so all of us can go for ice cream or something." Clara could feel herself trying too hard. She hadn't realized how desperate she was for a good friend. It was within her reach again, and she didn't want to lose it.

Shasta looked at Darren for confirmation that something was weird and got it when his eyebrows rose in surprise. Luckily, Bug was oblivious to the awkwardness of the situation and diffused it without even knowing.

"Dad said that they found a perfect place for the burial this morning. It has a slab of concrete already and it's really close to some cliffs." Bug was still anxious about the plan being executed, but she was also excited about her dad's success.

"That's what Darren was just telling me. He was there with Sheriff Buchanon this morning when our Dads made it out of the woods." She looked at Darren with a mixture of pride and worry.

"How long do you think it will take to do everything tomorrow, Darren?" Asked Clara who had moved to Bug's side.

Darren and Sheriff Buchanon had tried to come up with that answer on the way back to the hospital that afternoon. "Sheriff Buchanon thinks if we start first thing in the morning, we'll be finished by late afternoon."

"It's going to be a long day," said Bug. "But I'm glad you'll be finished when it's still daylight." Bug involuntarily shivered. *Where did that come from? Super weird.*

"I'm going to get going. I want to check on Mom. I have to talk to her about a couple of things." Darren bent down and kissed Shasta gently on her cheek. He could finally do that without her wincing at the tenderness of her skin. She was getting better every day.

He looked at her straight in the eyes. "Don't worry about me tomorrow. I promise I'll be very careful. Get yourself home and comfortable and I'll see you tomorrow night."

Shasta's eyes suddenly filled with tears. She was so scared about what might happen to him. They had already been through so much. Blinking them away, she tried to smile. "I'll try. I really will. See you tomorrow."

Darren said goodbye to the other girls and left the room. Bug saw a box of tissues and held it out to Shasta. Clara looked like she was about to cry too, though. Bug didn't know which girl needed the tissues more, so she just held onto them.

Clara stepped closer to Shasta's bedside. Bug was right, there were tears in her eyes. "Shasta, I'm so sorry. Not about Darren. Well, I'm sorry about Darren, but I'm more sorry about… Oh, I don't know what to say. I'm just sorry that I've been so horrible the last few years. I don't know what I was thinking, and I just want you to know that I feel really bad about everything." She grabbed one of the tissues out of the box Bug was holding and started to dab at her eyes.

Shasta had stopped crying when Darren left, but she was really touched by Clara's apology. "Thank you, Clara, really. That means a lot." She didn't know what else to say. She was still a little confused by this new Clara. She thought maybe Clara had somehow been affected by Hansen's death.

Bug and Clara left the hospital about an hour later after chatting with Shasta about the latest Hollywood gossip. It seemed to be understood that the topic of the burial was off limits. Everyone needed a break from the constant stress.

———

"Are you nervous?" Hunter asked Eli.

They were sitting in the lawn chairs in back of the Massey's house. They had just finished eating dinner when Sheriff Buchanon had shown up to give them all an update about the trail into the woods. It sounded like a great spot. Hunter and Eli were going to be driving Bill Port's Blazer. He was going to drop it off later that night and pick up Eli's Fusion to use tomorrow. Everything in the plan had been settled. Now all they could do was wait.

"I'm not nervous," replied Eli. "I just want it over with. All the damage it's caused. I mean, Mr. Jackson, Hansen and Mr. Just. That's horrible enough. But sometimes, I just can't believe Heather's gone."

Hunter felt awful for his friend. He knew Eli was hurting. Hunter was too. The guilt that both of them felt was almost overwhelming.

"Eli, I feel horrible, too. But you know what my Dad said? He said that anyone in the world could have come upon that box. And ninety-nine percent of them would have done the same thing we did. It's natural human curiosity." Hunter had felt a little better when his dad had told him that. He wondered if it made Eli feel any better. "He also said that there was no way we ever could have imagined what was in that box. If we had imagined it, we never would have taken it out of the woods. That makes sense, doesn't it?"

"It does, and I know you're right. I just can't stop feeling responsible. I mean, it was my stupid dog that led me out there in the first place." Eli was rubbing his temples, as usual.

"Well if you're going back that far, then it's Mr. Jackson's fault for digging it up, right?" Hunter thought he made a good point.

"I know. I'll just be glad when it's over tomorrow." Eli stood up and stretched. "Do you think you can take care of switching out the cars with Mr. Port? I'm beat and my head is killing me. I just want to go to bed."

"No problem, Buddy. I'll handle it. Go get some rest." Hunter reached out for the keys that Eli was handing over.

"I'll see you first thing," Eli said.

"First thing," echoed Hunter.

———

The three of them stood in the driveway next to Bill Port's Blazer. Lara Andrews had quiet tears running down her face as Gina Massey put her arm around her friend. Hank Massey was giving the boys last minute instructions on the Blazer's GPS and Darren was standing with his mother. They were going to drop Darren off at the Sheriff's Department where the bulldozer was stored. From there, they would follow Darren down Route 68 West. Sheriff Buchanon and Deputy Clay were to pick up the dump truck and rendezvous with them at the gravel road.

Hunter and Darren were in the front of the Blazer. Eli sat in the back seat. The day seemed very gray to Eli. He knew it was early, the sun wasn't all the way up, but the sky had a strange darkness to it.

They made it to the Sheriff's Department without passing one car. The sheriff had said that the impound lot would be unlocked when they got there, and he was right. Darren got up in the bulldozer and cranked the engine. It sprang to life.

He remembered getting in it yesterday for the first time since his father's death. He hadn't anticipated his strong reaction to his father's smell. It had been meticulously cleaned since Claymont's death, but his father had been in the rig almost every day for the last twelve years. Darren had closed his eyes and taken a deep breath. It had felt a little like hugging his father. He had needed a moment to collect himself before driving the rig out of Tony Clark's construction site.

Today wasn't as big of a surprise. He expected the smell. He even welcomed it. Darren felt like his dad would be there with him today. "Let's go to work," he said.

The boys made it to the gravel road off of Route 68 without incident. Sheriff Buchanon was already there with Deputy Clay. It was weird seeing both men in street clothes rather than their uniforms. The boys pulled the Blazer in behind Darren in the field.

"Morning, Boys," Sheriff Buchanon greeted. "How'd everybody sleep?" He could tell by their eyes that they had gotten as much as he had – none.

"I figured as much," he said. "Before we start, I want each vehicle to have one of these." He motioned to Deputy Clay who walked over to the Blazer and handed Hunter a walkie-talkie. Then he went to the Cat and gave one to Darren.

"We're on frequency four. If for any reason, one of you feels funny or has any kind of problem, we're aborting this mission. Don't hesitate, Boys. It's not worth your lives. Understand me?" Sheriff Buchanon used his most intimidating voice on them. He didn't want any heroes out of the three.

The boys all nodded their understanding as Hunter leaned out of the window of the Blazer to vomit yellow stomach acid onto the ground. The safe with the rock was in the back of the Blazer. It had taken longer to affect Hunter today, but Eli's head was hurting badly.

Sheriff Buchanon saw Hunter puke and decided to get the show on the road. "We'll start out in front. Darren, you follow us and Hunter, you fall in behind Darren. We're going to chug along at as fast a pace as we can manage. If you start to fall behind, notify us ASAP." He looked at the nervous faces of the boys and thought to himself, "What the hell am I doing, these are just kids. What choice do we have, though?"

To the boys he said, "Let's roll."

───────

They were all in the living room at the Port's house in Meadowview Acres. Shasta had been released from Community Hospital that morning. Soon after she and Val had gotten home, Agnes had shown up. Clara, Bug and Ann Hamilton arrived a little after that. Margy Buchanon was there, as well. Val had called her the night before to ask her to wait with them.

Bill and Mark were outside talking. Their plan was to park at the edge of the gravel road to wait for news. The men felt like they were part of this plan and didn't want to be left out, even though they couldn't be close to the safe with the artifact.

Shasta was comfortable on the couch. She had a soft blanket covering her that didn't hurt her skin, but her cough seemed a little worse. The doctor had said that was to be expected. Her lungs were still clearing.

Bug and Clara were sitting on pillows on the floor close to Shasta on the couch. Agnes and Ann were in chairs while Val flitted around bringing the women drinks or snacks. She was much too nervous to sit down. Margy wandered from window to window as if she expected her husband to show up at any minute.

Bill poked his head in the front door just then and said, "Hey, Hon? We're going to head out now."

Val rushed over and hugged him. "You all be safe, okay? And call if there's any news at all, you hear?"

Bill hugged her back and said, "Promise. I'll check in with you after a while." He went to the couch and kissed the top of Shasta's head. "Bye, Sweetie."

"Bye Dad, be careful," she answered.

Bill then went to Margy Buchanon and gave her a little hug. "He'll be fine, Margy. He's a tough one."

She looked up at him, glad that Don's old Army buddy would be near, and nodded.

Mark came in then and said goodbye to Ann and Bug. "Don't worry about us. We can't get near the site; we're just there in case they need something."

"We won't worry, Dad," said Bug.

The men left and the room was quiet. Finally, Margy went to Val and the two women hugged. Val knew that Margy was remembering when their husbands were overseas for that last tour. Val looked at her friend and said, "At least this is just one day, not a year."

Margy looked back at her and said, "Yes, but why does this feel scarier?"

———

Sheriff Buchanon felt like his head was about to explode. For the past hour, Deputy Clay had been talking non-stop. Don knew it was only nervous energy, but he needed Michael to shut up. Don was entertaining thoughts of strangling him.

"...couldn't have known there was a chicken down there, too. So I said, "How we gonna git 'em out?" and he said, "Well, shoot, Mike, I don't know. Reckon we can...""

"Mike!" Sheriff Buchanon interrupted abruptly. The deputy stopped talking at once. "Do you think we could just have a little quiet for a minute? I'd like to go through some things in my head, and I just can't think with you rambling on like that."

"Oh sure, sorry, Sheriff," Michael replied, a little hurt. "I'll be quiet."

"Thank you," Don breathed a sigh of relief and checked his rearview.

Darren was still right behind the dump truck. He had practically kissed his bumper all the way in so far. Don guessed that was nervous energy, too. Behind him was Hunter, bringing up the rear. Don could see the poor boy's head pop out of the window every once in a while to retch. He was alright though, Don could tell. He was mostly worried about Eli. The boy's color had been pasty white this morning and he had been holding his head in his hands.

They were roughly twenty-one miles in. They had made good progress. The information from Bill and Mark about the terrain had been extremely accurate, the trees flanking the path had been easily taken down as the dump truck rolled over them. A little over ten miles and they would be at the destination.

The GPS from the Blazer had been transferred over to the dump truck, but they had hardly used it. There was only one way to go on the rough path. Don figured they might need the GPS when the path gave out.

The walkie-talkie crackled to life.

"Sheriff? Sheriff Buchanon? This is Hunter. Are you there?"

Michael handed the device over to the Sheriff who pushed the button and replied, "I'm here, Hunter. What's up?"

"Um, Sheriff. I'm kinda worried about Eli. His head's really hurting. Do you think he could ride in the dump truck with you?" Hunter's reply had been broken up a couple of times with dry heaves.

The sheriff had a better idea. "Darren? Are you there?"

Darren answered immediately, "Yes, Sheriff."

"Good. Everybody stop." Don slowed the dump truck to a stop and put it in park. He jumped out of the truck and walked back to the Blazer.

"Unlock it, Son," he said as he passed by Hunter's open window.

He heard the pop of the lock and opened the hatch. The safe was there. It looked the same as it did the last time he had seen it, when they welded it shut. Sheriff Buchanon lifted it out of the Blazer and bright blue flashes of light assaulted his vision. He wasted no time walking to the back of the dump truck.

"Michael! Hey! Can you jump up on the back of the truck so I can hand this off to you?" Deputy Clay hopped out of the truck and ran around to the back. He jumped up on the bumper and climbed up so that he was standing on the top of the back tire.

"Here you go, Sheriff, I got her," he said as he reached for the safe.

Don gladly handed the thing over and watched through flashing lights as Michael brought it over the side of the truck to lay it on top of the gravel mixture.

"There she sits," Deputy Clay said, "Snug as a bug in a rug."

He hopped down from the truck, and Don noticed that the man was clammy and white.

"You okay, Mike?" he asked.

"I'm fine, Sheriff. Just feel light-headed's all."

As the men walked back to the front of the dump truck, Michael said, "Hey, Sheriff, did I ever tell you about the time Uncle Tim fainted in church? Now that's a funny story. It was one Sunday when my mom and I was sittin' way up front with him near the preacher and he..."

Sheriff Buchanon, hoping the engine would drown out Michael's story, started the dump truck.

"Is that helping," Hunter asked Eli. He had been seriously worried about his friend for the last several miles, when finally he had decided enough was enough. Against Eli's protests, he had notified the sheriff and now the safe was resting in the back of the dump truck.

"It's easing up a little bit, I guess," Eli replied. "I honestly can't remember what it feels like not to have a headache. I wonder if I'll have one tomorrow after the rock has been buried."

"I know what you mean," Hunter agreed. "I'm going to eat so much food! Just knowing I won't be puking it back up sounds awesome! What should I have?"

"Everything you've been puking for the past ten days. Man, has it only been ten days since this thing started? It seems like months to me," Eli said.

"I know, Man," agreed Hunter. "But today it ends, and then the feasting begins."

———

Darren had been thinking about his dad all morning. The smell inside the cab of the bulldozer was comforting. It had helped him remember all kinds of things that he and his father had done together. He remembered playing ball, of course. He remembered learning how to fish with Claymont hooking the worm on his line. He remembered a summer movie that the three of them had gone to where Claymont just couldn't stop laughing. Darren and Agnes had finally made him go to the lobby to get himself under control. He also remembered a family vacation to white, sandy beaches where Claymont had let him drive a Jet Ski with his father holding tightly to him from behind. "Where was that," He wondered. "I'll have to ask Mom."

The whole trip into the woods so far had been a really nice trip down memory lane for Darren. He had been able to completely let go of the anger that had been enveloping him since Claymont's death.

As he followed the dump truck winding its way through the trees, he was peaceful – relaxed. For the first time since his father's death he felt as though things would work out.

Shasta was back in his life. They were closer than ever because they didn't have to hide their true feelings from each other. She was everything to Darren. Whatever happened from this point on, their paths would be intertwined. He would make sure to never lose her again.

There was a break in the trees up ahead. Darren could make out a little shack up there. The windows of the cab were cracked a little, and he could smell sea air coming in. They had arrived. This was the site for the burial.

He followed the sheriff to where the dilapidated shack stood. Not sure about the plan, he parked the rig but left the engine idling.

Sheriff Buchanon had parked the dump truck on the far side of the shack. He was walking over to the rig, so Darren let his window down all the way.

"There it is, Son," he yelled over the motor. He motioned to the little hut. "Take her walls down and pry up the floor. Then we'll dig us a damn grave."

CHAPTER 36

The Burial

D arren had taken down the only two remaining walls of the outbuilding in no time at all. The sheriff marveled at how the boy wielded the machine. He was a pro. He knocked down the walls then scooped up the rubble to deposit in the woods.

The concrete floor was next. He got the bucket of the rig underneath one side and started to pry it up. The rainfall from yesterday wasn't much, but it had loosened up the ground. The concrete slab came easily away. Darren balanced it atop the bucket and set it aside to be used later.

While Darren worked, the others just stood around and watched. Their part would come later when filling the hole was necessary.

So far, the team was feeling only mild effects from the rock. Well, everyone except Darren. Sheriff Buchanon had a headache and was still seeing sporadic spots of blue light. Deputy Clay was a little lightheaded and weak. Hunter was, of course, burping stomach acid, and Eli's head was still hurting.

The dump truck with the safe in the back was parked about thirty feet away from the work zone. The woods became a little denser around the building so it had been hard to get it further away. If Darren kept working at his fast pace, however, they could be finished in a couple of hours and the Rock of Varuupi would be entombed.

Sheriff Buchanon jogged over to Darren in the rig and yelled up to him, "Start digging the hole where the floor was! You feeling alright?"

Darren nodded and gave him the thumbs up.

Don backed out of the way and wondered what they would have done without Darren and the Caterpillar. His head was getting worse, and he could tell the others were feeling it too. He knew they never would have been able to dig that deep before one of them fell to the effects of the curse.

Darren backed up the rig and put the bucket down. Moving the Cat forward, he scooped a big mound of dirt out of the ground. Backing up again and turning to the right, he deposited the load on the ground. The hole was going to take a while to dig, but he knew he could make shorter work of it if he used a steeper ramp. Darren turned back and moved the rig forward, scooping another bucket of earth out of the ground.

———————————

Gina and Lara had joined the others at the Port's house. Bill had called about a half an hour ago to say that they hadn't heard anything yet, but were going to wait at the entrance to the woods. Everyone was basically just sitting around making small talk.

Clara felt like she was going berserk with boredom. She didn't know why they had to sit around doing nothing like a little pack of hens while all the guys got the important jobs. Clara didn't want to hang around there all day waiting for news. The rock hadn't affected her at all. She knew she should be a part of the dig with Hunter. She decided to wait a while longer and then make an excuse to leave. She would get her car and go out there herself.

Shasta and Bug were looking at a magazine, and the other women were talking about how the neighborhood will have changed after the crazy event was over. They talked about Claymont and Heather of course, but they also mentioned Hansen and Mr. Just. While they were discussing the people who had died, Clara thought just how lucky she had been. She was standing right next to Hansen, the rock had been at her feet. She could just as easily been the one to die.

She thought Hunter and Eli were the luckiest ones. They had been around the artifact many times, and they only became sick. She wondered why they were alright when all the others had died on the spot.

Clara was making herself antsy. She wanted to get out of there to go find Hunter. She was walking over to say goodbye to Bug when Shasta suddenly cried out…

The work was still going at a steady rate. Darren was about six feet down. He had managed to create a steep ramp into the pit. He would get to the bottom and scoop out another bucketful of dirt, then back up the ramp and deposit the dirt on top of the now quite large mound. The work was progressing and Darren was holding up well.

Sheriff Buchanon had driven the dump truck over and positioned it so that the back lined up with Darren's pit. The safe holding the Rock of Varuupi had been removed from the back of the truck. It now rested with the concrete slab on the far side of the dig.

The rest of the group was slowly getting worse. The bright sunshine wasn't helping either. Deputy Clay was sweating profusely and had started a nose bleed. Don had sent him back to Bill's Blazer to get him farther away. The other two boys were back there, too. Hunter's stomach was cramping, and Eli looked like hell.

Sheriff Buchanon was happy with the pace Darren was keeping. He was starting to get a creepy feeling and wanted this over with. The blue flashes of light were starting to mess with his head.

The sheriff walked closer to the pit and saw that it was a little deeper, maybe eight feet down. "Four to go," He thought. "And maybe one more for good measure, depending on time." He was just about to walk to the Blazer and check on the others when he heard Darren yell.

———————

Darren was happy with the progress he was making. The easy repetition of the controls in the cab didn't take much thought. As a result, Darren's mind was wandering. He could see the end of this nightmare and felt almost hopeful. A few more hours and they would all be back in their homes in Meadowview Acres with their families.

He and Shasta had talked about what they would do that night. After all of the horrible business was over, they would finally just sit together and relax. No big talks about the future were necessary. They had no big plans. They just wanted to sit and be together.

Darren scooped out another big load and brought it to the top. He could tell that he was almost eight feet down. He dumped the load and turned back to the ramp. That's when it happened.

His nightmare came out of nowhere and hit him like a ton of bricks. He was falling into the pit. His mind saw the steep ramp before him coming closer as he and the bulldozer tipped forward together. He tried to make the controls listen to his head screaming "Back UP! Back UP!" Something wouldn't let his hands move the right way. They weren't listening to his brain.

"No," He thought. He couldn't die in this rig like his father had! He saw Shasta's face in his mind and willed himself to scream.

"Sheriff, help!"

Sheriff Buchanon was at the side of the Cat in a flash. "What is it? Are you hurt?" He yelled.

Darren had put the engine in park, but was helpless to move any more. He gathered his strength and yelled out the window, "I can't move. My arms, my hands, they aren't moving. And I'm falling! Help me! I'm falling into the pit!" In Darren's mind, he was still tipping forward into an unending abyss.

Don had too much experience at being efficient in a crisis. By the time he had jumped up to the cab of the Cat, he had already called for the others to help. He had yanked the door of the cab open by the time they made it to the rig. He had pulled Darren's solid body out of the cab by the time they had figured out what was happening.

Deputy Clay got underneath the sheriff as he reached for Darren's weight. Hunter could see what was happening and moved forward to help Michael carry the young man away from the site. Eli grabbed Darren's legs as they passed, dragging on the ground. Together, the three of them got Darren to the Blazer and lay him down in the back of the truck.

———————

Val was at Shasta's side, "What is it? Are you in pain? What's wrong, Honey?"

Shasta couldn't speak. She didn't know what was happening to her. She couldn't explain it. She had an undeniable feeling of falling, but she could clearly see that she was still safely on the couch.

"Shasta!" Bug said firmly. "Tell us what's wrong right now!"

Shasta started moving her lips, trying to form words that would make sense. She thought she had a sentence and then it would escape her thoughts again. She closed her eyes and concentrated. She could feel the panic in the room.

"F, fall...falling," she managed. "I f,feel like I'm f,falling."

Valerie looked at Lara and Ann for help. With one a Neonatal nurse and the other a Physician's Assistant, surely they would know what to make of this. Ann stepped forward and grabbed Shasta's wrist to take her pulse. Lara seemed to freeze. The others thought she was most likely remembering Heather's death.

"Her pulse is racing," Ann said. "Shasta, Honey, look at me. Let me see your pupils. Okay, fine. Steady your breathing. Are you in pain?"

"No, no pain." Shasta was beginning to recover from the episode, but was no less confused. "I just had a real feeling that I was falling forward. It was almost like when you have a dream, and something wakes you up at the last second. Do you know that feeling?"

"She's still acting super weird," said Bug. "What's wrong with her?" Bug was going through her card catalog brain looking for anything remotely connected with a sensation of falling.

"I don't know, Bug," her mother answered. "Her pulse is slowing a bit, though. I think she's getting over whatever that was."

Clara was startled at the scene. She had a strange feeling when Shasta cried out. Clara instantly thought that it had something to do with Darren. "Shas? Did you see anything when you felt like you were falling?" she asked.

Shasta squinted her eyes together trying to clear her head and remember. "I feel like there was something, but I can't remember what it was."

"Keep trying," said Clara. "It may be important."

Agnes walked over to Clara then and asked, "What are you thinking of, Missy? You have an idea. What is it?"

It was Clara's turn to stumble. "I, I just had a feeling when Shasta screamed."

Agnes looked at her. "What kind of feeling, Clara?"

All of the eyes in the room were on her. Clara felt hot and uncomfortable. She wished she hadn't said anything. She thought she would just make something up because what she was thinking was a little far-fetched.

Bug spoke for her, though. "You thought something happened to Darren, didn't you?" Bug asked Shasta.

Shasta's eyes got wide. "Yes, I did! I remember I was falling forward and I saw dirt. A lot of dirt." Shasta was getting worked up again because of the recollection.

Valerie put an arm around her daughter to steady her once more. "Calm down, Shas. It was just a weird little dream. I'm sure Darren is fine."

Shasta looked at Bug, and Bug looked at Clara. They were all thinking the same thing. Bug said, "It might not be a dream. Twins have this thing where they can feel what the other one feels. Maybe Darren and Shasta are connected like that. Maybe they can feel when the other one is in danger."

Bug was obviously not thinking of Agnes's feelings. If she had, she might not have said that in front of Darren's mother. The look on her face was one of horror. "I'm going out there," Agnes said and rushed to the door.

"I'll drive," yelled Clara, running after her.

———

Feeling came back into Darren's arms and hands as soon as he was lying in the back of the Blazer. His sensation of falling was fading. The curse had certainly taken its time getting to him, but then it packed a wallop.

He was exhausted. He was too tired even to sit up. Being far away from the safe was better, but the damage had been done. Sheriff Buchanon was not about to let him anywhere near the dig.

"We'll have to do the rest with shovels," he said. "Darren, don't you move from that spot. Are we clear?"

Darren nodded his head with effort. He wasn't going anywhere.

The band of four retrieved the shovels and went toward the pit. Hunter stopped at the top of the ramp to look inside the cab of the Catepillar. He knew how to drive a stick shift. He didn't think it looked much different. He thought if he played with it a minute he could get the hang of it.

"Hey, Sheriff! You mind if I give this thing a go? It doesn't look too hard." Hunter was standing at the door to the cab.

Sheriff Buchanon thought for a second then said, "Ten minutes! Go ask Darren for a few pointers and then you've got ten minutes. After that, you're digging with us! We can't afford to waste time! That thing's getting to all of us!" With that, he jogged down into the pit with the others.

———

Clara drove like a mad woman all the way to the woods. They were there in record time, pulling up to Bill and Mark in the Hamilton's car.

Rolling down the window, Clara told the men, "We're going in as far as we can. Shasta had some kind of weird vision; we think something's happened."

Bill spoke up first. "No way, young lady. You're not going anywhere near that site. What's happened with Shasta?"

Just then his phone rang. It was Valerie. Snatching it up, he said, "Val! What's going on with Shasta?"

On the way to the site, Agnes and Clara had discussed the possibility of meeting with resistance. They had decided that since Agnes hadn't been around the artifact, she would distract the men so Clara could drive on through. Clara looked at Agnes and said quietly, "I'll be as fast as I can getting back with news."

Agnes winked at her and said, "Be careful." She got out of the VW and walked over to Mark's car. Clara took the opportunity to throw the car into first gear and take off down the gravel road. She heard shouts behind her but she didn't stop. The VW Bug was bouncing all over the gravel. It was barely staying on the path.

Clara was exhilarated. She didn't need to stay at home waiting for her man to come save the day. The VW hit a low spot on the road forcing Clara to hold tight to the steering wheel. She wasn't sure how far her car would make it down the path, but she was determined to get to Hunter.

Deciphering the instructions from Darren had been difficult. He was so weak. Hunter thought Darren was more affected than they realized. He didn't seem to be getting any better. Hunter knew time was not on their side. He bolted from Darren to the Cat and climbed up into the cab.

It smelled earthy and musty in there. There were pictures of Agnes and Darren taped to the dash. It made Hunter sad to look at them. He turned the key and the engine came alive. Remembering the instructions from Darren was easy – putting them into action was a little harder.

Hunter found the clutch and the gas pedals. Then he played with the controls for the bucket. Up, down, tilt, left and right. He repeated those several times. When it came time to actually move the bulldozer forward, there was an awful screech from the motor. He had obviously done something wrong.

Looking out the front of the cab, he could see the other three shoveling dirt. The sheriff looked a little panicked and Hunter knew Eli felt horrible. Deputy Clay's shirt sleeve was covered with the blood that he continuously wiped away from his nose.

"I've got to get this," Hunter said to himself. He felt the responsibility sitting heavily on his shoulders. He spit more stomach acid out of the window. His stomach cramps were all but natural to him by this time. Pulling together all of his concentration, he moved the controls and the Cat crept slowly forward. Hunter practiced a scoop with the bucket. He got some earth and backed up the rig. Repeating this a few times, he seemed to get a little more efficient.

"Hunter!" Sheriff Buchanon yelled from below. "Have you got that thing under control?" He had been watching Hunter's progress as he shoveled. He had given him more than the ten minutes because he could see that Eli and Michael weren't going to be able to shovel for very long, and it looked like Hunter might be able to work the rig.

"I think I've got it," replied Hunter. "You all get out of there and let me try!"

The three vacated the hole and watched as Hunter guided the rig shakily down into the pit. He scooped a small amount of earth, but on his way back up he lost control of the bucket and dropped the load onto the ramp. Cursing to himself he tried again. He did better that time and better, still, the next load.

Sheriff Buchanon said a silent prayer as he watched Hunter improve. He didn't want to let on, but he was really worried now. Eli had mentioned a couple of times how strange it was that it was getting dark so early in the day. The Sheriff looked at the dappled sunlight shining through the woods. He looked back at Eli. The boy was squinting at the bulldozer. Sheriff Buchanon wanted him out of there.

"Hey, Eli!" He called to the boy. Eli came jogging over ready to help.

"Yeah, Sheriff?" He squinted up at the sheriff with a questioning look.

"Go back there and keep an eye on Darren for me, would you? I don't feel right leaving him alone." He thought that was better than saying, "You look like hell, and I think you should get far away from that rock."

"Sure, but what about shoveling?" Eli was determined to help put that thing into the ground.

"I'll call you if we need you. Right now, I'm more concerned about Darren. Go on now." Sheriff Buchanon felt relief as he watched the boy leave the site.

Eli trotted back to the Blazer and Sheriff Buchanon turned his attention to Deputy Clay. "How're you holding up, Michael?" He asked.

"Reckon I'm fine. Just that sickly feeling and this dang blasted nose bleed," Michael said. "How much longer you think this'll take?"

Sheriff Buchanon looked back at Hunter on the rig. He was getting better with each pass but still a far cry from Darren's expertise. Maybe another hour until the hole would be deep enough. Would that be too long? The spots in front of his eyes were sparkling bright blue.

Clara was making good time on the path. Her little VW was just light enough that it felt as if she were on an ATV. She had left the gravel path some six miles behind her. The dirt one she was on now was easy compared to the gravel. The path that the convoy had left was easy to find. The tire tracks from all the heavy vehicles stretched out before her like a beacon.

"I'm coming, Hunter," she said to herself inside the empty car. "I waited too long to get you to lose you now."

Shasta had been frantic after Clara and Bug's theory had been revealed. She was convinced now that something horrible had happened to Darren. She knew their connection was strong. She had no trouble believing it was possible for her to sense that he was in trouble.

Val and Ann had calmed her down as much as possible. Val had learned from Bill that Clara was on her way down the path to find the site of the dig. Shasta seemed to settle down a little after hearing that. Help was on its way. She didn't know exactly what Clara could do, but maybe she could get him out of there and back to safety.

The room had taken on a stressful quiet. Bug had retreated to one of the chairs by the window. She looked small and frightened as she gazed outside. Her mind was frantically working – willing someone to come back.

Margy Buchanon was sitting with Lara. They were holding hands and looking somber. Communication wasn't necessary. Everyone in the room was thinking the same thing.

Come back safely...

———————

"Stop!" Shouted Sheriff Buchanon. He was sure about twenty minutes ago that Hunter had hit twelve feet down, but he had wanted him to go a little farther for peace of mind. Now he was positive – it was time to bury the safe.

Hunter backed up the ramp, cut the engine and hopped out of the cab. He bent over to spit then asked, "Are we there? Is that it, Sheriff?" Hunter was pumped. He had gotten into the rhythm of the work. The repetition of the controls had made it easy for him to improve steadily and, forty minutes later, they were finished.

Eli had heard the shouts and run back to see what was happening. He got to the dig just in time to see Sheriff Buchanon struggling with the safe. He seemed to be stumbling. Eli could tell that it was getting darker outside, but he could see well enough to help. He ran over to the Sheriff and relieved him of the load.

"Let me take it, Sheriff. I'll get it down there," he said. As the weight of the safe transferred over to him he felt a shift in the earth, like a bump, and his knees buckled. He recovered quickly and started down the ramp with the safe.

Sheriff Buchanon didn't argue when Eli took the safe from him. The flashing blue lights were assaulting him with fierce brightness. A sharp pain had started over his left eye. He watched as Eli walked down the ramp with the safe. The scene had a strobe-like quality. "Bury that son of a bitch," he thought.

Hunter was still standing on top of the bulldozer. He watched as Eli took the safe from the sheriff and started down into the pit. "Go,go,go...," he chanted in his mind.

Eli was back quickly, sauntering up the ramp as if he had just gone for a Saturday afternoon stroll. He had a peculiar look on his face. Hunter was about to yell down to him when they all heard something. It was the engine of a car. Hunter looked back the way they had come and saw Clara's bright yellow VW Bug tearing toward them, a puff of dust stirring up in her wake.

"What the…," Hunter began.

Sheriff Buchanon walked crookedly back down the path to the Blazer. Clara had just parked the VW and was getting out. Hunter jumped down from the cab and jogged over, too.

"Well, hello guys," she said coming over to plant a kiss on Hunter's cheek. "We thought you could use a little girl power."

The sheriff had no intention of refusing help. Actually, he was pretty happy to see her. He was alarmed at how quickly the situation was deteriorating.

"We sure could, Clara. Darren's in the back of the Blazer. He needs to get out of here. I want Eli to go, too. Can you do that for me please?" He blinked continuously now, trying to clear his vision.

"Eli?" Hunter said. "Why Eli, what's wrong?"

Sheriff Buchanon looked at Hunter and said, "I'm just a little worried about his head. I'd let you go too, but we have to get the slab into place with the dozer."

"I'm fine," Hunter said as he spit once more. "And good luck getting Eli to go. He wants to see this end as much as I do."

Hunter looked at Clara then, proud that his girl-friend could return the favor he owed Darren. "Take Darren out of here, we won't be long." With that he walked over and slipped an arm around Clara's waist. Pulling her to him, he kissed her cheek gently, then looked at her and said, "I'll see you soon."

Clara was overjoyed at Hunter's reaction to seeing her there. She was ready to do whatever he said. She followed the sheriff to the Blazer and helped with the doors as he and Hunter lifted Darren out and got him settled in the VW.

Hunter winked at her and sauntered back to the Caterpillar. Sheriff Buchanon said, "Thank you, Clara. And please tell everyone that we're alright and we're almost finished." With that, he wobbled back to the dump truck.

When he got to the truck, he saw Deputy Clay in the driver's side. Michael started the engine and leaned out the window.

"Am I good to go, Don?" He yelled down.

Sheriff Buchanon was happy that Michael had taken over the job. His vision was worse than ever. "You're in line, Mike. Let her go!"

The dump truck made a series of grunts and squeals as the load started to tip. The gravel and sand mixture trickled out slowly until the bed was far enough that the whole load seemed to fall at once with a mighty "Whoosh." The back flap slammed against the truck three or four times, banging loudly.

Eli felt like crying. Standing beside Hunter, he felt more tired than he had in all of his sixteen years. He had aged a lifetime. He understood exactly what Professor Monroe had felt.

Hunter knew what his best friend was feeling. He felt it too. He clapped Eli on the back and said, "It's almost over, Bud. Let me put the cap on this thing."

Hunter jumped back up into the cab of the bulldozer and started it up again. He maneuvered the Cat over to pick up the concrete slab. Gently, he got it balanced on top of the bucket and slowly made his way over to the site. He rolled over the gravel and sand mixture to pack it then positioned the slab on top of the hole. He slowly lowered the bucket and rolled the Cat backward until the concrete slid off with a solid thump.

The Rock of Varuupi was entombed.

The four of them looked at each other. No one was smiling; there were no jumps of joy. This had taken a toll on them all. They only wanted to go home.

"Hunter," Sheriff Buchanon said. "Put a few buckets of that dirt over the slab. We'll help with the shovels."

Feeling better than he had in over a week, Hunter started on the last job of the day. He felt his stomach start to unclench. The bile in his throat was receding. He scooped up load after load of the discarded dirt and poured it atop the concrete grave of the beast. With each scoop, he felt stronger.

Sheriff Buchanon's headache was subsiding, but the lights in his vision were still sparkling. They weren't as bad, but they would take a while to go away completely, if they ever did. He noticed that Deputy Clay's nosebleed had stopped as well. He said a silent prayer of thanks and looked around for Eli. He spotted him over by the bumper of the dump truck and went to the boy.

"Good job today, Eli. I know this has been really hard on you," he said. The boy looked like hell, but he guessed they all did. "How about we get out of here? Since Hunter has to take the bulldozer out, why don't you drive the Blazer?"

Eli was staring off into the distance. "I don't think that's going to be possible, Sheriff."

"What's the matter, Son. Are you still feeling pretty sick?" He asked, concerned about Eli's head.

"No," Eli answered. "My head feels fine. It's just that...I can't see anything, Sheriff. I think I've gone blind."

CHAPTER 37

Meadowview Acres

Clara had eased off of the gas a little on the way back out of the woods. She noticed that the farther away they got from the dig, the better Darren seemed to feel.

At first she was afraid. To see Darren, this guy who was so strong and intimidating, be so out of it was unsettling. She was nervous that something could happen to him on the way back. Her nerves calmed a little when he started to come around.

"Wha...what's happening?" He asked as the fog lifted from his brain. He was surprised to see that he was in Clara Stagg's car. He had no memory of her at all.

"Good morning," she said, glad to see him awake. "You've been out cold for a while. Sheriff Buchanon asked me to take you away from the site. I guess the rock was starting to affect you."

Little pieces of memory were starting to come together. Darren remembered the awful feeling of falling into the pit. He thought that was just a dream, but then he remembered more. His hands and arms didn't work. They wouldn't move. He brought his hands up to his face to check. Wiggling his fingers, he remembered more. They had put him in the back of the Blazer. Hunter was asking him questions about the controls in the Cat.

"Did Hunter finish digging the pit?" he asked.

"They were just finishing up when we left. I'm not sure what was left to do, but the sheriff said that it wouldn't be long." Clara eased back on the gas a little more. They were almost to the gravel road. It would be a much rougher ride.

Darren was still confused. "Why were you there? How did you get there?"

Clara wondered how much she should tell Darren. She didn't want to stress him out about Shasta, so she said, "Well, we were all at the Port's waiting this thing out, and Shasta got a little nervous. Then your mom got nervous. I just decided that we should come out and check on things." She saw his brow furrow with worry. "It's fine, though. Shasta was feeling better when we left, and your mom is with Mr. Port and Mr. Hamilton at the entrance to the woods. I told her I'd bring information back as soon as I could."

"Nice work, Stagg," Darren said as he closed his eyes and laid his head back on the seat. He was still exhausted.

Clara smiled to herself feeling proud. "Yeah, nice work, Stagg," she thought.

———————

Sheriff Buchanon looked at the boy. His eyes were focused on some far off point in the distance. He was praying that it wasn't happening – that Eli wasn't blind.

He grabbed Eli by the shoulders and stared into his face. "Eli, can you see anything? Anything at all? A shadow, a blur?"

Eli was calm when he answered. "No, nothing."

Hunter had finished scattering the pile of dirt over the concrete slab when he noticed the sheriff grab Eli by the shoulders. He cut the engine of the Cat and hopped out. By the time he was behind the sheriff, Deputy Clay had arrived as well.

Sheriff Buchanon gave each of them a sorrowful look. Hunter thought he saw tears in the big man's eyes.

"What's happening?" Hunter asked. Moving forward to Eli, he said, "What's wrong, Buddy. What's going on?"

Eli, still looking far off into the distance said, "Hunter, remember what happened to Professor Monroe? Well, it looks like I've been cursed the same way."

Hunter felt a blow to his stomach. The effects of the curse on him had been steadily wearing off. He just assumed that Eli would be feeling better, too. They all had.

"Eli, are you sure? Maybe it's just a temporary thing. Let's get out of here, and it might get better." Hunter was grasping at anything to give his friend hope, but he knew as well as Eli did that there was none.

"I think I've known all along," Eli told them. "The headache never went away, even when I wasn't near the rock. And every morning when I woke up it seemed like it took longer and longer to clear my head. This morning was the worst. I think I've been waiting for this all day."

"It's time for us to leave. We need to get you out of here, Eli," said Sheriff Buchanon. "We've done what we came to do. Now let's get you to the hospital."

There was no arguing with the big man. No one wanted to anyway. They were all emotionally drained and physically fatigued.

"Michael, you're driving the dump truck," he continued. "Hunter, you're on the Cat. Eli and I will take the Blazer."

He took the boy's hand and guided him to the passenger side of the SUV.

Bug had been watching Shasta for about half an hour. She seemed a lot better. Shasta wasn't aware of it, but the whole room had been using her as a barometer since Clara and Agnes had left. As weird as it seemed, the girl's emotional attachment to Darren was the only link they had to their missing loved ones. Considering the strangeness of the last two weeks, maybe it wasn't so weird after all.

"They're finished, aren't they?" Bug asked her.

Shasta's head popped up as if she had just woken from a dream.

"I think so," she said. "I just feel really calm."

"Oh, thank God," said Margy, and she started to cry. The fear she had been holding inside finally escaped.

Val and Ann looked at each other and smiled thinly. Lara and Gina hugged each other tightly. All they wanted was to hear something, anything, that would give them hope.

The phone rang and Val, pushing the talk button as she did, scooped it off the table. "Hello?"

"Honey, it's me," said Bill. "Clara and Darren just made it back. He's had some sort of reaction, but it seems to be wearing off. Mark's taking him and Agnes to Community right now."

"Hold on," she told him urgently. To the room she said, "Clara and Darren are back. Mark's taking Agnes and Darren to Community. He's okay, but needs to be checked."

She punched the speaker button on the phone and back to Bill she said, "What about the others?"

His voice came through the speaker so everyone could hear. "Clara said that Don told her they're finishing up, and it shouldn't be much longer. She said it didn't look like anyone else was having a problem except that Don was a little wobbly."

The sighs in the room were audible to him over the speaker.

"It looks like this might be over," he finished. "I'll call back when the rest of them come through. I'm going to wait here with Clara."

"Thank you, Honey," Val said. "We've been dying for news."

She hung up and looked around the room. The women all had expressions of shock. They were worn out from worry, but they all seemed relieved – all except Bug. Clearly distressed, she was still looking out the window.

"What's wrong, Bug honey," Val asked. "It sounds like everything's alright now."

Bug turned from the window and said, "I'll just feel better when we see all of them for ourselves."

"I know what you mean," said Shasta. "Mom, will you take me to the hospital? I want to see Darren."

———————

The scene at the hospital was organized chaos. Everyone had split off into small groups. Sheriff Buchanon told the medical team that the group had been part of a training exercise. That accounted easily enough for Darren's exhaustion and Hunter's dehydration.

The sheriff's headache had subsided as they made their way out of the woods. The flashing lights disappeared. Deputy Clay's nose bleed was gone, as well as his light-headedness. That left Eli.

Dr. Hill had told Lara that the blindness was most likely a delayed result of his experience in the fire. She said that it was "ocular trauma". Only the residents of Meadowview Acres knew the real cause. Lara was upset, but eased somewhat by Eli's mood. He was remarkably calm about the whole thing.

Eli was sitting up in the hospital bed when Hunter went in to talk to him. Lara was in the hallway with Dr. Hill, so the boys were alone.

"Hey, Dude," Hunter said as he walked in. "Guess who?" Hunter immediately wished that he hadn't said that, but he saw Eli smile.

"Hmmm...let's see," said Eli. "It kinda sounds like my Grandma Andrews. Hi Granny, nice of you to visit."

Hunter was caught a little off guard by Eli's joking attitude. He didn't quite know what to say.

"Um, sorry, I didn't really think before I said that," he told Eli.

"It's fine, Hunter," Eli responded truthfully. "I'm alright with this. I really am. It's like I said at the site; I've been expecting it for a while, so it's not that big of a surprise to me." Eli thought for a moment and then added, "I think I've been expecting to die this whole time, Hunter. I really have. I'm almost thankful that this is all that's happened."

Hunter sat on the edge of the bed. "I don't get it, Eli. Why? I didn't have any lasting effects, neither did anyone else. So why would you?"

"It's just the way the curse works. It affects different people in different ways. Professor Monroe and I were the ones who took the rock from its resting place both times. Maybe that had something to do with it. I don't know. This is my first time being cursed." He giggled again.

"It's really weird how cool you are with this," Hunter told him. "Maybe it touched your brain and made you weirder than you already were." Hunter was starting to get on board with lightening up the situation. He guessed that Eli was right. After what that curse had done to the others, they were lucky.

"So what are we going to do when you get out of here?" he asked Eli.

"I guess you're going to have to Shazaam me some kind of titanium walking stick with motion detectors and secret compartments." Eli thought of something else then. "Unless you'll be too busy with your new girlfriend," he added.

Eli couldn't see Hunter blush. He said, "I won't be too busy with Clara. She's cool, you'll see."

"What do you mean, "I'll see"?" Eli tried to look offended but he couldn't help laugh when he heard silence from Hunter.

Finally, Hunter caught on and joined Eli's laughter with his own.

———————

Bug was sitting on Shasta's lap in Darren's hospital room. He had checked out fine, but the doctors wanted him to have some fluids before he left.

"I think all of us are super lucky," Bug was saying. "I didn't tell everyone all of the things I read about in

Curses of Ancient Tribes. Some of those things are brutal. Well, I guess this one was super brutal, too." She thought of pretty little Heather, with her hair styled all wrong, laying in her casket at Peaceful Hearts.

"We were lucky, Bug," said Shasta looking at Darren. "Even though we all lost special people, we still have our loved ones with us."

Darren winked at her from the hospital bed. "I can think of one more thing that would help me recover," he said.

Shasta smiled, "What's that?"

"An extra-large deep dish with everything from Hot Slice! Let's get one on the way home tonight," he said. He had just noticed that he was starving.

"That sounds amazing," Shasta agreed. "Want to come with us, Bug?"

"Nope, I'm way behind on my reading and there's a documentary on tonight about how toxins and chemicals released into the atmosphere will ultimately destroy our race." She had been waiting for weeks to see that one. Luckily, she was free tonight. *Knowledge is Power.*

"Alright, then," said Shasta. "Tomorrow we're going for ice cream with Clara, right?"

"You bet! I need a double scoop after all of this," she said.

"It's a date," said Shasta.

Bug got up from her lap and went to Darren. She gave the man of steel a big hug and said, "Thanks for getting rid of that thing." Then she left the room.

As she walked down the hallway to the waiting room where her parents were, she thought of Eli. It had been surprising to everyone when Sheriff Buchanon had broken the news about his blindness. But it hadn't been surprising to Bug.

As she waited for news while looking out the window of the Port's house, she had been replaying everything in her mind. She began with the day she followed the boys into the woods, the feeling that she had sitting on the fallen tree. She remembered how Eli had looked that day. He was a different boy now, she realized. As she stared out the window, she tried to think what he reminded her of. She remembered how he looked when she and Shasta had gone to speak with him and Hunter about the rock. He looked different then, too. What was it?

She had realized, sitting in the Port's living room waiting for news, that Eli's face had become Preston Monroe's, the lines around the eyes, the strange dullness of color. Every time she saw Eli, his eyes had become a little less blue. How could she not have noticed sooner?

When Bug got to the hospital and heard the news, she wasn't surprised. That was his fate, just as it had been Preston Monroe's. Eli would be different, though. Bug was determined to make sure Eli didn't spend his life worrying about the curse. He wasn't going to end up the way the professor had.

She passed a room on the way to the waiting area and overheard laughter from inside. It sounded like Hunter. She crept over and peeked in. Hunter was on the side of Eli's bed, and they were both laughing. Maybe she wouldn't have to worry about him after all.

EPILOGUE

Clara was sitting in a pedicure chair at Curls for Gurls. She was waiting for Shasta. It was prom night and they had decided to get ready together. The two had become close again over the past six months. She couldn't believe it had only been six months since the nightmare had been buried. To Clara, it seemed like last week.

Life had slowly returned to normal after the burial. Darren and Hunter had recovered completely. There had been no new instances of the curse affecting anyone. The gravel road and entrance to the woods had been cleverly disguised by Sheriff Buchanon. He'd had Darren use the Caterpillar to cover the gravel path with dirt, not all two miles of it, but enough so the road could no longer be seen from the highway. They had thrown out grass seed which had taken hold in no time. No one could tell there had ever been a path into the woods.

Lara Andrews was coming to terms with the loss of Heather. Eli was helping her a lot. He was doing really well and had attained almost Rock Star status at school. Most people were under the impression that he had been injured in the fire at Hallston High; only a few knew the real reason for his blindness. His positive attitude regarding his loss of sight was inspirational to everyone. He seemed to be a different guy in a lot of ways. He seemed lighter somehow.

Clara noticed Shasta's truck pull into the parking lot and smiled as she watched Bug hop out. Clara was glad that Bug could make it. It was a special day, and she didn't want her little friend to be left out.

Coming in the door, the girls scanned the shop and found Clara waving them over.

"Hey," Bug chirped happily, hopping into the pedicure chair beside Clara. "We're a little late because Shasta had to finish her paperwork for college."

"Yeah," Shasta confirmed. "I've already filled out all of the initial paperwork for my scholarship, but this form is for the school newspaper, The Dixon Times." She took the chair on the other side of Clara and plopped her feet into the warm water. "I'm actually on staff now."

"I'm so excited for you, Shas," Clara said. "I'm going to miss you so much, but I know Dixon University was your number one choice."

Shasta's eyes sparkled as she said, "I still can't believe I actually got in. I really thought it was a long shot."

Shasta was excited about her future. When she had received the letter outlining her scholarship award, she had almost fainted. Dixon University was a two hour drive south of Hallston. It was still close enough to come home for weekends and Darren's games were going to be a top priority. He would be playing for State College in Chester since Agnes had decided to stay in Meadowview Acres.

Bug squirmed in her chair; the lady doing her toes was being ticklish. She had started getting pedicures regularly because Clara had told her it was "Necessary Beauty Maintenance". Clara was teaching her a lot about girl stuff since she had decided on attending the Beauty School in Shale. Bug was sad about Shasta leaving, but she was glad Clara would still be around.

They chatted about their plans for the evening until their nails were polished and dry. They were getting ready at the Port's house so Darren and Hunter would pick them up there. Then, they were all going to meet at Emily's for group pictures. From there, the group would be hopping into a limo for the trip to Glovercroft for dinner.

Bug watched the girls getting ready and wondered if she would ever be asked to a prom. Maybe she wouldn't even want to go. *There might be a super good documentary on TV that night.*

Later that evening, as the disco ball above the dance floor circulated beams of light around the room, Clara was genuinely happy when Shasta and Darren were voted Prom King and Queen. The happiness she felt now that she was herself again was better than any bejeweled crown. She and Hunter swirled around the dance floor then headed over to where Eli and Angie were sitting.

Angie was dying laughing as they came upon the two. Eli was always cracking people up; his new outlook on life was amazing.

"Hey!" Eli said as Hunter and Clara sat down at the table. "I smell something weird, Angie. Maybe we should find another table."

"Haha, very funny," Hunter said good-naturedly. "We got tired of dancing. Why weren't you out there smacking people with your stick?"

"That's for later in the evening. I don't want to peak too early." Eli was having a ball. He loved the sounds and the music. He was feeling better than he had in a long time, maybe since before his dad left. He still missed Heather and would always feel a certain amount of guilt, but he would be fine.

Darren and Shasta walked over then. Darren huffed, "This dancing is killing me. I've got to sit down." He took the chair next to Eli and dug into the bowl of nuts in the center of the table.

Shasta laughed and said, "Man, what a wimp! Are you sure you're football material? Maybe you should look into a knitting scholarship!"

That started all of them jabbing at each other and joking. Eli just sat back and listened. He thought of the people around him. They had been through hell and back. Six months ago, the span of just two weeks had turned their lives upside down.

Darren had lost his father and then almost his life trying to save Eli and Hunter in the fire, and then at the dig site when the curse hit him so hard he had been in serious danger. Shasta had been seriously injured in the fire, too. Clara had watched Hansen die and then been so fearless driving out to the dig site to help. Getting Darren out of there had been critical.

Then there was Hunter. He soldiered through right by Eli's side. The whole time he had been solid, doing whatever was necessary. Eli knew that Hunter was a friend for life. They would spend their senior year together next year and after that they would stick together. Eli knew they would.

Mr. Just had been sorely missed at the high school. A memorial had been held and Eli didn't know for sure, but it sounded like the whole town of Hallston had come to show their respects. Poor Ms. Leezil had taken a job in Shale. She said that Hallston High had too many memories for her to continue teaching.

Then there was Bug. Eli couldn't get away from her. She had started coming over right after he had gotten out of the hospital. She had insisted on teaching him Braille. Then she had helped him set up the Braille internet reader. He was cruising the web in no time thanks to her.

Eli thought that Bug would have suffered some lasting effects from the turmoil with the cursed rock, but if anything, she seemed more mature. If he told himself the truth, he was glad that she came to see him all the time. She just needed to find another word to use besides "super".

The dance was breaking up into little groups going to after parties so the friends said their goodbyes. Hunter and Eli, with Clara and Angie, headed off for a party in the neighborhood and Darren and Shasta headed home to Shasta's house.

They were at the front door when Shasta grabbed his arm and pulled him down to sit on the stoop. Darren could tell that she needed to talk.

"What's going on in that crazy head of yours?" Darren asked.

"I don't know," she replied somberly. "Tonight made me realize that things are really going to change. I'm going to be leaving, Darren. Isn't that weird to think about?"

"Well, I'll be leaving too, Babe, but we'll be coming back home. Your parents are still going to be here, and my mom. We'll be home for weekends and holidays, too. It won't be that bad." He was trying to make himself believe it, but in his heart he knew that he would be miserable without her.

"I guess you're right. I just feel like we lost so much time together. We need to make sure we don't let anything like that happen again." She leaned her head against his shoulder and closed her eyes. That was where she wanted to be. Was she crazy to think of leaving?

"Look, we have all summer long to be together. Then we'll just make a plan. We'll look at a calendar and plan when we'll be together. We can do that, right?" He put his head on top of hers and smelled that citrusy Shasta smell. He would miss that.

"Yeah, we can do that. I'm sure it will all be fine. I guess I just got a little dose of reality," she said.

"Yeah, stop being so serious. You're ruining prom night," he teased her.

"Hey, you can't talk to the queen like that!" She laughed and stuck her crown back on top of her head.

Motioning to the bejeweled crown, he said, "I can tell that thing is going to be dangerous. I may have to hide it."

They sat on the stoop looking at the stars and talking about their future. It looked brighter than ever.

———————

Two hours south of Hallston, in the neighborhood of Plantation Springs, Rebecca Scott had just returned home from her night class at Dixon University. She didn't mind the night class; it wasn't as crowded as the ones she took during the day, but sometimes she wished she lived on campus instead. As she pulled into the driveway of her parent's home, her headlights flashed on something at the end of the drive.

More curious than afraid, Rebecca put her Mustang in park and grabbed her book bag from the seat beside her. The thing outside had looked like an animal. Usually, they only got opossums or raccoons around Plantation Springs. The thing on the drive looked a little bigger than those, though.

She climbed out of the car and locked the door with the key fob. With a little more caution, she walked slowly toward the end of the drive. The moon was bright, casting shadows everywhere making the night seem more eerie than normal.

She peered into the darkness, trying to focus her gaze on the spot where she saw the thing in her headlights. Rebecca was taking smaller steps, she was starting to get a little afraid.

She remembered the tiny flashlight her Dad had given her to put on her keychain. She found it on the ring and pushed the button. A bright stream of LED light issued from the small opening. Pointing the bright beam of light at the end of the driveway, she moved it first left then to the right trying to see what was there...

ACKNOWLEDGMENTS

I'd like to thank my parents, Bud and Wanda McGaw for their constant support and encouragement during the writing of this book and for sharing with me a great love of reading, my husband Chuck and sons Chase and Eliot for giving me the confidence to continue this journey and for remembering who the Princess is in a house of men, my sister Terri whose written word has always left me speechless and whose strength is unending, my amazing friend Margy for her honesty after reading the first draft, my copy-editor Pam Shuster for her expertise, to my brother Chuck and sis-in-law Pam for their great sense of humor and fun in all situations, to Audrey for letting me borrow her nickname of "Bug", and to Andrew, Samantha and David for each being inspirational to me in their own way.

Look for PLANTATION SPRINGS

Coming in 2013…

the story continues

Donna Cain lives with her husband, Chuck, just outside of Louisville, Kentucky. Her two sons, Chase and Eliot are currently in college. She spends most of her free time spoiling her dog, Moose, and writing her second book, Plantation Springs.

www.ingramcontent.com/pod-product-compliance
Lightning Source LLC
Chambersburg PA
CBHW030927020726
47498CB00001B/137